Chaos and Destiny

FAE RISING

MIRANDA LYN

Copyright

Fae Rising

© 2020, Miranda Lyn

Cover Designer – Tairelei – www.facebook.com/Tairelei/

Editor – Second Pass Editing - https://secondpassediting.wixsite.com/website

Proofreader – Mel Smith www.LinkedIn.com/in/melsmith42

CONTENT WARNING
Violence, Language, Sexual Situations

Also by Miranda Lyn

FAE RISING

Blood and Honor

Fate and Flame

ALEWYN

THE BOG

THE MISTS

WIND COURT

WESTERN GAP

DREGAN MOUNTAINS

EASTERN GAP

MAZE FOREST

TRESA

HYTHE

HRUNDEL

ROCSBREW

MARSH COURT

ERAST

NAGA RUINS

DUNES

FLAME COURT

SEA COURT

Dedication

For Duck ...

NEED A RECAP OF BOOK 1?

After Ara's parents died, she went for a vacay with the old lady Aibell, per her mother's request. Then, learning she was Alewyn's Promise (kind of a big deal), she decided she couldn't hide away forever. Especially because that was only half of her prophecy. But she had nothing to survive on, so she became a vigilante as she traveled to get the book from King Coro's library. She went to the city, saved her friend Nadra from a terrible relationship and watched the moody southern prince and his little lackeys save two lesser fae. After that, she snuck into the castle, and the prince captured her and locked her in his rooms.

Temir created a truth serum. He wanted to use it to run away with Oleonis and Gaea. That didn't go to plan. After Oleonis died tragically, Tem used his secret death magic to kill Thane because the truth serum revealed he'd touched Gaea without her permission. Speaking of her, they had sexy bath time, and then Oleo died and now she's a mess because the timing could not have been worse.

1

KING TOLERO

*T*wo thousand years was an exceptionally long time to live, but it was an even longer time to rule.

I moved my aged hands through the long blades of grass covered in dewdrops and wished the memories were more tangible. Everything was fleeting when time passed slower than the sun. It seemed the moments I wanted to remember most were barely there, and the ones I didn't want to remember at all would never leave me. I placed my palm to the dirt and wished the gods would give her back to me.

"Do you remember, my love? The things that I cannot. Do you hold those moments for me?"

I stood and cleaned myself of the soil from that most sacred isle, the land that would one day hold my ashes until the wind carried them far, far away. I never thought it was fair that a mate could die and leave the other behind. I'd wanted to die every day from my broken heart and severed soul, yet still, I remained. The gods were not done with me yet.

"It feels the same, Efi. Our son is grown and gone, and they said in time I'd heal and one day breathe normally, but the absence of you has never lessened. The gaping wound in my soul remains, in case you were wondering."

I spent more time on Efi's Isle than I should have. I knew an entire kingdom needed me as much as I needed them, but certain long days were harder without her than others. My mate. Gone far too soon and far too fast. I never recovered from the loss of her. One day she walked the palace halls with light and laughter flowing behind her, and within days of that, she was gone. Poisoned. There were no answers to her death. My son would never come to the isle. He stood in his rooms at the palace and watched her funeral pyre burn from a heartbreaking distance. He never healed, but I supposed neither had I. Perhaps I was to blame.

I laid a fresh wreath of silvery flowers on the pile with all of the old ones and rowed back across the calm waters of the bay, leaving half of my heart behind, as I always did. Somewhere, deep within me, a tiger rested. I locked him in a cage the moment I lost her, and he had since slumbered.

"Your Grace." Inok bowed and took the wooden oar.

He was my hand. But more than that, he was my brother in all things but blood. He was far younger than I was, but then most of the fae were.

"Thank you, Inok." I patted him on the back as he handed my lengthy staff to me. I would have liked to say it was for royal vestment, but in truth, it was just a glorified walking stick. "We're getting too old for this walk, my friend," I said as I began the trek up the red sand hill toward the palace.

"We are getting too old for many things." He chuckled.

"You know what I was thinking about today? What is the benefit of living this long? At what point in our lives do we just welcome the blade and move on?"

"We've surpassed it," he huffed beside me.

"That we have."

"Do you feel the tension in the air? The animosity and uproars from the north? Does it remind you of the Iron Wars?" I asked as my staff sank into the shifting sand.

He looked at me a bit surprised but did not answer right away. I had learned there was truth in silence. Especially with Inok, who observed more than he spoke. He held wisdom in his fawn-colored eyes and showed it through his ash-colored beard. He had aged well.

"I wish I could say otherwise, but it does feel similar. Some days the news is worse than I remember it being. Do you think we are ready, my king?"

"I've done everything I can for the last fifty years to remove the Flame Court from the northern hostility, as you know." We stepped into the cool shadow of the castle, the relief from the scorching sun welcome.

"Do you think sending Fenlas north changes that? Do you think the northern fae pushing into our kingdom does? You may do all you wish, my king, but do not think for one moment they don't have a target on us."

He was right, of course.

"I really wish you wouldn't call them northern fae, Inok. Just as we do not address our people as lesser and higher, like they do in the north, we will not draw a geographic line between types of fae," I said, pausing.

"Apologies, Your Grace. But you're missing the point. Do you remember during the Iron Wars, when King Autus took the entire northern territory? It was because the former king, King Graf thought he was immune to Autus' hatred. He thought if he hid behind his walls, his neighbor would not see him as a threat. Where is he now?"

"Graf is dead because he was playing a game he had no right to play. Autus believed that land to be his own. His mother was the rightful heir, and Graf refused to yield because Autus already ruled the Wind Court."

"No right? I believe half of the Wind Court would disagree with you. Graf held the kingdom because Autus' mother chose to leave."

I shook my head. "A thousand years ago, the Iron Wars were long and brutal. I don't wish to repeat that. The northern kingdom were as savage as the blizzards that consumed them. Autus' court was small, Inok. He took the western half of the north and doubled his size."

"Precisely." He planted his feet, and his pointed look did not escape me. "The fae are talking, Your Grace. He's itching for war. He wants the whole world."

"Greedy fae always want what they cannot have. He won't have it. Just as he was denied that privilege a thousand years ago. I don't fear him. Even now. Even when they talk and the air feels the same as it did. The Flame Court is a long way from the Wind Court."

The low tones of desperation in his pleading voice caught my waning attention as he continued. "You must do something, King. It took him fifty years of bloodshed to be pushed back into his frozen hole. He's been scheming ever since. I promise you that. He's betrothed to Morwena now. That will make him king of the sea as well. He will rival the numbers of the Marsh and Flame Court then. And so far, Coro isn't doing a thing to stop him."

"That's why Fenlas was sent to barter an alliance, Inok. I'm not completely oblivious to this tumultuous world. I've lived in it a long time. Most are too young to remember the Iron Wars. Autus was still a child when he conquered the other half of the north." I tucked my hands beneath the folds of my robes.

"Imagine what all these years have taught him." Inok looked away, his eyes fading, as if he could see Autus plotting in the distance.

"I prefer not to think of him at all."

His focus snapped back to me. "That is precisely the point and the problem. If you do not think of Autus, Coro, and Morwena, you will not see them coming. You've been withdrawn for so long, you're the easiest target."

"Or so they would think," I answered. "What would you have me do? What do you advise an old king?" I asked as he began to pace before me, his feet sinking heavily into the deep scarlet sand.

"Get a message to Fenlas to come home. I don't claim to know all things, Your Grace, but I would bet anything he already has a target on his back."

I forced a smile. "He is smarter than you give him credit for."

"I never said he wasn't smart, but is he wise, my king?"

"When I was a boy, my father expected me to marry for the sake of the kingdom, as most royal fae eventually do, but it was my mother who encouraged me to wait. My Efi was worth the wait. Worth the fights with my father. The day our mating bond emerged, we were wed by midnight, Inok." I paused a beat as I remembered. "Though some mates are fated and prophesied, she was my surprise and gift in all ways. I wasn't wise then either. But I knew what I wanted."

We walked back to the castle in amiable silence. I navigated toward the kitchens as I always did after visiting Efi's Isle. There was nostalgia in the kitchens—memories we had there as young lovers. I rubbed my chest and leaned against the door to the larder, letting the tart smell of elderberry distract me.

"Another bad day, Your Grace?" Loti asked from inside.

She stood to about my waist, and I don't think I had ever seen her without that apron on. Her sandy curls were wound tight to her head and perfectly in place each and every day.

"Will it always be this way?" I asked the cook as she shuffled through the vegetable baskets. This was the other reason I came to the kitchens. Of all the fae in Alewyn, she too had lost her mate. Long, long before I had lost mine.

"Always." She nodded. "It's been fifty years since Efi passed, my king. Has it gotten any better since that first day?" She handed me three large potatoes.

"It comes and goes."

She released a heavy sigh. "That's about as good as it gets. Take those to the cutting board for me, would you?"

5

The greatest lesson I'd learned as a king is to treat the people who take care of you like you are also taking care of them. In any other kingdom, Loti would work for nothing and likely never see the face of her king. In the Flame Court, I hoped all of my subjects saw me as their leader but also a friend. Loti made a fair wage for her work, as did everyone else.

While the other royalty ruled with a heavy hand and fearmongering, I chose to rule with compassion. The world didn't know it, but the ability to enchant the mind was weakening. Morwena's siren song was still immensely powerful, but perhaps that's why the others were scrambling for war. Before enchantment was gone forever.

"Where are your staff? The kitchens are empty."

"Aye." She huffed as she crossed the room with arms full of more potatoes. "Jima was needed to help at the market, and both of the new girls are out. I'm afraid you're stuck with just me today."

"I suppose it's a good thing Efi taught me how to peel a potato then."

"I was hoping you'd say that." She smiled and held out the knife. "Do you remember, Your Grace, the first time she pulled you down to these kitchens. By the Mother, I thought you'd chop all your fingers off by the time you were done," she laughed.

"She never did give up on me, did she?" The corners of my mouth lifted.

"She was far more patient than I would have been."

"Far more patient than you are, even now. You swore to the heavens when I burned the rolls."

"I thought you'd fire me right there for cursing at you." She laughed, placing a pot that was nearly larger than her onto the counter. "Now look at you, working in the kitchens like a commoner."

"Don't tell anyone," I said, smiling as I sliced into the first lumpy potato.

"Your secret is safe with me, my king. Imagine the crowds we would have to fight off if people knew how many meals you've prepared in this kitchen. They would line up just to watch."

I plopped a potato into her silver pot. "Are you ready for the Trials to begin?"

"Are you ready?" She sliced a knife through the peel of the potato without taking her eyes from me.

"My involvement is merely ceremonious at this point. Perhaps the change in atmosphere is just what we need around here."

"Are you sure you will not open the castle for guests this year?"

"Yes. I'd prefer to keep the crowds in the city. We will have open meals and that is all. I'll make sure Inok lets you know how many to expect, and, as always, you may bring in extra staff as you need them, Loti."

Some time later, I sat at my desk waiting for Inok to join me, letting my eyes land on the smooth surface of the old desk Efi had gifted me. I peeled them away to study the print on the couches she'd chosen. I had hated the oversized pillows because they were always in the way of comfortable naps. But now I loved them. They were hers. They held the laughter she'd filled the room with when I grimaced at her decorative choices. She was everywhere. And nowhere.

Inok hastened through the room and took his seat across from me. Never late. Never absent. "The schedule for this afternoon, Your Grace." He handed me a rolled parchment.

I took the paper and unrolled it, shaking my head. "Why are we meeting with Attoc and Muth? They were in the open council meeting just days ago."

"They were, Your Grace. Both have champions to present for sponsorship, and they cannot come to an agreement. They have requested a private council."

"I should have known. Tell the pit lords I will not meet with them again. Instead, send Brax to each practice yard. Let him observe and report to me. I'll make a decision then."

"Yes, Your Grace." He paused, glancing at the paper in my hand. "And the other?"

"Other?" I looked once again at the message. "Oh. Right. I was trying to avoid this one." I let out a deep breath and handed the note back to him. "Tell her to meet me in the throne room."

"You know she hates that." He smiled.

"I know," I replied with an answering grin.

ARA

I'd seen him die.

Over and over again, I pictured all the different ways I would kill the southern prince and watch the blood leave his still and lifeless body. I'd tie up his lackeys and make them watch, just for locking the door.

I should have been more careful. I should have stopped to consider the power of the royals. But what kind of prince spends his free time in a library? I turned around and glared at the stacks of books on the desk across the room. Maybe I'd kill him with those. Can you papercut someone to death? I added it to my list of options.

I went to the window first. Several stories up, the only thing it offered was a clear view of the furious thunderstorm wreaking havoc outside the castle. Rather than using the simple lamps that sat collecting dust, the room glowed in the dancing flames of hundreds of candles spread throughout the masculine chamber. Even the embers of the fireplace snapped, giving warmth to the ambiance of the Marsh Court suite.

A tall-backed, red leather chair sat beside the fire, and, had I been here for any other reason, I would have dared to call the room cozy.

Printed rugs lay flat along the wooden floor while several surfaces held trinkets of random things. The dresser, void of candles or books, held an open felt-lined box—an indication the prince kept his prized weapons secure. I ran my fingers over the flasks of wine and lifted a half-drank jug of ale, sniffed, and then promptly corked it. The bitter scent was horrendous.

The printed drapes matched the wood tones of the towering timber beams that crossed the ceilings and reflected the calming glow of the candelabras. I moved in front of the fireplace and let the heat warm me as I studied the painting above. It was a simple painting of a farmstead, likely depicted from somewhere within the Marsh Court. I was sure the prince hated it; therefore, I liked it.

I checked behind the wall hangings and under the bed. I spent hours tracing my fingers along the tiny gaps in the floorboards for anything that would help me, and I even rolled up the rug on the floor. I found nothing but a stashed pile of dirt a sneaky maid had been hiding below.

Knowing the sentries weren't posted outside the door based on the silence on the other side, I flopped onto the bed that was way too soft and used my knife to clean beneath my nails as I plotted. I'd gotten out of this situation before; I could do it again.

I eyed the leather-bound book I'd risked everything for. It pulled me, suffocated me, encased me. I was terrified to open those tattered pages and find the truth to be more than I had bargained for. Nealla was the only one who could tell me the reality of Alewyn's Promise and my full prophecy. She was also the source of most of my childhood nightmares. Once I learned of my prophecy, there was no turning back, and the thought of losing my own free will sickened me.

Skimming through the textured pages of the book of magic, I wondered if I could use it to escape. I'd crushed a sea fae's arm before, so surely a door would be easier.

Unfortunately, the book was not a step-by-step guide on how to use magic. There was a lot of information about the rooted origins of magic and how the intensity of magic used to be much more powerful, but overall—though I tried—the book was pointless. I tossed it aside and looked again to the other book, feeling the power thrum. I would read it. Soon.

The room was so large, but every corner was filled with him: his books stacked along the furniture, the Flame Court sigil embroidered on a tapestry hung along the wall, and even the pillowed bedding smelled of him. I pulled open the heavy wooden drawers of his borrowed dresser. Though he had been here for a while, his room was fairly bare. His perfectly folded trousers and shirts hardly filled the drawers. The cloak he had worn in the tavern the previous night hung over the post of his bed. He definitely hadn't planned on capturing me, and it seemed like he would walk in any moment, based on the way he'd left this room.

I searched through the nightstand for hidden papers or secret messages—anything. It was empty. Did he truly have nothing to hide? I knew that wasn't true. I'd seen him save those two lesser fae in the alleyway. I knew he was hiding something.

Watching the sun set below the horizon, I realized I had been in the castle for a full day. Tilting my head against the window frame for a moment, I thought of the last time I was here as a prisoner. It seemed like a lifetime ago. I still had parents back then and I was also blissfully unaware of who I was—that I was Alewyn's Promise.

Shaking my head, I refused to think of those days. No matter what, I would get out of this opulent room and find my own place in this broken world. Hopefully, Prince Fancy Pants would show up soon, so I could kill him and be on my way.

The door flew open and I was instantly moving. A small lesser fae skittered in, dropped a tray on the floor, and ran out of the room. A great wind pulled the door shut just before I could reach it. *Damn it.* I needed to stay focused.

I sat crossed-legged on the floor and stared at that steaming tray of questionable food. Would he poison me? It was possible that he was working with Morwena, and she definitely would. I was starving but still just scowled at the tray, trying not to think about how delicious the food smelled. There was a restlessness in my legs, in my arms—my entire body. I couldn't stay in here, yet, I couldn't find a way out. The mere thought kept my heart racing.

I rubbed the faint calluses on my palm. I hadn't trained with weapons in a long time, and I was certain my father would be ashamed to learn I'd not only been taken prisoner, but had missed a chance to escape. I crossed the room to the bed, pulled off the blankets, and dragged them behind me across the room.

Slipping out of the elaborate dress Nadra's mother had weaved her magic into, I opted for one of the prince's oversized shirts hoping he'd find out later and be pissed. I rubbed it against my armpits for good measure. It was simple and hung to my knees, far more comfortable than the gown. Laying on the floor next to the door, I wrapped myself up in his stupid, cozy blankets.

I closed my eyes and breathed in the scent of Prince Fenlas. I didn't want to like it, didn't want to notice the smell of the summer sun and sandy beaches. I hated him. I hated everything about him and his arrogant, commanding attitude. I knew he felt the same way because I saw the way he looked at me. He could hardly hold back the revulsion. Why would he even want me in his rooms, going through his things?

The floor was ice cold. I tossed and turned and, after several hours, realized I couldn't sleep here. I had two options. I could either commit to staying up for the night, or I could lay in his bed and try not to think about him. I threw the blankets off and shoved them into the corner. There was no way I was sleeping in his bed.

I crossed the candlelit room and picked up the book I had been avoiding.

It's just a book. Open it.

Laying on the patterned rug in the middle of the room, I slid the book under the sliver of moonlight shining on the cool floor, pressed my hand to the textured leather and closed my eyes, letting my fingers feel the fabric beneath. I could totally do this. I'd worked hard to get this book in my hands. I couldn't let fear control me. I opened the book and pressed it flat against the floor.

Again, I could feel its pulse. This book was alive. I wasn't sure how or why, but I knew the minute I read these pages, the trajectory of my life would change forever. But then I'd known that the moment I left Aibell's, and still I came, searching.

The pages of the book were so thin, I thought they would disintegrate between my trembling fingers, but they didn't. I thumbed through them. Skimming. But as I drew closer to Nealla's story, I could feel it. Her. I pulled my hands from the book and closed my eyes.

"Are you in there?" I whispered.

Thankfully, she didn't answer. I'd probably forfeit this whole fucking plan if a book started talking to me. Especially one that seemed to haunt me more than help me. I knew what the tales said about her, but somehow, she was the answer to my questions, so it was time to learn the truth.

I couldn't breathe. The moment I found her name, the breath rushed from my lungs and hung somewhere in the room I left behind as I was yanked into the aged pages of the book. Panicked and shrouded in darkness, I left that castle behind. The scent of the prince was faintly there, grounding me only slightly as I began to work my way through this otherness. This separate world within the dark magical book. The truth became abundantly clear: I had no business being here at all. Whatever had called me to open this book was not friendly.

My body jerked forward as I was pulled by invisible hands. I wanted to panic. I wanted to scream, but my control had fled like a whisper in the wind. I became limp as I moved through the obsidian expanse and toward whatever entity called me. I was going to die. Within the deepest parts of my mind, my soul, I knew it. The imminent death sat just beyond reach, dragging me forward. Again, I tried to breathe, but I couldn't. I tried to move in any capacity, but I was paralyzed by either my own fear or lack of control. I wasn't sure which.

My ears tingled as my fae hearing picked up a small echo somewhere far, far away. I was breathing. I just couldn't feel my chest rise and fall. I wasn't paralyzed, but instead completely numb. This wasn't my body. I'd left my body somewhere behind, and now only my soul lingered in this unknown space.

"You must come to me," a smoky voice hissed through the uncomfortable darkness.

I couldn't speak. Still could not move.

"Beyond, child. I am beyond. You must come to learn, or you will fail this world."

Completely weightless, I tumbled forward. *Who are you?* my mind screamed.

"I am the one you fear, the one you seek, the one you need, child."

Where must I go?

"Beyond The Mists."

There is no 'beyond The Mists.' You step into them, you die.

The heated anger filled the blackest night, and somehow my aura sliced into pieces with fear.

"You dare question me after all I've done to help you?" the grated voice roared. "I've locked away your secret! I've forbidden the world to speak of you, and still you prove the fae are not worth saving."

Agreed. They are not.

There was a pause, and then the anger around me shattered like glass, and the room was full of emptiness once more.

"Come find me beyond The Mists. There's more."

More what?

I drifted backward, trying to hold on, trying to force my soul to stay, but it was in vain. I slammed back into my corporeal body. Lightheaded, I reached my hand up to the tears that streamed down my slackened face. I pulled my fingers away and saw the blood. Head spinning, I nearly passed out as I ripped the bottom of the prince's shirt and used it to clean my face, then threw it into the roaring fire.

'Beyond The Mists' the voice had told me. No one went to The Mists unless they wanted to die. The journey to get there was treacherous enough. I couldn't think of one time someone had traveled there and returned. Not only did that thing want me to travel to them, it also wanted me to meet them on the other side. I'm not sure how, but I knew it was Nealla. I had felt the truth of her when she'd spoken into my mind.

Exhaustion like I'd never known crept through me. I stumbled through the room and dragged the prince's blankets back to his bed. I didn't care if someone came in. I didn't care if I'd have one single chance at escape. I wanted nothing more than to crawl into that massive feather bed and sleep until the world was a brighter place.

The storm that commanded the sky beyond rumbled its concurrence, so I settled into the warmth of the thick blanket around me, trying not to think of the last person who had slept there. The crackling of the fireplace snapped in tune to the rain pounding the window, and I fell asleep easier than ever.

3

TEMIR

"Why are your horns so long, Temir?" the stable boy asked as we sat on the old dock, throwing flattened rocks across the frozen lake.

"I'm letting them grow."

"But why?"

"Listen, no one will ever accept us for who we are if we can't accept ourselves."

"But why are we different?" He reached to the side and plucked a flat rock from the ice-cold mud beside him.

"When you look at Gaea, what do you see?" I threw the rock in my hand and glanced at him. His face twisted as he considered what might make her different. The innocence of children always beguiled me. He shrugged his shoulders, shaking his head. Naturally, we were all the same in his eyes. "I have horns, some call them antlers. She has feline eyes. And you?" I reached over, poking the blue markings on his face. He pulled away and giggled. "You have these handsome markings and longer ears than I do. The lesser fae are still fae, boy. We just share features with the animals of Alewyn."

"But our hearts and souls are the same?"

I wrapped an arm over his shoulder and he scooted closer. "Exactly the same. Though some would say our hearts are even better. Have you thought about what I asked you?"

"I have, but I dunno. It's hard."

"I won't call you 'boy' forever. You'll have to come up with something eventually."

"Alright, if it's such a big deal, you do it." He threw the last rock he had found.

I waited for it to chirp across the ice before I responded. "You want me to name you?"

"I don't know nothing about namin' boys," he mumbled.

"Alright, how about," I lifted my finger to my chin as if I were really thinking hard, "Rock?"

He laughed, and it made me smile. I couldn't remember the last time I'd done that.

"I don't wanna be called Rock, Tem." He turned his face to mine, and the blue ice faerie markings along his cheek shimmered like a spackling of glitter.

Where did he really come from? How did he come to be a stable boy? He just showed up two years ago, barely walking and stumbling around the barn.

"Well then, what *do* you want to be called?" I threw my own flat stone.

"I already told you, I don't know." He smirked. "Let's ask Gaea."

He had grown a crush on her, and he, in return, was her new favorite person. I certainly wasn't. I had other things to worry about, though, so I didn't push her.

"We can ask her tonight at dinner." I patted his shoulder.

I was certain the boy was enjoying his newfound freedom, but I was equally confident Marte was working him harder for it. Though I had threatened him severely, some dogs just never learned. It wasn't within

17

my power to pull the boy from the stables forever, but I allowed him to join us as often as he could. The lonely life of a stable boy could crush your spirit if you weren't careful.

"Time to get back, Rock." I ruffled the nearly white hair behind his elongated ear. "I've got a council meeting to get to."

"That's not my name, Tem." He pushed my arm away.

"Better think of a good one then!"

After dropping the boy off at the stable, I crossed the bailey and entered the stone castle. Several sea fae gathered near the door, and as I walked past them, they eyed me suspiciously. Unlike most of the Wind Court, the castle's visitors had not been enchanted to accept me as high fae. I would have hated that before, but I no longer cared what they thought. I had joined the rebellion, and my end goal was to prove them all wrong anyway. I lifted my chin higher and strode through the stone castle that had been my home for so many years.

Somewhere between loving Gaea and losing Oleonis, I'd found myself. It pained me to know Oleo would never see this side of me, but somehow, he had known it was within me, even when I hadn't.

I walked through the halls and stopped for a moment before I opened the council chamber door. I twisted the ring on my finger and took a deep breath. Though the king would not be able to enchant me, thanks to Gaea's gift, I needed to sink back into the fae I was before I'd joined the rebellion. I didn't want the king to grow suspicious.

I hadn't done anything significant for them yet, and most of the rebellion did not trust me. I'd prove myself eventually. Fortunately, the leader, Rook, knew what he had in me. I reminded myself of that as I pushed the hefty door open and strolled into the most coveted meeting room in the Wind Court as a spy.

I took my seat across from Gaea and kept my eyes down. This meeting was to officially release Thane from the council, and though I'd killed him, only she and I knew that.

I had thought, even hoped, that with Thane gone, the tension in the room when only the council and the magical fae were present would lessen. Instead, Eadas eyed everyone suspiciously as he sat twirling the scruffy tufts of his hair and boring his beady eyes into mine like he always did when I looked in his direction. He could be dangerous. He had always held the king's ear, and I'd never stopped to wonder why.

Beside him, Bolgan shifted on the chair that was somewhere below him. He used to be the leader of the trolls in the Dregan Mountains, but he had forfeited his title when the king asked him to join the council. It was a political gain without marriage, but as vicious as trolls could be, they weren't the most intelligent.

I tucked my head low and stared at my hands until the door slammed open, cracking against the wall. The king barreled in, stomped across the room, lifted Thane's chair, and beat it repeatedly against the wall until there was nothing left but mangled and shattered pieces. He screamed and the call reverberated around the hollow room.

"Eadas!" he shouted. "True or false? The leader of my fucking military has been murdered in broad daylight, and not a single damn fae has any idea how that happened."

"T-true," he stammered.

He yelled again, and I caught Gaea's flinch out of the corner of my eye. I would not look at her. "And how the fuck does that happen?" he roared.

"I-I don't know."

The king moved to the head of the council table, sat in his oversized chair, and slammed both fists so hard against the tabletop I thought the ancient wood might crack. "I want some gods-damned answers. By whatever means necessary."

I knew what was about to happen before he started. I tried to look as mechanical as I could while the magic of his voice saturated the room. Of the seven members left, three of us were going to have to be very careful to keep our secret. Gaea and I were immune to the king's enchanting, but I'd wager Oravan, the blacksmith, was also.

"I've prided myself on having a council that was so loyal I would never have to use magic to extract honesty. I can see now that isn't the case. In times of war, I must never be too careful." His voice shifted into song. "My private council now consists of only three members. That is more than enough for a powerful king. But I've invited the magic wielders to join us out of the kindness of my heart. Going forward, you will all be considered members of the council and are therefore all required to attend every single meeting that is called. Nod," he demanded, though I heard a falter in his voice I'd never noticed. A struggle.

I fixed my eyes on the cracked stone directly in front of me and nodded my head as he commanded.

"If you or someone you know has worked against me or are thinking of working against me, stand." No one moved. A room of blank faces aside from the king's ire. "If you know why my commander is dead, stand," he barked. Again, no one moved. "You will find out who did this and bring them directly to me."

He stood and left the room, leaving us to sit until the magic dissipated. I think I was the only one to notice the sheen on his forehead. I waited until Ragal, the king's cousin, shifted and then did the same.

I looked up to find Gaea's beautiful eyes on mine, and I knew she was worried. We would now be hunted.

Later in my rooms, I waited for her to spirit in. The moment she appeared, she plopped down on my couch and raised her legs over the arm as she had done a lifetime ago. "Hey, Tem."

"So, you're not worried?"

"There are far more concerning things in the world than the king's temper tantrum, hun."

I tried so hard not to look at those glorious legs. So hard. "I've told the stable boy he needs a name," I said, changing the subject.

"Well, of course he does, poor thing. Is he coming to dinner?"

"I believe so, unless Marte piles on his chores."

"He will," she scoffed. "Better go down and get him ourselves."

"The traditional way?" I asked, surprised when she stood and walked to the door.

"I could use the walk." She shrugged.

We wove our way through the stone castle. Walls I'd seen a thousand times before felt distant until, at long last, I realized why. They didn't feel like home. Since childhood, they hadn't brought me peace or comfort in familiarity. Maybe the rebellion was home, because this was not.

"Temir?" Gaea asked before we reached the barn.

"What?" I'd been lost in my own thoughts.

"Where is your mind lately?"

"It's here. I'm here." I forced a smile.

She stopped and crossed her arms. "You're not here, Temir. You're exactly the opposite of here. I've stopped by several times, in fact, when you were nowhere to be found. Tell me what's going on. I hope you know you can trust me."

It was so hard to look into those feline eyes and lie, but I had made a promise to the rebellion, and until it was time to recruit Gaea, I would have to keep her out of it. For both of our sakes. "I've been around. Usually in the garden rooms or my solar. The more inexperienced soldiers we have coming in to train, the more demanding the use of my healing is."

Her eyes looked back and forth between mine as she tried to ascertain the truth, but I held her gaze, and eventually she gave up, leading the rest of the way to the barn.

As she had guessed, Marte stood just inside talking to the boy. "You've got to get the mare out of the pit and get her into the third stall before nightfall. You leave her tied up to the post too long, we will have a repeat of last week."

"Yes, master. I've done that already."

"And you—"

"Ahem," Gaea interrupted.

The stable master turned to see us waiting and took a step back into the barn. He'd been careful around me ever since I threatened his measly life. I was still not ashamed. I watched him clutch the whip in his hand, and knew I'd do it again if needed.

"He's just finishing up his chores now, my lady," Marte said.

She sauntered across the barn, touched a finger to his small hand, and with his jaw on the floor, she pulled the whip from him.

"I don't think we'll be needing this today, will we?" she asked in a tone that stirred something feral inside of me.

Sometimes I forgot that I wasn't the only male enthralled by her beauty though, as far as I knew, I was still the only male she'd acted upon those desires with. If only she would come back to me. If only I didn't spend half my time pining over a female I loved who would not love me back.

She hung the whip above the tack table and winked at the smiling boy.

"You may go, boy," Marte managed to get out.

"Thank you, master." He dropped his saddle on the workbench and ran for the door. "Hey, Tem." He bounced on his feet.

"Hey, Rock," I answered, turning back to the castle.

"Gaea, tell him not to call me Rock. It's not a name."

She chuckled and looked at me questioningly.

I shrugged. "He needs a name."

"Oh yes, he sure does." She smiled down at him. "What would you like to be called, then?" She took his hand in hers as we walked back to the castle.

"I dunno. Hey," he said, stopping. "I thought you said we could go to the river for dinner this time." He dropped his hand, giving her a pouty face.

"Come on, kid. Dinner's already inside."

"No." Gaea lifted her palm to stop me. "I did promise, and a deal is a deal. Hands in." She held her palm out.

I scoffed, and she gave me a death glare, so I shook my head and took her hand, smashing the boy's hand between ours. One moment we were standing in the cold snow outside the castle stables, the next, we were surrounded by lush green grass and the sound of a river rushing by on the edge of a dense forest.

"What will we eat?" the boy asked.

"Should have thought about that before you insisted we leave," I grumbled.

Gaea swatted my arm and knelt before the kid. "Leave it to me." She was gone before I could protest and then back again moments later. "Shall we?" She held a towering tray of food I knew she had stolen from the kitchens.

"I hope the cook doesn't get in trouble for that missing food," I whispered in her ear.

"Don't worry. I told her it was for you. Those ladies just love the 'strong and handsome Temir,'" she said in a singsong voice.

I held back my eye roll and reached for a biscuit.

She smacked my hands, and I pinned her with a hard look. "Let the boy eat, Temir. Look at him, skin and bones."

"I make sure he's fed," I answered defensively.

"Why do you guys talk about me like I'm not here?" He took a vine of grapes.

"Sorry, dear." Gaea shoved the tray into my hands with a wink and spirited away. She was back within seconds with a woven blanket to lay on the warm ground.

"I wish I could do that," the boy said to her.

"No, kid. You don't. Trust me, it's safer these days to just be a plain fae with no magic."

"But why?" he asked.

"Because if you have magic," she leaned into him, "the king will steal you away forever."

"I'd get to be with you guys, though. So, I don't see the big deal."

Gaea and I exchanged a look, knowing we'd never be able to explain it to a child his age.

"How about that name?" I asked, slowly reaching for the biscuit I had put down.

"How about River?" Gaea asked.

"Hm. It is my favorite place."

"Mine too," she answered with a sweet smile.

Gods she was beautiful.

"Okay, River is my name, then." He shoved an entire block of cheese into his mouth.

"Do you want to fish when we're done eating, River?" she asked.

I stood to look for a good stick, knowing what his answer would be.

"Mmhmm," he mumbled.

He opened his mouth to speak and Gaea raised her palm to stop him. "A gentleman does not talk with his mouth full."

We were somewhere within the Marsh Court, but I wasn't sure where. The trees were planted so close together, at times I had to turn sideways to get through. The brush crunched beneath my feet, and birds sang melodiously high above me. I found a stick long enough for fishing and followed the sound of the river back to them. Just before I left the cover of the forest, I stopped, leaning my shoulder against a towering oak tree. I watched them on the blanket and felt my heartbeat stop. I saw the way she looked at him, and I knew, in that moment, that was her dream. To be free to care for a fae child. To escape the chains that bound us both. Nothing in her life contrived.

Without warning, her head snapped up and turned to me. "Temir!" she screamed. "Get out of the forest right now."

I turned to look over my shoulder and ran for them. Before I was halfway through the clearing, she stood, grabbing River and holding her hand out to me.

"Faster," River yelled.

But I wasn't fast enough. The claws of the attacker ripped into my flesh as I was slammed to the hard ground, smashing my head into a jagged rock. The cries from the distance were muffled as a lavrog, a massive horned feline, bellowed in my ear, saliva dripping down over my face. I could feel the torn skin on my back as the beast continued to hold me down. I managed to look up and see the absolute horror on both faces in front of me.

"Take him ..." I whispered. "Take him back."

Gaea shook her head in terror. Her eyes unblinking as she watched and held the boy firmly to her chest. She needed to go.

I began to pull my magic forward. "Do it," I rasped.

Tears streamed down her face, but she nodded, and they vanished. I rolled, feeling more skin rip, and the shock of it nearly stunned me. One moment the beast was on top of me, and the next I rammed my death magic into it, and it rolled, crumpling to the ground.

Before I could begin healing myself, Gaea returned. "Temir? Oh gods, Temir," she cried, kneeling beside me. "Your back."

I dug deep and pushed the magic through my body, letting it flow. It stung, causing me to nearly call out, but I bit back the pain and willed my flesh to stitch together. I lay panting.

"I don't understand what happened," Gaea said as I rolled over. "I thought for sure I'd come back and you'd be ..." She couldn't finish.

I sat up and let the world below me right itself as I pushed my thumbs to my temples and forced the nausea and spinning away.

"I don't know," I lied. "It was about to kill me and then howled and fell over.

She took a few tentative steps toward the fallen monster. Its legs were longer than Gaea was tall, and though she wasn't sure if it was truly dead,

I knew better. She looked back to me and then at the beast again and shook her head.

"Perhaps there is a hunter in the woods. We should go."

She nodded, eyeing the cat warily. She took my hand, and before we knew it, we were back in my rooms. My wound had nearly healed, but using the death magic was incredibly draining when I also had to heal myself.

"Your clothes are ruined, Temir." She gripped the edges of my shirt and pulled.

My heart caught in my throat, remembering the last time she had pulled my clothing from me. I lifted my arms, and her knuckles grazed my ribcage as she moved. I tried not to think of her that way, but I couldn't help it.

She dropped my tattered shirt to the ground and stepped closer to me, resting her small hands on my bare chest. "Does it still hurt?" she asked, scarcely above a whisper.

"There are plenty of things that hurt far worse." I stroked her cheeks with my thumbs.

She looked to the floor, and I thought she would step away, but she didn't. "I know I've been distant, Temir. I know it isn't fair to you or to us. I can't force my heart to heal. Every time I think of being with you in that way, I get flashbacks of his body lying in a puddle of blood on the floor, and I can't get past it. The guilt is eating me alive every single day."

I pulled her tiny body to my chest, wrapped my arms around her, and rested my chin on the top of her head. We stayed like that for a long time. "I'm not in a rush, Gaea. I've got all the time in the world to let your heart heal. I know Oleonis was like a father to you. I'm here, though. If you need me."

"I think I'll always need you, Tem." She looked up at me with those beautiful eyes.

I wanted to tell her so many things, but I didn't know how. The rebellion was not my secret to share. I couldn't tell her about my magic.

I would never tell anyone. But, also, I loved her. In whatever capacity a broken male could love a wounded female. And those words would only send her running, as she so often did when she couldn't deal with reality. Oleo had told me she was like the wind, but I was beginning to think she was more like a storm. Once she was free, life would be on her terms only, and she'd settle for nothing less.

CHAPTER

4

KING TOLERO

"Umari." I looked down the steps to the leader of the draconian fae with her raven-colored hair and high cheekbones. Her watchful eyes were cruel and unforgiving as she stared at me.

"Your Grace." She bowed low and gracefully, though I knew it grated on her nerves to show such reverence to me.

"How are our people fairing?"

The storm within her cracked through her glare. There were visits when it was hard to look at her at all. She looked so much like Efi it pained me.

"Fine," she snapped.

"Are you ready for the Trials to begin?"

She looked around the throne room and rolled her eyes as she tapped her bo on the tiled floor, the wooden staff echoing throughout the chamber. She leveled her gaze to mine. "Shall we?"

"I'll meet you there," I said, rising from my throne.

She stormed out of the room before I could do it first. She resented me more than anyone in the world, but we were both stubborn enough to keep a promise, even if it meant nothing now.

I crossed the castle and exited the main grounds, with sentries accompanying me on both sides, as we traveled down the worn road to the open pits just outside the packed city below. I sank slightly into the sand of the arena floor and looked to the crowds of fae filling the seats around us. I supposed watching royalty belittle themselves was a spectator sport in the southern kingdom. I dipped my head to the accumulated fae as I waited for Umari to join me. She had to wait on the sidelines for the king. I could barely hide my grin at the upper hand.

If looks could kill, I'd be dead already as she stomped across the arena, never taking her eyes off mine. The traditional fabrics she wore tied around her distracted me. I knew she didn't do it on purpose, but I looked at her and saw only a shadow of my mate. I held my staff in both hands as she bowed once more to me, and then the dance began.

Practiced steps from years of training with her helped my precision. If I was even a step behind, she would crack her bo on my shins. She relished those moments. Beating up an old fae more than twice her age was probably the only thing that brought her joy anymore. That and the cetani.

Block high. Block low.

"Palm down," she scolded.

We crossed our long wooden weapons in the middle, and the crack reverberated through the air. I swung my staff and connected once more with hers. She became the aggressor pressing me backward. I knew these steps. Though older and far less strong, they were still ingrained in my memories. It was only for the show after all.

"Ha!" she screamed as she moved.

Fighting with the bo was a specific technique that the draconian fae specialized in. Umari, as their leader, was the best among them. Though rare, whenever the draconians were blessed with a child, they were taught to walk with bos in their hands, and rather than attending any form of traditional schooling, they trained with their weapons and their bodies day after day. My dance with Umari was just for show. Unless I enchanted her—which I never would—she would always have the upper hand in a fight, and she knew it.

She snapped her bo across my fingers. "Focus."

I stared her down as we continued.

There was a line. She'd gotten close to it a handful of times over the years. Perhaps I was too kind to my people. Perhaps I was too lenient. But she had pushed too far, and I've had to make it clear in the past what behavior would not be tolerated. I knew she hated me. Blamed me. But no more than I blamed myself. And if the folk of the southern kingdom thought they could all get away with her conduct, I'd have a lot more problems on my hands.

One time. One time I enchanted Umari, and I'd never apologized for it. I'd never taken it back, and I never would. I wanted all the fae in the Flame Court and throughout Alewyn to have the freedom to think and feel as they chose. I never wanted anyone to fear my ability to enchant their minds. It was a power I used so rarely, I'd nearly forgotten how until she had insulted my mate. She thought she had the right as the leader of the draconians, but she didn't. No one had that right. Not even me.

Even still, I wanted to like Umari. I wanted to love her, even. But that would never be. Though I knew it would pain my Efi, I would never be closer to Umari than I was in that moment, and we were worlds apart.

She stopped and slammed the tip of her bo to the mat.

"Where is your mind today, Elder King?"

"Perhaps I am just too old for this."

She scoffed. "You promised her."

"Do not remind me of the words to my mate. I know what I said to her."

The fae along the walls began to shift uncomfortably. There had always been animosity between us. Some days, I believed they came for that show and not to watch Umari show off the skills of her people.

"Where is my grandson?" she asked.

"He is away on a mission."

"Will you tell me anything else?"

"There is nothing else to be said."

She bowed and left the arena. We were only halfway through our ritual, but I think we both had reached our limit.

"That went well," Inok said from behind me.

"Considerably." I handed him my staff. "This old fae needs a drink."

"Yes, I believe mothers-in-law have that impact on everyone, Your Grace. The crown is no exception."

"Indeed."

When the draconian fae fled the Wind Court during the Iron Wars, they settled in the dunes of my kingdom. Efi was sent by her mother as a liaison to barter peace. Our mating bond did not emerge right away, and she was as fierce as her mother during negotiations. Eventually, we settled on an agreement, though Efi drew a promise from me that would always bring me and her mother together. Every ten years, the southern kingdom held the Trials, an event known across the world for its showcase of fighting technique and talent. Come war or peace, life or death, I promised that her mother and I would perform a choreographed bo fight to officially open the Trials, which would then follow a month later.

Soon, warriors from all over the kingdom would fill Halemi, the thriving city adjacent to the castle. Several events took place during the Trials. Once they officially began, we would have dancers, fae beast taming, and the pit fighters would perform, fighting through a bracket of trained males entered by the pit lords. At the very end, the traditional Rites would take place, allowing any fae who lived in the southern kingdom to show off their fighting skills, hoping to become a member of the royal guard.

Days later, I woke to Inok throwing my heavy curtains open and urging me from bed. I sat at the edge and wished my body was as lithe as it once was. Glancing out of the window, I noticed the sun hadn't risen. I pulled my long gray hair behind me and stretched. "What is the reason for waking me at this ungodly hour?" I groaned, rubbing my eyes.

"There's been a murder, Your Grace."

"What? Where? Who?" I tumbled through questions as I dressed quickly and hustled out the door.

"One of the guards. Favic."

"No." I stopped in the hall. "He was just married."

"I'm afraid so, my king. They found his body at the gates."

"Do we have any idea who killed him?"

"Some of the townsfolk are blaming the draconians that were here with Umari. They said Favic was the guard in charge of their arrival."

"No. I just can't believe it would be them." I shook my head. "Umari may hate me—may blame me for the death of her daughter—but she honors fae life. She wouldn't kill, or order her draconians to kill, without cause."

"I'm only reporting what I heard, Your Grace."

"Of course, Inok. Lead the way."

The long hallway carried the sound of our hustled steps. The occasional staff we passed held knowing looks of concern and somberness. Though early morning, word had already spread. Unlike the northern kingdoms, death was a great loss in the Flame Court. I trailed the halls with Inok close behind, wondering what I could say to bring comfort. My private council would already be waiting for my late arrival.

"Have you called an open council for later?"

"I have. Though I believe sooner rather than later would be wise."

"Yes. I suppose so."

Days like these made me grateful for Efi's eye for details. I could feel her in the halls as I walked. I looked at her paintings, the drapes she chose, and the hand-woven tapestries and willed them to bring me comfort so that I may give it to others. I entered the quiet room and stood before my council as they sat shoulder to shoulder at the lengthy table with long, somber faces.

"Do you see these empty chairs?" I gestured to the lines of vacant seats behind me. "In a short time, these seats will fill as my people beg for solace and answers. A widow will sit in that chair and look into your faces seeking something, anything to change the way she feels. As we continue this meeting, I want you to think of her."

They dipped their heads in a slight bow, and I walked up the stairs and took my seat in the middle of the lengthy table.

"With all due respect, Your Grace. You know where the blame will be pointed," Jacon said timidly, his eyes never fully meeting my own.

"I know," I answered.

"And what will your response be, my king?" Igrer asked, taking notes as he always did.

"We cannot close our borders to those seeking refuge. We do not yet have answers on the boy's death, do we?" I looked to Adom for clarification.

He stood and shuffled through his own notes. "My king." He nodded. "Favic was found early this morning, propped against the portcullis. His neck was sliced open and an ear missing."

"An ear?" Igrer curled his lip as he wrinkled his nose in disgust.

"I can't make sense of it, but yes. There is no other evidence, other than he didn't die there. They deposited him. Which meant they intended to leave a clear message and likely also intended the death."

"What message could they possibly be sending with murder?" Sabra asked.

"If I may, Your Grace?" Madu asked, standing.

He was quiet for longer than I thought he might be. I allowed him to continue. I knew where he would land. We all did.

He walked down the stairs, turned his back to the empty chairs and faced us all, just as I had upon entering. He was nothing if not dramatic. "I think I speak for several when I offer two suspects. Two choices, I suppose." He crossed his hands behind his back and paced, looking at each of my council as he passed them. "The draconians—"

"Stop," I interrupted, rising. He bowed low and waited. "I will let you speak, as I always do, Madu, but you will speak only with facts of this council meeting and not your own prejudice. Radical suspicion will derive no answers. Be mindful of your words, but get them out before my people are in attendance."

"Of course, Your Grace," he said behind a forced smile.

Inok and I exchanged glances as Madu continued.

"As you all know, I represent the borderland owners. We have all witnessed the fair amount of lesser—forgive me—fae," he corrected, "entering the Flame Court. If you would, my king, what happens when a fae of the lower class, according to the north, is killed in the north?"

"Madu, enough with the dramatics. You know the answer, spit it out." I was far too old and impatient for his ways. He held a council member position on a rotating schedule with the other border lords, but I appreciated his input the least. Still, it was fair to give everyone a voice.

"Right," he said, rubbing his hands together. "The answer is nothing. No one in the north cares if another dies. I've attended a ball where three deaths happened, and the music didn't stop. I only say this to point out that it is possible the fae filling our lands for safety may not know what is expected of them in the south."

I looked to Sabra. She did not wear her emotions well. She clutched the table with whitened knuckles and was biting the inside of her cheek to keep herself from speaking out of turn.

"Sabra?" I asked, giving her the floor.

She flew out of her chair. "Your Grace," she bit out. "I would like to remind the council that fae who come into this kingdom are coming here to avoid death. I make it my personal mission to welcome most of them and make sure they understand the way the Flame Court treats each other. I cannot sit here and let fearmongering," she twisted her lethal gaze to Madu, "convince this council, or anyone who will join us later, to believe they are to blame. Unless you have proof, Madu, I suggest you sit down and mind your tongue."

Madu held both hands in the air in submission. "I only mean to submit a possible guilty party. I think we have to call out everyone to narrow down the suspects."

"Thank you, Madu. Please take your seat."

I stood and nodded to Inok. He went to the doors as I addressed the council. "For the current meeting, let me address my people. I will not allow questions at this time, since we don't have answers. I would ask that you also avoid answering questions with your suspicions. I expect your support in silence until we have more information."

They would do as I asked. My council was granted more freedom than most other councils, and they knew it.

Inok opened the main doors, and fae of all shapes and sizes filed in. I looked in the eyes of Favic's widow, and for a brief minute, we understood each other. Our losses made us the same. In only a short time, the room was full of grieving and concerned folk, each bowing before taking their seat. Many had come. I was not surprised.

The room went still and quiet, and even the sobs vanished. The power of a king was immense. "It is with the greatest sorrow that I have to tell you that we have lost a great warrior today. A faerie of honor." I paused, bowing my head.

It was so hard to look at them all. The pressure to give them peace when I didn't have it myself overwhelmed me. I was reminded daily, with the loss of my mate, that peace was only a fragile state of mind. Rarely attainable.

I walked down to the people and leaned heavily on my staff as I stood before Favic's widow. "Favic was a good fae. I have many fond memories with him. I am sorry to report we do not have answers." The murmuring began. "I am sorry for your loss." I looked in her sorrowful eyes. "The council has met already this morning. We do not believe anyone has a reason to fear for their safety, but we also do not know what happened. If anyone saw anything suspicious, please see Inok, so we can investigate. We will say our final goodbyes tonight at sunset." I paused, looking down. "As is tradition, you may all now rise and pay your respects to Favic's widow."

She burst into tears at the word, and I reached for her trembling hand. I knew how much that title hurt. She rose from her seat and bowed before me.

"I am sorry for your loss," I said before leaving the room. Inok trailed behind me, and I stopped, facing him. "I need a moment, brother. Please see the people out of the council room, and for the sake of everyone, get Madu out of there before they start asking him questions. We don't need him staining the minds of the people with his bullshit."

"Yes, Your Grace."

It was rare that I didn't open the floor for questions or comments from the folk, but I knew where it would go, and I needed to keep everyone unified. A divided kingdom was a weak kingdom, and this was not the time for that.

I wanted to crawl back to Efi's Isle, lay in the sun, and wait for my soul to leave me. To finally find her again. I knew that was not how it worked, but as the days passed, I found myself more distant from the demands of the crown. With my son gone, I realized I was slowly losing my will to live, and for the sake of everyone, I needed to find it. I didn't know how the soul was supposed to go on when half of it was gone forever, but I needed to find a way for the legacy that I would one day leave my son.

Before I realized, I'd found my way into the kitchens.

"I heard what happened, and I knew you'd be torn up by it, my king," Loti said, setting a plate of chocolate cake in front of me. "Don't start thinking you're anything special." She smiled.

I lifted the small fork and let it glide through the creamy chocolate frosting. I didn't say a word for fear of revealing my true emotions. Instead, I let that chocolate cake take me back. Back to the first time I'd ever tasted it. To my mother's laughter and the shadows of my childhood. Where the world seemed much smaller and far less complicated. I'm not sure what kind of magic Loti hid from the world, but she poured it into that chocolate cake with such perfection, I counted my blessings that she knew me so well. Better than I knew myself, it seemed.

CHAPTER 5

ARA

*E*merald eyes watched me.

I ran through the fields as fast as I could, trying not to look over my shoulder, but no matter how far I got, I could not escape them. The blades of grass turned into sharp knife edges and ripped my legs to shreds as I continued to run. I called out, but to no avail. I'd lost complete control of my body. I could feel the daggers, and then suddenly they were snakes, each single stem a poisonous serpent biting into my already damaged legs. I forced myself to look down, only to see blood and sinew pouring from me. When I reached the edge of the field, I skidded to a stop atop a cliff, tumultuous waters slamming the rocks below. Panting, I looked over the edge, and I heard her. That smoky voice dipped in death.

"I know what you are, girl. Come. Swim."

I tried to turn away, but couldn't. A gale blasted me, and before I knew it, my body was hurled off the cliff. My scream was the only thing I could hear as I fell until my body shattered against the freezing water. The giant waves hurled me like a tumbleweed, and the water burned my empty lungs. I tried to break my arms loose of the spell that held them at my sides. Again, I failed. I watched the sun grow darker and darker until I was sure I had drowned in the sea.

I blinked my eyes in the water a final time and within that fraction of a second, the water became flames. The ground, solid beneath me once more, rattled as the flames licked up the sides of my tattered legs. I watched the flesh melt off my bones until I lifted a single hand and realized bone and ash were all that was left of my broken, lifeless body. I shuddered, convulsing so hard, I collapsed screaming.

Somewhere in the distance I heard a loud crash and my eyes flew open.

A dream. It was only a dream.

I squeezed my eyes shut and opened them again, remembering whose prison I was in. I peeled myself up off the floor, realizing falling from the bed must have been the crash I had heard. My forehead dripped with sweat, and the tray with fresh breakfast grated on my fucking nerves. The servant had again been in and out before I'd even had a chance to catch her. I quickly checked to make sure I still had my knives strapped around my thigh and breathed a sigh of relief when I felt them. They had become a second skin.

By midday, I turned reckless. I threw every one of the prince's leather books into the glass panes of the single window trying to shatter it. Two broken food trays later, still not a crack. I couldn't lift the leather chair, or I probably would have tried that also. I searched the bathing room for any kind of weapon I could use, but there was nothing. I eyed the gilded feet of the claw-foot tub for a moment, knowing they would be heavy enough, but obviously, I'd never be able to remove them. I tried several candlestick holders, but they didn't work either. I was beginning to wonder if the glass was charmed.

Eventually, I gave up and perused all of the titles of the prince's stupid books. The rumors claiming the fae of the south were great warriors must have been true. Most of his books were either stories of heroes fighting great battles or technique-styled books on all kinds of fighting. I opened the book on the nightstand. A picture slipped out of it, drifting gracefully to the floor. Tossing the book back on the table, I dropped to the ground and grabbed the portrait, flipping it over and back, studying it. Three cheerful faces stared back at me. One was a beautiful fae female, exotic even, with long dark hair and sharp cheekbones. Beside her stood an older fae, muscular and graying. His eyes were kind. The crown set atop his head gleamed in the light of the image. Between them was a boy with familiar green eyes, sun-kissed skin and raven hair, like his mother. The Elder King looked nothing like what I had pictured growing up. I had always heard he was fierce and a walking weapon, but the male in the picture seemed friendly, enamored with his family. The words on the back were written in a light feminine script.

My dearest boy,

The heart is the strongest weapon of all. No matter where the world takes you, always remember where you came from.

~All my love

I forgot the prince actually had a family. He was his mother's twin. Even as a child, he still resembled her. He'd grown since the image was captured, but the same eyes that haunted my dreams looked back at me now.

I slipped the portrait back into the book, knowing that the southern queen had died and that might have been the only one he had of her. I still planned on killing the bastard, but I wasn't an animal.

Later, I decided to work on my knife-throwing skills. I slid the chair across the massive room, stood on it, and wrapped a piece of cloth around my eyes until I couldn't see. It would be just my luck that the door would swing open and someone would see me dressed in nothing but the prince's massive shirt, blindfolded and standing on a chair in the middle of the room with knives in my hand. I hoped not. Actually, that would be hilarious. Plus, I'd still be able to hit them.

I lifted the blindfold a bit, peeking at my target. There was a wooden beam on the wall directly across from me. That would do. I threw the knives and listened as each thunked into the wood, only inches apart if my aim was right. Just as I let the last knife fly, a crash came from behind me. I spun, forgetting I was standing on a chair, and my feet flew out from behind me as I tumbled to the hardwood floor. I raised the blindfold and looked around, but nothing was there. Nothing moved. I closed my eyes and let my fae ears listen for movement or breathing. Still nothing. The vibrations from my knives hitting the wall must have knocked something off a shelf.

I followed along the wall until I found a metal cup laying on the floor. I rolled my eyes and put it back on the shelf. Being locked up in the castle and left to my own regard for two days was definitely starting to get to me. Last time I was terrified for my parents, that they would have to live alone without their child, but this time I had only myself to worry about. I'd also killed a male since then. Several, in fact. I just wasn't the same person.

I pulled my perfectly placed knives from the beam and smirked at the gouges they had made. I hoped he hated them. I did push-ups until my arms shook and then pull-ups on the bar across the top of the posts on the bed. I made a rookie obstacle course and forced myself to train. I had nothing better to do with my time, and by the end, I was dripping with sweat, and the shirt I wore stuck to my body. I slid my back down the wall by the door and stooped my head between my knees, attempting to control my breath. I listened for noise, anything, outside.

"Just let me out already," I begged.

I wiped my arm across my damp head and crawled to the bathroom, my muscles refusing to lift me up. It had been a while since I worked out. I felt my palms, and only faint bumps remained of the callouses I once wore like armor when training with swords with my father. My knives had become an extension of me, but I promised myself when I escaped this place, I was going to work twice as hard to earn those back.

I reached up and turned on the bath.

Fuck it. If they wanted me to just stay in this gods-forsaken, prince-smelling, book-riddled, nightmare-inducing room until I grew old, at least I'd take advantage of it. I let the steam from the hot water fill the room until the air was heavy and every surface was damp. I lowered my naked body into the scalding water and tilted my head back in complete euphoria.

I moaned and sank down until I was entirely submerged. I ran my fingers through my hair and wondered if Nadra would kill me for not using the right products. When I couldn't hold my breath any longer, I came out of the water and heard the door click shut.

"You have got to be kidding me."

Once again, I had missed the damn servant. At this point, I was beginning to think they were watching me somehow. I hadn't touched a single thing they had brought into the room either day. I stood from the bath and dried with the towel, letting my wet hair fall down my back as I walked into the bedroom. I pulled out another of the prince's oversized shirts and put it on, followed by his trousers. This was practically my room now, so these were basically my clothes.

The luscious scent of food shot through the air like an arrow. I looked to the tray and then turned my back to it, willing myself to pretend like it wasn't there. I failed. And not just kind of. That gods-damned tray haunted me. It was just sitting there like a glowing light beam screaming my name every five seconds. I lifted the cover and steam billowed out. Groaning, my stomach growled in response. Thick potato stew filled a bowl with several rolls and different cheeses off to the sides. A slice of roasted meat sat on a plate, smothered in a savory sauce, and inside a small glass dish were several pastries.

"You know what? Screw it. I give up. Do you hear me Princey Poo? I bet you do. Can you hear this?" I gave a crude gesture to the locked door.

Being the prince's prisoner had absolutely made me a moody bitch, and if I was going to be Alewyn's Promise, or whatever the fuck they wanted to call me, I probably wasn't going to die by poisoning. I was sure those were someone's last words, but I didn't care. I followed up my dinner by locating a decanter sitting atop a table in the corner. I helped myself to that, too.

I started with a glass, then two, and then suddenly I was lying upside down, half on the floor with my feet up in the chair singing every bawdy tune I could think of at the top of my lungs.

"Their hands were so greedy, their mouths mighty crass
So she hiked up her skirts and showed them her ass."

I giggled until I was roaring with laughter. I flipped over and rolled onto the floor, spilling my drink on my shirt and the pretty rug.

"Did you see that, Prince Fancy Pants? I ruined your stupid rug." I hiccupped. "Oops."

I pulled the shirt over my head and stood naked in the room. I crawled into the bed and wrapped the covers around me.

"You know what? I'm just going to be a prisoner forever. I don't even want to get out of here," I slurred.

Then I began to giggle again, and I leaned over the edge of the bed and reached as far as I could for the decanter I had left on the floor. I was almost there. Almost. With my legs still tangled in the blankets, I fell, flopping like a fish. And then I remembered that I was as drunk as a fish and that was hilarious because fish don't even drink. So I just sprawled on the floor twisted in the blankets and laughed until I couldn't breathe.

I heard a sniggering coming from the corner, but I couldn't decide if I had made it up, if it was actually my own laugh, or if I was really just losing my mind.

"Welcome to prison, Freta," I told my new imaginary friend as I lifted a glass. "Try not to break all Prince Pissy's things."

Laughing again, I kicked the blankets off my legs and stood, wobbled, grabbed the edge of the nightstand, and heaved the blankets back up onto the bed, crawling back in. I tossed back the rest of whatever was in that liquor bottle and laid my head on the doughy pillow.

The drunken stupor faded, and I found myself deep within the same nightmare I had the previous night. The grass turned to knives, then snakes, the wind that shoved me off the cliff, the drowning that morphed into burning until I was screaming and screaming inside and outside of my dream.

"Open your eyes, child," I heard a voice say. "Leave that place before you cannot return."

Heart racing, I gently opened my eyes, peeking into my ornate prison. I'd fallen to the cold hard floor, again, but a familiar face stood above me, looking down and shaking her tempered head as I lay racked from the nightmare.

"I leave you alone for such a short time and look at all the trouble you've caused."

"Aibell?" My voice cracked.

"Embers," she said, looking up to the bed and back to me on the floor.

"Embers?" I looked back to the bed and realized she was right.

"Setting the castle to flame is one of many ways, Ara."

"Oh my gods, you have to help me." I peeled myself from the floor. "Water, Aibell. We need water." I looked back to the bedding and watched it burn until the glowing flecks turned into flames. I ran across the room and grabbed a pitcher of some kind of liquid and tossed it onto the fire. Instead of dousing it, the flames roared to life, until nearly the entire bed was aflame. "Aibell!" I screamed. "Do something."

"Such demands warrant no response."

I jerked my hand toward the fire. "Does burning down the fucking castle warrant a response?"

She simply turned away and sat on the scarlet chair sitting in front of the fireplace.

I ran and grabbed another pitcher as the room filled with smoke before turning back to Aibell as she picked loose threads from the seam on the arm of the chair.

"Aibell, please," I urged her. "Would you please help?" I coughed as burning smoke filled my lungs.

"Oh, finally. Manners."

I rolled my eyes and turned my nose into the bend in my arm, trying not to inhale any more smoke. Aibell only looked at the bed, and the flames were gone, taking the smoke with it. Coughing, I doubled over, my throat already sore from screaming through my nightmare.

"Where the fuck did you come from?" I choked.

CHAPTER *6*

TEMIR

I'd only been down the tunnels a handful of times since joining the rebellion. Being a member of the king's inner circle, I knew I had to be more careful than most. I also knew a lot of the rebels didn't trust me yet. I didn't blame them. I'd kept my head down and my ears open most of the time. I wanted this. More so, I needed this. But they had to want me too, and I'd bide my time until they did.

I walked next to Roe, who had summoned me for the rebel leader. Like the rest of the rebels, Rook was a lesser fae–a satyr. We entered the open cavern hidden within the maze of tunnels below the castle and beyond the battlements. It still shocked me that the rebellion was hidden directly under the king's nose. In many ways, it made sense, because it was easy enough for the castle fae to slip in and out as needed. The entrance was not within the castle itself, and I didn't think many even remembered the tunnels existed.

I had never seen the cave empty before. When I looked to Roe with a hiked brow, he only shrugged and continued on until we met Rook. He stood at the front of the room looking over a few giant maps laid out on the table, scratching the base of the curved goat horn atop his head.

"I brought Tem, like you asked, Rook." Roe slipped the hat from his head and squeezed it between his stubby fingers. "You want me to stay?"

"Not this time, Roe. You can wait for him in the tunnels. This should only take a few moments."

I watched him walk away until he turned the corner, then looked back to Rook to see he had done the same. He folded his arms behind his back and paced before me, his hooves echoing off the floor and throughout the large empty space.

"Sir?"

"Yes, yes, just a moment." He walked back and forth a few more times. "Ah." He lifted his finger into the air, then walked over to his map, wrote something along the side, and finally turned to me. "Business as usual," he gruffed. "I'll cut to the chase, Temir. I don't want to waste either of our time today. I have a job that needs to be done. I think you're just the male to do it."

I had known this was coming. I was surprised it hadn't happened sooner. The rebellion planned to test me. But what was the point of being in the rebellion if you didn't do anything?

"Is someone hurt?"

"No, no. Nothing like that this time." He went back to his pacing, and I waited until he had all of his thoughts lined up. "There's a high fae in the castle that I need you to kill."

He dropped that truth like an anchor and waited for my reaction, watching me carefully.

I hid the surprise. "As you know, it's my nature to heal and help others. I cannot take a life." I swallowed the bile rising in my throat as I said the lie aloud.

"I thought you'd say that. Let me tell you a bit about this fae, and we will take it from there. His name is Arol." He halted his march to raise an eyebrow. "Heard of him?"

"In passing. I don't know him personally."

He rubbed one of the curved horns atop his head. "He's been abusing the servants. Last week, a rebel who works at the castle found the body of a sprite crammed into a box and shoved in a wardrobe. The sprite, we believe, was working within the castle."

"Sick," I answered. "How do we know it was Arol and not his wife? She has quite the reputation."

"Has she now?"

"Indeed. She goes to dinner in the hall nearly nude, she snaps at the servers and has been caught by her husband with both male and female faeries. I've not heard much of Arol, but she is fairly well known for her antics. I believe the king finds her entertaining. I wouldn't be surprised if she has visited his bed a few times also."

"I see. I suppose we can't say for sure if it's the husband or wife, so you might need to do some digging. Either way, we need the problem taken care of. It's time to prove yourself, Temir."

"It won't be easy. Especially within the castle."

"If it was easy, it would have been done already." He walked back to his maps in dismissal.

I started toward the door but he stopped me.

"There's one more thing. We need Oravan." He jutted his chin toward my hand. "I need more of those rings."

"You want me to reveal the rebellion to another member of the council?"

It made sense. I knew why Oravan would be a good fae to have on our side, but he'd been approached and denied the recruiting attempts from the Marsh Court. If that didn't persuade him, I doubted a small gathering of angry northern fae was going to do the trick. He nodded as he reached for the map, lifting it as if he was looking through it by the light of the sconces scattered through the room, rather than at it.

"And how am I supposed to do that?" I asked.

"I'm sure you'll figure it out." He folded the paper, turned, and left the room.

I wasn't sure how to read Rook. Sometimes he seemed approachable, at other times it was a hard wall of demands and orders. I supposed that's what a good leader was though. He had to give the jobs to those he saw best fit for them. I could respect him for that. I met Roe in the tunnels, and we made our way back to the castle.

"Wanna talk about it?" he asked.

"Not really." I let out a deep breath. "Let's just say this is going to be a very interesting week."

"Iva's been askin' ta come see you. Think you'll have some time?"

I shrugged. "I might need her help getting into another room later today." I rubbed my temples, lacing magic within the touch to push the budding headache away.

"That bad, huh?"

"The king is in a dangerous mood, and I'll have to be careful."

Later, in my rooms, I pulled the truth serum from its hiding place on the shelf. Mixed in with all the others, it looked like an ordinary elixir. I had told Roe to have Iva meet me in the hall just outside Arol's rooms. I tucked the vial into my pocket and walked out the doors. I came around the corner of the long hall and expected to see Iva waiting for me. What I did not expect was to see her pinned to the ground with Arol covering her mouth so she couldn't scream.

I ran for her. "What the fuck are you doing?" I tackled him to the marbled ground.

"This little monster was standing outside my rooms. Thought I'd teach it a lesson."

I slammed my fist into his face. "What gods-damned lesson do you think you should teach her?"

I punched him over and over again, until Iva rested her hand on my shoulder, breaking the spell. Blood from his broken nose poured, and the desire to heal him didn't come.

"It's okay, Tem," she whispered. "I'm okay."

"Open his doors and meet me in my rooms in twenty minutes."

"Gonna have a little fun with it?" Arol asked, choking on his own blood.

I dragged him through the open door and Iva slid back into the hallway. Looking down to her, I clenched my jaw. "Tell no one you saw me here, nor that you came yourself."

She nodded and walked away. I only suspected Roe had told her I was summoned by Rook. She likely knew what was happening.

Arol's room was simple. A bed sat along the wall, a dresser and a wardrobe filled the rest of the space. I looked at the damn wardrobe and shuddered. I knew what he had done. Probably in this very room. Pulling the corked serum from my pocket, I poured it down Arol's throat as I held him pinned to the ground. "How many lesser fae have you killed in this castle?"

He pinched his lips and turned to the side, but he could not resist for long. "Four," he finally answered.

"Where are they?" I gripped his shoulders so tight he began to squirm.

He looked to the wardrobe and back to me.

"No, surely not all four of them?"

He nodded reluctantly.

I stood and slammed my boot into his ribs. "Why?"

"Because they are tiny, impure beasts, and I'm doing the world a favor every time I slice one of those bastards into pieces."

"I want you to look at me and tell me what I am." I bared my teeth, a sharp breath the only sound between us.

"You're a high—" The serum forced the truth into his mind.

His body froze, and his entire bloody face changed. "You're a monster, just like them. How have you been hiding it from the king? Why doesn't anyone know who you really are? I'll tell. I'll tell them all."

"They know what I am, you sick fuck. But like you, they have to treat me like a high fae because the king demanded it. That does nothing for you though. Would you have killed that fae outside of your door today?"

"What's it to you? She your lover?"

My grip tightened so much the blood flow left my fingers. I reached a hand into my pocket. "No, she isn't. She is my friend though, and she deserves so much better."

"I would have killed her. I would have wrapped my hands around her throat and watched her skin turn blue. I would have felt her body convulse beneath me, and I would have added her to my collection. She is nothing. No one."

I sank the knife I was hiding into his chest—I had stolen it from a sea fae after Roe left me—and within minutes, the gargles turned to faint wet breaths, and moments later, the room was silent. It was the loudest silence I'd ever heard.

I had just killed a high fae. I'd taken his life and didn't feel an ounce of regret. This was who I was meant to be. A weapon. A killer. I'd spent so many years hating the possibility of that truth, but at this moment, I relished in it. Gaea may have been the wind or the storm, but I was death incarnate. Deep within me, my power surged to life. More aggressive than I'd ever felt before. I'd accepted my purpose. Not easily, not happily, but I had.

I left Arol's body on the floor, the sea fae's knife in his chest, and crept back to my rooms, where I found Iva waiting for me. Her cheeks were flush, and she shook standing outside my door. I glanced over my shoulder and hustled her into the room. "Iva, if you'd been seen waiting for me, it would have raised suspicion. You must be more careful."

"I'm sorry." She burst into tears.

I froze. I was awkward, had spent the majority of my life in seclusion as often as possible. I knew precisely nothing about comforting anyone. "I'm sorry," I said, vigorously patting her on the back with my fingers. "It's my fault."

"He would have killed me if you hadn't shown up," she sobbed.

"I didn't know, Iva. I wouldn't have asked you if I had known. I only wanted you to let me into his room. That's all."

"It's not your fault," she sniffled, smiling behind her tears. "You can stop patting me now, Temir."

I dropped my hands to my side. "Oh, right." I poured her a glass of her favorite honeysuckle wine and guided her to the couch, where I moved a few notebooks I had been working on.

"Honestly, Temir. I'm coming to clean this room whether you like it or not. It's a disaster. How do you even find anything?" She swiped her hands over her cheeks and forced her sadness away, as if happiness was a mask she was used to wearing.

"It's only a disaster if you don't understand my perfect organizational process. Everything is exactly where I need it to be."

She shook her head. "I'll put everything in a nice, organized pile. Your dust has dust, Tem." She smiled at me, and her cheeks flushed.

I nearly forgot she had a small crush on me. Here we were, alone in my rooms, as I gave her wine and tried to console her. I jumped from the couch and scratched the back of my head while stepping away. "Uh. Yeah, okay then. As long as you don't feel like you have to." I couldn't make eye contact with her. "I've got to find Oravan to deliver a message. Take as long as you need."

I grabbed a full flask and headed for the door.

"He'll be in the forge," she called after me.

Obviously. Where else would the blacksmith spend his time?

Oravan had a small forge in the bailey near the lists. Most of his work was done with magic, so he didn't need much space to work. I had only been there a couple of times, but as I opened the door and the heat of the small building struck me, my eyes watered, and I had to take a moment to see past the large fire in the middle of the room.

"What is it?" I heard him call from the other side.

"Got a minute to talk?" I hollered over the clanking of his hammer.

"Not taking orders right now," he yelled back.

"No. No, I'm not putting in an order." I took a step onto the soot-covered floor and moved to the side so I could see him beyond the flames. "I just wanted to talk to you."

"No one ever wants to just talk to the blacksmith." He continued to beat on his project, though his magic swirled, heating the tip of the weapon.

"Alright. I just wanted to say thanks for the ring. It works great, but I'm sure you knew that already."

The hammer stopped as I walked back to the door.

"Wait." He set the hammer down and ambled over to me. His long white hair was tied back in leathers—as it usually was—his hands permanently stained black from his work. "Don't think I haven't seen you with that ring on since I made it. You've had it for a while. Why come thank me now?"

I thought back to the king's order. He enchanted everyone in the council meeting to make them hunt for suspects in Thane's murder. I hoped Oravan wore his own shield against enchanting, but I couldn't risk it.

"Care for a drink?" I asked.

He tilted his head, pressing his lips into a fine line. "S'pose I could spare a minute or two."

I pulled the flask from my pocket as he pointed at two folded chairs in the corner. We took our seats, and I held the flask out to him first.

"Woah. Rough day?" he asked, indicating my split knuckles.

"Just a little training. Can't be too careful these days."

"Too true." He lifted the flask to his mouth and swallowed nearly half the liquid. He handed it back to me and wiped his dripping chin with the back of his dirty arm. "Your wine tastes awful, Temir."

"Yeah. I'm working on it."

He looked at me curiously but didn't say anything.

I held the flask to my lips and faked a swallow. "Are you protected from the king's enchantment?" I asked as casually as I could.

"Of course."

"Why didn't you join the Marsh Court when they tried to recruit you?"

"Ah, Gaea did tell you the secret, then. I don't know why I trusted her to keep it."

"It didn't come easily from her, if that's what you're worried about. I don't think she will tell anyone else."

"I told them no because I've known for a long time King Autus was not going to be happy conquering only the other half of the north. He believes himself to be a greater ruler. His mother's ties through Coro's lands drive him. I was here, you know. During the Iron Wars. I know that gleam in his eye. If I had left him for Coro, he would have only killed us both once he moves south."

"Did you want to leave?"

"Yes." His brow furrowed, and I guessed he would have preferred to lie about that.

"I'm going to tell you something now, but I need your word that you will not repeat it."

"I'm not sure that's a bargain worth taking." Oravan fidgeted with his hands.

I shifted in my seat and leaned in. "I won't force you to accept, but if you're interested, there is another option outside of the court's rule."

He looked at me for a long time until his gaze shifted as he studied the flames of the forge's fire. "What's in the drink, Temir?"

I stared at him. Only Gaea and I knew of the truth serum. If I told him, I wasn't sure I could hold him to his word. Still, the rebellion was testing me, and I needed to prove myself. I'd joined to make a difference, and that's what I was going to do.

"It's a truth serum, Oravan. Now that you've consumed it, you will either be stuck telling the truth until, one day, it eventually wears off, or

I can give you the antidote right now." I patted my other pocket as his eyes lifted.

"Alright. A secret for a secret. You know I only stayed out of fear, and I know you have the ability to make a very dangerous weapon."

I glanced around the room noting the blades covering the walls. "You can also make a very dangerous weapon, Oravan."

"Yes, I can. There's one in particular you might want to know about." He looked at me expectantly.

"I won't give you the other information until you verbally speak the bargain out loud. You must promise that this will stay between you and me, no matter what."

"Okay, I promise I won't speak a word of anything we have discussed on this day as long as you make the same bargain to me."

I paused, realizing he had me. It was a game we were playing. He had something else to share, and so did I, but could I promise not to speak of it? A promise under the truth serum wasn't even binding, though I didn't tell him that.

I nodded. "It's a deal. You first."

"The king asked me to duplicate a weapon. It is a blade forged in magic replicating one I'd only heard passed down in stories. Terrible stories."

"So he wants a new sword?" I didn't see the issue.

"It's not just any sword, Temir. Once I've finished this, it will be kin to the most powerful sword ever created. I think he has a plan for it, I just haven't been able to determine what it is.

"Can you give him a fake?"

He shook his head. "I don't think so. The amount of power this thing needs will nearly drain me. Evin knows it. The king will have him test it, as he always does. If I don't put enough magic into it, he will know."

"Shit." I'd forgotten about the king's personal magic detector.

"Your turn," he said, eyeing me.

"Right. Well, I'm not sure how to say this other than bluntly. The rebellion wants you to leave the king and go into hiding with them. They need your skills, and I've been sent to personally ask you to join us."

"Wait." He stood. "Holy fuck, Temir." He ran his hands through the hair at the top of his head. Eyes wide, he looked away and back to me. "Are you telling me there's an organized rebellion against the king?"

"I am," I said, nodding.

"And they want me to join?"

"They do."

"I don't know." His heavy steps were a cadence to his indecision as he paced the room. "On one hand, I'd love to get my family the fuck out of here and go into hiding. On the other, a rebellion could be a death sentence."

"Well," I said, standing. "You don't have to decide today, but you must keep this between us. If you want to join, find a way to let me know, and the rebellion can have you and your family out of the castle and in hiding before the king even knows you've left."

"What about you? You've joined them but remained in the castle?"

I shrugged. "Spy, I guess."

He was shocked, rubbing his aged hands down his face in disbelief. "And Gaea?"

"She doesn't know. Not yet, at least. I won't keep her in the dark much longer. The rebellion could use her too."

"Where are they? The rebellion."

"That's information on a need-to-know basis. You decide to join, I'll introduce you to the leader, and he can determine for himself what to tell you."

"Holy fuck," he said again.

"Do you have any intentions of sharing this information, Oravan?" I asked him.

"No," he answered.

"Good." I handed him the antidote and walked out. I wasn't sure if that had gone well or not, but I'd at least covered my own ass. For now, anyway.

KING TOLERO

"*I*nto lightness and darkness, into shadows and mist, may you rest for eternity. Over the mountains and beneath the sea, let your spirit find peace. May nature keep your soul, the wind hold your memories, the river bless your spirit, and the fire carry you away."

I took four reluctant steps through the deep sands on the crowded beach toward the pyre and laid the torch within. As the flames grew higher and the bard sang to the heavens, I gave the signal, and the pyre was pushed into the water. I held my breath as the widow beside me crumpled to the ground. I knelt and helped to lift her. "You may cry, but never fall."

"Yes, Your Grace," she wept.

I put my arm around her trembling shoulder and stood solemnly beside her as the pyre drifted away. One by one, the fae surrounding us lifted a hand to her. Until there was no room, and then those in the back lifted a hand to the fae in front of them and so on until we were all connected by hands and fingertips, watching Favic leave us.

"Please, come back to the palace grounds. We will have the dancers perform and drinks will be provided. Let us turn this tragedy into a reason to celebrate the soul of a fae we knew well and loved."

As I sat amongst the fae outside, listening to the celebrations, I thought I might drink heavily that night. It left a bitter taste in my mouth though, so instead, I let the fire dancers entrance me while the drums thundered through the night and my people danced the traditional Jabari.

The fae of my kingdom were proud and ritualistic. In moments like these, life was breathed into me again. I felt our pride and our purpose. I watched the warriors dance, and my soul moved within me. A tiny bit of that tiger I'd locked away shifted. I'd almost forgotten he existed, as my people were surely beginning to forget. Would they remember me as the fierce king I once was, or would I be remembered as the shell of a male I had become? I handed my cup to Inok and took myself to bed. Even I didn't want to be around myself anymore.

I spent the next few days moping until, finally, I pulled myself up and out of bed with conviction. I would not live this day as I had the others before it. I dressed and went to the stables. The powerful fae horses stamped and grew agitated as I walked through. Their massive, fearsome muscles shuddered, and their restless hooves kicked up pillows of sand around them, creating flashes of memories through my mind. Memories of my happy childhood. Memories of stolen kisses and fervent wishes of a boy so incredibly young and naive.

"Yes, it has been a while, boys."

"Who in the—" The stable master noticed me and balked. "By the mother, Your Grace. I'm so sorry, I didn't see it was you. Can I help you?" He fell to his knees.

"No, no, Rah. I'm sorry to cause a disturbance. It's just ... I require something of you."

"Anything," he answered.

"Is there something I can do here to help? Any job that needs to be done that I could assist with?"

He recoiled, curling his lip. "No, of course not."

"I won't be in the way. I just need something to change my mindset a bit. I could muck the stalls?"

"No, Your Grace. You couldn't."

"Rah, my father sent me to the stables all the time when I misbehaved. It's been a long time, but I know my way around a couple of horses."

I could enchant him. I could force him to give me a job. I just wouldn't.

"Well, Your Grace, if you insist. The tack is all lined up there. The horses need to be brushed down and saddled. Be careful with Bette on the end. She's feisty on her good days and downright mean on the others. She may nip at you."

"Great. I'll start with her."

"Are you sure?"

"I'm sure, Rah. Just go about your business and pretend like I'm not here."

"Oh, um, okay. But can I help you? I could carry the equipment, if you like?"

"I'd prefer to do it on my own. See if I can still manage."

I stood in front of Bette with the heavy bridle in my hand. I had learned long ago to place my forearm above and between the ears and guide it on, directing the bit into the mouth, but she shook wildly and bit me twice.

I finally remembered to press my thumb into her gum, and she opened, letting me complete my task. For the first time in a while, I was challenged and felt a small victory. I looked up to see Rah watching me, but at my gaze, he went back to whatever busy work he could find. I saddled two more horses, catching his eyes every time I looked up until, finally, I couldn't take it anymore. "Is there something you want to talk about, Rah?"

"Oh!" He jumped up and threw his rag on the workbench. "Yes, Your Grace. If you don't mind?"

"Well, I don't see how either of us is going to get much work done until you speak your mind." I walked to the stall of the next fae horse, and he followed me.

"Me and the guys were talking and, well, I was just wondering. Do you think the dracs have anything to do with Favic's death? They were the only ones here and all."

I sighed, handing him the reins. "I don't think the draconians had anything to do with it, but I suppose this is going to keep coming up until we find out for sure. Ready four more horses. I'll be back shortly."

Within an hour, Inok, myself, and two guards were on our way to the dunes. I sat atop the fae horse and watched the clear water jugs sway with each step the leading horse took. I considered the conversation I would have with Umari and knew no matter what I said, she would take it as a threat, and we were going to have larger problems on our hands. But what was a king's job, if not to have difficult conversations?

"Any predictions on how this is going to go?"

"She'll kill us all just for asking," Inok said.

"I do not fear the draconian fae and nor should you."

"Oh no, it's not the whole group of them, just Umari. She's a beast."

He laughed, and the sound was so infectious I laughed with him, and before I knew it, the guards were laughing as well. For all her beauty and traditional values, she really was a brute.

We came upon the towering dunes by nearly nightfall. There was nothing like watching the burning sun settle into the scorching sand, surrounded by a million colors painted across the endless sky. The draconian village sat nestled deep within the canyon with a small body of water, an oasis, in the middle. There was no way to approach the village unannounced. The draconian guards marched along the hilltop with eagle eyes and lethal grace. Even against the setting sun, their silhouettes showed their large, muscled bodies.

Pride coursed through me as I watched them stride back and forth in total unison.

We were approached long before we made it to the village. In one fluid motion, the draconian fae fell to bended knees before me. It had been so long since I'd visited, I let them hold their bow longer than I normally would have. I had come to question them. It needed to start with respect for the crown.

"Rise." My voice lingered in the chilly night air. I looked sideways to Inok as we were guided to the village, and he did not waiver. His head remained forward. His chin held high. In everything but blood, Inok was my brother, and I could feel the tension rising within him as we moved closer to the village.

"Where are the fae?" I asked as we approached.

The village was still and silent. The draconian people lived as a unit. Often taking all their meals together, sleeping together, and training together. They lived as one, usually outside of their homes. I'd never seen the village bare before.

"They are in prayer, my king," a sentry answered.

"Is something wrong?"

"It is not my place to speak of it. We have sent ahead for Umari, and she will join you soon. Please, rest." He handed me a flask of water. They only drank wine or ale on certain holidays and funerals, so that confirmed no one had died.

We were led to a building where I took the head table, the guards standing at the door, and Inok to my right. I sat with my spine straight and listened carefully for any sign of the draconians as I waited for Umari. I caught myself yawning. The soft breeze that followed us to the dunes began to build, and before she arrived, the winds had grown so strong, even within the building, I could hear nothing else. Desert winds could be dangerous. They were the warnings and creators of sandstorms.

The door slammed open, and Umari marched in, leaving the door open as she adjusted her clothing, dusting the sand from her. I nodded to a guard to shut the doors so I could hear beyond the storm as she stalked forward.

"This is an unwelcome surprise," she said, kneeling before me.

"I won't apologize for my intrusion. These are my lands, Umari. You'll do well to remember that. I've given you the freedom to govern your own, but don't forget yourself."

She simply nodded and rose, jamming her hands to her side as she waited.

"Where are your people?"

"They are in prayer, Your Grace," she hissed. She was so protective of them. I'm sure giving any information at all felt like a betrayal.

"What is wrong?"

She stared at me for a long time. Her measured breaths were the warning of her brittle mood.

"Umari, please. This war between us will only grow until we are forced to do things neither of us wants to do. I won't apologize again for what happened to Efi. I know you loved her very much, but you must see how I suffer as well. The loss of a mate is the greatest punishment of all. We have to move on."

Her tanned skin reddened, and I braced myself for the explosion. Instead, she let her shoulders sink and whispered, "It is the cetani, Your Grace."

"What about them?" I moved to the edge of my seat.

She swept her hand toward the door, her stacks of bracelets clinging together at the motion. "Please, come and see. I do not have answers."

I followed her out of the building, and, as the sand beat into my skin, I forced each step through the high winds, hearing nothing around me as we moved together through the building storm and toward the hollowed caves built into the sandy hills.

The cetani, with bodies of great cats and behemoth feathered wings, built their own nest. They dug it into a cave on the side of a dune, and it took the draconian fae a long, long time to build a strong enough relationship with them so they could enter. That trust was the stipulation to the draconians being allowed to enter the Flame Court so long ago. The cetani did not care that I was a king. I was just another male, a threat to them.

We entered the cave, and Umari lit a long torch and indicated for us to follow her. Our shadows danced along the walls as the sound of the wind grew softer while the sound of singing draconians grew louder. The hall opened to a large clearing, and every one of Umari's fae who were not on patrol sat on their knees in a massive circle, arms extended to their sides to rest on the shoulders of the fae beside them. They swayed as one, letting the deep tone of their voices rise and echo through the room. In the middle of the circle sat the giant nest of cetani, all gathered together. Some with wings spread to cover others, some curled into themselves, some more still than they should have ever been.

"What is happening?" I breathed.

"The cetani are ill," Umari whispered. "We found them like this several days ago, and now they will not eat or drink, and none have left the nest. They will not let us close enough to see what is occurring."

"Why didn't you mention it when you were at the castle?" I demanded.

"Because I don't have answers to the questions you would have asked. It was difficult to come at all."

A tear escaped her, and I wondered if I had ever seen her emotional. Not even at Efi's funeral pyre had she wavered.

"May I get closer?" I asked, using small, slow movements.

"If they will allow it. Asha has been guarding them all fiercely."

Asha was Efi's cetani, their leader. I handed my staff to Inok, and he grabbed my shoulder.

"Please consider this, King. They are wild creatures. It is dangerous."

"All the same," I said, walking away.

I stepped over the extended arms of the singing draconian fae, and I was not sure they even noticed I was there, lost in prayer as they were. I inched myself forward, locking eyes with Asha. With a mane of a male lion and feathered wings as wide as she was tall, her enormous maw opened to howl at me, and I stopped. She lifted her body from the pile of cetani and moved around them to block me, never looking away. Her bone-white feathers reflected the warm flames of the torches mounted to the walls. The muscles in her paws were taut, ready to pounce should I move any closer. I looked into her familiar golden eyes and saw a reflection of myself, standing bare before her. It was rare but humbling to feel like I was just a male and nothing more.

I held my hand out to her and dipped my head as Efi had taught me, the proper way to greet a cetani. I heard her move in my direction, and as she placed her face below my hand and nudged me, the room went silent. I hadn't come to see Asha since the death of my beloved. I'd avoided the caves during each visit, knowing what it would do to my heart. But as I brought my head to Asha's and closed my eyes, burying my hands in her mane, I knew I had been wrong. We were exactly the same. Efi was the link between us, but we were still connected, even in her death.

"What's happening, Asha?" I mumbled into her silky neck.

She only moaned in my ear. The loss of the cetani would be great to the Flame Court, but it would be devastating to the draconians. They were a weapon to us all, a flying army of death and destruction, standing five times taller than any fae, even towering over the giants and trolls of the northern kingdom. The draconians though? They'd bonded on a much deeper level, nurturing and loving the beasts as if they were family.

I took a step back to pull away from her, but she pressed her face over my shoulder and pulled me back in. Several of the fae behind me laughed at her open affection, which was rare on any day, but probably more so now.

I looked back to Umari, who stood with a slackened jaw and arms dropped to her sides, then to Inok, who smirked and didn't seem at all surprised. Though he'd cautioned me against it, he'd never faltered in his loyalty. Asha continued to make noises in my ear as I threaded my fingers between her fur, petting her over and over again. She then moved around me and nudged me into the center of the cetani.

The gathered fae rose to their feet, several warning me against going any farther into the giant nest.

Inok's hard voice rose above the crowd. "Your Grace," he shouted. "You mustn't."

"Silence," Umari yelled. "King Tolero, please go on. She wouldn't allow you in if she didn't want to show you something. We have not yet had the honor, and if we can figure out what is wrong, perhaps we can save them."

The choice was made.

I moved closer, keeping my eyes on Asha. She would lash out the minute I went too far. I concentrated, stepping one careful foot in front of the other, until I stood at the outside ring of the nest. She rubbed her nose into my back and moaned once more, and I knew she was giving me permission to continue. The other cetani were not, however. Several growled and hissed, and I nearly turned away, until Asha moved in front of me, spread her wings as far as she could in the cavern, and roared so loud, my sensitive fae ears rang in protest.

The rest of the beasts cowered at her dominance, and I was allowed into the circle. Some of them moaned and shifted back, some of them only watched me as I lifted a hand to touch one of the more sickly-looking animals. His smaller size indicated he was male, and as he moved to hiss at me, I could see his heart was not in it.

"Guide me, Umari. What would you have me look for?"

"Can you see what they guard? In the middle?"

"They are tightly woven, I'm not sure that I can."

"We may never have another chance. You must try, my king."

My king. She had not addressed me as such in many, many years. An indication of the severity of the situation. Her cetani was buried somewhere within the others, and she was clearly worried. As I moved and they shifted, some being pushed back by Asha, it became hard to tell where one began and the other ended. After what must have been hours of careful maneuvering, the scent grew more wretched. I finally saw it, nestled deep within the middle of the cetani. "It is an egg, Umari. They guard an egg."

The gasps from the draconian fae resonated through the entire room.

"Out. You must get out right now."

I turned my back to the egg and looked at Asha. She spread her wings and would not let me pass.

"I'm afraid that's not going to be an option," I called.

"Is there anything else that she is trying to show you?"

I spun back to look. I took a few more steps forward, and my heart plunged into my stomach. I turned back to Asha and raised my hand to her once more. She lowered her head to mine, and I imagined the sound she made was her form of crying out to me. "You must let me leave, Asha. I promise I will come back. We will figure out what is happening." I spoke softly to her, hoping she would understand.

She moved to the side and let me climb my way back out of the ailing cetani. Once I reached the edge, I paused.

"You must eat, Asha. If not for me, then for her. For our Efi." I left her behind, and though Umari tried to stop me for answers, I had to leave the cave entirely.

"Stay here," Umari ordered the draconians.

I let the sandstorm beat against me as I walked all the way back to the sizable hut she met me in, and took my seat. I placed my head in my hands and tried to compose myself. I knew I'd have to say the words. I knew what this would do to them, what it would have done to my mate.

As part of our bargain, the draconian fae were challenged with taming the cetani so that they may become weapons should the southern kingdom ever need them. They took to the task with reverence and were bonded with the cetani faster than anyone thought possible. Perhaps they recognized the ferocious nature of each other. Efi was the first to bond with Asha, before we had finished our negotiations. As the bonds continued to happen with the draconian fae, they began to find purpose and new traditions in the Flame Court. All these years later, I believed the draconians would be lost without them.

"King Tolero?" Umari asked.

I looked to her and knew she could read the despair in my eyes.

"There is an egg," my voice shook. "There were two eggs."

"Were?" She looked down to her hands, her posture stooping.

"There is a sword." I paused, trying to clear the image from my mind. "There is a sword pressed into the second egg. I believe the second cetani egg holds only a skeleton. It's rotted from within."

"No," she answered, hand to her mouth. "They have laid no eggs in all the time we have been with them. Who would do this?"

"There is more, Umari."

Her eyes shot to mine, and mine dropped to the floor.

"A female cetani has died. She is wrapped around the eggs, and I believe they are not eating to protect her body."

"But how did she die?"

"I could not see for sure."

"But the other cetani are sick. It is not just that they refuse to leave the fallen mother, they can barely move. Asha's movements today were the most we have seen from any of them."

"I don't have any more answers, Umari. I wish I did."

"But this means someone has attacked the cetani. Even if it does not explain the illness, the second egg was a deliberate attack. Could you see who the sword might belong to?"

"The hilt was plain. No markings."

"Someone will die for this," she seethed, turning to leave.

"Umari," I ordered, stopping her. "The reason I came here today was to see if you had something to do with the death of a guard at the castle. Was it you or your dracs?"

She only shook her head and walked out into the storm.

CHAPTER

8

ARA

"So, I'm locked in a castle for two days and you just now decide to pop in for a visit?" I raised my eyebrows at her. I knew better. Aibell always had an agenda. I crossed my arms over my chest and stared her down. To my dismay, she only mirrored my stance and didn't answer. No surprise there, old hag.

"The world does not revolve around you, child."

I scoffed and checked the mental shields she had taught me to use. "I never said it did. I didn't ask for your help. I didn't ask you to come here."

"I've come all the same."

"Obviously," I mumbled. "So, are you here to help me or to take tea?"

"Oh, yes please. Tea would be lovely." She smiled and tucked her cloak over her arm.

I made an exaggerated examination of the room. "Looks like we are fresh out of tea this side of the prison door."

"I see the only thing that has grown since we were last together is your mouth."

"No, my mouth is the same, but my balls are bigger."

She pursed her lips. "Tell me child, have you found more comfort in the prince's shirts or his sheets?"

I rolled my eyes. "I'll answer that if you answer something for me." I crossed the room and sat at the table near the door.

She followed me and pulled out every chair until she found the one she liked. She sat, placed her hands on the table and waited for me to ask. She knew this was coming.

"Exactly how long have you known I have magic?"

"Since the moment of your birth," she said dully, as if I should have asked a more interesting question.

"Then why can't I use it?" I slumped back in my chair.

"Only rushing the river ends well."

"I opened the book, Aibell." My voice softened as I looked toward the table. I began to run my fingernail along a scratch in the wood. Anything to avoid those eyes.

"Yes, well, that is why you came here, isn't it?"

"I thought so. But it felt wrong. It felt dark, and it pulled me in. I've had nightmares for two nights because of it."

"Nealla herself is not dangerous to you, but there are plenty of things within that book that would rip your soul to shreds. You need to be careful with it."

"I'll leave it behind once I get out of here."

"No," she said, inhaling sharply. "You must use it later. That book should not even be in existence. It needs to be destroyed, and there is only one way to do that."

"I don't want to take that thing with me." I looked behind her shoulder at the book in question.

"You must take it to the waters beyond The Mists. You will find Nealla on the other side."

"But if you knew that ..." I stood from my chair and threw my hands in the air. "What is with everything being a fucking game with the fae? Why couldn't you have just told me that?"

"Think of the journey. Think of the lives you saved, the lives you changed, the fae you've helped. That was meant to be."

"But I don't want this. I don't want any of this."

"You are not alone, child."

I crossed the room, picked up the book, and set it on the table between us. "Why does it feel like it calls to me?"

"Because there are creatures locked within the book that would make Nealla look like a schoolteacher in your eyes. That book is dangerous."

"So, was my task to find the book for you or for me?"

She nodded.

Perfect. I refused to look down at the book. I tried not to think of running my fingers along the textured spine or flipping the seductive pages just to hear the sound it made.

Aibell snapped her fingers in front of me. "Control it."

"I don't know how."

"Think of your mental shield. Try to visualize it the same as you did before."

"No, I can't. Just take it." I slid the book toward her, and she nearly fell backward in her chair to avoid touching it.

"I cannot touch the book. I locked one of the creatures within. I don't want to release it."

"Holy gods, Aibell. How fucking old are you?"

"Older than most." She narrowed her eyes on me, her cheeks sinking in as she pursed her lips.

"What?" I huffed.

She snapped her fingers and I was dressed. Still in the prince's clothing, but at least not half naked. She lifted a corner of her mouth daring me to object. I wouldn't give her the satisfaction. Instead, I pulled the book back across the table and rested my hand under my chin. "Are we waiting for someone to join us or what?"

"Too late," she said, smiling. I looked again around the room, but it was still empty. I would admit I had missed the female but not the riddles. "Ah, finally. Move over one chair, Ara."

I looked around again and then slowly stood and moved over a chair, so I sat beside her and left one empty.

The door slammed open, and in walked the pompous prince and his three lackeys like he owned the damn place. Which he didn't. I pulled a knife and moved to jump out of my seat, but Aibell grabbed my hand and—though she smiled pleasantly—I was absolutely frozen in place.

"Let me go," I ordered, baring my teeth.

"Do as you're told, girl, and stay seated."

"I'll kill him," I whispered.

"Maybe someday, but not this one."

She let go of me, but I was still unable to move anything below my shoulders.

"Old One," the prince said, dipping his chin in respect.

"Holy fucking fuck," I sputtered. "Are you kidding me, Aibell?"

One of the lackeys in the back snorted, and I shot a death glare at him. He stood up straight and looked away.

"It was you," I breathed.

"You shouldn't have come here," he answered, his voice like honey, though his choice of words stung like bees. His sharp jawline was still covered in perfectly trimmed stubble, and I hated him just for that. And his stupid tanned skin. I hated that too.

"You were the one who came to Aibell's? It was the gods-damned prince?" I jerked my head to Aibell.

She only nodded but said nothing else.

"I heard your voice after I was poisoned. Why?"

He shook his head dismissively.

"Hey, asshole. I asked you a question. Let me explain. A question is when someone like me," I pointed at myself, "asks someone like you," I pointed at him, "a sentence expressed to elicit specific information."

A lackey in the back with messy blonde hair and ocean-blue eyes doubled over laughing and patted the prince on the shoulder. "You're screwed, Fen."

He swatted his hand away and looked back at me with nothing more than cold hard anger, and I was glad for it. At least we were on the same page. "I know what a question is, Ara." I refused to acknowledge the way my body responded to his sultry use of my name. "I would rather explain from the beginning."

"You know what? No. You don't get to call the shots here. I've been locked in this gods-damned room for two fucking days while you and your minions probably got drunk at that tavern you love so much."

The ire within me swelled until it didn't matter what spell Aibell had put on me. I leaped from my chair, and before anyone in the room could move a muscle, I had my knife to his throat.

"We're going to play by my rules now, got it?"

The three guards started toward me from the door, but the prince held up his hand. I looked to Aibell, and she only smiled delightfully as I realized I had just broken her spell over me.

CHAPTER
9

TEMIR

*T*he king called another council meeting, and the wielders were now required to join.

The line between the council and those of us with magic was becoming very gray. He sat in his oversized chair at the head of the table with an evil smile plastered across his demonic face. His comfort made my skin crawl as I sat prepared for anything. He kept his favorites close to his side, Evin with his ability to detect magic and Eadas, his advisor, with his nose in the air.

The king had been stomping through the castle for so long, there was hardly anyone in the halls anymore. Even the servants skittered as quickly as they could between the rooms. The suffocating tension had caused a lot of turmoil, and some of the visiting fae had left early. When he was like that, you'd lose your head for forgetting to blink. He was dangerous at good times and a ruthless killer at the worst. That was the king I had grown to fear.

He leaned forward with his elbow on the table, thrumming his fingertips together as he stared at Oravan's empty chair. "Where is he?"

Silence.

"Have I lost another?" He stood, screaming. "I asked a question! Have I lost another?"

I remained quiet with my head down as I always had. Of course, I wouldn't tell him that the rebellion had smuggled Oravan and his family out.

King Autus stomped across the room, his footsteps booming like thunder as he moved.

I hated this room. It was dark, cold and rarely did anything good ever come of it. I chanced a glance at Gaea, but her head was also down. She rubbed her fingers together, likely trying to cope with the trauma the king had caused her over so many years as his anger held us on edge.

"Temir," the king shouted.

My heart stopped, and I jumped out of my seat. "Yes, Your Grace?" I should have stuttered. The old Temir might have. I managed to keep my eyes down though.

"Tell me where Oravan is." His magical voice filled the council room like a thick syrup.

"I don't know, King Autus," I lied.

"Sit down."

I promptly did as he said. He worked around the table until he had tried to enchant the truth from everyone. When that failed him, he called in a servant.

"Go to the forge, find the blacksmith and drag him here by his head," he ordered.

The servant dipped in subservience and disappeared. Autus rarely used his enchantment. He was of the mindset all northern fae followed him explicitly and honestly. For that, I was grateful. Had he been less arrogant, the truth of the rebellion would have come forward a long time ago. Right now, we were in complete recruiting mode. That meant word was getting out, and inevitably, we would try recruiting a fae who would turn us over for favor to the king. We needed to tread carefully.

"We are all going to a special place today. Gaea, you will take us to Reith. I've got something to show you."

I'd heard talk of Reith recently. In fact, I was certain it was that tiny northern village from which a few rebels had just returned. The king couldn't have known that though. The rebellion remained undiscovered. I wondered what he could have possibly wanted all of us to see in that small village, but as Gaea spirited us in groups of two to the top of the hill overlooking the village, we were joined by two identical harpies I'd never met before. Both with dark hair and taloned hands, they stood in unison on the ledge, their ribbed wings tucked behind them.

"Allow me to introduce Arcon and Agrad. They work for me now. None of you speak to them. Ever."

Fortunately, I had no interest in the creatures anyway. Even if twins were incredibly rare, and it was hard to look away from them.

The minuscule village was only a gathering of twenty or so cottages built within a hidden valley below towering hills. We watched as a huge brigade of Wind Court soldiers poured out from behind a hill. They were death's army today, creating a perfect circle surrounding the unsuspecting villagers. They rode in that circle until the snow beneath the hooves of the fae horses became mud, and suddenly, from the top of our hill, I realized the king had painted a target.

Gaea stepped to me and took my hand as she grasped what was about to happen. I looked at the varying faces of each council member. Ragal, with his head down and eyes closed, whispered a soft prayer. Eadas and Evin, the king's new favorite pawns, didn't blink as they smiled beside their sovereign, knowing he would expect nothing less of them. But perhaps they did enjoy it. It seemed that way. Gaea already had tears streaming down her face. Bolgan stood watching, though I wondered if he even comprehended what was about to happen, because he looked around in confusion as the horse's thunderous tromps echoed off the sides of the snow-covered hills. The twins watched in eerie similarity.

The king lifted his hand into the air, and the horses came to an abrupt halt. As he dropped his hand, a soldier below called out.

"Exit your homes and present yourselves to your king who awaits you."

The heavy breathing of the troll beside me filled the still air as we waited. I begged the gods to show mercy. Gaea's gasp caught in her throat as the first of the villagers emerged from the safety of their homes. It started with only a handful of faeries, but by the end, nearly a hundred stood below us. If memory served me right, Reith was a village made up of lesser fae that the king had demanded hunt in the mountains, providing the castle with a portion of its meat supply.

"Turn!" the soldier yelled, pointing to the king and his advisors atop the hill.

My stomach rolled and lurched. I didn't want to be seen standing here. A monster among many. Still I refused to look away. Those were fae. Lesser or higher, it didn't matter. They were living, breathing people. Their lives mattered, and I would not blink as that right was stolen from them.

As one, the soldiers streamed into the middle of the circle with their weapons raised. I dropped Gaea's hand as I went numb. The stark white snow on the ground became stained with the blood of my brothers as guttural screams filled the cloudless sky. They were slain like pigs to the slaughter. I heard the king's maniacal laughter as a few tried to run and were cut down. Some fought back. Soldiers were pulled from their horses, but it only gave them a closer proximity to the bloodshed.

"Do you see?" The king laughed. "Do you see what happens when you defy me?"

"What have these people done to you, Autus?" Ragal dared to ask.

"They lived," he answered in anger. "I am the power. I am the God of Death *and* Life. It is by my will alone that you all remain standing here when I could so easily end your lives. You will remember this day. Look down and remember those faces. If any of you make a move against me, you will be next."

The king grabbed Gaea's arm so hard I thought she would cry out. She didn't. Instead, she disappeared with him back to the castle. Upon her return, she took the others, leaving me for last. I stood on the hill and prayed over the fallen bodies as I watched the line of soldiers ride into the cover of the distant hills, as if the God of Death had called them home. I fell to my knees and wept, folding my hands into my body. Perhaps I was nothing more than a weak male without conviction. My shoulders weighed a thousand pounds as the world shifted atop them. Why had I joined a rebellion when things like this still happened? How had no one known the soldiers had crossed the kingdom until now?

Gaea placed her hand on my shoulder and I stood. "Ready to go back?"

I shook my head, staring into the crimson sea of death below me.

"Temir, this wasn't your fault. You know that, right?"

But it was my fault. The king was angry because Oravan had left him. I had set that into motion. I had fueled this eruption of fire. "Go back to the castle. Leave me."

"I can't just leave you out here."

"I'm going down there. I won't leave them like that."

"What are you saying, Temir?"

"I'm going to light the whole village on fire, Gaea. They will have their pyre. I don't care how long it takes me."

"Let me help you." She drew her eyebrows together and lifted her hand to my arm. Not to spirit us away but in comfort. Something in the small gesture only hardened my determination to do the right thing. Their souls needed to be released to the Ether.

I nodded as I walked past her and started down the steep snowy hill. I lost my footing several times, skidding down the ice as I went, but eventually, I stood amongst the dead.

"How are we going to do this?" she asked.

"I'll have to move them together. You look through the homes and see if you can find any survivors or anything to start the fire."

I didn't find a single child as I worked my way through the fallen. I was grateful for that small mercy as I moved them. Most of the fae had corralled into the middle of the village, so I carefully added the others, one by one. I lifted a female with a sword in her back, and once I laid her down, I removed the violation to her body. Another male was too heavy for me to lift, and though I tried to move him cautiously, I had to drag him across the ground, atop the others.

"Temir!" Gaea shouted from a doorstep.

I jerked my head to her, and tears stung my eyes as I took in a single survivor. One short, old, gray-haired female stood wrapped in blankets beside Gaea. I took a step but then looked down and remembered I was covered in the blood of her family and friends.

"You may come, boy." She dipped her chin and waited.

I hesitantly closed the gap and watched as the female stared into the pile of bodies I had made. Her eyes misted over, and she shook as she held a hand out to me. "Take me to them."

I grasped her hand, and we took small deliberate steps until we stood before them. "My son," she whispered, pointing.

"I'm so sorry." There were no proper words to bring her comfort.

She reached into her blankets and pulled out a knife. She held it up to me, and I looked at her, tilting my head to the side.

"I've spent my life hiding from that wretched king and the others," she said. "My parents had the sense to realize I would have been collected. I will light my son's funeral pyre, but you will kill me when I am done. My entire life has died today."

"But we could hide you. Protect you," Gaea answered.

"And are you hidden and protected, girl? Are you safe from this?" she asked, indicating the massacre.

Gaea looked to the ground.

"I do not wish to see the world grow darker or more dangerous. It is the only thing I ask." She pushed the knife toward me, but I didn't take it.

I understood those words on a raw level. I knew what she meant, and although Gaea would not have agreed, I did. I nodded.

She turned to the villagers—to her son, her family, her friends—and lifted her fragile hands. I watched as she cast her magic forward and the entire village was engorged with flames, apart from a small circle around the three of us that remained safe. Gaea stood so close her arm brushed mine.

Life could have been taken from us at any moment: sitting in a room with King Autus, living in his castle, dining at his table. Every second of it was dangerous. These could be our bodies burning. We were far guiltier of treason than they were. But in this unfair world, with broken promises and unanswered prayers, we lived and they didn't, and that was the most unjust thing I could imagine. I had no idea why King Autus got to play a God and the rest of us were only cannon fodder, but Alewyn had once again failed us all.

We waited as the flames died down, and we stood in the center of a pile of ashes. The female began to whisper, and we joined her.

"Into lightness and darkness, into shadows and mist, may you rest for eternity. Over the mountains and beneath the sea, let your spirit find peace. May nature keep your soul, the wind hold your memories, the river bless your spirit, and the fire carry you away."

Finally, she turned to me and once again held the knife out. "I am ready." She dropped the blankets that covered her.

"Are you sure?" Gaea asked, tears slipping down her somber face.

"I will not be like you, girl. I've not lived my life according to his plans, and the longer you stay there, you only fool yourself. This world will never heal. I'll take my fire to the grave."

I took the knife and my hands began to shake. Could I do this? I looked to Gaea, but she only turned her back to me.

The female covered my trembling hands with her own. "Have peace, boy. This is my will and will not sit on your soul. I beg of you, send me to the gods. Let me find peace at last."

I nodded, feeling a calm wash over me. I would do this. For her. She would not be Autus' causality. She would die on her own terms. The knife slipped between her ribs. She smiled as she looked up to me while I laid her gently to the ground and held her until only her still body remained.

"It's time to go, Tem." Gaea put her hand on my shoulder.

I stood and turned to her. She wrapped her arms around my waist, and I hugged her back. In an instant, we were in my rooms. She wasn't quick to let go, and I understood. We were all each other had for comfort.

I aimlessly wandered the castle that night—unable to sit in my rooms and pretend like everything was normal—until I found myself sitting outside Oleo's old bedroom door. I leaned my head back and closed my eyes. Someday, I would learn who had killed him. And why. I thought of the old female and wondered if she had lived the opposite of Oleo's life. Were they mirror images of each other? Where one lived in hiding and the other as a servant? Was her life richer, though doused in paranoia and fear, or was his, even though he never made his own choices? I had to believe that, in the end, Oleo chose to love me and Gaea, and the king couldn't have stopped him.

CHAPTER *10*

KING TOLERO

A sandstorm could end as abruptly as it started but traveling through the frigid desert at night was also dangerous. With no lights to guide you, you'd wind up lost by morning, and that was if the cold hadn't sank in too deep. Umari sent males to direct us to a hut for sleeping. The guards stood watch all night, while Inok and I tossed and turned, neither getting a wink of sleep.

He finally gave up on the notion of slumber and asked, "Any guesses?"

"None. I can't stop wondering how anyone would have gotten into that cave without the guards seeing them." I stared up at the roof of the hut.

"I can't stop wondering why anyone *would*."

"My king," a guard called from the door.

"Yes?"

"There are riders approaching. It's too dark to see who they are. They've met up with the drac guards and are heading this way."

"I guess that's our cue, Inok."

"I guess so."

Within minutes, the new company had arrived.

"Hima, what are you doing here?" I asked, surprised to see a castle guard.

"My king," he said, kneeling. "Forgive me for interrupting your rest. I bring grave news."

"More?" Inok jumped to his feet.

"Yes, sir." He nodded. "Two more have been murdered in the city." Inok and I shared a glance.

"Out," he ordered the guards. "Everyone waits for us outside. Be ready to leave immediately."

"Yes, sir," they said in unison and walked out of the hut.

"Say it," Inok demanded. I raised an eyebrow and waited. "You know what is happening. Say it out loud, Tolero."

He only called me by name when we were in private and tensions were high. All the signs were there.

I whispered, "Someone is attacking the Flame Court. We must keep this to ourselves for now, Inok. Just like we used to. I don't want to involve anyone we don't need, and I don't want to draw or give attention to them."

"I don't know, Your Grace. This feels bigger than that. Sporadic deaths draw their own attention."

"We have no idea if the cetani illness has anything to do with what's happening in the city. For now, we will act as if they are unrelated until we find reason to suspect they are."

"Yes, my king."

"As soon as we get back, arrange a meeting with Murtad. Let's go."

I didn't like to let a fae horse run in the desert. Though fully capable and able to make the trip in a fraction of the time, it was hard on them. All obsidian in color, the sun just wore them down. We stopped more often to water them but were still back by late afternoon.

"Better give them a good wash down, Rah."

"Yes, Your Majesty," the stable master said, giving me a wary eye.

"Is there something you wanted to discuss?" I asked him pointedly.

"No ... uh, no, King Tolero," he stammered.

I knew he wanted to ask me about Umari, but he would hear what I had to say as soon as everyone else did. It was best to keep everyone at arm's reach until we knew what precisely was happening.

"You're sure Murtad is coming?" I asked Inok sometime later.

"I'm sure. He said he'd be here. He will be."

We traveled cloaked and without guards to the meeting location. Pressing my palm to the old door, we entered the abandoned building and stepped into the shadows. The walls had begun to rust, and a thick layer of dirt settled atop the dilapidated floorboards, but when it came to Murtad, he liked his secret spots. Sitting together waiting on a rebel leader was not something I believed I would have ever done, but the world was changing. Alewyn had made her move, giving the world her promise, and as the days passed, it looked as if it was time for us to make ours.

A rustling at the front door came, and we jumped to our feet and withdrew weapons. We were meeting in the back of an abandoned shop on the outskirts of the city. Inok and I had made an agreement ages ago that if we were doing recon work, which we did often back in our prime, I would have to enchant fae if we were ever discovered. So, we took extra precautions to avoid that.

"You rang, Your Grace?" Murtad said as he sauntered into the place like he was just out for an evening stroll. He left his golden-brown hair in a disheveled mop on top of his head, but there was no hiding his horns.

"I'm going to cut straight to the chase, Murtad." He bent only slightly at the waist and smirked at my comment. "What do you know, if anything, about the recent deaths in the city?"

He shrugged and picked invisible lint from his jacket. "What should I know, Your Grace?"

"This isn't time for your games, Murtad," Inok snapped. "King Tolero helps fund your rebellion, or have you forgotten?" Inok leaned toward the rebel leader.

He raised his hands in the air and took a step backward. "Calm down, Knocky Knock. I'm not here to pick a fight."

Inok grumbled, and I stepped between them, giving him the eye. "So, you know nothing?"

He casually leaned his shoulder against the wall, examining his hands as he spoke. "Here's what I know. Umari was the first suspect, obviously." He drew out the last word. "But she and her flunkies were here and gone, and Favic was seen sending them off. Couldn't have been them. I have heard someone else kicked it, but no further details."

"Kicked what?" I asked.

"I believe he means to say another person has died, my king," Inok explained through gritted teeth. I had forgotten how much he hated the rebels. The principal concept of a rebellion grated on his nerves.

"Pre-cisely." Murtad nodded.

"Well, the count is up to three." I tossed him two large bags of coins. "I've never asked the rebellion for a thing. I've supported you from afar and anonymously because I believe it's needed. I won't make demands of you, Murtad, but if you could keep your ears out for me and let me know if anything happens or you hear of anything suspicious, I would appreciate it."

"And you do owe him, Murtad."

"You got it, Kingo. See ya later, Knocky," he called, giving a two-finger salute and dancing out of the building.

"This generation—"

"Don't start, Inok. That male is over three hundred years old."

"A baby."

"Close to it." I smiled. "Let's head back. I've still got that meeting with Brax about Attoc and Muth, and I have to make a decision before I meet with them later."

"Ah yes, our people are dying, the cetani are dying and we have to host the Trials, which begin soon," Inok grumbled.

"Better keep that sour face or they might start suspecting something's wrong."

"Funny," he mocked. "What will we do about the last two deaths? We need to address them quickly. Their absences will be noticed. One has a family."

"Let's hold off for now, get the Trials opened and hope that's a big enough distraction. We will hold a private ceremony for the fae with family, and I'll discuss discretion with them while we investigate. Deal?"

"Deal." He kicked a rock on the ground through the empty building.

"The minute we get back to the castle, you better go see Loti for some cake," I laughed.

"Cake will not save the world from its problems," he answered.

"No, but it is delicious."

"If it wasn't far, far below me, I'd roll my eyes at you right now, Tolero."

"Think of it this way, at least we have something to keep us busy. We haven't gotten to do this in over a hundred years."

"Don't be so cheerful. It's not like you."

"I'm the King of the Flame Court. I can do whatever I want," I teased.

"If only Efi were here to," he paused mid-sentence. "I'm sorry, my king. I didn't mean …"

His words trailed off, taking my smile with them. "Let's just head back before anyone notices we are gone."

Somedays I forgot that I wasn't the only one who lost her—that she had bewitched the entire kingdom, and they also felt her gaping absence. Even now, years later.

***

As we sat together in the study later, I asked Brax, "So Attoc, then?"

"Honestly, I'm not sure I trust any of their approaches, but if I'm looking strictly at the fighters, Attoc has the better male."

"What did you find wrong with their approach?"

"The fighters don't seem to be committed to their lords."

"What makes you think that?" Inok asked from beside me.

"Sir," he said, turning toward Inok. "You've always taught the southerners that fighting with pride and purpose would make you a better fighter. I see it in the men's faces every day as we train. But that fire is not there with any of those males."

"Tell me, Brax. What do the Trials mean to you?" Inok asked.

"Well, a lot. I don't much care for the pit fighting. Attoc and Muth train those males for years to fight for bets of blood and glory. The drac ceremony is fun to watch. I like the way they fight, like they can fly through the air without wings. I always try to watch the traditional Rites. The part where the prospective soldiers try to win a slot in the guard. That's where the passion is, if you ask me. Someone fighting for something they want."

"And you think the competitive fighters don't want to win?" I asked.

"No, I think they do want to win. I just …" He paused, scratching the back of his head, and turned away. "I think something is going on down there. Both training fields I went to, the fae were just really apprehensive of me poking around."

Inok and I shared a look. It was just another thing to add to the rapidly growing list of potential problems.

"I have a meeting tonight with both owners, and I have a proposition. I would ask another favor of you, Brax."

"Anything, Your Grace." He nodded eagerly.

A loud raucous in the hall pulled my attention away. I recognized the screaming voice, though it grated on every nerve I had. "Inok will meet with you later." I stood as Umari charged into the vacant room.

"Was it you?" she seethed.

"You will bow before your king and watch your tone, or you will lose your head, Umari. Don't mistake the liberties your king chooses to give you," Inok intervened, stepping in front of me as he motioned for the guards to enter the room.

Umari looked around and slowly bowed, though she held her breath and reddened as she waited for my order.

"Rise," I drawled.

"Was … it … you?" she asked again.

"What specifically?" I asked.

"Did you have anything to do with the illness of the cetani?"

"Umari, what in the Mother's name are you talking about. Of course, I didn't. Did you leave just after we did to make it here? You could have asked last night. If you were so concerned."

"They let me in, Tolero. The sword was my own."

"If it was your own, then why do you accuse me?"

"The same reason you accused me."

"The rest of your people believe I am to blame? Though I was here when it all started?"

She lifted her chin and drawled, "Were you?"

"Umari, I will not defend myself to you or anyone else. I had nothing to do with the cetani illness."

"Not the illness. The egg. You were the first to see it, and no one else was allowed into the circle before you." She clenched her teeth, the tension in her jaw increasing her ferocious nature.

"Why? Why would I ever steal your sword, which I didn't even know you owned, and kill a very rare cetani hatchling? The cetani have been mine, in the Flame Court, long before you came here."

"Was that why? You didn't like that they made the draconians even stronger? Or was it the fact that you didn't like how much they reminded you of my daughter?"

My words became low and lethal. "I'll give you one chance to leave this room unharmed. But do it now, Umari, or you will be taken to the dungeons."

"I have nothing more to say anyway." She got all the way to the door before she stopped. "Stay the hell away from my beasts and my people," she finished, stomping out of the room.

"Shall I retrieve her, Your Grace?" Inok asked, already walking toward the door.

"Let her go. She knows she has a losing fight on her hands. She's worried about the cetani. Just let her go."

It took him several moments of shaking his head and pacing between the desk and the door, but he did as I ordered. "You give her too much freedom, my king. Like a snake, she will eventually have the ability to turn around and bite you."

"I make the best of a terrible situation and have compassion, Inok. It does not mean that I am not still holding her accountable. Send a message to draconian fae that half are to remain with the cetani, and the other half are expected to perform at the Trials."

"But, Your Grace—"

"Inok, now is not the time. We will follow the ritual, and I expect them to do the same. Send the message and let the pit lords in, please." I jammed my thumbs to my temple, making clocklike circles until the tension dissipated.

"Yes, my king," he gritted out, leaving the room.

Within minutes, two males followed him back into the study. Muth was a tall, slender fae. I noted the look he gave me as they entered. Disdain? I looked to Attoc, but he was just as aloof as always with his short gnome-like features. He grabbed the tail of his long white beard and bowed as he kept his eyes to the floor.

I stood. "It's been brought to my attention, per your last meeting request, that you would have me choose between your fighters, rather than deciding amongst yourselves as we have for the Trials for centuries. Is this correct?"

The pit lords looked to each other with blank faces. Definitely odd. They usually hated each other. Both competitive by nature, they could hardly stand by each other some days.

"Yes, Your Grace," Muth said, snapping the last two words like they physically hurt him to say.

Inok cleared his throat.

The males looked to him and stood a bit straighter.

"Don't forget who you stand before, Muth. Your fighting pit is open because I allow it." He said nothing, only stared ahead blankly. "I will not choose either of your fighters to sponsor this year." I waited for the arguing to start, as I knew it would, but instead, they remained still and silent. "Brax will fight in the pit bracket this year as my fighter."

"So that's why he was snooping around my training grounds," Muth spat.

"No, he was there to decide who was the better fighter. Since neither seemed good enough, I've decided to go a different route. Perhaps he will remind you of your place in my kingdom."

"Perhaps." Muth's bitter smile didn't reach his cold eyes.

"That will be all."

They were escorted out of the room, and in that one moment of peace and solitude, I crossed the study and placed my hands on the windowsill, looking out to watch the heat of the sun begin to fade behind the horizon. This was the second day in a row that I had been able to watch the sunset.

"Your Grace?"

I turned to see Inok standing in the doorframe waiting for me to give him another order. I lifted a shoulder. "Shall we take the night off?"

He shook his head. "Muth's always been an impudent twit."

"Sometimes I think the older you get, the less you like your job as my second."

"Oh no, Your Grace. I like my job just fine, I just don't like dealing with disrespectful imbeciles."

"You're in the wrong line of work, then." I smiled.

He shrugged. "Maybe I need that night off after all."

"Go see Loti for some chocolate cake. Find Brax tomorrow and let him know he has a new job," I answered, patting his shoulder. "I'll see you in the morning, old friend."

CHAPTER 11

ARA

"Put the knife down, Ara," the prince demanded with his pretty fucking scowl.

"No, I don't think so. You know, I'm looking back and I'm trying to think of one single time you've been even remotely kind to me, and here's a twist. You haven't. So, I think I'll keep it here." I lifted the blade so it sat below his chin. "I'm going to ask a question, and you're going to answer it, and that's how this is going to go."

He nodded, though I could swear steam came from his long, lovely ears.

"Why do you treat me as if you know me when I've never met you before?"

"It's a long story."

"I have an incredible amount of patience. I think I'll make it through."

"If you would just put the knife down and sit, this would be so much easier."

I pressed the knife in a little closer.

"Okay, fine," he said, throwing his hands up.

I didn't consider how close we were. I didn't consider that we were touching. I didn't even think about it.

"Let me start by saying you're the one demanding this truth."

My voice fell as flat as my stare. "Thank you for clarifying that."

"I knew your mother and father. Your real mother and father, and the pair you knew to be your parents."

"What?" I nearly dropped the dagger as my head whipped to Aibell.

"They will always be the parents of your heart, child."

I shook my head. "What are you saying?"

"You had four parents. Two who gave you life and two who raised you. You've lost nothing. You've only gained."

"Don't," I warned. "Don't sit here and tell me I've lost nothing. I don't believe either of you."

"Why would I lie?" the prince asked.

"I don't know why you do any of the shit you do. Why make me sit at the end of the table at a banquet? Why force me to go home during a ball? Why lock me in your room for days without a single fucking explanation?"

I realized I'd nicked his skin, and as he sucked in a quick breath, I almost apologized for it.

"Put the knife away, Ara," Aibell ordered.

"No. I'm not your puppet, I'm not his puppet, I'm not the world's puppet. You can't just walk in here and be like, 'Oh hey, you know that guy that raised you? Yeah, he isn't your father.' There's not a single thing either of you can say to me to take that title away from him. Get on with your story so I can decide for myself if it's true."

"You are Alewyn's Promise. Because of that, your blood is powerful. It's why Thas—" He paused. "Your father has always taught you to dispose of your blood. It's why your parents knew they would have to die as soon as your prophecy was given. Let me start from the beginning."

I dropped my knife and he turned in his chair to look at me then reached out to take my hand. I stepped backward. "Don't touch me."

He looked to the floor and then rested his hands on his lap.

"Your real ..." He paused. "Your other parents came from the Flame Court. They were high fae living in the court. Your mother was friends with my mother a long time ago." He swallowed and continued. "Everyone was thrilled when they announced you were on the way. As a gift for her friendship, my mother brought in a seer the day you were born. The seer revealed not only half of your prophecy, but all of mine as well." He took a deep breath and scratched the back of his head.

"Do you want to tell this part?" he asked Aibell.

"No. It is you who must tell her."

His shoulders slumped as he released a long sigh. "When the seer announced that you were Alewyn's Promise, your parents knew, if they lived, you would likely die."

"But why?" I shook my head, heavy denial settling in the pit of my stomach.

"Because if anyone discovered who you were, they could use them to get to you, or possibly use their blood, which runs in your veins, to control you with magic. They had no choice. They took their own lives to give you a chance at one. Thassen and Viola, the only parents you knew, were then enchanted by my father to never speak of your true nature or purpose. While they probably wanted to tell you numerous times, they couldn't."

I paced back and forth as he told his tale. My tale. He couldn't have known that I'd been taught to hide my blood. But didn't everyone?

"Your parents were chosen to be your protectors because of their strength and cunning. Your mother was so smart and your father, as a member of the Wild Hunt, would go undetected. Thassen knew my father when he met my mother and trusted no one else."

Deep pride melted over me, knowing my father had been chosen. He was worthy of so much more, as was my mother, who really was a cunning fox. I'd always thought I got my auburn hair from her, but maybe I hadn't. That hurt more than I thought it would.

94

"Go on," Aibell encouraged him.

"The seer was later killed when we learned she gave your secret away. My father had not thought to enchant her, and that's when we knew we had made the right decision. Thassen and Viola lived and worked in the Marsh Court and would keep you safe but hidden in plain sight. Word traveled about Alewyn's Promise until suddenly, one day, no one could speak of you. Nealla had made a blood oath to Alewyn to protect you. Even Aibell is bound from telling all she knows."

I looked at her, and she confirmed with a soft smile. So maybe she wasn't purposefully withholding information.

"If no one else can speak of this, what makes you so special?"

He glanced at Aibell and back again. The fact that he referred to the old hag for every damn thing was slowly eviscerating my last nerve. "Because while you were fated to be Alewyn's Promise, I was fated to be your Guardian."

A subtle shift in the room didn't go unnoticed as the two guards exchanged knowing glances. I'd think about that later. I had enough to process. "Is that it? I'm just supposed to believe my parents weren't my real parents because you said so, and now you have to save me from the big, bad guys? Well, where the fuck were you when I was killing fae just to get to the castle? Where were you to save me from the queen when she captured me? How about capturing me yourself? Just fulfilling your fated duties, Fenlas? No thanks. I don't need a Guardian. I can take care of my gods-damned self."

"I thought you were with her." He tipped his head toward Aibell. "I thought you were safe. I did help you escape the queen. It was one of mine who freed you."

I snagged the book off the table, the dress off the floor and moved toward the door. The three douchebags tried to block me. "Don't make me hurt you." I glared.

"Let her go," the prince commanded, and reluctantly, they let me walk out.

I didn't think about the queen, I didn't even think about Coro, I just stormed through the castle until, finally, I was outside of it. I wanted to fall to my knees with the weight of what they had said. But how could I believe any of them? My parents were gone. All four of them, if the prince were to be believed. My vision clouded with the onset of tears I forced away. Aibell was wrong. I had lost everything. I *was* alone. Irrevocably.

Walking down the worn road, I went directly to the inn where I had stored my things. I'd spent two unpaid days locked in that castle and it was going to be an issue. I was in no mood to deal with issues. Stuffing the book into the waistband of the prince's oversized trousers, I realized I looked like a homeless street wench. *Oh well.*

"Where are my things?" I asked the owner, knife out and ready.

"This isn't a storage chest. You can't come and go as you please without paying for the room." He looked down at my knife, snorted and turned away.

They never took me seriously. I threw the knife in my hand, letting it embed in the wall inches from his face. "I asked where my fucking things are."

"Y-your friend came and got your things."

"I don't have friends," I sneered.

"Yes," he shook. "The pretty one with the red hair. H-her mom is the seamstress."

I hopped over the counter, jerked my knife from the wall, and walked out. I would have paid him had he not added fuel to my growing internal fire.

I had barely thought of Nadra during my isolated time at the castle. I never claimed to be a good friend though. She was probably still mad at me, but at least she had come to get my things. I wasn't sure I would have thought to do the same for her.

I entered her mother's small shop and the glass door squeaked as I walked in. I didn't recognize the place at all. The last time I had come, there were bolts of discarded cloth covering every inch of the floor and rhinestones and beads everywhere. Buttons laid spread out on the counter, and the shelves were unorganized and crammed to the brim with different materials.

Now, the entire place was perfect. The fabrics were organized by color and texture along the walls, a dedicated shelf of jars for all the small trinkets held no dust, and it smelled like wildflowers.

"What happened here?" I asked Nadra's mom. I should probably have known her name, but I didn't. And I wasn't about to ask her now.

She spun at my voice. "Mother above, Ara. Where in the gods' names have you been?"

"Oh, just lounging around the castle," I answered.

"You could have sent a message that you wouldn't be coming right back. Nadra's been worried sick."

"She has?" I asked, twisting my face.

"Of course she has. She's your friend. She hasn't even been sleeping. She cleaned the whole shop to pass the time." She swept her hand through the tidy room.

"I mean, it does look beautiful."

"It's atrocious," she snapped. "I can't find a thing in here."

I smiled. Some people just thrived in chaos. "I'm sorry you were worried. I didn't have a chance to send a message, I was stuck in a room for a couple days."

"Good heavens. The dungeons?"

"No," I said. "The prince's room."

She dropped the scissors she was holding and they clanged to the floor.

"It's not like that," I assured her. "He had some information for me and I had to wait to get it, that's all."

"Oh," she said, her shoulders drooping as the disappointment crushed her. What was it with this female and coupling people?

I handed her the gown she had let me borrow. "Where's Nadra?"

97

"She's in her room. I doubt she's asleep up there."

I started to walk up the stairs but she stopped me, resting her hand on the railing. "I've completed the second outfit you asked for."

"Perfect. I'll be down to try it on in a minute."

She smirked and I knew she was excited.

"Nadra?" I called, knocking on her bedroom door.

"Ara? Good gods!" She swung the door open, and I could see the cleaning spree hadn't spread to her room. "Come in."

I stepped over a pile of clothing and dug my feet down until I was standing on the solid floor, ankle-deep in her mess. "Did you clean the shop to piss off your mom?"

"She's been yelling about it since I finished. It's only fair."

"I'm—"

She held up a hand to stop me. "Listen, before you apologize, which you totally will, I know he was a jerk and didn't deserve me. I'm fine, really. But you should have told me. My mother shouldn't have meddled, and I should have found out about Odir in my own way."

"You're right. If it had been me, I would have wanted to know, too."

"Friends?" she asked, sticking out her hand.

I took it. "Friends."

"Also, thanks for punching that jerk in the face. It's the only thing that has gotten me through. I just think about it over and over again, and then I feel better."

"We can go find him and I'll kick his ass if you want? I need to let off some steam."

"Girl, you are scary as hell, do you know that?"

"I do my best. Listen, I've got to get going. I can't stay in Hrundel. I have to head north."

"Unless you are chasing that beautiful King Autus, why in the world would anyone want to go north? I heard the weather is miserable."

"First of all, that king is not beautiful. Stop saying that. It's creepy. Second, I have some things I need to take care of, and I can't explain it all, but I promise one day I'll come back and I'll let you drag me back to that groomer."

The room filled with her high-pitched laughter. "He's a stylist, Ara. A groomer is for animals."

I shrugged. "Hair is hair, so whatever." She snorted, and I couldn't help but laugh. "Your mom's finished something for me, want to come check it out?"

"Yes! She hasn't even let me peek. Oh, I have your stuff. I was worried when you didn't come back. I thought the innkeeper would have tried to sell it."

"He definitely would have. Thank you."

She crawled atop her mess, and in the corner was my pack, sword, and a small pile of folded clothes. "My mother added a few things. She said when you came, you probably wouldn't stay, but you would need more than a change of clothes."

For the first time, she looked me up and down and scrunched her face. "What in the hell are you wearing?"

"Uhm, Prince Fenlas' clothes?" I lifted a shoulder and looked down. I mean, it wasn't that bad.

"Shut. Up. Tell me everything."

"Nadra, no. It wasn't like that. You're just as bad as your mother." I saw the sting across her face and tried to backtrack. "No, I mean ... it just wasn't like that. He caught me and locked me in his room for a couple days while he was gone, and it was just complicated. I got out though, and no, nothing happened. He's a terrible fae and he disgusts me."

"You don't mean that at all." She smiled. "Your words don't match your face, Ara."

I glared at her. "You have no idea."

"Mhm," she answered, bounding down the stairs.

"Are you ready?" Her mother stood before a mannequin covered with a long piece of navy fabric. "I've added in a few more things than what you asked for. This is quite possibly the greatest thing I've ever made." Her eyes gleamed, her smile filling her entire face.

She ripped the cover off the mannequin, and with it, the air from my lungs. It was literal perfection. She reached up and removed the black hooded cloak by unfastening a silver clasp on the front neckline.

I reached out to touch the material. "What is it?"

It was gods-damned perfect.

"It is made from a fabric that I've created to be whatever you need it to be. If you are hot, it will cool you. It's as light as silk and as hard as metal."

It was such a dark black material, the details on the bodice, the textures all melted into the shadows, sitting in the middle of a well-lit room. It was a full-piece black suit with intricate metal that covered the chest and various spots along the legs, arms and bodice. The metal wrapped along the back and resembled wings that did not extend beyond the frame.

"Will I be able to move in the armor?" I asked, reaching out to feel the seductive material.

"It is quite light and not restricting."

"Can I try it on?"

"As if I'd let you leave here without seeing you squeeze your hot ass into this," Nadra said from behind me.

It fit like a glove, and just as I had asked, it could carry all my weapons easily.

"Why hasn't the king stolen you away from us?" Gold flakes trimmed the full-length mirror I stared into. The reflection did not do the material justice.

"Oh, I work for him when he demands it, but he lets me stay in the shop. As long as I'm easily accessible, apparently that's good enough for him. No one with magic is immune to the capture of royalty."

"Right."

I strapped my weapons on, added the cloak, and told Nadra she could keep the prince's clothes. She awkwardly hugged me, and her mother did the same. And then I left, promising I'd see them again one day.

CHAPTER
12

TEMIR

"Tell me, Temir," the bitter king asked from his elevated seat at the head of the table. "Why the hell do I even have a council when no one fucking councils me?"

It was our third mandatory meeting in a week. The king was interchanging the wielders and his council. Probably because they were dropping like flies around him no matter what he did.

"I can't speak for the rest of the fae here, but I cannot, in good conscience, offer council on a subject I know nothing about."

"So, you're worthless?"

I didn't want to respond. The words didn't even sting. His negative opinion of me was irrelevant. I was only here for the rebellion. "Perhaps. I will try to speak up more frequently." I pinched my knuckles under the table to try to keep my face neutral.

"Yes, well, if everyone would come with that conviction, maybe we would get somewhere." He turned to look at Ragal.

His cousin did not waver.

"May you all be as ambitious as Temir," the king said, leaning his elbows on the table and looking between each member.

A pointed foot crashed into my shin. While I was confident it had come from Gaea, she didn't appear to have moved at all. Sneaky little vixen.

"I need a replacement for Thane. Temir, since you've decided to speak the fuck up finally, who should it be?"

I looked around the room and considered my options. There weren't many. I looked to Ragal first, but the barely perceptible shake of his head was enough of an answer from him. The dark twins were new, I couldn't rely on what little I knew of them.

"Today," King Autus shouted so loud I jumped.

"Eadas," I said instantly, choosing a random member.

"Why?" he asked firmly.

"What else does he contribute?" The words were out of my mouth before I could filter them, and while I'm sure Eadas was infuriated by my comment, Bolgan's laugh filled the chamber, and I thought even the king raised a corner of his mouth.

Eadas turned his nose up. "I do a lot more than you, Temir. I give my king anything he needs."

I bet you do.

"Precisely. The Wind Court could use that devotion in other areas as well," I answered blandly. I enjoyed the red tint to his face as I barely responded.

"All members in favor of Eadas taking over as general of my army, raise your hand."

Confused, Gaea and I looked at each other. Evin timidly raised his hand, and Autus slapped him in the back of the head.

"Don't be an idiot, Evin. We don't fucking vote around here. You do whatever the hell I say, and that's it. Eadas, you start with the soldiers tomorrow morning."

The twins ducked their heads, snickering, their wings shuddering behind them at the movement. It was strange. When I went to the meetings at the castle, we sat in the largest, most hollow room where only Autus had a voice and the rest of us were really there to fluff his feathers and do as we were told. The room was quiet and cold, and each person sat a million worlds apart from the next, apart from them.

Later, I sat crammed in the rear corner of the rebel's compound surrounded by so many fae I couldn't count them all as they shifted. Each one with their own stories—their own memories of Autus and his hateful court. I didn't matter here, and I was okay with that. I was one more male. One more person with one more set of painful memories. It was hard to see the rebellion as anything but strong and united when the king sat in his giant castle, surrounded by fae that feared him, but each of these faeries had made a decision to be here.

The hushed tones of the crowd grew silent as Rook stepped forward, placed his hand to his chest and thumped his fist. The crowd did the same, and you could have heard a pin drop as he began. Although his voice was quiet, the cave carried it through to everyone easily.

"I'll start by asking anyone with news to raise their hands."

A few scattered fae raised their hands in unison with my own. Some looked surprised, but no one said anything. I was new. Even though I had done a mass healing in front of nearly everyone here, even though I'd revealed a secret that I carried from my childhood, they still hadn't accepted me yet.

"You, please come forward," Rook said, gesturing to a female in front.

She stood and faced the crowd. "I've news of a distant cousin to share. She lives within the Marsh Court, but her mother writes to me that she has shown signs of magic." The crowd gasped, and Rook raised his fist to silence them. "We believe she manipulates the air somehow. She's had no proper training, but her mother has agreed to send her to the Weaver."

The fae in the room waved their hands in silent applause at the potential win for the rebels as it was still necessary to keep our volume low. The kingdom functioned above us, even if the main hall was somewhere below the outside of the battlements based on my quick estimate.

Magic was so powerful. Anyone who we could bring to our side was a great leap forward. The female melted back into the crowd, and Rook asked for raised hands. Again, I raised my own.

He pointed to a fae in the crowd with great stag horns like mine should have been. My heart leaped as I wondered if he was of any relation. I had no idea who my parents were. I had grown up in the stables as a discarded lesser fae.

The male stepped forward and bowed his head. The silence grew thick in the air as the crowd anticipated bad news. "My boy," he said as his voice cracked. "My boy was summoned by the king." He began to shake with sorrow or anger, I wasn't sure. "The king accused him of stealing from the village and ordered him killed. Not just killed, he was slaughtered."

A cry rang out from the crowd, and the male stepped back to comfort a wailing female. The rebels reacted in a way I hadn't seen before. Surrounding the couple, they reached for them, and then the next layer around touched for those in front of them, until the act stretched all the way to me along the rock wall in the back. I lifted my hand to the fae in front of me, and as one, we were all connected. It was a powerful statement. Possibly the most moving thing I had ever been a part of. We shared the loss of the boy with the male and female and sent our comfort forward, as though it were a palpable, tangible thing.

After several moments, the crowd dropped their arms and again Rook stepped forward. This time he called on me, and the rebels parted so I could step to the front of the room.

Before I addressed the crowd, I leaned into Rook's ear. "This will be heartbreaking. Do you want me to tell you first?"

"No. Address the masses. We are one."

I nodded and turned to face them. At least a thousand fae eyes were glued to me as I pulled off my hood and took the deepest breath I could muster. "Three nights' past, the king forced the council to stand on a hill just above Reith. We were made to watch as the soldiers poured in around the town and killed all but one old fae female."

The cries throughout the room were so loud, Rook had to raise his fist and then clap his hands to quiet them down.

"We were recruiting in Reith," Rook said quietly behind me.

"I know. But I can assure you, no one is left, and if you send anyone there, he will be watching. Waiting for them."

"What happened to the old female?" someone asked from the crowd.

"After all the others had left, another council member and I went down the hill to create a pyre for the citizens of Reith. She searched the houses while I—" I stumbled over the words, and Rook put his hand on my shoulder. "I moved the fallen bodies to a pile so that we could release their souls to the Ether. It was not pretty, and I'm not proud." I steadied myself. "The other council member found the female hiding inside of a home. She said she had spent her entire life hiding her magic from the king. I can't say I blame her. She wanted her life to end on her own terms, and I could not deny that to her after she had witnessed the death of everyone she knew."

"That could not have been easy," Rook said.

"But I have relations in Reith," a male called from the crowd. "This cannot be. Surely we would have gotten word by now if this was three nights' past?"

"How? No one is left to speak of it but the soldiers who would kill you for that knowledge. You must be careful to speak of it even now," I told them. "One other thing." I turned to face Oravan in the crowd. "He has enchanted several others to kill you and your family on sight. You must be extra cautious."

He nodded graciously as he buried his hands into his beard.

"Come see me after the meeting ends, Temir," Rook said in a hushed tone behind me.

Nodding, I walked back through the crowd to my place in the back along the wall. I was greeted with a few pats as I settled in. If I continued to prove myself useful, knowledgeable, I hoped they would accept me more readily. I hadn't fit in my entire life, and it had never mattered until now. Joining the rebellion was a risk for me, but it was also a risk to all the other fae who disappeared into the tunnels each time there was a meeting.

They had a system. Rebels would pass each other and give hand signals or send symbols to indicate when the meetings would be. It was always days out, so word could be spread cautiously. Then, the fae would descend into the tunnels in small groups for a full day leading up to the meeting so that no large group would be detected.

To my knowledge, the tunnels were no longer accessible from inside the castle. Several other access points had been forgotten ages ago, and the rebels used that to their advantage. Although the cavern was not directly below the castle but just to the west, it still felt as if we were meeting right under the king's nose. The other rebels seemed fine with that, but I knew it was a dangerous game.

After the meeting was over, I weaved in and out of the gathered fae toward the front to speak with Rook. He stood with a huge male with black raven wings that contrasted his stark white hair.

"Temir, this is Rhogan."

The male placed his fist to his chest, and I did the same. "Good to meet you, Temir," he said in a gruff but kind voice.

"Likewise."

Rook got right to the point. "I need to send you on a mission. Can you get away from the castle for a week?"

"No. I push it even coming to the meetings. The king keeps me close at hand."

"I see," he said, the dejection clear.

"What's going on? Maybe I can help in another way?"

"There's a potential magical fae hiding near Narth, but he won't talk to anyone. We thought if we sent another magical fae, we could convince him. We were going to send Oravan, but he doesn't want to leave his family, being so new to the rebellion."

"I'm not sure I'm the right fit anyway. If he recognizes me, he isn't going to listen."

"I trust that you can do this, Temir. If you traveled with Rhogan, he would help. He knows the family of the fae."

"I might have a way to get there, but I'd have to travel alone. Can I send word and have you meet me?" I asked the winged male.

"If you travel alone, I can fly and get there faster. I will need a little over a day to get there though, so you'll have to let me know ahead of time."

"I will do my best."

"That's all we ask," Rook said, turning away from us to talk to someone else.

"Think we can do it?" Rhogan asked me.

"Convince the fae to come?"

"No. The whole thing. Do you think the rebellion can overthrow the king?"

I thought about that for a moment. I realized I had never questioned the end goal of the rebellion aside from fighting for something better and helping protect the lesser fae. "It's hard to say. I hope we can."

"I'll tell ya something. I never put hope in anything. I'm an all-in kind of male. I'll die for this rebellion if I have to."

I considered that, crossing my arms over my chest. *Would I?* "How long have you been a rebel, Rhogan?"

He shifted his feet, adjusting those heavy wings. "I was one of the first in the north. Rook and a few others joined up. One of them asked me to join, and then we found the access point to the tunnels and started recruiting. And here we are. I think the tables will turn soon though. The rebellion can't continue to only recruit. We are going to have to move against the king eventually."

"Don't you think there is an advantage to remaining hidden for now? He has no idea the rebellion exists."

"As far as you know he doesn't." He watched me carefully.

I bit my tongue. "What do you think the first strike from the rebellion should be?"

"I'd love to set the barn on fire and send a really clear message about who we are."

I thought of River and fear gripped me. "There are innocent fae who live in that barn. Would you condemn them to send your message?"

"No, of course not. I'd make sure the barn was clear of fae first, then light it up."

I nodded, noticing Rook had stopped talking and his ears had perked. He was listening to us now. "That would certainly send a message, but what would the rebellion actually gain other than targets on our back?"

"That's how I know you've been living in that castle while the rest of us are barely living. We already have targets on our backs. We were born with them. We sleep with them. We name them and take them out to dinner. Don't forget that, pet."

If I bit any harder on the tip of my tongue, I was going to bite it off.

"Listen, I've spent my entire life in limbo. I'm not good enough for them, I'm not tortured enough for you. I don't belong and I get that. But don't for one minute think I'm doing a single thing for that asshole's benefit. I'm not his pet. I'm not his friend. I attend those meetings to bring information directly to the rebellion, and I have done so faithfully since the day I came here. Don't think that because I've lived a different life than you, I've had anything better. You start drawing those lines and you're no better than he is."

He slammed his hand to my back, flashing me the biggest smile I've ever seen. "Glad to see you've got some fire in you. I was beginning to think you were all talk and no walk." He winked, but the damage had already been done.

"If you'll excuse me." I slipped away. I caught Oravan waiting for me just before I reached the door.

"Just wanted to say thanks for getting me here." Oravan held a hand out to me. I took it and found an object pressed between our palms. He leaned in. "It's another barrier charm. In case you know someone in need of it. As a thank you."

He wasn't ready to tell the rebellion about his ability to block the king's enchantment, and I'd let him do that in his own time. I hadn't told them about the truth serum yet, so we were on equal terms. I'd share that with the rebels soon. I just needed to have a few barrels of storage before I did, so they had enough on hand to start questioning each member. I imagined it was the same for Oravan. He'd have to make a large number of charms, like the one on my finger, and they likely took a lot of time and magic.

"Thanks. I'll see you around," I said, walking out.

He smiled a genuine smile and walked back to his family.

I'd never seen a real smile from him, and I was, once again, reminded of the importance and necessity of the rebellion. Rhogan had meant only to test my reaction to his jeering. I really shouldn't have expected anything less.

CHAPTER 13

KING TOLERO

*T*nok would have some choice words for me when he discovered I'd gone out without him, but I'd decided to go anyway. He was loyal to a fault, but he was buckling under the stress of the past few days.

I remained cloaked in shadow as I watched the people of my city fill the evening streets. With long dark robes wrapped in black ornate steel plating, I let my sharpened twin blades show as I moved. Should anyone get any bright ideas, I hoped it would deter them from starting a fight they would never win.

I kept my head down as I made my way toward the slums of the bustling city that seemed more alive at night than day. Judging by the crowds of fae moving in one general direction, Muth had his pit fighters working tonight.

As I approached the outdoor arena, two of his males worked their way through the crowd towards me. Still, I kept my hood up and chin down, trying to avoid them. While most fae in the north carried blades, in the south, I probably drew more attention than I wanted once I moved from the shadows into the crowd.

"You there," a guard called in my direction. I walked on, pretending I hadn't heard him. "In the black," he yelled, trying to push people out of the way to get to me. He grabbed my shoulder with firm fingers and I rotated to face him.

I let my magic loose ever so slightly. "You do not see the face of the king. When the others ask, everything checks out."

"Yes, everything checks out," he mumbled, his eyes blank.

"Good lad. Continue on."

My throat pinched as I pulled the coursing magic back in and shuddered. It called to me. Roared at me to let it soar through the world. There were few things I disliked more than taking away someone's free will and memory, though I'd felt the purity and strength of that magic fade over the years. It was not what it had once been.

Moving back into the flow of the crowd, I found an empty bench and sat. I looked down at the sandy pit below and watched as large black beasts paced back and forth, panting so heavily their shoulders lifted with each breath and saliva dripped from their elongated teeth. Fae hounds.

I watched the anxious crowd as we waited for the fighters to come. With extra sensitive hearing, I listened to the conversations around me. Everything seemed relatively normal, apart from the hounds. Admittedly, I didn't frequent the pits, and I was unaware that hounds were ever used for training. I'd have to find out if this was something new.

"Welcome," the deep timbre of a male's voice called from below.

The anxious crowd roared, their cries echoing off the walls of the stadium.

Four males held the fae beasts at bay with whips that cracked through the night as the announcer continued. "Tonight, you will have the pleasure of witnessing some of the most exciting and brutal pit fights you've ever seen. As you all know, the Trials are just weeks away and, as our best, most ferocious fighters prepare to climb their way to the top, we bring you an evening of entertainment and bloodshed. Now, get on your feet and show your due respect to the male that makes it all happen around here. Our fearless leader, a fae who can build someone from nothing, a male who can spit at the feet of the elder king and walk away, a male who cares more for you, his loyal patrons, than for his own fighters. The one and only, Muuuuuuttth."

The crowd laughed and jumped to their feet, stomping on the rafters and screaming through the night air. At least Inok wasn't here. He likely would have jumped into the pits just to teach the announcer a lesson.

True, I had become much more complacent in recent years, keeping the tiger in hibernation. As the world began to fall, they would learn to fear me once more. Perhaps I had made the Flame Court too comfortable.

Never let them forget who you are at the expense of becoming what you think they want you to be.

My son's final words to me before he left to find his destiny echoed in my mind. Alewyn had fulfilled her promise, and I only hoped the southern kingdom was on the winning end of the battle to come. Inok was right. I couldn't ignore the northern kingdoms and simply hope they were also ignoring me. Maybe it was time to call in a war council and start talking about our defenses.

Shaking my head, I tried to bring my thoughts back to the arena where Muth stood rambling on about his fighters and why they were the best.

"Alexi, Alexi, Alexi," the crowd chanted.

"Yes, yes. I know." Muth's snake-like smile plastered across his face as his voice echoed. "I will think about letting Alexi make an appearance tonight. He will not be fighting, but perhaps I'll let him come say hello."

"Boo!" the crowd jeered.

Muth held up his hands and let a fake, staged laugh roll from him. "Fine, fine," he said. "One fight. The final fight."

The crowd roared louder than it had all night, and obviously, they had played right into his hands. They would stay for all the lower-tiered fights, ordering drinks and placing bets, lining Muth's pockets. Likely,

Attoc was doing the same thing in his fighting arena. Attoc had a nicer establishment on the other side of the city, and while his fighters were fewer in number, his patrons made higher bets.

Muth stepped out of the pit, turning the stage back over to the announcer, who stalked forward, held his hands out and spun in a circle as he spoke. "Tonight, your unprecedented experience will start with these feral beasts. Starved for a week, they would certainly eat anything. Even a fae. Especially a fae. Please join me in welcoming to the pits, for his very first fight, Lere."

The crowd quieted as a young male entered the pit. He carried only a chain with a heavy spiked ball on the end. He looked to each of the beasts and straightened his back as he swung the mace in slow deliberate circles above his head.

The four males guarding the beasts moved to the exit as one, and the crowd gasped as they watched the beasts begin to circle their prey. I looked from the pit to the crowd and back again. I searched for Muth but was unable to find him. My heart raced as I realized what was about to happen.

The crown allowed the pits to remain open because no fae died. They fought, but never to the death. We bred and built warriors from birth, so fighting was in our blood. It was our right. But this? This was murder for entertainment, and I needed to stop it. I didn't see how this boy would walk away from this fight.

I stood, leaning forward as the boy began to turn. I grabbed the rail in front of me and squeezed as the dogs moved. The boy swung the mace, forcing them back a few steps, but still, they surrounded him like the target he was.

One of the hounds lunged for him, catching his lean calf and locking its jaw. The boy didn't make a sound as he swung the mace and it crashed into the hound's side, spikes impaling his fur. I forced a breath. The hound fell away and didn't move, only whimpered as the three hounds closed in once more. Again, Lere, took the mace and created a physical boundary between him and the beasts. Half the crowd were on their feet, silent as the boy moved.

"Look out," someone screamed as the one in the back jumped at him.

But the boy was smart and turned his body with his arms, the mace colliding with the head of the beast.

Two down, two to go.

I blinked, hardly believing what I saw. I wouldn't have bet a single coin that boy could defeat one hound—but the battle was only half won.

They didn't give him time to reset his feet from the last hit. He rotated, and a hound growled fiercely from behind, distracting him as the other dove forward. This time, it caught him by the arm that swung the mace. Dark red blood seeped down the boy's arms, and his poise shattered as he screamed and tried to pull away.

Instead of mercy, the beast from behind clamped his jaws on the boy's leg. They pulled in opposite directions, attempting to rip him into two.

"Stop," someone from the crowd yelled.

"Stop this, he will die," another yelled.

I looked again to where Muth was known to be, but he was absent. I looked at the announcer, who only smiled and watched.

"Stop this at once," I called, realizing no one could hear me over the screaming crowd and the screaming boy. I leaped, and before I knew what I was doing, pushed my way forward and jumped over the edge of the arena, landing gracefully on my feet. I'd physically regret that later, but for now, I didn't even think of it.

The crowd went still as I removed my hood.

"It's the king," someone shouted.

"Save him. Save the boy."

I pulled my swords from my back and crossed the arena. "Release," I yelled at the fae hounds with as much magic as I could possibly force into a single word. One beast whined and let the screaming boy go. "Stay," I demanded.

I looked to Lere and saw nothing but terror on his face. Of me, or imminent death, I wasn't sure. Enchanting beasts could be tricky if they were of no intelligence. The opposite could be said of the fae. It was a well-guarded secret that those of stronger will and mind were harder to enchant.

The hound at his leg still growled low as he pulled at the boy, but his eyes were on me as I moved. I swung my swords in each hand and held his gaze as I spoke to the boy. "As soon as he lets go, you are to run to the gate, do you understand?"

"But what if he attacks you?" Lere's voice shook.

"I am not afraid, and you will do as I command." I swung for the dog, but he moved, dragging the boy with him.

I stalked them both, watching the hound back himself into a corner. Faster than I remembered I could move, I ran for them just as he hit the wall and plunged my sword into his side. It whined and dropped the boy, and though he limped, he did as he was told, leaving a trail of blood behind him. The hound watched him go, remaining on his feet. Before he could attack again, I buried my second sword in his neck and walked away, refusing to watch him die. The crowds cheered until I held up my hand to stop them.

"The northern kingdoms kill for pleasure, we do not. These fights are over. Go home." I moved to the gate. "Muth!" I yelled. "Come bow before your king."

The crowd stood but did not leave, watching for Muth to come out. He took his precious time, but fortunately for him, he also obeyed. He dragged his feet through the sand, scowl on his face and eyes to the ground the entire way. The crowd murmured to each other, but they watched intently. When Muth stood before me and lifted his head, I looked pointedly at the ground and back to his face. I heard a low rumble, but he did eventually bow, though only slightly.

"Lower," I growled. The tiger in me stood to attention, the first time he had woken in ages. Muth bowed lower, but certainly not low enough for my forgiveness. "On your knees, nose in the sand, Muth."

He jerked his face to mine, and his shocked expression told me he didn't believe I had it in me anymore. He wasn't the only one though. The volume of the crowd grew.

"Now," I demanded. "Before I make you do it."

He fell to his knees and bent all the way to the ground until he inhaled the soot and sand. The crowd seemed to disappear in their own silence.

"Now hold it," I ordered him.

I pulled out my twin blades and held them like scissors at his neck. "Who are you, Muth?" He shook but did not respond. "Answer."

"I-I am no one."

"And who am I?"

"King Tolero."

"I am your king. I am king of the south. King of the desert. King of the Flame Court, and you are no one."

The tiger paced on padded paws deep within my tattered soul.

"Remind me," I shouted. "When did you ever spit at my feet and walk away?" I tightened my grip on the swords placed around his neck.

"Never, my king," he said, barely loud enough for the dirt he kissed to hear.

"Louder!"

"Never." His voice echoed through the pit.

I took a step back, planted my swords into the ground and bent so that only he could hear me. "You will leave this night with naught but your life. You've forgotten these pits are mine. That boy would have died on your watch, and where were you to save him from that fate?"

He visibly shook. "Please don't take the pits, Your Grace. I'm sorry."

"You're sorry? Do you expect an apology to be an adequate exchange for a life? I'm done with your attitude, Muth. The disrespect you have shown me has gone too far. Send these people home. You are to report to

117

my throne in a week's time. I'll let you know my decision about the pits then, and not before. You're lucky I'm considering it at all based on what I witnessed tonight. Get these people out of here." I yanked my swords from the ground, crossed them on my back, and walked to the gate.

"The fights are closed for the night. Everyone, go home," Muth's shaken voice called out.

The crowd moved as one. I replaced my hood, though it would do me no good now, and walked out. As I passed the announcer, he took a step backward, and I squeezed my fist, opened it, and squeezed once more. "The next time you mention me in your intros, I would be very careful about what you say. That is not your crowd, they are mine, and I'll have your head if I ever hear of it again."

I walked away before he could lift his jaw from the ground. I had grown too lax in these last years. When my fae were more surprised by my presence than a direct insult, I was doing something wrong.

I stepped back into the deep shadows of an alley and watched the rest of the crowd pass. Some leaned in close, full of harsh whispers, some left more silent than the dripping of a nearby gutter. Out of the corner of my eye, I saw something I hadn't seen in hundreds of years. I squeezed my eyes shut and opened them to make sure I hadn't imagined it. Not one, but two selkies attempted to blend into the crowd of fae. Tall, slender beings with watchful eyes and iridescent skin that shimmered in the moonlight caused dreadful realization to slam into me like a mace to the chest. The sea fae had come to the southern kingdom, stirring more trouble than I needed and likely making everything worse.

CHAPTER 14

ARA

*F*orests had officially been ruined for me.

Spending days wandering and wounded in the one north of my cottage had permanently damaged me. I stood at the edge of the tree line and stared into the next leg of my journey. Reluctantly, I took that first step, and then the next, until I was moving at a steady pace.

I thought my plan was simple: I'd travel north from Hrundel, through the forest, then go west along the foothills of the Dregan Mountains, which divided the Marsh and Wind Courts. Typically, travelers followed the edge of the mountains the opposite way, toward the ocean and then through the Eastern Gap. I hoped to find the Western Gap and travel through the ravine rather than having to scale a mountain or travel for days in the wrong direction. From there, I'd keep going until I hit The Mists, and then I wasn't sure. I'd wing it and see what happened.

No one had ever come back from The Mists, so there were no tales of what they really were or how to navigate them. It was said that when a fae lost their mate, they would travel to The Mists and forfeit their own life, so their shared soul could be together again. They said that losing your mate was like losing yourself, and you could never recover from that.

The concept of sharing a soul was absolutely ludicrous to me. The only thing I really knew about mates was that the bond sometimes took a long time to emerge. When it did, your choice was to either accept it and live in saccharine bliss or deny it, and sever your soul in two pieces again and try to find a way to recover alone. I'd never known if my parents were truly mated, but if they weren't, they were still happy beyond measure.

The thought of my parents stopped me short. They were everything to me, all I had ever known, and now if I was to believe the prince, they weren't even my real parents. I reached my hand to the necklace I wore and closed my eyes, rubbing my thumb over the jagged edge of the simple stone that lay inside.

"Maybe I was never yours, but you were always mine," I told my mother, hoping she could hear me from the Ether.

I shifted the pack I carried, and the weight of the book reminded me of Nealla. I was more determined than ever to find her. I needed the truth, the whole truth, from the beginning all the way through. I knew there was more to my twisted story. I couldn't trust the prince and his tale, even if that meant admitting that I also couldn't trust Aibell. It was difficult and confusing because my mother had sent me to her, though she'd sent me to Mikal first and the final message she had left with him was to trust no one. Maybe my mother was telling me not to trust Aibell? But I knew her well enough to know she would never send me into the arms of someone I couldn't rely on. I'd never been more confused in my life as I tried to work through every emotion raging through my body.

The prince thought he knew more about me than I knew about myself, and that was probably the worst of it. I was a whole person. I was more than my birth story, more than a prophecy. But he thought me to be weak. He had captured me with ease, and I hated him for it. For his words, his cocky attitude. All of it. He could have been nice. He could have found a better way to tell me anything he needed to. Send a fucking messenger for all I cared. Instead, he chose to be an asshole, and if he thought I was going to play nice after that, he was wrong. I might have been a bit of a pain, but I'd backed down from him every single time at the castle, as my mother had taught me when dealing with royals, but there were no rules anymore and somewhere along my journey I'd lost all the fucks I had to give.

By midafternoon, the density of the trees had grown so thick I could no longer tell which direction I was going. Several times I had to climb a tree to look above the forest canopy, and twice found I was going in the wrong direction. I stayed alert and kept my fae ears perked, fully aware that danger lurked in every forest, and the closer I got to nightfall, the more wicked the woods became. I had heard the snapping of twigs and branches many times, but whatever it was that followed me kept their distance. I still carried a knife in my hands, just in case.

I didn't risk a fire the first night and probably wouldn't the second either. I thought of the knovern and shuddered. There would be no peace here. Certainly no security.

It was day two of being turned around in every direction. Once scarce and intriguing, the symbols I had discovered etched into scattered trees became more frequent until I was surrounded by them. I'd passed the same symbols and the same pattern of symbols over and over again until my mind was numb and all my sense of direction had left me once more. Someone was definitely following me, and while I wanted to focus on that little gem, it hadn't felt like a threat. Now though? I felt the eyes of something far more terrifying much closer. I slowed my pace and perked my ears until I heard the distant clinking of iron chains. I paused, and so did whatever it was that tracked me. I closed my eyes and listened for breathing. Silence answered. I searched my memory for clues to the symbols.

What did I just walk into?

I spun in a circle, and at the same time whipped the blade from my back. My cloak trailed behind me, and the sounds of the forest went deadly silent. My own heartbeat thundered through the clustered trees like the beat of a hollow drum, and I knew it had betrayed me, as the glowing red eyes of the largest fae horse I had ever seen stepped out between two trees in the distance.

Atop him sat an ethereal beheaded rider linked to the beast with chains. In one hand, he carried the rotted remains of his own head, and in the other, he carried a long barbed-wire chain whip that he cracked through the musty air.

It snapped inches from my face and broke the spell.

I swung my sword and rolled to the side, wracking my brain for any knowledge I might have to slay an undead. If not for the glowing red eyes of the beast, I likely wouldn't have known where he was in the dark forest with the trees effectively blocking out any light I might need.

Run.

It sounded great in theory, but this was his territory that I had encroached on. Also, he was on a horse and I was, well ... not. It had to be the symbols. It's the only thing that made sense. I couldn't kill the horse. From what I remembered, the only way to kill an undead beast was to either make a deal with a dark demon or to restrike it with the same weapon that had killed it in the first place. Neither of which were options, but if I remembered right, the dullahan was not as tricky. The symbols on the trees were part of the charm that held him here.

I wasn't sure what would happen to the beast once he was free of his rider, but I had to worry about that later. The whip cracked again. The sound of the chains was more disturbing than the putrid stench of the rotten skull he carried like a trophy. I kept my face to him as I backed into a tree and felt for the symbol blindly. He stalked forward, and as I slid the blade across the deep marking, I said a silent prayer that I was destroying a charm and not a ward. The last thing I wanted to do was unleash a dead horseman on Alewyn.

I bolted for the next tree, but I couldn't find a symbol. Then again to the third. This time, when I damaged the bark, the horse reared up on its two hind legs, screamed into the darkness and charged at me full speed. The horseman pulled his own sword, balancing the chain in his other hand, and I barely moved fast enough to block him from taking my own head.

As he turned the beast around, I quickly scratched the next symbol and then crouched low to the ground. He couldn't hit me with his sword at this level unless he leaned way over on his horse, and though I was sure he was a skilled rider, I could easily tumble to the side if that were his tactic. A small tingling tapped on the shield in my mind, and I realized he was trying to break it. I reinforced the wall as I moved to the next tree. Again I sliced, and again the horse screamed with fury as they charged. I leaped behind the welcomed trunk of a broad tree, and he had to turn sharply to avoid crashing into it.

Shit.

I couldn't remember how many symbols I had to remove, and to be completely honest, I wasn't entirely sure I was doing it right. Still, I moved to the next one, and to my surprise, this one was already scratched out, but it wasn't from my own blade. Perhaps the last victim of the dullahan hadn't been as lucky as I hoped to be.

He charged for me once more, and this time I held my sword firm as he came, spinning out of the way at the last minute. While I thought I'd nearly had him, the sound of his blade whooshing by my ear made my heart stop. I had been hoping his lack of mobility on the horse, in a forest no less, would be to my advantage, but I had forgotten this was his game. Several long minutes passed with him charging me and me doing my best just to block him or avoid the following crash of his whip through the air.

Finally, I thought I had him. He came barreling forward, and rather than moving from one side to the other, I stayed on his left. Changing the pattern did just enough that my sword sliced through his thigh, though he didn't bleed. He grabbed his wound though, which gave me reason to think I had hurt him. I tried it for a second time, but he anticipated it and turned far too soon, snapping the barbed whip.

It ensnared my wrist.

I screamed in pain, the first sound I had made. Instead of trying to pull my arm out of the whip, which I was sure is what most fae would have instinctively done. I punched my arm forward, loosening the chains just enough to twist and jerk my hand out of his hold. I crawled backward. There was no fucking way I was going to escape this certain death. I looked to the forest floor and saw the scattered trail of blood I'd left behind. I didn't even care that it could be used to bespell me. None of that mattered when I was going to die anyway.

Still, I lifted my sword again. I had to use my left hand, which was now the stronger one, and regain my footing. A bit wobbly, I stood. I held my sword straight toward him, and the glow of the fae horse's eyes brightened. Perhaps even he knew they had me now. But one moment my hand held the sword before me, and the next minute it vanished.

I tried to gasp, but a smooth hand covered my mouth.

A feminine voice whispered so lightly I could barely understand, even with my sensitive hearing. "There are three more of those symbols behind him. We need to circle around to get them. If you even breathe, he will hear you."

That voice—it was familiar. I'd thought of that voice for ages, full of questions. She'd been the one to free me from Morwena's guards the day my parents died. She was his. *It was one of mine*, he had said. Prince Fenlas. He'd been playing his hand in this faerie game for longer than I'd known.

I nodded in understanding, and when the firm hand fell from my face but held my arm tight, I felt like a gods-damned fool. I thought of all the signs and everything I knew and replenished my hatred for Fenlas as the female and I slowly crept around the circle, invisible to the dullahan. I could not see her, but I knew she was there, her magic encompassing us both.

The horseman shifted left and then right atop his steed. Confused as hell, he moved forward to where I had been standing before, and we were able to get behind him. Sure enough, three trees were still marked. I moved quickly to deface them all and then turned to watch the horse whinny as his rider fell to the ground and shook. Tendrils of smoke rose from the creature, carrying with it a putrid stench of rot, death and decay, until the body was gone and only a discarded pile of threadbare clothing was left behind.

The horse bolted from the forest, free of his master, and I said a prayer to the gods that he would find the final death he would likely search for. His own. I watched him for a moment and then jerked my hand from the one that held mine.

"Show yourself," I demanded.

A beautiful female appeared before me. Her thick, shoulder-length brown hair matched perfectly to the leathers she wore and her soft summer tan. My stalker. She lifted her hands in mock surrender. "Look, before you say anything, just know that I was totally against this whole thing, and I told Fen it was a terrible idea."

"So, you *are* one of his lackey's?" I asked behind gritted teeth. I balled my fists, ready to give her the beating he deserved. The only thing that held me back was that she'd saved me. Twice.

"I'm going to say yes to that because I can't think of a better term at the moment, but believe me, I'd like to punch him in the face as badly as you would. I mean, I never would do that, but I want to."

"Oh, I don't just want to punch him in his pretty face. I want to send him back to the hell he haunts me from."

She smiled. "I thought I was going to like you as soon as you started drunk singing back in his rooms, but now I know for sure. I'll hold him down, and you can beat the snot out of him as soon as they catch up to us. I'm Wren, by the way."

I took a step away from her. "Wait, back up. I gathered a bit too late that you've been following me and spying on me since I was in the castle. But what do you mean as soon as they catch up?"

"You didn't think he'd really just let you leave, did you?" Her cobalt eyes searched the grey of my own.

"Nothing that male has done since the day I met him has ever made sense to me. I don't need a fucking babysitter."

She looked at me pointedly and then down to my wrist and back to my face.

"It's just a scratch." I lifted a shoulder in a shrug.

"I'll clean up the blood on the forest floor, you get something tied around that arm."

Bossy. But she probably had to be if she were the only girl among the rest of them. I decided I would hold my thoughts until she pissed me off and then make my final judgment. Because even though it grated on my nerves, I had to admit, it was my own fault for not catching her sooner. And if I were the prince with a magical fae who could literally disappear, I probably would have done the same thing. You could never learn more about a person than by watching them when they thought they were alone. As I wrapped a bandage around my wrist, I smirked. She had seen way too much of me to not even give her a chance.

"So," she said, walking back over. "We've got some time, wanna mess with the guys?"

"There is not a single thing you could possibly say to convince me to sit around and wait for him to get here. It's not personal, but I don't want or need the company. You all clearly don't trust me, but I don't trust you either. For obvious damn reasons."

"You're two days deep into the maze forest, Ara. You need Kai. He's an amazing tracker. He doesn't have magic, but you'd think he did if you watched him. He can have us out of this hell hole sooner than we would ever manage on our own."

I noticed her use of the word we and cringed. I was confident it was visible, but she ignored it entirely. I shook my head. "Trust me, you don't want to go where I'm going."

"Actually, I do. Because like it or not, Fen is like family to me, and it matters to him, so it matters to me."

"Fine!" I threw my hands in the air, mumbling. "I don't even know how to get rid of a disappearing fae anyway."

"Great, so now that we have that squared away, let's fuck with them."

"Will it piss the prince off?" I asked.

"A girl can dream." She rubbed her hands together.

I tried to hide my smirk. "Lead the way.

"Can you climb with that?" She jutted her chin toward my new bandage.

"Yes. It's just a scratch."

"It bled. Scratches don't bleed."

"How far behind us do you think they are?" I asked, walking away. She joined ... of course.

"Well, I'd say probably not much. All the circling you did probably slowed them down a bit."

"Intentionally," I lied.

She grinned and pointed to a good climbing tree with stepping branches placed evenly apart. "You'll have to get yourself up there. And try not to touch the tree too much."

"How the hell am I supposed to climb a tree without touching it?"

"Right, well, just try your best and let's see what happens." She spun, scanning the dense forest around us.

Once I reached the highest point I could while still being able to see below me through the branches, I called down. "How's this?"

"Perfect." She climbed up behind and sat near me.

"I cannot believe I agreed to this. Must be the lack of sleep."

"Listen, if you want to get down right now and keep moving, we can. But I promise they are going to catch up with us sooner than later anyway, and we seriously need Kai if you plan on going north."

"Well, we're already up in the tree now. We might as well see it through."

"He is going to kill me," she laughed.

"Nah, I'll kill him first."

"Well, the fight will be fun to watch."

"Indeed." I pulled out a knife to give my anxious hands something to do. "Is he terrible? The prince?" I didn't want to let that burning question seem so damn vulnerable, but it did.

"No. He isn't really." She passed her hands through her hair, and a smile lit her eyes. "Passionate, stubborn, asshole? Yes, but terrible? No. My sister and I grew up with him at the castle. She serves on the council now, but Fen and I have just always been closer. I think he has spent his whole life thinking about you, and now that you're here, he isn't sure what to do about it."

He sure had a funny way of expressing obsession. "And the others?"

"Oh gods, they are terrible." She laughed. "Kai is Fen's best friend. He is the quintessential definition of a southern fae warrior. You can't take a single thing he says seriously, but there is no one Fen trusts more than Kai, except maybe Greeve." She shifted on her branch and leaned back against the rugged bark. "When Fen's mom died, he wouldn't eat or sleep. So, Kai moved into his rooms at the castle and refused to as well. He told Fen if his best friend was going to starve, then he was too. So, Fen ate and slept just to make sure Kai would. They've always taken care of each other like that. Like brothers."

"And the other two?" I asked, pushing the picture of a starving little boy from my mind.

"Well, Greeve is a wind cleaver and a drac."

"Which means?"

"Oh right, sorry. Northerners."

"Call me a northerner again and I'll leave you dead in this damn forest."

"You could try," she said, lifting an eyebrow.

I scoffed.

"The draconian fae used to be from the Wind Court until Fen's mom convinced his dad to let her people come south during the Iron Wars. I guess it's a long story, but basically, all the dracs live in a communal way. They are fierce southern warriors now, and no one messes with them. They can be scary. Greeve travels on the wind too with his magic."

I ran my fingers over the deep grooves etched into the cool handle of my blade as she continued. I knew what a draconian fae was, of course. But she didn't need to know that. I didn't have time to care, but she talked a lot. And as my mother said, even useless information can become a weapon at the right moment.

"Well, when Greeve was born, they knew right away that he had magic, so they sent him to the castle to be trained. He was the third wheel with Fen and Kai for a while, but now they don't go anywhere without each other. I'm pretty sure they piss in a triangle."

I snorted and she continued.

"Lichen is a whole different story. He's a lot older than the rest of us, but he used to be an important advisor on the council. When the queen died, the king reduced the council size. Lichen was sort of gifted to Fen so he could learn the ropes. He's nice and all, for an older fae, but—"

I jerked my hand up to quiet her as I heard a movement somewhere in the distance. "I think they're coming," I whispered. "No one is talking though."

"Probably them then." She reached out to take my arm. We were gone in an instant, and my body jerked in response. I had to grab on to the tree to keep from falling.

"Can't he see through your magic?" I asked.

"He can, but the others can't," she whispered back.

We watched, and just when I was about to tell her I'd gotten it wrong, several figures moved into the space below us. An older fae with white hair trailed in the back. The one I'd recognized, that locked me in the prince's room with his magic, had to be the draconian. He was covered in tattoos and his long, dark hair was pulled back, probably to keep it out of the way during the fight he was waiting for. Lackey three, the one with messy golden hair that thought he was funny, led them. I'd never noticed how attractive he was until now, seeing him in his element with keen eyes, helping his prince. They all were, really. Stupid fae bastards.

They were good though. Using hand signals to communicate movements and words. All armed and weapons out, the prince moved to the exact spot I had been injured, and he ran his hands through his hair. My anger flared just seeing him. Over and over, I heard the click of that damn lock on the door to my recent prison—at his own command. He locked his hands behind his neck, and his muscles strained. I grimaced. I wanted to hate him so bad, but hating someone you were also attracted to took a careful level of determination.

"Fuck," he whispered. He made a few more hand signals, and then the one who I assumed was Kai made a vulgar one back.

Wren covered her mouth with her hands to smother the laugh.

Kai looked around frantically, trying to find where our trail continued, wiping his curls from his face. He pressed his finger to the side of his nose, and Fen shook his head. The four of them walked in a circle below us for a while, and finally, the prince yanked out a knife and haphazardly threw it into the half-dead tree across from him.

"I don't know," Kai said. "They were definitely here. There was a fight though. See all the scratch marks in the trees? And it looks like there was a horse also. There's skid marks on the ground and..." His voice trailed off as he paced back and forth. "It smells weird. Like old Knocky right before his monthly bath."

Wren snorted, and the gig was up. The prince's head snapped to the trees, and his face was redder than that fae horse's eyes.

"We are so dead," she said.

I slid my hands along the rugged bark and leaned forward so I was laying like a feline across the heavy branch. I smiled and waved a few fingers to the asshole until he shook with anger. "Cat got your tongue?" I asked in a sickly-sweet voice.

"You're hurt."

"Oh, this old thing?" I held up my wrist and showed him the oversized bandage.

"What the fuck happened, Wren?" he sneered.

"We stopped for a nap," I answered.

She turned her face so he couldn't see the smile, and it only encouraged my desire to taunt him.

"A nap? Was that before or after the dullahan?"

How did he even know about that?

"It was after. We invited him to join us, but he was too busy dying. Care to join him?"

"Come down from the tree, Ara," he commanded.

"Mmm. No thanks." I stretched a bit farther and yawned. "It took you so long to find us, we've bored ourselves into exhaustion."

"Hey!" Kai called from beside him, crossing his arms.

"I mean, it did take you two days, Kai," Wren called down.

"You kept fucking turning in circles."

"Maze forest," I said, spinning my finger in the air. "That's the point."

"How long are you going to act like a child?" Fen growled.

"I think maybe ten more years. Give or take a few, probably. Fifteen max."

"I can't deal with this shit right now." He stormed off.

"Time to climb back down, Ara," Wren said, her face serious.

"Fun hater." I smirked.

We climbed down, and I didn't care that the males wouldn't look at either of us.

"The forest is dangerous, Wren," Kai whispered.

"We had it under control," she snapped.

I didn't wait for their argument to start. I just began walking. They could follow or stay behind and have a picnic, I didn't care. Unfortunately, it only took about twenty paces until the clingy prince was hot on my trail and mad as a grendel. I could only smile as I continued to walk ahead of him, pretending I didn't notice the way he huffed in anger as he stalked behind me.

"I'm sorry," he mumbled.

"Oh, look at the handsome prince. So sorry he kidnapped the poor tiny female for reasons her little ol' brain was just too small to understand. No need for a reasonable adult conversation to explain things, just a fucking shit load of chaos wrapped in a pretty package of forced destiny. But you're sorry, so it's fine. Tell me, did it physically pain you to say that?"

"Yes," he said. "I locked you in my rooms to make sure you were safe. I don't know how this is supposed to work. How is this going to go if we can't find a way to get over it? I'm just going to follow behind you and rush in at the last-minute hoping to save you every time you do something stupid?"

"Call me stupid one more time, you alpha fucking male asshole. Then we'll see how this is going to go."

"No. I didn't mean that. Damn it. You are so infuriating."

"Hang on one second. Let me find you a mirror."

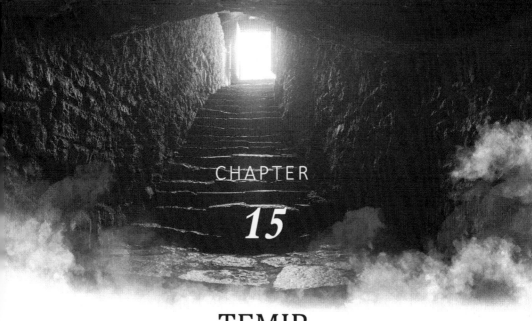

CHAPTER

15

TEMIR

*W*here were you last night?" Gaea asked, jerking her head in a tilt.

I sat in the leather chair behind my old wooden desk and took a lingering deep breath. "Please, come sit down. I have something to tell you."

Her face lost all color as she crept to the worn chair across from me. She sat and folded her hands into her lap, waiting for me to drop a bomb on her. It seemed that was all we had been doing lately.

"What is it, Tem?"

"I was out last night." I shifted in my seat. "There's something I want to tell you, but not here."

She moved her hand across the desk and I took it. We scattered into pieces, and then we were standing whole, in the middle a tall grass field surrounded by soft rolling hills and a breeze that blew her long chestnut hair around her. I took both of her gentle hands into mine. She looked at me, quietly patient as I tried to find the right words, but nothing came.

"I'm not sure how to say it other than just blurting it out," I said.

"Mother above, Tem. You're killing me with anticipation. Just spit it out already."

"I joined the rebellion."

She dropped my hands. "You what?"

"I joined the rebellion." I scratched the back of my head and raised my eyebrows.

"I knew it." She shook her head and walked away, turning her back to me. "It's so dangerous, Tem. Do you always have to be the righteous one? He will kill you."

"I know it's dangerous, but so is everything else. Living as a lesser fae is dangerous."

"But you're not," she snapped. "You live in the castle."

"No, but I could be. If I didn't have magic, I would either be stuck in that fucking barn or dead long ago. I won't sit by and do nothing anymore. I won't dream about escaping only to be hunted. I want to actually do something. Make a difference to someone."

"You make a difference to me and to River. Isn't that enough?"

"No, it isn't, and you know that," I said, frustrated. "They need me to travel to Narth, and since I can't take the time to walk there, will you take me? I know it's a lot to ask, but I can't think of another way. I ... we would potentially be saving a magical fae."

"Of course I will, Temir, but they aren't smart, you know? At least not all of them. I still listen in the halls. I spirit around, and they talk too much."

I made a mental note to talk to Rook about that. "You could join."

She moved her fingers through her hair and looked up to the clear skies, taking a deep breath. The pleading tone to her voice nearly undid me. "I would never. You can't trust them. You can't trust anyone. Only me, Temir. Only me." She walked back to me and wrapped her hands around my waist, laying her head on my chest, and for that one single moment, I was lost in her.

She was my comfort. She was my home. But she pulled away too soon.

"Why won't you let me love you, Gaea?"

"Because I'm just as broken as you are, Temir. There's nothing to love in broken things." She looked away, her hair trailing behind her like wings. As if she could fly away. But then she could, if she wanted to.

"You are not broken." I moved a step toward her. "Your heart is broken, but it will mend. Oleonis would not want you to live in this constant mourning. Please come back to me, and it can be like it was before."

"It can never be like it was before."

She shattered me with those chilling words. I'd waited. I'd wanted her for so long from afar, and she'd just ended it right there.

"There's to be a ball at the Marsh Court, and we are required to attend," she said dully. "That's how I knew you were gone last night. We leave tomorrow after dinner. You're to wear something sharp."

Her voice was quiet, and though I was hurting too, I couldn't see her like this.

"Listen." I stepped in, sweeping my finger below her chin and forcing her gaze to mine. "It is just going to take some more time, that's all. We have all the time in the world."

She shook her head, and a tear dropped down her cheek. "How do I even deserve you?"

In that moment, I had begun to wonder the same thing. If I was being shamefully honest, would it ever work when my feelings didn't seem to matter at all? It killed me to think that because her feelings mattered too and everyone grieved in their own way. Maybe we weren't being fair to each other. Or maybe I was trying to force something that wasn't meant to be.

***

I stood before the long mirror in my room and pulled the wrinkles from the sleeve of my jacket. It seemed the first few times I had gone to the rebels I felt like an imposter, but now, as time had passed, I felt like an imposter here in the castle instead. I was questioning where I stood with Gaea, Oleo was gone, and the only real work I was doing was making as much of the truth serum as possible and hiding it any way I could.

I left my rooms to meet in the great hall as we always did before leaving the kingdom. No one traveled with luggage, because unlike other kingdoms, Gaea would have us all home before morning.

The king was the last to arrive, as usual, and it seemed even he was dressed for finery tonight. The customary travel companions had come. I stood between Autus in his layers of furs and Gaea, as beautiful as ever in a long black-sequined gown. Next to her, Eadas adjusted his stiff collar and Ragal stood still as a statue, waiting. We would go in pairs of two. I always wondered how Gaea's magic worked. It seemed so different from mine. She never seemed tired or drained.

"Before we go," the king announced. "Keep your eyes on the details of the Marsh Court. The next time we leave for this palace, it will be to take it as our own."

Within mere minutes, we stood in a group just outside of King Coro's dining hall. The folk rushed about or stumbled depending on their level of inebriation. The air was full of the sweet scent of wine and laughter, and though the night was meant to be full of jubilation, something in the sugared air turned my stomach—as though fate had already predicted the night to be a tragedy. Our party held blank faces as we stood together but so far apart. The Wind Court would always be the hindrance, the hateful, the hammer. Autus cultivated nothing else, and unless you escaped his heavy hand, you were just a pawn.

The air was different here, but so was the atmosphere. It was a warmer, humid climate with a stronger scent of the gardens than we got in the north. I envied the south for that. Droves of lesser fae were invited as guests to the ball, not just servants, and though I had been to the Marsh

Court hundreds of times over the years, the stark difference between their court and ours was nearly inspiring.

It bothered me that lesser fae were still unpaid servants in this court— put together and fed last, with less freedoms than the high fae. Even so, it was worlds apart from the Wind Court and Autus loathed coming here because of it.

I thought perhaps Morwena was the reason we came, but oddly enough, she didn't seem to be in attendance. The king stopped for none of the exaggerated revelry as he crossed the cavernous hall bedecked in gold foil wallpaper and took his royal seat beside King Coro at the head table. We sat close by as a group.

Food was promptly served and devoured, and then everyone was moved toward the ballroom for the dance to begin. I noticed Gaea taking in all the small details and even occasionally smiling at one passing thing or another. I supposed that was just another difference between us. The details didn't seem to matter to me anymore.

We stood atop the stairs and were introduced to the room just before our king. As we began our descent, a lesser fae moved into King Autus' way, and Gaea clamped her hand on my arm. She sucked in a sharp breath in warning just before the king planted his enormous foot on the back of the butterfly winged fae and kicked him down the lavish stairs. The room stopped only long enough for the fae to scream out in pain, and then they all went back to what they were doing like it hadn't happened. The king took his seat. I watched the fae out of the corner of my eye as he crawled inch by inch out of the way across the marble floor.

I looked to Gaea, and she shook her head. But how could I just leave him?

She grabbed my arm again and whispered, "You can't, Temir. He will see you."

I had forgotten. The king believed that only the council and Morwena knew of my magic, knew why the king who passionately hated the lesser fae would allow one to stand with him. Gaea looked like a high fae in every way except her feline eyes. Me? I had rapidly growing stag horns. They were hard to miss.

"I have to. Just distract him."

She nodded slowly. She did not agree, but she would always have my back. "Be quick about it," she snapped.

I knew deep down she wanted to help, but Oleo's death had scared her into submission. Maybe not to the degree the king would have liked, but enough that she was afraid to move against him.

I disappeared across the room while she made sure to keep the king facing away. I managed to get to the fae in the corner easily enough.

"We need to get out of this room right now. I can help you, but not here."

He moaned and shifted from the fetal position he was in to look up at me. He lifted his arm high enough to point to a small, discreet door in the wall not too far from where he laid.

"This is going to hurt," I warned, looking over my shoulder to Gaea. She had a fake smile plastered on her face, and I knew I had only seconds to disappear.

I grabbed under his arm and dragged him into the small closet hidden below the stairs. He breathed heavily. I laid my hands on his damaged wing, and he sighed in relief as I called my magic forward and pushed it through to him. The king had broken not only his patterned wing but also his back, several of his ribs, and it sounded as if at least one of his lungs had been punctured. Left on his own much longer, he would have died in that corner without a soul to even notice his grave suffering. Alone.

The healing was only slightly draining, but I worked as quickly as I could in the dark, lit only by the small bit of light coming from below the closed door. The ambiance from the ball was only marginally muted. The fae sat up with my assistance and twisted back and forth.

"How?" He sucked in a deep breath and pulled his head away from me in awe.

"Magic," I responded.

138

"Thank you," he whispered. "Without my wings—"

"No time. Listen. You need to follow the phoenix symbols throughout your city until someone finds you. Trust me, they will. No lesser fae is safe. No matter what anyone tells you, war is coming."

He nodded and took my hand, shaking it frantically. "Thank you, sir. Thank you."

I stood and cracked the door open to peek out. I could barely see the king across the crowded room, but still his back was to me. I slipped out and left the male behind, hoping no one had noticed. I kept telling myself he would have died. His fragile life was worth the risk.

I grabbed several wine glasses from a passing tray and hustled back to Gaea. I gave a barely perceptible nod, and her shoulders relaxed as I handed her a glass. "Sorry. They must not have enough servers around here. I had to chase these all over the room."

I handed Ragal a glass also, and I could tell he didn't quite believe me as he searched the room, but said nothing. As more fae filled the dance floor, I drifted back toward the comfortable shadows along a far wall. I watched them dance and spill wine and laugh, and the fury within me grew like wildflowers. How could they? How could they find joy in this world? How could they stand in the room with anything but understanding and fear of what was to come? Could they truly be so oblivious to what King Autus' betrothal to Morwena meant?

I looked to Gaea as she moved through the room, taking dances with the males who asked. The king would expect nothing less of her, and so she would play the part.

I caught a glimpse of fire-red hair, and my body reacted before I realized. I had taken two large steps toward the female before I stopped, confused. My breath was stolen as something I could only describe as foreign magic weighted my entire body down until I could scarcely draw in a breath. I placed my fingers to my temples, willing away the pressure as King Autus left his diminutive throne and descended the steps to speak with the female I'd seen and someone I presumed to be her mother. They

139

were similar in stature and shared facial features but something about the younger one felt *off.*

I watched as the king leaned in and whispered to her. I saw her eyes glaze over, and my stomach lurched when I realized he was enchanting her. She pulled away laughing, and her mother smiled broadly. The king reached for her hand and pulled her up to the throne. He sat her on his lap, and they whispered back and forth, smiling like lovesick children.

I turned back to the room and saw Gaea watching me. I walked over to her and pulled her hand to my mouth for a gentle kiss. "I hate seeing that and knowing it was done to you."

"I don't want to talk about that tonight." She pulled me to the packed dance floor and pressed her body to mine. We moved back and forth until I forgot about everything and everyone in the entire world. She had a way with me. One day we were fine and the next we would never be fine, but for now, that would have to be enough.

She spent the rest of the night in my arms, and while I caught King Autus watching us on several occasions, I didn't care. Couldn't.

It was well past midnight before Gaea took us all home, and we stood together in the darkness of my rooms. I couldn't help but think of the last time we were here, in this position, after a ball. We had lost Oleo that night. I knew she thought of it too, but she had drank and drank at the ball, and it was a miracle she was able to spirit us home.

"Take me to bed, Temir," she slurred.

I rocked her back and forth and ran my hands up and down her exposed back, leaning in and kissing below her ear. It would have been so, so easy to finally break through this wall she had built between us. I tipped my head back and moaned. She stood on her toes to kiss me, her soft lips massaging mine, and I breathed every ounce of her in.

She tugged on my arm, and we collapsed to the couch. She swung her legs over my lap, and the slit in her dress gave me easy access to brush my fingertips along her soft thigh. I closed my eyes and remembered what it felt like to be between her glorious legs. I could have gone there—she would have let me—but she probably would have regretted it in the morning.

"I'll take you to bed, my love. But I can't stay."

"You can," she answered.

"You'd hate me in the morning," I whispered as I carried her to my bedroom. I covered her in layers of blankets and went back to the couch. Walking out of that room was one of the hardest things I'd ever had to do. My heart called to her, but hers did not respond.

The next morning, I woke early. I had dreamt of fire-red hair and a tyrant king with the voice of poisoned honey. I was unsurprised to find Gaea had spirited away in the night. That spoke to me as the distance between us grew. Shaking off my hurt and disappointment, I went down to the lists to check on Eadas who had seamlessly taken over training the soldiers, and I was curious to see how well he led them. I passed the twins watching and whispering. They always seemed to be plotting something horrendous, though I never saw them do anything.

I had hoped for far worse than what I found. He did not yell and scream at them but ran drills, and the males moved in fluid motion with each other. I thought Eadas taking over as commander would benefit the rebellion, but I was so wrong.

I sent a message through Roe that I needed to speak with Rook as soon as he could find a way, and by nightfall, I had a message to meet him by the eastern tunnel entrance.

"What's going on, Temir?" he asked, business as usual.

"Well, several things actually. All important. I can run the mission with Rhogan. I'll get there on my own, so just have him meet me there in three days."

"I'll make sure he is ready. What else?"

"The king plans to sack the Marsh Court castle the next time he goes. I'm not sure when that will be, but he cozied up to a female and her mother while we were there, and I wondered if they were important to his plans. It's not a lot to go on, but it's all I know. Also, we need to talk to the rebels about using code words and being more discreet. I know for sure that one council member has learned of them on her own by listening in the hallways."

"Fuck. I'll try to get a plan in place as soon as possible for another meeting."

"Last thing," I said. "Eadas took over the Wind Court army. He trains the sentries and soldiers as their new commander. I thought that was going to work in our favor, but I think I was wrong. He's always been sneaky, and if he brings that tactic through the military ranks, we're more likely to be ambushed. He's smart. Cunning. We have to be careful."

"Half the soldiers are only there because they have to be. Not because they want to be," he said. "I have to believe that when it comes down to it they will drop their weapons rather than fight against us." He leaned against the rugged trunk of a nearby dead tree and put his hands in his pockets.

"You want to believe that, but if the king begins to enchant them, they won't have a choice." I thought of the last time he'd enchanted a group and seemed to struggle, but I didn't mention it. "The minute he learns of the rebellion, he will start doing that. He won't make the same mistakes he did in the last war. He will control the minds of the world before he loses anything."

"About that. Oravan revealed his secret to me. The barrier charms." He looked down to the ring on my finger and back to me again. "I've wondered how you've managed to avoid the king's mind control, but now I see. He plans to make as many as he can so we can keep ourselves safe. We are looking into other methods he can use." He turned his head to the side and his goat horn struck the tree, but he didn't seem to notice.

"Make sure he isn't making all of the same jewelry. If everyone wears the same thing, we will be easier to hunt. Also, this won't make as much sense to you, but make sure he isn't draining himself. Make him rest."

"I'm already on it. Our time is coming, Temir. We will make our first move soon. Are you ready for that? Can you handle the king's scrutiny and suspicions, or will you leave the castle?"

"I plan to stay as a spy in the council meetings for as long as I can." I shrugged. It was the only answer I had.

"Good. Just watch your back with Autus. He's never trusted a soul, and his suspicion is deep-rooted." A whistle sounded in the distance. "Time's up for this little meeting. You can always call for me or send a message."

"I'd rather not write anything down that can be intercepted."

"Smart mind. I'll see you soon. Good luck with the new wielder."

I nodded and hustled back to the castle. I could handle the king's suspicious nature. It was his relentless wrath I was worried about.

16

KING TOLERO

*S*he misses you, I think," I told Efi as I lay in the sacred grass and let my toes sink in. "I'm sorry I haven't been back to visit her, but it was so hard to be with Asha without you there, my love. Do you think she felt your soul in mine and that is why she allowed me into the circle?"

I breathed in the deep scent of the salted sea and closed my weary eyes. I knew Asha had responded to me because of my mate's deep connection with her. She had seen and grasped for the fragment of Efi's soul that remained within me. I didn't need to ask, but I still wished she could answer.

"There are so many things that need to be done here. The Trials are going to be a disaster. I'm sure the draconians are only coming because I demand it. I've got one pit lord I may have to shut down. The cetani will not show. Last night, I saw two selkies in the crowd at the pits. And our people are dying with no explanation. I wish you could be here."

I laid my head back, closed my eyes and let the fiery sun warm my skin. I listened to the lulling waves gently crash into the isle and took slow measured breaths until I drifted off to sleep.

I saw her then. In my dreams. She caressed my face and placed a phantom kiss upon my lips. I could smell her there with me as she whispered, "Look at Asha and think of me. Let loose what slumbers within."

I knew I was dreaming, but she was so real. Tangible. She stood before me so corporeal I could feel her smooth velvety skin against mine.

"Don't let me wake, Efi. Let me stay with you."

"You cannot. You must protect our son."

"He is grown. He doesn't need me."

"You are wrong, Tiger." She took a step away.

I reached for her. "Wait," I cried.

"I must go, Tolero. Send Asha my love. Remember what I said, look at her and think of me. You must let loose the beast."

"What do you mean? I look at the simple sun and think of you. I look at the halls and think of you. I always do. How can you not know that?" I took a step toward her.

"Tolero." She slowly faded away. "Tolero."

Her voice melted into that of a male's, and I was abruptly woken from my dream.

"King Tolero," the masculine voice called again.

I sat up, disorientated from the vivid dream, and took a moment to remember where I was. She was so real. She was right here with me, and then she was gone.

"King Tolero," Inok called again. He stood in a boat beside mine along the shoreline.

"I could kill you right now for waking me," I scolded.

"Forgive me, my king." He bent at the waist, rocking his boat with the gesture. "You must come now. There's been a fire."

"Where?" I barked, lifting myself from the grass and hustling down the hill to the small beach and into my boat.

"It's Trig's farm. They said no one made it out alive."

"No one?" I asked.

"I believe there are ten dead. The barn and the house were set aflame."

"Do we know who did it?" I asked, grabbing my oar.

"There is talk there were guards seen leaving the property." Inok pushed offshore just behind me with his own oar.

"Which kingdom's guards?" I asked, moving through the water.

"Ours," he said gravely.

My hands froze in place. I met his eyes for only a moment before he looked away in sorrow. "My guards killed ten of my own people? Do we know which ones? Who saw them?"

"We don't know which guards. Witnesses saw them from a distance riding away from the farm. That's all we know."

"Hurry, Inok. We have to get back right away."

"The welcome may not be warm," he warned.

"Call an open council meeting immediately."

"But sir, wouldn't you rather have a private meeting first?"

"No. Call everyone who wants to come to the throne room. Let us hear what the people have to say. I've always been good to them, Inok. They will not believe the lies."

"Can you be so sure that they are lies?"

"Why would my guards do that? Of course they are lies."

Hours later, I sat upon my throne with my staff in hand, letting my long robes drape to the floor as I stared straight ahead and waited for the room to fill with the fae of the Flame Court.

The traditional flames were lit along the walls as thousands of people entered the cavernous room, silent and wary. My council filled the first row, and only Inok and I remained on the dais. My son's seat beside my own was noticeably the only vacant one in the room. My dream from earlier held me on edge as I looked to Inok and dipped my chin.

He stepped forward, and I felt more than saw the gathered fae take in a breath as they waited for an answer. One I could not give.

"It is with the deepest sorrow that I confirm the fire and tragic deaths at Trig's farm. The king was just as surprised as you were to learn of this news today. We have no explanations for you, but we would like to hear from you. First, we will call forward the witness. Amil, if you will step to the front." He gestured for Amil to move to the base of the steps before me.

He did, bowing low and graciously before standing straight and waiting for my questions.

"Please tell the room what you witnessed, Amil."

"As you know, my king, my land sits adjacent to Trig's goat farm, just north of the city. First, I heard a bit of screaming, so I went outside to see what the cause of it was. I saw the smoke before the flames in the distance, and then witnessed the guards racing back down the road toward the city. I hopped on Gana, my horse, and rode as fast as I could to Trig's, but I was too late. There were no more cries by the time I got there."

The crowded room grew in volume as they heard the witness' tale. I held my hand in the air for silence, but it did not come.

"What will you say for your guard's actions?" someone called out from the middle of the room.

"Did you order it yourself?" another asked.

"Were they related to Muth? I heard you attacked him in the pits."

I stood and slammed my staff into the floor. "Enough." The room fell silent, but the stares were deadly. "You've heard the witness and now know as much as I do. I did not give an order to have anyone killed. I don't know which guards were responsible. You will be respectful, or you will be taken from this room by force, understood?"

Silence.

I looked to my council. They whispered amongst each other but said nothing out loud. Perhaps I should have consulted them first.

"Can you describe the guards to the room, Amil?" I asked, taking my seat once more.

"N-no, Your Grace. I did not see faces, only the guard's ensemble as they rode off."

"So, we have no way of proving they were actually our guards and not imposters wearing stolen uniforms?" I asked.

"No, Your Grace."

"Okay then. I have given testament that I have not ordered this tragic event. The witness has agreed that he cannot prove the soldiers were mine. Does anyone have anything to add?" I could see the disdain on their faces, but no one spoke. "You are all dismissed."

All but my council rose from their seats and exited the room. No one left satisfied, but in that we were the same.

"King Tolero," Madu stood.

"Yes?" I thrummed my hands along the arm of my jeweled throne.

"Is there anything more you can share with the council aside from the information given to the people? The death toll in your kingdom is rising. What will you do?"

I stood once more and strode with my tiger's intensity. I knew what it looked like. I knew what they thought. But they were all wrong, and I would answer to no one.

"You've been given all the information to this point. Don't think for one moment that I owe you or anyone else an explanation of my own innocence. You're welcome to visit the northern kingdoms if you need a reminder of what life could be like here."

Sabra stood with Madu. "I think what he means to ask is what will we do? Should we warn the people to use more caution until we can discover what is happening?"

"You may use your own discretion. If you feel concerned, use caution. Now go, all of you."

I didn't watch the shock on their faces as they left the room. For a long time, I leaned on my council. The tumultuous relationships between them were not helpful though.

"Inok," I whispered, sitting back on my throne. "Please bring Muth in."

As I waited, I closed my eyes and tried to send myself back to the dream with Efi.

Let loose the tiger, she had said. Didn't she know? Didn't they all know how dangerous that would be? If I did not control myself?

Muth entered the emptied hall and knelt before me, placing his nose to the ground without prompting. This morning, I would have yanked the pits away from him without thought. Now, I realized the fae, the ones questioning me and my intentions, needed to be reminded of my mercy.

"Rise," I commanded. He slowly rose to his feet yet kept his chin tucked and his eyes to the floor. "You have one minute to convince me to let you keep your title as pit lord. One minute to explain why you should have a place in the Trials." He was silent. "You're losing time, Muth."

"Your Grace," he said, barely above a whisper. "I can only apologize for the sight you witnessed and beseech your forgiveness. I have taken my liberties too far, and I am regretful."

"Do you understand that you nearly made hundreds of fae watch the death of a boy for entertainment? Did that feel entertaining to you?"

"I'll admit, I should have used more restraint with Lere. He showed great potential with the mace, and I thought he could win."

"Did you starve the hounds as well?" I clasped the edge of my seat to push back the fury.

"I did."

"And do you believe you are above punishment?"

"I do not." He shook his head.

"You will be allowed to keep your position for now, Muth. Not because you deserve it, but because I do not have time to deal with you right now. Your recruits may fight in the Trials but heed my warning. I will be watching you closer than you ever imagined possible and, if for one second, I think you are doing something you shouldn't be, I'll kill you. I'll put your head on a stake and display it in the middle of your beloved pit so your crowds are reminded who is really in charge. Do you understand?"

"Yes, Your Grace," he answered solemnly.

"As for your punishment, you will report every morning to the lists here at the castle. You will check in with Brax, and you will do whatever he tells you to do until further notice. If he needs the soldier's weapons sharpened, you will do it. If he needs the stalls cleaned in the stable, you will do it. If he needs you to remain on your hands and knees for an entire day, just to show your humility, you will do it. Am I understood?" He nodded but said nothing. "You are dismissed." As his footsteps echoed through the room and he reached the door, I stopped him. "One more thing, Muth." He spun back to face me. "Your announcer will fight the first battle in the Trials against Brax."

He bowed and walked out.

"Brax will kill him," Inok said from my side.

"If only," I answered.

"The lords are beginning to fill Halemi, and I imagine the city will be buzzing tonight, my king."

"I'm counting on it. We are going hunting. Ready your weapons."

"You're going out again?"

"*We* are. I have a selkie to catch, and I'm going to need your help. It's time to put the puzzle pieces together."

He nodded and joined me as we walked into the bustling hallway.

"Your Grace." A messenger handed me a sealed letter. "Someone left this for you."

I looked down at the familiar phoenix imprinted on the wax seal, thanked him, and tucked it into my robes. I would open it into the solitude of my rooms.

We had to weave through the people in the castle. Some curtsied, some bowed, several gave me looks of concern and derision. Even in my own palace they had brought hatred. In all my years of ruling, I had never felt the abhorrence of my fae as much as I did now. That worried me. It was like a poison spreading through them.

I halted my steps and sucked in a breath. Exactly.

"Good gods, Inok. Get to the stables and tell Rah we need the three fastest fae horses ready immediately. We have to get to the dunes right away."

"If we go there, we will never be back by tonight."

"I guess we are just going to have to ride fast then," I answered, hurrying to find the healer.

Look at her and think of me, she had said in my dream.

I slammed the apothecary door open and likely startled the poor male half to death.

CHAPTER 17

ARA

*P*rick. Prick. Prick.

I wasn't sure why they called him a prince when prick was so much more appropriate. We had been walking for hours. Hours. All six of us. Barely a word had been spoken, and the southerners were doing their weird hand signal thing again. I found it so difficult to concentrate with the wrath boiling me from the inside. Every time I looked at him and tried to let it go, I saw myself trapped in that room. And maybe that wasn't the biggest issue. Maybe it was my own fear of being trapped by my prophecy while he got to make his choices and call the shots on everything up to this point, and that just didn't work for me. So, be it his mistakes or my own fears, I kept my distance.

They let me lead, but I could tell it was driving Kai nuts. He kept making grunting sounds every time I went in a direction he didn't think I should—Prince Doom and Gloom had to give him a look several times to get him to stop—but I was pretty sure I was headed in the right direction. I weaved in and out of the trees and tried to go fairly straight.

It was all going well enough until I found a tree with the dullahan's symbol on it.

Panicking, I continued forward, watching for another set of glowing red eyes in the dark. Soon, the symbols became more frequent until we reached the small circular clearing similar to last time. But the clearing was not only similar, it was exactly the same. I had led us in a full circle. I closed my eyes and cursed the gods for my own stubbornness.

Kai started to laugh once he knew I'd finally realized what I had done.

I turned and gave him a look that would stop anyone else, but he was too busy laughing to notice. Two pricks. How lucky was I?

"Ready to work as a team yet?" Fen asked, running his hand through his dark hair.

"Work as your own team and just leave me the hell alone. I wouldn't have gotten turned around if I didn't have five extra people trailing behind me, distracting me."

"I've already told you. I am your Guardian. I can't just leave you."

"Listen." I stepped closer, that boiling rage about to blow. "I don't need a Guardian, though it's awfully fucking noble of you to want to be one now when you didn't have a problem leaving me with Aibell."

He shook his head and walked away. I relished in the victory.

"He's not so bad when you don't anger him all the time," Greeve said quietly from beside me.

"Who asked you anyway?" I snapped back.

"Woah, Ara." Wren stepped between us. "It's been a long day. Why don't we just set up camp here for the night and figure the rest out tomorrow?"

I took a deep breath and rubbed my face. "Whatever." I dropped my pack to the ground, and that was enough of a clue for the others to do the same.

"You called?" Aibell's withered voice rang out. She waltzed through the trees, grinning as if she had been there the entire time.

"No, I most certainly did not."

"Fenlas, come here." She crossed her small arms over her chest and buried them in the folds of her robes.

He was there in an instant. So kind and respectful to everyone else, apparently.

Aibell grabbed my arm and his arm and winked at me. She vanished, and I looked down to see iron chains linking us together.

"Are you fucking serious? Aibell? Get back here, you old hag!"

Her cackle lingered in my mind as I caught the crooked smirk on Fen's face.

I snarled. "Something funny, Prince?"

He shook his head and looked away, his smile instantly gone. We simultaneously took a step in opposite directions and were jerked back toward each other.

"Could you just cooperate for once in your life and come this way so I can grab my bag?"

"Let's try this: 'Hey Fen, I need something this way, would you mind?'"

I huffed at his tone and jerked him in the direction I needed to go. I heard the oomph and the laughs from the others and ignored the furious look on his face. His stupid pretty fucking face.

Within minutes, they had a small fire going, which I thought was incredibly stupid, but apparently, they were all so much smarter than I was.

"Any guesses why she did this?" Fen asked me.

"You're the know-it-all secret keeper around here, you tell me," I bit out.

"Listen, Ara. I'm sorry. I can't change any of that now. But here we are, stuck together, literally." He raised the chain between us and shook it, causing my arm to swing also. "We might as well make the best of it."

"Don't tell me how to feel about being handcuffed to the one person I've dreamed about killing for weeks. Months, even. I might be a stubborn bitch who doesn't listen, but you are a cold-hearted asshole who doesn't care, and I'm not sure that's any better."

He leveled eyes with me and tugged on the chain until I was inches from his face. His gaze melted through my hatred like a flame. Why did I want to lick him? "We're chained together until we get along, I'm guessing, so you might as well try."

I stared him down, trying to shove my hatred toward him, but as we locked eyes, a flash of an apology appeared. It was gone just as fast as it had come. Vanished. I was so much better with anger. I understood it as a part of me, a language I spoke so fluently. Fury was a safety net. A wall. Attraction? That was the loss of control I so desperately feared. I pulled on the rage escaping me, willing it back into place, wrapping it around me. "Is this the part where the feral monster becomes the domesticated housewife and does everything she is told like a good little maiden?" I put the single free arm I had on my hip.

He rolled his eyes at me. Rolled. His. Eyes. "Just try to get some sleep. Greeve, take watch." His direct order grated on my nerves.

With one hand, I shook the blanket from my bag and tossed it haphazardly to the ground. He snorted and bent down to straighten it for me. It was an almost kind gesture. Almost. I laid down, jerking the prince with me, and listened to the soft voices of the others long into the night until the last of them drifted off to sleep.

I shifted on the ground several times and finally gave up on sleeping. Every night since I'd opened Nealla's book, I woke screaming anyway. If the southerners' fire didn't draw a hungry forest creature, that definitely would.

"Can't sleep?" the prince asked, pulling on the stupid chain.

"Good gods, can't I be sleep deprived in peace at least?"

"Sorry," he answered.

"What do you want, Prince?" I sat up to look at him, pulling him to sit as well.

"Well, for starters, I'd love to know what we are doing in the maze forest."

"Okay, well first of all, I have no idea what *you're* doing here. I have to go west. This seemed like the quickest route."

"Depending on how far west, it might be, but not if you don't know how to travel here."

"How the fuck does anyone know how to travel here?" I sneered.

"We rely on trackers," he said in a flat voice.

"Then I guess you'll have no problem getting back to Coro's fancy castle."

"I've already told you, Ara. I'm not leaving."

"And I've already told you, Fenlas, I don't want you here. But apparently, words are like lesser fae around here. No one seems to care."

"Too far," he warned.

"Don't even try to play self-righteous with me. I was in that alley in Hrundel. I would have saved those two lesser fae if you hadn't because, unlike you, I'm not playing a part. I've been doing nothing but fight for them since I left Aibell's cottage."

He leaned back, and for the first time I think, he noticed the suit Nadra's mother had crafted for me with her magic. "What have you been doing?" Fire lit his eyes.

"Killing assholes for sport," I shrugged.

"This is not a game." He let his strained voice rise above a whisper. "What are we doing? Why are we in this forest?"

"I don't know why you're here. I'm just passing through."

He scowled and shook his head. "Where are you going?"

"That's my own business."

"I have imagined you a thousand different ways in my life. Not once did I think you would be a spoiled, selfish brat."

"Surprise," I said, smiling at him sweetly.

He growled, literally growled, and laid back down, turning over and jerking me with him, though he kept his arm behind his back. I heard a snicker from the sleeping pile of fae near the fire, and it sparked a deep embedded rage within me.

"Watch what you're doing," I snapped and laid back down awkwardly.

His fingers laid inches from mine in the dirt, and I knew he was just as wide awake as I was. I stared up at the dark forest ceiling and contemplated all the ways I could kill Aibell instead of Fen. I rolled to my side, letting my arm twist behind me. Hey, that had to be progress, right?

Greeve stood with his tattooed back to us, staring at the tree line. Of course he had heard us, but he kept his distance. His long black hair was tied back with strips of leather, and if any of the southerners felt dangerous, it was him. You could tell by looking at him and his long, curved sword that he was serious. Especially as a constant breeze followed him. Obeyed him.

There was something familiar about him, and as I thought about it, I realized he shared similar traits with Fenlas. With his broad chest and tall frame, they could have been brothers. But Fen had those emerald eyes. Those beautiful, haunting eyes that would not leave me.

"Why do you and Greeve look so similar?" I asked, rolling back over to face Fen.

"He is draconian, and my mother was as well."

I thought back to the picture I'd found in his room of him and his parents. "My mother died too," I said, forgetting who I was talking to.

"I know she did, Ara, and I'm so sorry." His face was inches from my own, and the sincerity in his voice was shocking. Maybe somewhere in there, buried way at the bottom of his angry soul, was a single drop of kindness.

Something small sparked within me, like a bated breath, a lingering moment of desire.

I rolled back over and closed my eyes. I didn't sleep at all that night. I refused to consider him as anything but an asshole. My mother had told me not to trust anyone, and as far as I was concerned, that included him and his lackeys. Wren was okay, but still, what did I really know about any of them?

We traveled for several long days attached by that damn chain. My overwhelming hatred had faded to bored disdain, and though I caught him staring at me from time to time or found myself lost in thoughts of him, I still held him at a distance. As far as I could, anyway. He'd tug on me and I'd pull on him, and overall, whatever Aibell's purpose was, the only thing it had done was teach me how to do everything with one hand.

"Would you just stop for a minute?" he asked me one day as we followed Kai through the endless mass of trees and foliage.

"They'll get too far ahead," I grumbled.

"They won't. Look at me." He planted his feet and yanked me backward.

"Ow," I said, pulling back on the heavy chain.

"I'm sorry. I wasn't trying to hurt you."

"Rule one of not trying to hurt someone, don't fucking yank them around like a rag doll, Prince."

"You are so gods-damn maddening. What do you want me to do? I've apologized. I've tried talking to you. I've tried to help you. I've given you space."

"Ha!" I snapped. "How are we supposed to have space like this?"

"I think if you would just get over your anger, the chain would go away. If you could let it go, Ara."

"Let it go? So, you get to treat me however the fuck you want for however long you want, and the moment you're over it, I have to be too? I don't get to feel angry because you've decided I shouldn't?"

"No, I'm not—" He turned and stomped the ground, clearly frustrated. "I'm not trying to tell you not to have feelings, I'm asking you to calm down. How can you walk around so pissed off all the time and not age a thousand years? I'm sorry I was an asshole and didn't handle everything the way I was supposed to. None of this came with directions."

"If you would be kind to me, you would probably get the outcome you're asking for."

"I've been nothing but kind to you from the moment the handcuffs went on," he seethed, leaning in to bark in my face.

"You just ..." I paused. He was right. I'd been the asshole. But he deserved it, and I wouldn't apologize for it. "Fine. I'll stop yelling at you. But that's the best you get. I still want to murder you in your sleep, Prince."

"Ah, the budding sounds of friendship," Kai hollered from the front of the line.

"Shut it, Kai," Wren said.

The tensions in the group were high, and I was the reason. They all leaned on Fen for leadership and support, and I could tell they genuinely respected him. But as we traveled and the two of us bickered, that negativity had poisoned the group. The first day, they all smiled and laughed and joked as we moved. Now they were quiet as everyone was on edge.

"You realize they're here by choice, right? I never asked any of them to come north with me."

"I'm sure it's been a lovely vacation." I bit back my grin. For the first time in days, he shared that adoring smile with me, and, distracted, I stumbled over a rock. He reached out to grab my arm, keeping me from falling. "Thanks."

He jerked up, held out a hand, then brought his fingers to his lips. He pointed to the side and then to his ear. I listened carefully, and sure enough, two heavy sets of footsteps crept toward us. The rest of the team halted, and like perfect stealthy warriors, they faded into the trees nearly unseen. I pulled a dagger and loosely held it in my steady hand. My favorite.

"I will handle it," he whispered.

"Not on your life," I answered smoothly. He made some more hand gestures. "I don't know what the fuck you're saying to me. Just let the bastards come, and we will figure it out from there."

"Put the knife down," he ordered.

"You've got a lot to learn about me, Prince."

"Thirty seconds max," Kai said from behind us.

I hadn't even heard him move, but I realized quickly the group had formed a circle around us. "gods-damn it, I'm not a child."

The prince snorted, and I'd never wanted to use my sword on someone so badly.

"Careful, Fenlas," Wren warned. She'd seen me use a weapon.

"Quiet," Lichen's deep voice boomed.

I'd nearly forgotten about him. He had watched me intently as we walked through the forest, but I couldn't recall him ever saying a word. I readied my feet, and though I was attached to the prince, my dominant hand was still free.

"Stubborn brat," the prince mumbled.

"And pretty," I added.

Wren laughed, but it was interrupted by two tall hunters stepping out from behind the distant trees like a form created from shadow. They wore those familiar black outfits. A flash of the sea fae I'd killed in the cave came to me.

Fen moved forward. "Who are you?"

"None of your business, Prince. We've come for her." One pointed a sword at me.

"Come and get me then," I taunted.

"No, I definitely would not recommend that. Who do you work for?" He may have been the prince, but he was not very bright. Kai was fuming beside me, and I could tell he was barely holding himself back. "It's two against six here, boys, are you sure you want to start this fight?"

"Two girls and an old male don't count," one of them said.

Without another word, I threw a knife, and it landed so hard into the other sea fae's skull, it threw him backward.

"You were saying?" I asked the one still standing.

"Holy fuck," Kai whispered.

The sea fae took a step backward. I pulled another dagger and flipped it in my hand while I gave him a moment to reconsider.

He retracted another step and another until he backed right into Greeve, who had used his magic to cleave behind him. He shrieked in surprise, and Greeve snapped his neck, tossing him to the ground.

"No fair," Kai whined. "It was my turn."

"I forgot." Greeve shrugged.

"Nice shot," Lichen said from beside me as he sheathed his sword.

"It would have been nicer if we learned who they were first," Fen argued.

"They were sea fae," I answered.

"How can you be so sure?" Wren asked.

"Black coats, subtle shimmer to their skin, evada pearl in that one's ear. And for your information, Prince, I'd bet you a fae horse those weapons were poisoned, so next time, kill first and ask questions later."

"They're still hunting you?" He moved in front of me with a mix of anger and confusion on his face. He'd probably thought Morwena had only sent the one that poisoned me outside of Aibell's cottage.

"Yes. But I don't know how they found me here. They shouldn't have been able to do that." I unintentionally brought my hand up to my mother's necklace tucked beneath the magical fabric I wore.

Lichen cleared his throat. "Let's discuss this as we move. We need to get out of this damn forest before you two start fighting again."

"For the love of the gods, Kai, get us out of here. I smell like dirt and wet leaves," Wren begged.

"Can we stop bickering and move a little faster?" Fen asked, quirking an eyebrow at me.

"Fine." I rolled my eyes.

"And can I be the official line leader?" Kai asked.

"Seriously? I guess," I said. "Give an inch, take a mile."

"Yes!" He shot his hands into the air and abruptly turned to march away, high knees and all.

"And I'm the child?" I asked Fen, walking back to the fallen males.

He grinned at me, and for an instant, the anger I'd been wrapped in whisked away. The moment it was gone, the one I'd been hoping to avoid hit me like a ton of bricks. Desire. And that feeling scared me more than anything. I looked away, trying to remember why I hated him. Why I didn't want to be his friend or his lover, but as the days passed, it was getting harder and harder to remember.

"I make no claims about these two assholes." He pointed toward Kai and Greeve. "So where are we headed?"

"The Western Gap."

Everyone stopped short. All of them.

"You're kidding, right?" Wren asked.

"No. That's where I have to go."

"Why?" Fen asked.

"I didn't tell you all to come. That's just where I'm going, okay?" I yanked my knife out of the sea fae's forehead. I didn't trust them enough with my whole truth. Maybe once we made it to the gap, I would explain. Maybe.

"We better hunt before we leave the forest," Kai said, changing the subject.

"Are we allowed to do that, Princess?" Fen asked with more sarcasm than I knew him capable of.

"Be my guest." I curtsied for good measure.

Kai and Greeve left to go hunting while Wren, Lichen, Fen and I stayed behind to set up camp.

"Tell me," Lichen said, digging through his bag. "What's it like?"

"What's *what* like?"

"Being the ..." He stumbled over his words. "I guess we still aren't able to say it then."

"I am protected by Nealla. You won't be able to speak of my fate until she breaks the binding."

"Right." He nodded, pulled out a book and a pen, and wrote something down.

"What are you writing?" I reached into my pack with one hand, yanked out my blanket, and shook the wrinkles from it.

"Oh, I just like to journal things in case we need to reference them later. I find the best way to advise is to reference facts."

He was strange but seemed kind.

"Let's go see if we can find some water," Fen suggested, pulling me away from Lichen's question.

"Thanks," I said after we were far enough away. "I hate questions."

"I can see that." The corners of his mouth lifted into a half-hearted smile.

I stepped over a rock and followed the sound of rushing water ahead. "Do they all just cater to your every request?"

"I wish. They are all assholes. Trust me."

"Must be a Flame Court thing," I mumbled as he pulled on the chain.

"We've all known each other for a long time. We have a history. They listen because that's my role. Just like Kai's role is resident smartass and Greeve's role is to keep us from killing each other or getting killed."

"And Wren?"

"Wren is Wren. She's a decent fighter and she mothers us. I guess she filled a void we needed. She keeps us in line too."

"I can see that." We stepped up to the bank of the river. "Let me ask you a serious question though. Where does this end for you?"

"What end?"

I held the chain up and wiggled it.

"I don't think this chain is here because of me, Ara. I think it's really up to you. If she wants us to get along, that's probably all it's going to take."

"It stinks, you know? Not getting a single say in any of this. My whole life is lined up before me, written in a prophecy, and I just get to walk the path and let life happen to me. I swear to the gods, if I have to be mated to someone on top of all this shit, I'm going to sacrifice myself to The Mists."

"That bad, huh?" He knelt and rubbed his hands in the running water.

I joined him, and when he was done with our shared limbs, I washed my face, taking a deep breath. "It's the last thing I'd want in my whole life. Give me the monsters, the murder, the evil royals, but spare me the forced love."

"I would have never guessed you even considered love with all your sarcasm and death threats."

"I wasn't always a murderous assassin, Prince."

CHAPTER 18

NADRA

*C*old. I had never been so cold in my life. My jumbled mind was not my own, but still the aching desire was. The way he looked at me, the way he spoke to me like I was the only person in the whole world. Lies. Pretty, festering lies that twisted my mind into believing I was his beloved. He spoke of the others with me. At night, when he came to my rooms, he spoke of them. My mother. He wanted her too. Not in the same way he claimed to want me, but she would one day be his. With honeyed words or her own conviction, I wasn't sure, but the king always got what he wanted. At least that's what he said to me.

I laid in my giant bed alone and confused and felt the pull of my heart. North. We had traveled. I was to be his lover, and my mother his prize. He hadn't taken me though. I'd begged him to find comfort in my arms. He'd slapped me for my forward words. Broken. I laid broken on my gifted bed wishing for sleep that would never come. The fog within my brain was suffocating.

CHAPTER
19

TEMIR

"*Y*ou're sure you want to do this?" Gaea asked as we stood in her bland room. No trinkets. No books. No color at all.

"I'm sure. It should be quick. If you can get me to the town, I'll have a simple conversation and meet you back wherever you drop me off within an hour. If I can't convince him in that amount of time, nothing I say will do it."

"You can and you will. Just listen before you talk and believe in yourself." She offered me her hand. "Ready?"

"Now or never." I grasped her fingers within my own.

In an instant, we were in the middle of a small village like the one I had watched burn to the ground. Rhogan leaned against a fence post not too far from us. He was hard to miss with his giant raven wings extended. He tied his hair back, flashing a big smile to Gaea.

"Who is that?" she asked, her eyes wide.

"Come, I'll introduce you."

"No, Temir. I should go. I'll meet you back here in an hour."

I pulled her into a hug, and as soon as I let go, she vanished.

"Who's your friend?" Rhogan asked, wiggling his eyebrows.

"Someone who doesn't want to get involved with us. You know where we are going?" I asked, deflecting.

"Seems like she's already involved with one of us," he said, pushing his shoulder into mine.

"Something like that."

"The wielder is right up here. His parents are waiting with him."

We walked to the house, and Rhogan entered like he owned the place. We sat down in two chairs opposite an older fae boy and his parents.

"Before you even start, just tell me why you told them, Rhog," he asked.

I looked at him and back to the boy.

"Cheb, you know I wouldn't be here if it wasn't important. I would have never told your secret if I didn't know this was the best way to keep you and your parents safe."

"Why would I join the rebellion and not stay in hiding or go to the king? I heard if he sees my powers, he will protect me. Might even let me live in the castle. Seems like a good idea to me."

Rhogan gave me a look, and I nodded. My turn.

"My name is Temir. I trust that everything we say here today will stay here. Is that a fair thing to ask? Even if you decide that the rebellion is not the right place for you, can you keep this meeting between us?"

"Yeah, yeah, we've already promised Rhogan he could kill us if we talked." He looked at Rhogan, who grinned from ear to ear as if the threat were something to be proud of.

"I actually live in the palace with King Autus. I thought about leaving that out of the meeting, but I think it's best to just be honest with each other. I can tell you firsthand that being someone's slave, being at someone's beck and call all day every day for the rest of your life is no way to live."

"I can't believe hiding and running for your entire life is a way to live either," he answered, looking at his parents.

"No, but I think joining the rebellion would be the middle ground. You wouldn't have to hide from everyone, and everything you did would make a difference. You could help change the world."

"Is that what they told you?" he asked.

"Actually, no. I'm not even sure the rebels wanted me when I first joined. But I wanted them."

He bit his lip, studying me. "What is your magic?"

"I'm a healer, what's yours?"

"They didn't tell you?"

I shook my head. "Should they have?"

He motioned toward a bucket in the corner and then stood, drawing the water in a thin stream through the air and into a bucket in an opposite corner. He concentrated so hard I thought he might start sweating, but eventually, one bucket was empty and the other full.

"I'm just learning, and there's no one to teach me, so I know it's not much, but it's getting better."

"Can I show you?" I asked.

He looked to his parents, who nodded, and I stepped toward him. "You've already figured out the hard part, and that's the initial spark to let your magic move. Close your eyes for me. Now picture your magic like the water in the bucket. You've only got so much to perform the task. No matter how big or how small the task, your power is limited."

Hope lit his eyes. He nodded, and I could see his understanding.

"Before, when you moved the water, I believe you pushed it constantly with your mind until the task was done, but your bucket was also almost empty. You'll never have a bigger bucket. Your magic will never grow to be more expansive than it is right now. And you should *never* use the last drop. The key is rationing your magic, letting it do the work for you. Keep your eyes closed and think of moving the water again. But this time, I don't want you to actually move it. I want you to just see it happening. Watch the full process in your mind. After you are done, take that entire process and wrap a small bit of magic around it. Put your magic into the process and not the actual action as it happens."

"Okay, I'm ready." He rubbed his palms together and bounced on his toes.

"Now, just let your magic build around it, just a little bit, and release it."

He opened his eyes, and we all watched as the water moved in a beautiful arc from one side of the room to the other without a single drop spilling. "Woah." He sucked in a sharp breath.

"It's different, isn't it? Before, when you moved the water, you were nearly drained. The second time, it took almost nothing, but you didn't gain extra magic between the first and second time."

He looked to his parents, who seemed surprised. I couldn't tell if that was good or bad, but Cheb was clearly excited. "Can you teach me more?"

"I'm not sure. It would be easier to teach you if you were with the rebellion because I'm not able to leave the castle often, but there are other wielders there. Hiding."

"Do you spy on the king?" he asked.

"I do anything the rebellion needs me to do because I think it's the right thing to do."

He turned to his parents. "I think I have to do this. I'll never learn anything staying here, and we could help them."

His father stood. "Thank you for your time. Let us discuss this as a family. We will get back to you soon."

"In the meantime, please be careful. The king is hunting wielders more now than he ever has before. If he catches you, I can't promise we can save you," I told him.

He reached out his hand, and I took it. "Thank you. Must have been hard enough to get away."

"It will be worth it," was all I said in return.

The boy's mother shoved a heavy basket of food into Rhogan's hands. He tried to refuse, but she insisted. "If your mother knew I had seen you and didn't feed you, I would have never heard the end of it. Just because she's gone doesn't mean I won't still feed you, boy."

"Fine, fine." He took the basket and leaned down to kiss the top of her head.

I followed him out, but I still had some time before Gaea returned for me.

"He'll join," Rhogan said as we waited by the fence.

"How can you be sure?"

"Did you see his face light up when you showed him how to move the water? I think his father has been itching to join the rebellion for a while anyway, but his mother worries. Now that she's seen he could benefit, I bet we will hear from them before the week's end."

I nodded, looking at the town in the distance. "How long do you think we have until the king figures it all out?"

"Weeks at most. There are just too many of us now. I know the northern rebellion has over a thousand members, and it's hard to keep that many discreet. They can't be too quiet or it's suspicious, and they can't be too loud or they draw attention. I doubt many of us are actually aware of that balance."

He was smarter than I initially gave him credit for.

"What's your end goal, Rhogan? When has the rebellion won in your eyes?"

He shifted, and his light blonde hair caught in the breeze. "When there isn't a single lesser fae on Alewyn who's afraid to lay his head down at night. When a high fae female and a lesser fae male marry and no one thinks twice about it. When a warrior's biggest job is protecting fae from monsters and not other fae."

"It stands to reason that fae are actually monsters in their own way."

"Indeed." He jutted his chin forward. "Your ride awaits." He smiled that giant grin of his and wiggled his eyebrows as if we had a shared secret.

I turned to see Gaea scrutinizing us as we talked. "See you around?"

"See you around, Tem."

His giant raven wings pounded the air, and he was gone within seconds, fading into the sky.

"Did you play nice with your friends?" Gaea teased.

"I think so."

"Let's have dinner in the hall tonight." She held her hand out for me.

"Okay."

Later, we sat at our place just down from the king. The red-haired female had come. I should have known the king would see that fire-red hair and feel the pull to her as I did. Something about her captivated me. She and her mother had arrived days ago, and while she was given rooms beside the king, he had moved her mother to the opposite end of the castle.

I knew this game he played. The daughter was just the toy to get the mother to play nice. She had magic. She could weave charms into clothing to make his armies stronger. She could tie leather onto the hilts of swords that would make them fatal in one strike. King Autus may have been a brute and a beast, but he was not daft. He would do the same with her mother as he had done with the rest of us. He would force her to choose a place on his council, though there really never was a choice, just constant scrutiny and ire until you agreed. He wouldn't enchant her because of pride alone. I worried he would push too far this time though. A mother's love of a child was a different kind of bond.

"What do you think he's doing with her?" I asked Gaea at the dinner table, nodding toward the female and her mother.

"Nadra?" Gaea asked. "He's doing what he always does. She is her mother's weakness. He wants to conquer the mother, so he will use the daughter."

"Nadra," I repeated, committing her name to memory.

"You okay, Tem?" Gaea snapped her fingers in front of me.

"Yes, I'm fine. I just hate to see the king use an innocent female, as he did to you."

"Who says she's innocent?" Gaea nipped.

I pulled my eyes from that curly red hair and looked to Gaea. "What's wrong?"

"Nothing. I'm just not feeling well. I'm going to head back to my room."

"Let me help." I reached for her hand.

"No. I'm fine, Temir. I'll see you tomorrow." She spirited away before I could protest.

The king had been strange at dinner. He looked around intently as he ate. He and Eadas may as well have been in their own room, as he spoke to no one else through the entire dinner. I certainly didn't want to have the king's attention on me, but as he continued to study the dining hall, I began to wonder if Gaea leaving was in her best interest.

I had seen Roe enter the hall several times and make awkward eye contact with me as he served. I'm not sure he had ever served dinner, so by the third time of him entering and exiting the room, I had to call him over to take whatever was on his tray just to show him I understood what he needed. What Rook needed. Roe was the messenger, and Rook needed to see me asap.

I couldn't leave though. The king was watching, and if I got up and left the table, he would condemn me and Gaea. Whatever Rook needed, it would have to wait.

I pushed my food across my plate and caught myself looking to the head of the table again and again. The king's odd behavior, Nadra and her mother, Roe's constant presence. Something was stewing in the Wind Court, and sadly, I was right in the middle of it all.

After what seemed like ages, the court dispersed. I waited until a few people were gone and then stood to leave myself.

"Temir," the king boomed. "Come see me."

I drew in a sharp breath and bowed slightly as I did what he commanded.

"It is a fine night, is it not?" His eyes bore into me.

"Yes," I answered blandly.

"Where did my Gaea go?"

"She was feeling tired and thought to rest. Shall I get her for you?"

"No, no. I've got my eye on other sport tonight." He smiled viciously at Nadra.

I refused to turn my head. I did not want to see her long for him.

"I don't believe you've met her yet, though you've met her mother, Megere in the Marsh Court. This is my darling Nadra."

I tried to hold back my groan as I gave her a quick, short nod before turning back to the king.

"Isn't she lovely?" he asked.

"Quite so. What does your betrothed think of her?"

His head snapped to me, and rage filled his face, mirroring my own billowing within. The words had escaped before I could control them. He stood and grabbed me by my arm. I wanted to lay into him, but I let him lead me away from the table.

"I didn't mean to offend you, my king. Only remind you that such outward affection may have been okay before but might be hurtful to your future bride. We must think of our alliance. Or did you not want my opinion anymore?" I held my breath.

He deflated, patting me on the back. "I can always count on you to look out for me, Temir. You are quite right. Morwena has too many spies in the castle these days. I must watch myself closely. Not that I'm afraid of that wench," he said, stopping short.

"No, of course not, King Autus. But you don't need a female scorned on the eve of your nuptials. If we are in fact on the eve. I never did ask when you planned to marry."

Hopefully, the subject change would be insightful as well as effective.

"She's yet to pick a date, and I'm in no rush."

"You always were smarter than me," I scowled behind my smile.

"I would hope so," he said. "I am a high fae king after all, and you, with all your privileges, are still a lesser fae. Still lucky to be alive."

"I have only you to thank for that."

"Thank me later. I've got a beautiful female to see."

As soon as I was dismissed, I stormed to my rooms, grabbed a vial of truth serum, just in case I needed it for anything and headed to the tunnels. I was extra diligent to make sure I wasn't followed, due to the king's odd behavior, but I walked as quickly as I could to the tunnels, and it didn't take me long until I heard the screams and cries from within. Instantly, I was running. Something had happened, and if I had to guess, I would say the king, with his odd behavior, had discovered the rebellion.

CHAPTER

20

KING TOLERO

"How educated are you on poisons?" I panted, staring down the healer I'd just startled half to death.

"Well enough, my king. What is it?" He set a glass jar on his dusty table and wiped his soiled hands down the front of his apron.

"Do you know anything about the poison that took my mate from me?"

"Yes, a bit, but my lord ... that poison does not have an antidote. It comes from the waters beyond The Mists. One sip, a single drop on a finger, and it will kill a fae. It is nearly impossible to acquire."

It was her then. All these years and now I finally knew. My tiger roared within me. The room swayed from below. I closed my eyes and tried to focus.

"What about a beast? Would it kill a cetani?"

"Well, they are quite massive, but yes, I believe so. If it didn't kill them, it could make them very sick, my king."

"Could you do anything to help them?"

"I may be able to flush the system of the beast, but I typically work on fae, Your Grace. I wouldn't know about the cetani."

"That will have to do. Bring whatever supplies you may need and meet me in the stables as fast as you can."

He rushed around the room, dropping jars into a long leather satchel at his side. I left him to it and hustled down to the stables to find Inok waiting with three massive horses. They felt the urgency. The ground thundered beneath their hooves as they twitched with anticipation. I mounted my ride, and he threw his head back to whinny to the others.

"Who will be joining us?" Inok asked.

"The healer."

He nodded, and we waited until, finally, the male scurried out of the castle doors with his arms full of more things than he should be able to carry.

"Good gods," Inok said, dismounting his horse. "Rah, bring a second saddlebag."

He helped the healer pack everything he carried and quickly got back on his mount. "You're sure you want to leave?"

"I don't see that I have a choice, Inok." I planted my heels into my horse's flank.

We rode as fast as the horses could take us. We had to travel through the winding cobbled roads of the bustling city, and I ignored the looks and calls from the people as we moved. I wasn't sure if there was an antidote for them either, but I'd deal with that when I got back.

As always, the sun beat down on us, but still, we ran those horses. I kept an eye on the healer, guessing he had never traveled like this before, but he managed to keep up better than I gave him credit for. Eventually, we had to stop to water the horses down. I leaped from my horse and noticed the healer did not.

"Do you need a hand down?" I held my own to him.

"No, Your Grace." He smiled at me, though it didn't look sincere.

176

"Are you sure?"

"Oh yes, quite." He looked forward with white knuckles on the reins. "I'm afraid if I get down now, I'll never talk myself into getting back on," he chuckled.

Inok and I shared a laugh but understood him entirely. Riding a fae horse at full speed was like riding lightning. The wind didn't just blow on your face, it pelted you. At times, you had to turn your head just to take in a full breath.

I poured a canteen over my beast's face and brushed the water back along his long neck. We traveled with bitless bridles to easily and quickly allow the horses to drink. Once again ready to go, we tore off into the endless desert, and it was nearly evening before we approached the dunes. At that point, I wasn't sure if I'd make it back before the celebrations in the city died down. There was only one way I could think of, and the thought alone unsettled me.

We were greeted cautiously and taken to the same meeting room as last time. This time, however, the room was full of draconian fae. I expected cold stares, but instead I received wide eyes and a sense of awe as the room collectively took a knee.

I looked to Umari at the head of the room and saw exactly the opposite. "King Tolero," she said, rising from her seat. She dipped her head, but I knew that was as far as she would take it.

"Leave us," she ordered, and the draconians filed out of the room, some reaching out to touch me as they followed. Some had tears in their eyes as they passed.

"I can see your people do not hold as much contempt for me as you do, Umari," I said once the room has emptied.

"They believe you to be the prophesied one," she answered.

"Of what divination?"

"Why are you here, Tolero?"

Inok shifted beside me, and the healer stepped behind him, shrinking a bit.

"I've brought a healer for the cetani, Umari. I believe they have been poisoned."

"Well, I could have told you as much," she said. "What I cannot tell you is why my sword was in that hatchling's egg or why I have guards missing pieces of their memories, if not for a king with the ability to control minds."

"Interesting," I answered. "Umari, would you allow me to enchant the guards? To see if I can find the truth. I believe the cetani have been poisoned with the same fatal liquid that Efi was."

Her body jerked at the mention of her daughter. "First tell me why you believe that to be true."

"You do realize he could do it without your permission, do you not?" Inok intervened.

"He could try," she answered.

Inok pulled his sword and stormed toward her. The healer yelped.

"Stop, Inok," I ordered.

He visibly shook but remained in place, only an arm's reach from Umari, who was not at all concerned.

"Umari, when Efi was ill—"

"Poisoned," she corrected me.

"Yes, when she was poisoned, she was unable to eat or drink. We only learned after she left us that the poison was from the waters beyond The Mists. I believe it's the same poison because I think someone is trying to send me a message. I believe only one person in this world has the ability to acquire that poison. Can you not think of whom? Can you not see the full picture?"

"Why would she?" Inok seethed. "Why would she allow reason to seep into her world of hatred?"

Umari stepped down the stairs and brushed passed Inok until she stood before me. "Are you telling me you believe Morwena to be at fault, Tolero?"

"I am."

She looked to the healer. "Do you think you can help them? Are the cetani stronger than the fae?"

"Not stronger," he answered, straightening. "Different."

She spun back to me and looked long into my eyes before she spoke again. "Many years ago, before we came to the Flame Court, there was a prophet among the draconian fae. She was the reason we traveled south before the Iron Wars destroyed our people. She told us that we would be charged with befriending the cetani. We knew before we left the north, though we did not tell you."

"So, all the negotiations with Efi ..."

She held up a hand to stop me. "Had I not sent my daughter to you, you would have never met your mate, so I'll not apologize for that."

I nodded. She was right. I would do it all again for naught.

"The same prophet told us that the cetani would be barren until Alewyn called upon them, and though twin eggs would arrive, only one soul would enter this world, but that is where the prophecy divided. We knew one of the first hatchlings would die, but the prophecy was clear. Either one of our people would rise to save the cetani, or they would all perish before the next war would come.

"For years, we thought this prophecy spoke of one of the draconian fae, but now I realize, she made you one of us, just as you made her one of you. We are one and the same now, Tolero. Efi was the bridge of our people. You are the prophesied one. You must save them."

"The blood of a king," the healer whispered.

"What of my blood?" I turned to him.

"For years I've researched. Since the loss of our queen, in fact. I was beside myself when she died, knowing that I couldn't save her. I knew then that the poison was from the waters beyond The Mists because no antidote worked. I've dug into legends and read through the tomes of the elven ancestors, and only one single paragraph speaks of those waters. The words do not translate easily, but now that I hear the prophecy, I believe I need your blood, my king, to save the cetani."

"You will not have it," Inok gritted out. "You'll find another way."

"That is not your choice to make," I bit out.

His face became red with anger. "How can you even consider this? You've said yourself you believe the sea queen is behind this. Your blood is powerful, Tolero. You cannot consider this. What if she has enchanted the mind of this healer? What if the moment he has your blood, she curses you with it? This is madness."

"Answer truthfully. Have you been in contact with the queen or her people?" I let my enchantment pour into my words before he could prepare himself.

"No, my king," he said blandly.

"Do you have ill intentions toward the cetani, myself, or the draconian fae?"

"No, my king," he repeated.

I faced Inok and raised an eyebrow. "Good enough for you?"

He pinched the bridge of his nose and shook his head. "You will be the death of me, King."

"Umari, take us to the cetani."

We rushed from the room and raced to the cetani's cave. The putrid smell hit me long before the light from the cave within could be seen. We had to cover our faces with our arms as we walked.

"They still will not leave the cave," Umari's muffled voice shouted. "They have let a few of us into the circle, but we've not been able to remove the fallen hatchling's egg or the mother. That is the reason for the smell. We probably will not be able to stay long."

The beasts had spread a bit since the last time I saw them, and only a few draconian fae were inside the cave. They had tied cloths around their faces to protect themselves from the smell as they continued to try to feed the beasts.

The healer stepped forward and took in the horrid scene, dropping his hands to his sides. He looked back at me and then took a careful step forward. "Based on the size of the cave entrance, I would never have guessed they were so large. I've never been this close."

"That is the point, healer," Umari said to him. "They are harder to find when we underestimate them."

He nodded. "Where should we start?"

"You can start with Asha, if you'd like. She has been moving less and less. She is strong though, so hopefully that will help."

"Please tell your people to remove all the food and water they have been trying to feed the cetani," he ordered. "We need all fresh food. All from a different source than you are used to using."

"I'll have it done at once," she answered, walking over to one of the fae in the room. Within minutes they were carrying out all traces of meat and water.

My stomach lurched, but still, I stepped forward. "I'll find Asha." I moved into the nest and spotted her right away. She was the largest, but also, as I drew near, she moved her head to me and purred. "I told you I'd come back," I said, doing my best to step around the beasts as I made my way to her.

I reached out and buried my hands into the fur around her thinning face. "She came to me," I whispered to her. "She is the reason you will be saved. I am not the savior. She was. I need you to let us try to save you, Asha." She dipped her head as if she understood, and I gestured for the healer to move closer. "That fae is going to enter the nests. You need to let him come. Can you do that?"

She purred again, and I knew that was going to be the only confirmation I would get. I looked into her distant eyes and could feel the well of pain within her. She was here but so very far gone. It felt just as it did with Efi the day I lost her. She had fallen sick, and shortly after, she was gone. It was not drawn out at all. Though painful, I barely had time to say goodbye.

"Your hand, my king," the healer asked, pulling me from those sickening memories.

I held it out to him, and he dug through his satchel. He pulled out a small dagger and a few vials. "I'll do my best to keep this as pain-free as I can."

"Just do what you need to."

He took my hand in his and drew the sharpened blade across my palm like it was a knife to silk. As the blood poured, I turned my hand over and let it fill vial after vial. When we were done, he wrapped my hand in cloth and tied it before I moved back to Asha.

"You're not going to like this part, but you'll do it anyway. Okay?"

She laid her massive head back on to the cetani beside her, and I took that as her answer. I nodded to the healer, and he stepped closer to her. She hissed like a cat, her open mouth every bit as terrifying as I remembered.

"You will let him, Asha," I demanded, though I knew I didn't have the right.

The healer stepped closer still, and I could see her breaths coming faster and faster, but she did not move again. He slowly reached a hand toward her face, and I stayed beside him, stroking her neck as he moved.

"Open," I told her.

She did not move.

"Asha. You will die if you do not let him closer. Is that what you wish? Will you choose to leave all of your family behind?"

Her large golden eyes met mine, and my heart stopped. Was that the lesson I was to learn in all of this? I thought of all the times I'd laid on Efi's Isle and wished for death to find me. Would I also choose to leave my family? I understood now.

"I will stay if you will," I whispered to her. "If you choose it, so will I. We will stay and we will lead together, Asha. You will become mine, as you were Efi's. I choose you. Live, my girl. Just live."

She shifted her head closer to the healer and opened her maw until her dry, gray tongue was visible. He mixed my blood with a solution and forced several drops into her mouth. A deep shudder wracked her entire body as she threw her head back. I grabbed the healer's arm and yanked him backward as she convulsed.

"What is happening?" I yelled, pulling him by the collar until his nose was even with mine.

"It is a spell, Your Grace. Give her a moment. The waters are s-spelled. That is all. It does not work like other poisons." His body trembled in my grasp.

I stared him down until I saw her body go still out of the corner of my eye. I could tell he was just as panicked as she was when I released him. I darted to her, and for a moment she did not move. Did not even take a breath. But then, as if resurrected, she stood and roared to the heavens.

ARA

"How much water can one person actually consume?" I asked Fen as he drank from the flowing river while holding me in place for nearly ten minutes. "You realize the more water you drink, the more bathroom breaks you'll need, and I'm already annoyed with your tiny ass bladder."

"You should drink more, it's good for you." He sat up, wiping his dripping stubble-covered chin.

The smile fell from my face as I felt the ground move below me. I jumped to my feet, pulling Fen. A thunderous booming and the ground shaking meant only one damn thing. We took off toward Lichen and Wren in a full sprint. He kept my pace easily. Danger emanated from him as he moved, his muscular body completely unaffected as we darted through the forest together. Adrenaline rushed me forward as Wren screamed for help. It was time to separate the fighters from the friends.

We made it to them seconds before Kai and Greeve. Weapons out, we stared up at the giant before us. With layers of animal skins sewed together for clothing, his bare feet were worn and bleeding and his long dark beard nearly touched the ground.

"Why the fuck is there a giant in the forest?" Fen asked. "Giants live in the mountains."

"Food," the giant answered.

"Running low on goat?" I asked.

"Not time to piss off the giant," Lichen warned.

"Trust me, it doesn't matter if we piss him off or not, he is going to attack," I said.

"Food," the giant said again.

"Listen, we have to get him to his knees. Once he is down, watch his fists."

"What makes you a giant slayer?" Fen asked, pulling his sword.

"I've been trained," I said, pulling out the rope the weaver had given me.

"Food."

"Yeah, yeah. We get it. You want to eat us, and we're going to kill you."

The density of the trees here would be our advantage. Unless he snapped them all off in a fit of rage before we could bring him down. His mobility would be limited, which we needed. He was stronger but slower than all of us, except for maybe Fen and I tied to each other.

"Wren, take Lichen and disappear. Greeve and Kai, take left and right. I'll take forward. Ara, stay behind me."

"Are you kidding me?" I fumed. "Greeve, you cleave Lichen into a tree way over there," I said, pointing. "Wren and Kai can work together and twist this rope around his legs to knock him down. Fen, Greeve, and I will keep him occupied. If we can keep his attention moving back and forth between us, he won't be able to decide and we'll have a better chance of not, oh, I don't know, dying. Once he is down, it's going to take more than just one of us to take him out."

"I don't care what we do, but you two better decide quickly," Kai said.

I looked to Fen and raised an eyebrow. His subtle dip of the chin was all I needed. I tossed the rope to Wren, she grabbed Kai and they both disappeared.

"You go clockwise, and I'll counter," I heard Kai tell her.

Greeve dropped to the ground behind the giant, who twisted back and forth, watching, trying to decide who to eat: Fen and me or Greeve.

I pulled a knife and threw it, but he moved just in time, and I missed him completely. Fen jerked my hand, and I watched as he formed and threw actual fire.

"Magic?"

"You don't know everything about me either, Princess."

"Gods, Fen. Don't forget we are still in the middle," Wren cried out, knowing we couldn't see them.

"Watch those fucking flames. Greeve, if you hit me with an arrow, I will kill you," Kai yelled.

"You could try."

"Enough chatter," Fen ordered.

"NO," the giant roared. "FOOD."

"He's going to draw every damn creature in this forest to us. We have to hurry," Wren scrambled.

"I'm out of rope, Wren. Meet me at his legs," Kai said.

"Start backing up, Fen." I pulled on the chain.

He grunted, and I could tell he didn't like orders. But he did it anyway. Visible again, Wren moved to the side while Kai circled around him until he was close to us. Greeve did the same. As soon as all of the giant's targets came together, he tried to step toward us but crashed to the floor. I grabbed on to Fen to steady myself. I'd only ever seen half-giants. This guy was enormous. Closer to the ground, I could see the anger on his face as he pounded his leathery fist on the dirt, trying to smash everyone.

186

"I need both hands for magic, Ara," Fen warned. "Let me do this."

I narrowed my eyes at him but put my knife away. "Okay, teamwork then. You do your magic voodoo shit, and I'll try to direct them."

He nodded.

As we stepped farther back, I watched Greeve and Kai dive and roll as they avoided the giant's pounding. He laid on his rotund belly with the thick rope tight around his legs, flailing like a fae child throwing a tantrum.

"Water!" Greeve used his magic to move back and forth, slashing the giant with his long, curved weapon as he moved.

I watched as Kai stepped in front of Fen and I with his sword out while Fen bowed his head. I sucked in a sharp breath. "No, you can't stand still. He can't reach us, just keep moving."

"Kai," Wren shouted, running back into the chaos.

I pulled a knife back out and tried not to move as Fen continued to concentrate on his magic.

Kai bolted to the side, and Greeve continued to cleave through the air, circling the giant and slashing him left and right.

The giant reached out and snagged him mid-swipe.

I threw my knife as hard as I could without jarring Fen. I missed his eye, but it still stuck into the side of his face. My tiny throwing knife in comparison to his size made it look like nothing more than a thorn.

"Nicely done," Fen said from beside me.

It worked. The giant roared and shifted his attention to me long enough for Greeve to jam his curved blade into the monster's hand so that he would release him. He landed with a thud and scooted backward.

Further enraged, the giant screamed until he was choking and gasping for air. He dropped his fists to the ground and swiped them back and forth.

"Look out," I shouted just as he was about to collide with Wren and Kai.

They went in opposite directions, rolling on the ground as the giant continued to choke. He stopped flailing as he brought his massive hands to his throat, and I watched in silence as the others moved to stand beside us while the giant drowned in Fen's water magic. Even moments after the giant was clearly dead, no one moved. Fen not only had magic, he had more than one core. I'd seen fire and water. Two elements. As far as I knew, that wasn't possible.

"Well, that was fun," Kai finally said. "Can't believe he caught you." He punched Greeve's arm.

"He got lucky," Greeve answered, scowling and jamming his sword back into the sheath on his back.

"Not bad," Fen said, nudging me.

I smiled at him. "Not too bad yourself, Prince."

"Calm down you two." Wren raised her brows to me. "Someone will think you can actually be civil."

"We certainly wouldn't want that," Fen smirked.

I noticed the subtle way he pulled me closer to him and tried not to read into it. I could potentially think about possibly being friends. That had to count for something. Right?

"At least you make a good team," Wren said, watching us closely.

"Not like we had a choice," I answered. "Let's get moving. I'm tired of this forest."

Kai played line leader, and we all followed, with Fen and I taking up the rear.

I held us back a little farther this time. "Why didn't you tell me you have magic?"

"You never asked."

"Well, it's not exactly something you go around asking the folk."

"Fair enough." He shrugged.

I didn't want to pry for information, nor indicate I was curious about magic. Instead, I tucked my tangled hair behind my ear and looked at our joined hands. "The first thing I'm doing when we get out of this is finding a pond and bathing."

"I could look away." His eyes were anywhere but on me.

"No thanks, Prince Pervy."

"Tell me something I don't know about you," he said, pulling us forward.

I thought about it for a moment. "I could ride a horse before I could walk."

"Somehow that doesn't surprise me," he said, and I hated the way his smile got to me.

"Tell me something about you."

"I have a cetani," he said, watching me closely.

My eyes doubled in size. I had heard about the creatures from my parents but never thought someone could actually ride them.

"What's it like?" I whispered for no reason.

"His name is Cal. I wasn't raised with the dracs, so no one really knew if I'd be able to ride one, but my grandmother allowed me to take part in the ceremony, and he chose me."

"What did you have to do?"

"It's pretty simple really. The whole village comes, and you're covered in warrior paint. They stand in a ring, and as the cetani pass, you hold out a piece of meat for them, or just your hand if you are brave, while you look away. If you are chosen, they take the meat or nudge your hand and allow you to ride them."

"Do you see him much?" I asked.

"Not really. I used to when I was younger, but I've been gone for a while, and he stays with the dracs. I stay at the castle. It's always the best when I get to visit though. He never seems to care that I've been gone." The prince smiled sadly, and for the first time, I actually felt bad for him. He was normalish. I was only now noticing.

"I had to let my fae horse go. It's not the same, but he was good to our family. I just knew I couldn't take care of him anymore."

"You gave him a great honor in releasing him to be free."

"Well, I left him in a forest glen and hoped for the best." I shrugged. I reached up and plucked a leaf from a tree nearby, picking at it to keep my hands busy. "I have magic," I blurted out.

"What?" He yanked me to a stop.

"I don't know how to use it or what kind it is, but it's in there somewhere."

"How do you know?"

"Well, I was in the middle of being a murderous bitch, and the sea fae I had tied up—don't ask—pissed me off, and I burned him somehow."

"That concerns me on so many levels." He pinched the bridge of his nose. "I could teach you."

"You would do that?" I grabbed his hand.

"I would do anything to make you stronger, to keep you safe."

My heart jumped into my throat, and I had to steady my ragged breathing. I'm not sure what kind of magic he was using, but I was living for it. I stepped closer to him, letting the world around us fade away. This was Fen. This was the male his friends looked up to. He was kind and caring and a little pissy sometimes, but he was good.

The weight lifted from my arm as the chain disappeared. Neither of us looked down. I swallowed audibly and tried to break my heated stare, but I stepped close enough to feel the warmth of his body a breath from my own.

"You did it," he exhaled.

"Did what?"

He laughed. A full belly laugh tossing his head back. He grabbed me around the waist and swung me around, and I laughed with him, realizing how dumb I was. We were free.

"What have you done with our prince?" I heard Kai ask.

"Yay!" Wren clapped. "Now we can leave the boys behind."

I realized Fen was still holding on to me, and I pushed away from him, stretching the arm that was so, so used to having him right there on the other end. We'd slept together all these nights, trying to get comfortable, and finally, I could have my beloved space. At least I was pretty sure that's what I wanted.

"Can you feel that?" he asked.

"Feel what?

"My magic is telling me there's water nearby. I can feel it."

"A bath?" I reached for him out of pure habit.

"Mhm," he smiled. "We can make camp here, and you can go if you want."

"Who are you?" I asked. "Just letting me wander off on my own."

"I trust you." He dropped his stubbled chin and the tone of his voice. "I've always trusted you."

"The locked door was a clear indication of that, Prince." I turned and ran off toward the water.

"Other way," Kai yelled.

"Oh, right."

"No fair, I want to come," Wren whined.

"You can go next," I heard Fen tell her as I went.

I found the small pond lit by moonlight not far away. I took off my clothes and the cold air ripped at my skin. I knew the charmed suit had been keeping me cool through the days and warm at night, but I hadn't realized how much until I stepped out of it and laid it on the bank with my pack.

I strode into the chilled water and knew if I didn't just jump in, I'd chicken out. I rushed forward and dove until the cold chilled my body and the soothing waters cleansed me. The moon's reflection rippled across the water and I had just enough soap left to lather and wash my dirt-encrusted hair.

"Mind if I join you?" The intensity of that familiar smoky voice jarred me.

I gasped and covered myself as I turned. "Yes, I mind. Turn the fuck around, Fen."

"I don't think you'd really mind at all though, would you?".

That crooked grin made my stomach flop. I looked back to the bank where all my clothes and weapons were and then back to him.

"So help me gods, Prince, if you even come a foot closer, I'll make all your nightmares come true. I don't care what just happened in the forest. I have boundaries."

He didn't listen. He took one step forward and then another.

I backed up, treading water as my feet left the sandy bottom of the deep pond.

He stepped into the lake. One minute he was fully clothed and the next his clothes vanished. He grinned as our eyes stayed locked on each other. My heart pounded in my chest. I opened my mouth to speak, but nothing came out as every single inch of his perfectly chiseled body lowered inch by massive inch into the chilly water.

"Do you like what you see, pet?" He tilted his head to the side.

I looked away, realizing I had been staring and he had fully caught me. "I'm going to kill you," I said behind clenched teeth.

"I don't think so, love. I think you're going to stay very still while I come to you. I'm going to show you what you've been waiting your whole life for, even if you didn't know it. Every girl dreams of her own prince, but you're the lucky one. You get to have me. And I'll have you. I'll do things to your body you didn't know were possible."

He continued to move step by languid step. His words spoke directly to my core, and I tried to push against the overwhelming need to have him.

"S-stay away from me," I said with less conviction than I hoped for.

"You don't mean that." He reached out to touch my hair, and I looked up to his perfect face. He moved closer, and just before I thought he would kiss me, someone called.

"Ara, stop. Look at me."

I turned to see Fen standing on the bank of the water, and then my head snapped back to the Fen in front of me. Only it no longer looked like him. I stared back at vacant eyes and elongated yellow teeth. I drew in a breath to scream, but it was too late. The water wraith dragged me under, the small bit of light from the surface vanishing within seconds.

TEMIR

he cries and shouting grew louder until I reached the open cavern of the rebellion meeting room and took in the horrific scene. Fae lay dead and wounded with trails of blood, leaving the rough finish of the floor red and slick. I searched the crowd for familiar faces and found Rhogan and Rook hovering over an injured fae. I squeezed my way through the chaos. Stalagmites hung above like great swords from the ceiling, and the jagged finish of the natural walls shimmered as the light from the sconces cast dancing shadows. I'd never noticed how horrifying it truly was until this deadly scene was painted within it.

"They have to be quiet, Rook. I could hear the screaming from the entrance."

"I've tried." He paused, looking around. "They are scared."

"Rhogan, come with me." He fell into step with me as we moved to the front of the chaotic room. "I need you to bat your wings. It will be loud enough in here to grab everyone's attention."

"Got it."

He did as I asked, and the rush of air through the cave as he lifted from the ground caused everyone to pause.

"Listen!" I yelled. "I will come to those quietest first and heal them. I could hear you above, which means that a soldier on patrol will hear you. If you don't all want to die down here, then stop and think. I want those who are healthy and uninjured to meet me at the front of the room. If you are injured, please stay where you are."

Rhogan landed beside me. "What now?"

"You're going to have to sneak out of here and bring back blankets, pillows, food, and water. As much as you can without getting caught. Can you manage?"

"I'll have to." He ran for the door.

I looked to Rook, who stood stunned, watching me.

The fae in the room began to move, just as I had asked them.

As the unwounded gathered around, I gave precise instructions. "I need you all to wash your hands. Then you will need to find an injured fae. You have to evaluate them. I'm only one person, so I can't do it all. If they have a non-life-threatening, non-emergent injury, stay with them and hold up an index finger whenever I call out. If they are bleeding but still coherent, you'll raise two fingers. If they are unconscious and you aren't sure what is happening, raise three fingers, and anyone with a fae who is close to dying, please remain standing next to your patient. Can you all handle that?"

Some nodded, some looked back and forth between each other.

"Hands washed. Now."

They sprang into action. Within minutes, we had a general evaluation of the medical attention needed. I pulled and pulled at my magic as I moved through the room. Some of the wounds were fatal, and the rebellion had lost four warriors before I even arrived. I healed gashes and removed arrows, healed a broken back and managed to save a female who had a lance through her middle. After the most severe cases, I had to take a break. Rest was the only way to preserve my magic, so I began to heal with more traditional methods. Stitching, bandages and the rebellion's generous supply of alcohol.

"Get these floors cleaned," Rook called from beside me.

I looked up to see him watching me again. Finally, he had done something productive.

"Mind telling me what happened?" I wrapped a shattered leg until I could do more.

"We heard there was a small town just this side of the mountains who wanted to join. The messengers said they wouldn't do anything until we showed them proof of numbers. We'd been hearing that a bit now, so I sent forty rebels. We had no reason to fear."

"No reason? I warned you. I told you the king was going to figure it out. I told you what he made us watch. He knew we were poking around in that little town." I stood and shook my head at him as an icy revelation melted over me.

Rook stepped backward. "I realize that now. It was obviously a trap, and though our guys figured it out, we still did not leave unscathed. I was cocky and wrong."

"Considerably," I bit out. "But it's worse than that. Now you have about two hundred fae locked in an underground chamber with only a handful of exit tunnels. If they were heard, if anyone saw the devastation as the wounded poured in, this place is a ticking time bomb. Eadas is smart. The king is smart. I can promise you they are watching. They probably even had sentries waiting to follow behind. Your hideout is compromised. You need to find somewhere else to go, and you need to start moving right now."

"I can't move the ones who are still badly wounded." His eyes grazed the horror scene in the room again.

"I'll stay behind and do my best to protect them. Do you have anywhere in mind in the meantime?"

"The space isn't as big, but there's a spot north of here I've been working on." He faced the quiet room, and everyone shifted to face their leader. "We have to leave right now. Anyone who can move needs to split up between the tunnels. If you are well, help carry supplies or help the others. If you are injured but mobile, use caution. We are headed to Bryer's Keep. Do you all know where that is?"

"Bryer's Keep was destroyed in the Iron Wars," a fae beside me called out.

"No. It wasn't. Well, not all of it, anyway. Upon approach, it will look desolate, abandoned. Continue to search and follow our symbol. You will find us. I urge everyone to use caution. I need warriors to volunteer to stay behind with Temir."

No one stepped forward, no one raised a hand.

"Are we a group of rebellious cowards, then? Is there only one male in this room who would stay to help the ones who would otherwise die?"

"I'll stay," a female with a staff said, crossing the room to stand beside me.

"I'll stay also," a large male called out, huffing across the room with a limp.

"I will as well," another called.

In total, I had six wounded who would stay behind with four guards and myself. Eleven of us would either die in this cave once the soldiers arrived, or the gods would show us mercy and we would somehow figure out how to escape them all.

"Rook," I called as he gave the others directions. "I've asked Rhogan to bring supplies here. Is there any way to intercept him before he is caught if they storm the tunnels?"

"Not that I can think of."

"Which entrance does he normally use?"

"I believe the one that runs under the castle."

I cursed under my breath. "I don't know how to navigate that one. Listen, the king's soldiers are going to tear this place apart looking for evidence and any information they can find. Make sure everything you don't want them to find is gone. And if you're smart, leave behind a few things you do want them to find."

I turned to leave, but he stopped me.

"I've not given you enough credit, Temir. I should have taken your counsel more seriously. I won't make that mistake again." He pounded his fist to his chest before he called the other leaders forward.

I let him form his escape plan as I began to direct my team.

"This isn't going to be an easy feat. I can promise you the soldiers are coming. I'm not sure how many, and I'm not sure when. These six have broken limbs and will not be able to move easily on their own. We will stay here, and I'm going to try to rest to restore my magic. After the others have evacuated, I plan to send you each at least partially down an exit tunnel to stand guard. Does anyone know their way through the tunnel that goes beneath the castle and out the other side?"

The fae laying on the only gurney we had grunted and raised his crumpled hand.

"I'd like to try to take that tunnel out of here if we can. A life may depend on it."

"How long will it take your magic to restore?" a male who joined as a guard asked, pulling an axe from his back.

"I'm not sure. If I could actually fall asleep, it would be faster, but my mind won't allow for that. For now, I'm going to that corner." I pointed. "I'm going to sit and try to figure out how the hell we are all going to make it out of here if the soldiers come. I'm open to any and all suggestions."

They looked between each other, but no one said anything.

"Right then. Guards, decide amongst yourselves who is taking which tunnel. The minute you hear even a peep of someone coming, even if it's a damn pixie, you get to the opening where all the tunnels meet just outside of this room and sound the alarm. You hear the alarm, you run like hell. Everyone meets back here and we head to the tunnel below the castle. Got it? The minute we hit those tunnels, no one says a word."

"Understood," the female said, walking toward the door.

It wasn't much of a plan, but it was all we had. I knew little about the route below the castle. I'd tried to find information in the library, but the rebels had effectively removed everything. I doubted even the king himself had a map when they were through.

Rook and the others may not have been as cautious as they should have been, but that didn't make them unintelligent. Every time I came to the rebel meetings and watched how they planned and moved and worked, I felt more confident about the future. It didn't mean we didn't have a mountain to climb, but even with this setback, I was sure we would prevail.

I sat heavily with my back against the wall and considered everything I knew about the castle. Obviously, some of the rebels were still inside. Roe and Iva included. If the rebellion was one thousand strong in the north with only two hundred in headquarters tonight, that meant eight hundred were still out there and had no idea we would be moving. I could only hope word traveled fast.

I rested until I couldn't sit still any longer. I tried to focus on replenishing my magic as I sat, but there wasn't much there. I was exhausted. The moment my adrenaline crashed, I'd be nearly worthless. I had less than one guard per injured person, even if I included myself. It would take two guards alone to pull the gurney if we planned to move quickly.

"Can you slide so that another may join you?" I asked the male on the gurney. He was my only hope at navigating the tunnels. "I won't be able to heal you, but I've got enough magic to take your pain away for awhile if you can. One of the injured is a smaller female who is unconscious. She won't be able to travel on her own at all."

He nodded as sweat poured down his head. I lifted the small female and slipped her in beside him. Two guards carrying the gurney left me, four injured, and two left to assist. Most had exposed bone and broken limbs, though one was a wing. I knelt beside her.

"I know you've stayed behind because you are unable to move on your own. If I tape up the wing that drags, you would be able to walk, but it will be painful. Will you be okay with that?"

She shook her head as tears filled her eyes. "It already hurts so bad."

"I just want to be clear. The only one of us large enough to carry you has a bad ankle. If you choose to leave this wing down and he has to put you down to run, you'll have to drag it like this through the halls. Are you sure that's what you want to do?"

She nodded. "I'll take my chances."

I walked away, trying not to be pissed. If we had to leave her behind, I'd never recover from making that call.

"Temir?"

I moved to the male with bandages around his head, arm and legs. "What is it?"

"There are blankets in the box. They left them behind for us."

"I know, but we can't carry supplies. It will be hard enough to get out of here as it is."

"No, you misunderstand me. We can use the blankets as gurneys. Take me, for example. I will need two guards on each side to stand. Both legs are injured. If you lay me on a blanket, you can drag me down the tunnel. I'm light enough, it would only take one guard."

"Your bottom half would be raw by the time we make it to the tunnel. I appreciate the thought, but in the end, I think it would only slow us down. We will still have to travel after we leave the tunnels."

"So what's that leave us with, then? You've got those two sharing a seat, so you'll need two guards there for sure. I'll need two to carry me, and the female with the broken wing will take the last guard to carry her. We will still have two more injured fae. Not to mention, at this point, our guards are only transporting and won't be guarding us at all."

I confirmed with a nod.

"If I can heal one leg, can you manage with one guard?" I would be pushing my magical limits.

"I don't think we have a choice."

I turned to face the room. "Listen. If I could, at the very least, I'd take your pain for this next part. I'm sorry I can't do that, but there is only one way we are going to make it out of here. I'm going to have to tie that wing up." I looked at the crying female. "I'll do my best to make it as painless as possible, but we cannot tie up a guard when you can walk. There is no choice here, unfortunately."

Facing the male that shared the gurney, I hung my head. I didn't need to say anything because he knew I couldn't take his pain away. He would have to endure the journey as quietly as he could while holding the unconscious female. I called my weak magic forward, placed a hand on the male with two injured legs and shoved it through him as much as I could. He cried out in pain. I saw that final drop coming closer, but I turned my mind away from it and pulled my hand from him.

"I'm sorry that hurt," I said.

He shook his head and gripped my hand. I pulled him to his feet, and with his other arm around me, he was able to hop.

"If you keep your good arm on the wall, can you manage alone?"

"I think so. Not fast, but I think I can do it."

"Good."

I crossed the room and pulled out the last of the medical supplies. I sat in front of the crying female, and as I laid my hand on her back, she jumped away from me.

"Just leave me here to die," she cried. "You don't understand. The pain in my wings is unbearable. You can't touch them."

"I won't leave you here to die. Tell me why you joined the rebellion. Tell me why you are here."

"Because I'm a fool, just like the rest of you," she snapped.

"No, you aren't a fool. You recognize the world needs something better, and you're willing to fight for that. If you weren't, you wouldn't have been there when the soldiers attacked. You were there and you were injured because you want something better. It's going to hurt, but I can promise you as soon as we get out of this cave, find safety and I have some magic restored, I'm going to heal you. You're going to fly again and there is going to be no more pain. It's only temporary."

She dropped her head, and I reached to touch her again. She jumped only a little and whispered, "Do it fast, healer."

I did my best to make it as painless as possible, but I had to crease and fold her wing. She shook from the pain, and I knew that wasn't going to go away until I could remove the tape, but as she stood on her feet and her wing didn't drag, I also knew it was our only choice. She did too.

That left me with two injured fae who would need guards. So, three and myself for transport, one for guard and two injured fae moving slowly on their own. It was our best chance. I made the bird call into the tunnels, and the guards all came running.

"Did you hear them?" the female with the staff asked.

"No, I didn't. But it's time to move. If we give ourselves a head start, we will have a better chance."

"But what if the king's soldiers use the entrance that leads to the tunnels under the castle?" the male with the hop asked.

"How many entrances are there to the compound? How many tunnels lead to us right now?"

"Seven," a fae I hadn't talked to yet answered.

"Okay, so it's a one in seven chance they will pick our tunnel, but we will have a good head start if they don't. I won't make this call alone. We will put it to a vote. All those in favor of leaving now, knowing they could come down that tunnel, raise your hand."

Six hands shot into the air.

"That's good enough for me, let's get going. We need the gurney in the front to set the pace and guide us. I'll take one side, someone else grab the other."

23

KING TOLERO

*E*very fae in the cave fell to the floor and covered their ears as the sound of Asha's roar echoed and shattered the stiff, sickly air. This was Asha. This was the cetani leader I remembered. I stood. She moved about the nest, carefully nudging and prodding her horde. She was healed but the rest still suffered. "Asha, the fallen hatchling and the mother need to be removed from this cave. Will you allow it?" I peered into the beast's golden eyes.

"It worked," Umari said in disbelief as she moved to my side. She reached out and took my hand, then knelt before me and placed it upon her forehead. The greatest show of reverence she had ever given me. "I am sorry, my king. For blaming you for her death, for hating you, for every wrong in my life, I am sorry."

"Stand, Umari. Let this world feel the peace that is now between us. Morwena has killed my mate and your daughter, and we now have a battle before us. She has made the first move, but we will make the last. Prepare your sentries, your warriors, and your beasts. Tomorrow, we will hold the Trials, as tradition demands, but after that, we will show her what the fire of the southern kingdom feels like."

Her eyes burned into mine, and for that one moment, we were connected in a way Efi would have only dreamed.

"I need to get back to the castle tonight, as soon as possible. If she is ready do you think Asha would let me ride her?"

"A cetani chooses only one rider for its entire life. I'm sorry, but I do not think, even as connected as you are, she will allow it."

"I need to try."

Inok cleared his throat, stepping through the room as he neared me. "Are you sure?" He would never outright disagree with me in front of the draconians, but the truth of his feelings were written across his face.

"I have no other choice. I need to get back. There is another poison spreading within my court. It's far more dangerous than this one."

"Another?" Inok asked.

"Have you seen the way they look at me? Their minds have been altered. Slow, subtle mind tricks. Morwena is behind all of this. She's the reason Umari's guard has missing memories. She is the only one with access to the poison killing the cetani. She needed them to be dead. The cetani are lethal, powerful beings, and she fears them."

I looked around the room, keeping my nose covered as I continued.

"She probably had no idea the guard would find the eggs when he set out to poison them. When he returned with that information, she came up with a way to frame Umari. She wanted to cause the same problems among the draconian fae that she has among those at the castle and within the city. It didn't work here, but it is working there. I must get back."

"What will you do? With the Trials beginning tomorrow, what can be done?" Umari asked.

"The Trials will be held as they always are. I will not sound the alarm just yet. I'll watch the crowds and think of a plan. For now, just make sure you and as many cetani and draconian fae as you can spare make it tomorrow. We will send our own message."

She smiled and nodded as I faced Inok.

"Borrow a fresh horse from Umari and begin the journey home. If you beat me there, say nothing but keep your eyes open. If Asha lets me ride her, I will see you in the morning, my friend."

"Go to the stables and tell the master you need to take Banok. He will understand," Umari instructed.

He ran for the cave entrance and disappeared without a word.

"How should I do this?" I asked Umari, looking back to Asha, who now stalked the cave, nudging the ill cetani.

"We have to get her out of the cave before we can do anything."

"Any bright ideas on how we can do that?"

"Not a single one," she answered.

"I have one, but it's absolutely ridiculous. She may hate me forever if it doesn't work."

"You're going to try to enchant her?" she gasped.

"I don't see any other options."

She nodded, taking several steps backward.

If Asha reacted with anything but full faith in me, she would tear apart half this cave in anger. I walked to her and held my hand out, dipping my head. I waited, but she did not come. "Asha." I looked up to her. Our eyes locked for a moment, and before she could turn away, I grabbed my magic and forced it out. "You must come out of the cave. You must take me home, Asha."

The melody echoed within the cave walls, and as we looked at each other, I realized she understood me. Even without the enchant, she knew what I needed. It was her choice, and though I attempted to take it from her, she did not yield.

"Please," I begged.

The minute I asked and did not command, she dipped her head and stalked to the door, tucked her wings in tight and walked out. I looked at Umari and then followed the cetani out of the cave. I was not, nor would

I ever be, in charge of Asha. I had never had more respect for a living creature.

Once outside of the cave, I looked back to Umari, and she shook her head. "This is your journey to navigate, Tolero. You must find a way with her on your own."

"That's helpful."

The draconian fae gathered outside. They hadn't seen a cetani leave since they fell ill, so if they didn't think I was their savior before, they certainly did now. I tried not to look at them, keeping my eyes on Asha.

She moved in a giant circle, stretching her wings as far as she could. Again, she raised her head and called to the heavens. The draconian fae went silent as they watched her move toward me.

I raised my hand and bowed my head. Finally, she nudged me with a cold press of her nose. I lifted my face and smiled at her as she bumped me again. The fae watching, laughed as she continued to push me until I was at the far tip of her wing, where she laid upon the ground with her wings stretched and looked to me.

"She wishes you to ride her," a fae called.

"Climb her wing," another said.

"But it is not done," a third objected.

I meant to stride forward, but just as I was about to take that first step onto her, Umari stopped me.

"Wait." She turned to her gathered fae. "Bring me Nuath." Two draconian fae dragged a third limp fae between them. "In front of your people, with my own beseeching, will you enchant the mind of this fae and help us to learn the truth of what has happened here." She faced the crowd. "You've all heard the testimony. He claims that he knows nothing; however, he is the only guard who cannot be accounted for the night the cetani turned ill. He says there are gaps in his memory. Today we will learn the truth." She gestured for me to begin.

I stepped toward the drooping fae as two guards held him upright. His face was bruised, and his lip split open. Umari had gotten her answers by force. I could only imagine how that pained her, knowing how close the draconian fae were to each other.

I stirred my magic deep and pulled a thin line forward as I spoke. "Wake," I sang.

The crowd murmured as fear or awe, I wasn't sure which, settled among them.

Nuath's eyes peeled open, and he cried out in pain as he remembered his own wounds.

"Tell this crowd the truth, have you had an encounter with the sea queen, Morwena?" I asked.

"Yes," he gasped as he searched his own mind for several moments while his eyes glossed over. "I remember," he sobbed. "No, no, no." He banged his fists to his own head.

"Stop," I demanded.

He stilled.

"Tell us exactly what happened from the moment you encountered her."

"She came in the night with a group of sea fae. I was standing watch, guarding the top of the dune above the city, but just as I was about to sound the alarm, she spoke to me. I was not able to move or call out. She made me ..." He tried to swallow the words, though it physically pained him to defy my order. "She made me tell her what the cetani eat and where we got it. I tried to lie. I couldn't. I couldn't." He grabbed his stomach, as if he'd be sick.

"What happened next?"

"She told me to steal a weapon of Umari's and kill the youngest cetani. Oh gods, I did. I entered the cave and found two precious eggs. I had no control. I plunged the sword into the smallest egg. She told me to forget once I was done. She made me forget it all. Everything."

"Did you report back to her about the eggs? Does she know?" I asked.

"She does not know. They were gone when I returned from killing the hatchling."

Wails from the crowd began. "Murderer," someone yelled at him.

I held my hand up and faced the angry fae. Their faces were hard, unforgiving as they reacted to his wretched testimony.

"Who called him a murderer?" I asked.

A female raised her hand and stepped forward. "I did. And I'll not apologize for it."

"Kneel," I enchanted her.

She was instantly on the ground.

"Sing to me."

She obeyed. Hideous as the song was, she continued.

"Now stop, lay on the ground and never take another bite of food again."

The crowd gasped as the rest of her body fell forward onto the ground. "But you'll kill her," someone said.

I walked over to the female and whispered in her ear. She nodded and stood. I held back my magic to prove my point. "Please tell the crowd what you have been doing these last few minutes."

"I've only just arrived. I was riding my cetani through the skies."

"Now you will remember everything," I sang to her.

She took a step away from me in horror.

"Do you see?" I asked her and the fae behind her. "This male will forever be haunted by what he has done, though he had no choice and no memory of it. You may be mad. You may be sad. But he is not to blame. He would have never chosen his actions. He was in the wrong place at the wrong time, and any of you who have had guard duty could have been in his shoes. I beg of you to show him mercy because I can promise he will never show it to himself. Nobody hates this male more than he hates himself right now."

They looked at each other in understanding.

Umari stepped forward. "I will not punish Nuath, and neither will any of you. Am I understood?"

"Hooh!" they all yelled in unison. The draconian warrior cry.

"The king has indeed saved the rest of our cetani, and now he needs us to fight for him. With him. Are you ready? Will you stand beside him against the real enemy? Against Morwena?"

"Hooh. Hooh. Hooh," the draconians chanted.

She turned to me, placed a fist on her chest, and took a knee. The crowd followed behind her. "We are with you, Your Grace. From this day until honor calls us home."

"Hooh. Hooh," the draconians called.

My skin was alive, my breath was alive, and the tiger roared from within. We would fight. I would find my mate's murderer, and I would find a way to kill her.

Facing Asha, she knelt to the ground once more, laying one wing flat. I carefully stepped onto her extended feathers, cringing at the thought, but she did not waver as I moved. She held fast as I took another step, and then another, until I stood atop her back. Slowly, I lowered myself to a seated position.

"Hold the skin at the nape of her neck," Umari called out. "Just between the base of the wings."

I plunged my hands in and grabbed on for dear life as she stood from the ground and sprinted toward the distant horizon. The beast pounded the ground until she leaped into the air and her wings flapped, deafening me.

There were few things I got to do for the first time anymore. When you lived as long as I did, you forgot what that feeling was like. I had traveled through wind with Greeve, but I had not flown. I caressed the billowing clouds that surrounded me like an endless sea, the moisture kissing my skin like fresh morning rain in the Marsh Court. The view of my kingdom from this far up was one of the most beautiful things I had ever seen as the desert sands melted into the ocean, and the scattered farms and villages were no more than a pinprick nestled within deep red sands, rich as flames.

"Hooh, hoooooooooooh," I called, throwing my head back and laughing as adrenaline coursed through me. And then I felt her. All around me, holding me, sharing my breath as we soared. My Efi was there, and for that moment, all was right with the world.

Let go, she whispered in my heart. *Trust Asha and let go, my tiger.*

And so, I did.

I thrust my hands out beside me as if they were wings, and Asha called into the night as she soared. We were one. The three of us. Efi, Asha, and I were one single soul as we surged through the sky. I'd never felt so alive.

We made it back to the castle faster than I ever knew possible. It was dark, but the busy streets were still full of fae. Asha landed on the roof. A dilapidated old shed sat to one corner, still standing though it had not been touched in fifty years. I pried open the rusted doors to the shelter Efi had demanded be built for Asha when she moved to the castle. The smell of old hay and stale dust filled my nose.

"I promise to have this cleaned for you tomorrow. Will it work for tonight? Would you prefer to fly home and return with Umari in the morning?"

She stalked inside, pawed at the ground, huffed as she plopped down, and curled around herself, resting her chin on her chest and closing her amber eyes. Without another word from me, she was asleep.

That was my answer, then. I took the steps two at a time and hurried back to my rooms. I ripped off my leathers and changed into my black steel-plated robes once more. Just as I was about to open the door, I remembered the messenger's note in my pocket. I reached back into the robes and pulled out the sealed letter. I slid my finger across the seam and cracked the red wax, watching the particles fall to the tiled floor. I took a deep breath, afraid to find more horrid news from the rebels.

King,

Urgent! Meet me tonight at the usual spot.

~M

Thankful I had made it back in time, I threw my hood up and stalked out the door to meet Murtad alone. The sad part was, at this point, I trusted the rebels more than my own people.

ARA

"He was a pretty male," the water wraith said below the surface as she pulled me deeper.

I scratched at her fingers holding on to me and threw my naked body as hard as I could to escape. My lungs burned and I couldn't see a thing.

"I think I'll enjoy him again later. Once my sisters and I are done with you."

Nails scratched the mental shield I had continued to build, creating an eerie feeling in my mind. I would not relent though. I would keep my thoughts to myself because there was no better way to torture a wraith. I wondered how long until I drowned, and then it wouldn't matter anyway. I didn't think she would let me die so easily, though. Water wraiths were intensely sexual beings that prayed on the emotions of others.

A second pair of hands grabbed me, and I knew they could only belong to Fen. We couldn't have gotten deep enough for her matriarchal colony to prey on me. And, at that moment, I wasn't proud. I needed him, and he was there. The wraith jerked from side to side, and then her grip loosened as Fen pulled me to the surface.

As soon as we were on solid ground, I flung my arms around him. "Thank you!"

"Ara," he said awkwardly, his body going rigid beneath me.

I took a step back and scoffed. "What? The chain is gone and suddenly my 'thank you' isn't good enough?"

"I'd definitely say it's good," Kai called from the tree line.

My entire life flashed before my eyes as I realized I was still naked and clinging to Fen like some kind of eager, desperate whore.

He pushed me behind him and turned to the others. "Find something else to do." His tone was deep, deadly, and fucking scary. His anger became its own entity, as if it were a thick fog he meant to conceal me with.

"Gods-damn it," I whispered, feeling like a total fool.

Kai whistled a tune and walked back into the forest. Wren giggled and followed behind him. I didn't watch the others go. My face flushed. Actually, probably my whole body flushed as I looked sideways to my clothes.

"Don't turn around," I commanded.

"I wouldn't dream of it," he bit out.

I wrung my hair out and tried shaking the droplets from my hands.

"What is taking so long?" His voice was strained and his balled fists were held firm to his side.

"I don't want to get dressed wet. It will take my clothes forever to dry without the sun."

"Come take my hand."

"Absolutely not. Repeat naked tackling? Surprisingly, not a life goal of mine."

"I can help you with the water." He shook his head.

"Promise not to look?"

"I'm not going to look."

I stood behind him, still trying to cover my naked body with one hand and put the other on his stupid shoulder. "Good enough?"

His shoulders rose and fell as a breath shuddered through him. He said nothing as he placed his hand over mine, and then all the water from my dripping body ran down and suddenly I was chilled but dry.

"Thank you," I whispered, still in awe of magic. I dressed quickly and put my pack on, lifting the hood of my cloak so he couldn't see my embarrassed face. And then I felt really dumb. I pressed my palm to my forehead, remembering the magical clothing would have dried me. "Okay, you can turn around."

He looked me over, and I felt a distant ache in my body from the water wraith's seductive words. I had to remind myself those were not his feelings or desires. We had only just lost the chain.

"What form did she take?" he questioned, trying not to meet my eyes.

He was just as embarrassed as I was, and gods help me, I couldn't let that go. Nor could I let him know the truth. I stepped so close to him his breathing hitched. I ran a finger up his muscled arm and whispered, "She looked like Greeve, naked." Without pause, I turned and sauntered away.

"You are such a gem."

"I know," I called over my shoulder.

Swaying my hips back and forth for good measure, I could feel the warmth of his gaze as he watched me go. I had frozen him in place, and I loved it more than I should. I turned back to face him, but he was right behind me.

"Enjoying yourself?" His voice moved like tendrils up my sensitive spine.

"Kind of." I smirked.

"Don't taunt me, Ara. I only have so much self-control."

"About this much?" I asked, pinching my fingers together.

"Every time I'm near you, I feel it all the way to my bones. I can't explain it. The minute I think you might be in danger, I'm overcome with this debilitating rage."

I crossed my arms. "I'm not in danger now. I'm sure the water wraith scared you, but she's gone now."

"I was not scared." There was that familiar ire. He jammed his fingers into his thick black hair and looked away. Struggling. "Just promise me you'll let us take this journey with you." He looked back to me, softening. "I trust you, I do. But I need a promise now that we aren't chained together."

I bit the inside of my cheek and tried to make it all work in my mind. I wasn't used to the company, the friendship, the chatter. I was used to being alone. But I couldn't see past the fact that he was worried for me. I hadn't realized how much I missed someone caring until those words wrapped around me like my father's arms, and somewhere deep within those arms was home. Not that he needed to know any of that. "I'll make a deal with you."

"I'll take it."

"Blindly? That's just reckless." I squinted my eyes at him.

"Yes, blindly, because I want you to see that you're in charge."

"Fine, the deal is you hand over your crown, and I'll kiss your ass like your lackeys do for five whole minutes."

"Ara," he growled.

"And that, Prince, is why we don't make blind bargains."

He pinned me with those eyes. Those fucking eyes that made my knees feel weak no matter how much I fought it.

"Fine, I take it back."

"What's the real bargain?"

"I'm not going to run off without you. I'll play nice and be part of the team, but you have to really teach me how to use magic, and you have to control your ragey alpha male shit that convinces you to lock me up for my own safety. I'm pretty sure I could kick your ass, so you're not saving anyone here."

"Deal. Done. I already told you I would teach you."

"And..." I paused. He raised an eyebrow, but I refused to notice the way my heart jumped while staring at those full lips. I had to look away. "And if I say I'm done, I mean it. If I don't want the company, you and your southerners have to leave. For good. You can't leave Wren behind to spy on me. You go, and you don't get to argue."

"I don't think I can agree to that," he ground out.

"Then I can't agree to go forward. That's the only way it works for me. It's either my choice, or there is no choice."

"Fine, but if you need me Ara, I will come. No matter what happens, I'll never really leave you."

"Okay, Prince Charming. Whatever you say."

He smiled, and my libido did a somersault. *Bastard.*

"Walk with me?" he asked, holding his hand out.

"We don't have to hold hands anymore," I said.

"I rarely do anything because I have to."

Well then.

"My friendship is not going to be easy," I warned him.

"Nothing worth fighting for is ever easy," he replied, his voice calm, though my heart might have stopped for a second. What was in that fucking water?

"So back to magic," I said, walking as he strode beside me. "How do you have two different kinds?"

"I have four."

"That's not even possible. A single person isn't supposed to have multiple types."

He shrugged. "I guess being the Guardian makes me the exception. What about your magic?"

"It's only happened that once ..." No need to mention the burning bed incident.

"Do you think you have fire magic?"

It felt like a secret. Like I shouldn't speak about it or I'd betray my mother's warning about not trusting anyone. But the chain had fallen, and he was good. I thought of what it would have been like to sit at that old table and tell her of the overbearing prince. Then I wondered where I'd be right now if they hadn't died.

"What's wrong?" Fen asked, pulling me from my thoughts.

"It's nothing," I lied. The pain of my parent's loss hit me just as freshly as it did the day I had lost them. Death was weird like that. It had a way of taking you right back to that single, tragic moment.

"I can see the sadness on your face." He stepped in front of me so I couldn't walk forward, then looked down, and the pull to reach for him was automatic.

"We aren't there yet. My feelings are my own for now." I stepped backward.

Something like hurt appeared in his features, but he took a deep breath and it was gone. We continued walking. "You certainly don't make it easy," he said, forcing a smile.

"I told you it wouldn't be."

"Will you tell me where we're going? Where we're really going?"

I took a leap of faith, knowing this was going to have to be a balance of give and take. "I have to find Nealla."

"What do you mean you have to find her?" Fire shone in his eyes as he jerked to a stop.

"Calm your rage, Prince. It's the only way to unlock the binding, but she also knows the second half of my prophecy. I don't have a choice. If I'm to be Alewyn's Promise, I need to find out what that means."

He paced in front of me, shaking his head. "What do you even know of her?"

"I have to believe she is good in some way. She did bind the world from talking about me to protect me. I don't know why, and I know that doesn't mean she is safe, but it's all I have to go on."

"Where exactly does that take us then?"

"Once we leave the forest, we have to get through the Western Gap. After that, we travel through The Mists, and beyond that, I don't know. No one does."

"And I'm just supposed to sit back and let you? No one just casually walks through The Mists. They go there to die. To rid the heartache of losing a mate."

"I'm not asking you to come," I said sharply.

His sharp jawline tightened. "And I can't change your mind?"

"No. I have to do this. I need to learn the truth."

"There's something I need to tell you, also. Something about Morwena."

"I already know she is hunting me, though I'm not sure why."

"That's what I want to talk about. You gave yourself away to her. Autus is ten times worse than Morwena on her worst day. She is cunning, but he is ruthless. If you break the binding, she will be able to tell him about you, if she hasn't already found a way, and you'll be hunted by them both. Autus collects magical fae, and he has a growing army. We have spies in the north, but every day he grows more dangerous."

"How did I give myself away?"

"The human." He watched me carefully for a reaction.

"I don't understand." I shook my head, trying to recall anything that connected the two.

"Remember when I told you the seer who delivered your prophecy began to talk, and my father had her killed? We believe she went to Morwena with the news, but before she could tell her everything, Nealla bound your secrets. So even though the sea queen knew of your existence, she had no idea who you were. She might have been told you and I were connected somehow, but beyond that, we don't think she knew anything else. Do you remember the day we met?"

"On the balcony? How could I forget. You were so kind to me. Shoving me out the door and all."

"Yes." Distracted, he took a step toward me and then caught himself. "I felt you before I even saw you. I was torn between telling you everything and getting you out of there. Do you remember the human walking through the room?"

"Yes."

"The human should have been unseen by any other fae there because of her magic. She saw you watching him as he walked back and forth. She set that trap searching for you. Hoping one day you would come, and sure enough, she found you. Only royalty could see through her enchantment. She must have realized Alewyn would have protected its Promised from enchantments also, or at least make you much stronger against it than others. I didn't realize it until I tried it myself and failed. You're a threat to her, Ara."

"Wait. You knew the enchanting didn't work on me?"

"I guessed it. My enchantment isn't as strong as my father's, but I could tell. I didn't really want to do it, but I had to know if that was her trap. I later learned that she was already pursuing your father to betray Coro and give her the power over the Hunt. Once she put all the pieces together, she begged Coro to have a luncheon you would be required to attend. I tried to keep you far away, by making you sit at the end of the table, but the minute you chased that damn human, she was watching. She locked you in the castle, and Wren helped you escape as soon as we were able to get her in and out without drawing attention to ourselves."

"I knew she was hunting me. I didn't know anything else. Did the human die?"

"She let him kill himself as soon as she was done with him."

A small wound opened in my heart for that poor human. I knew him for only a fraction of a second, but that was my job, wasn't it? I was supposed to be Alewyn's Promise. The savior. And I had failed him. I hung my head. "Is she still going after the Hunt?"

"I'm not sure. She hasn't been at the Marsh Court for quite some time."

"None of this changes anything for me, Fen. I still have to find Nealla. I have to keep going."

"Then let me do it for you. You can stay here or go back to the southern court where it's safe, and we will find your answers. I'll get on my knees and beg you if you want me to."

"No, but I'm half tempted to take you up on that offer just to see it."

"Do it!" Kai shouted from the trees.

"Do they ever go away?" I asked loudly.

"Nope," Kai answered.

"I mean it, Ara. Please."

I doubt that male ever had to ask for a thing in his life, but there he stood, asking for my permission because he was trying to consider my feelings.

"This is something I chose to do. I know I have to. I'm drawn to her. She wants me to find her. You can't do it for me, but I will let you come." I would not mention that I felt pulled to him as well. He was pretty. I'm sure everyone with eyes felt drawn to him. "You guys might as well come out," I yelled.

"We can move our camp to the clearing," he said.

"There's no way in hell I'm bathing in that water." Wren shook her head.

"Don't worry," Kai said, swinging his arm around her. "Fen killed the bad guy."

"Greeve, take Kai and go hunt. Wren and Lichen, make a fire and set camp. Make sure to fill all the flasks just in case we need to leave in a hurry."

"I wouldn't advise a fire, my prince," Lichen said, holding his hand out. "It's going to rain."

"Perfect. Go find something else to do then," he ordered, grabbing my hand and pulling me in the opposite direction.

"So, you guys make friends for one single day and we suddenly have to get lost?" Wren asked. She got a flash of Fen's angry face and raised her hands. "Not complaining." She grabbed Lichen and walked away quickly.

We walked in silence for quite some time, just circling the pond while he worked out whatever was on his mind.

"What are we doing?"

"We're going to build a fire."

"But the rain," I protested, halting.

"Let me worry about the rain and you worry about the fire."

"Okay." I rubbed my hands together. "Tell me what to do." I took a fighter's stance with my feet shoulder width apart, bent at the knees. This was training. This I knew.

"It does work a little differently for each fae, so we may have to try several times until we get it right. Don't get discouraged."

"I'm not a child, just tell me how." I dropped my hands.

"Close your eyes and search for the magic deep within you. It's there. It's always been a part of you."

"The only thing I see is the back of my eyelids."

"Imagine traveling down into your core." He moved so close I thought I could hear his heartbeat.

"I don't know how to do that."

"Think less literally. Just imagine it. If you had a store of magic deep within you, what would that look like?"

"What does yours look like?" I peeked through my lashes and saw the tender look on his face as he held me with his eyes.

"Mine is like the sands of the desert blowing in the hot wind toward the tumbling ocean," he whispered.

Giant raindrops began to fall. My clothing was dry though, and I wasn't sure if it was because of the magic woven within it or because of the prince's promise to take care of it.

"Can you see it?" he asked, pulling my thoughts back to my own magic.

"Maybe it was a fluke and I don't have any."

"It's there."

"I can't do anything with you looking at me like that," I whispered, hoping only he could hear me.

"I'm sorry," he answered, turning away.

"I wasn't complaining, Prince."

He looked at me again, with a roguish smile that melted me entirely. "Be careful how you taunt me, Princess."

"If that was supposed to be a threat, you failed miserably." I stepped closer, knowing it would rattle him.

He leaned down until his mouth was inches from my ear. "I'll try harder next time."

The vibrato of his deep voice sent shivers down my body, and my core tightened. "As will I, Prince," I answered, letting the seduction of my voice unnerve him as he had done to me.

"You will be the death of me," he whispered.

"Probably," I answered, quite seriously.

A crack of lightning filled the grey sky above, and thunder rumbled somewhere in the distance. One moment we were safe and dry, the next we were completely drenched.

"I thought you were supposed to be handling the rain." I laughed.

"I got distracted." Those damn eyes locked on my wet body.

"Let's go find the others. We can practice magic again tomorrow." I turned to see everyone staring at us in the rain. I guess they hadn't gotten far. We joined them, but I kept my face to the ground. I blamed the water wraith for getting me all worked up.

"Well, this isn't awkward and feels totally normal," Kai said.

Wren burst into laughter, and even Lichen laughed. Fen looked at me, and I nudged him.

"Help me with the fire, Greeve?" he asked.

As soon as they turned to walk away, Kai bumped his shoulder into mine. "Are you our mommy now?"

"Careful, Kaitalen," Fen growled over his shoulder.

"Fen, we talked about this. You can't just go around telling people my full name."

The prince walked away, grinning like a young child, leaving us to stand in a scattered circle while we waited for their return, the ground too wet to sit on.

"Hey, new mom," he whispered. "I think Dad has a crush on you."

"How does anyone ever take you seriously?" I laughed, though my thoughts were far from jovial. His joke didn't make me want to puke, which was a problem. I didn't want that attachment to Fen. I wanted mutual respect and honest friendship. It had to be that way.

"I honestly have no idea."

"We don't." Lichen took an eager step in my direction. "Ara, I've been hoping to ask you some questions, if you don't mind?"

I shrugged. "Okay." Of course I minded, but I had agreed to be a team player. Plus, he was old, so whatever.

"Is it okay if I take some more notes?" he asked.

"I guess." I looked at Wren and Kai, and they turned to have their own conversation, slyly removing themselves from this one.

"You've said you have magic. What form?" He pressed the tip of his pen to his paper.

"I believe I have fire magic, maybe?"

"Yes, is that all?"

"I can't be sure. I'm not able to control it. It stands to reason that if Fen has all four as the Guardian, then I might also, but without learning how to use it, I can't answer that honestly."

"Sure, sure." He scribbled. The sound of his pen scratching the paper felt like an invasion, though I wasn't sure why. I'd been on edge for far too long, and I felt guilty that I didn't fully trust the southerners yet.

"When did you first discover your ability?" He paused, lifting his wrinkled face from his notes.

"How is this relevant?" I asked, feeling defensive but trying to silence the warning bells going off in my mind. Not everyone was out to get me, and I had to keep reminding myself of that.

"It's not currently, but someday we may need to look back. I used to keep journals for King Tolero. Did you know he is over two thousand years old? His memories aren't quite what they used to be. I think he still references them from time to time."

"I see. Well, I don't really have much more to add. I discovered the magic by accident when I was pissed off one time, and that's all I know. It's never come back."

"Give her a break, Lichen. It's been a long day." Kai tossed a rock, and it thunked as it plummeted into the nearby pond.

He looked at me surprised, as if he hadn't noticed my discomfort at his questions. "Of course. My apologies. The scholar in me lives for education." He adjusted the long robes he always wore, even in the humid forest.

"Why don't you guys tell me a little bit about the Flame Court. I've never been."

"You were born there, Ara," Lichen corrected, tucking away his journal.

"Right, but I have no memory of that."

"It's basically a desert with an occasional oasis until you hit the ocean." Wren squeezed the rain from her chocolate hair as she looked off into the distance.

"It's far more than that," Lichen added. "The Flame Court is a land of pride and culture. We breed warriors, and our king is kind and caring." He sat and leaned forward, propping his arms on his legs, prepared to tell a story.

"Is he?" I couldn't help my surprise, though I should have guessed.

"Oh yes, quite so," he answered. "King Tolero is the only worthy royal among us. Apart from his son, of course."

"The Trials will be starting soon," Fen said as he came behind us carrying logs. "Greeve won them ten years ago."

He set the wood down, and Greeve followed behind. Fen touched his hand to the soaking wet ground, and all the water around us lifted and moved into the dangerous pond. My continued surprise at his plethora of abilities must have been written across my face because he winked at me. This was fine. I was fine. Not even kind of affected by that. Winking was stupid anyway.

We felt drawn to each other because of our twisted fate, that was all. I didn't want to get involved with him. I mean, I absolutely wanted to lick him, but that would probably be frowned upon. Friends. It just had to be that way. I couldn't let him distract me. This was my whole life I was trying to learn about.

No one else seemed bothered by the fact that there was a water wraith in the pond a stone's throw from where we set camp. Draconians were never afraid of anything, but maybe that extended to everyone in the south. The only one I caught eyeing the water suspiciously was Lichen, who had clearly resolved to keep his distance. We sat scattered around the fire, and I continued the conversation while purposely sitting between Greeve and Wren. "What are the Trials?"

"In a nutshell, it's an event that takes place every decade where warriors compete for top place."

"Pit fighters," Greeve corrected. "And then the whole kingdom is able to try to join the royal guard."

"You're a pit fighter?"

"Yes and no. I lost a bet with Kai and Fen, and I had to enter under one of the pit lords." A soft breeze surrounded him as he remembered, and it lifted the tips of my hair with it. "I trained with the army more than I trained with the pit fighters, but when King Tolero chose me as his champion, I was determined to win, bet or no bet. It was pretty easy though. We don't fight to the death, and most of the fighters forfeited after a few blows because it's hard to beat a wind cleaver."

"Oh yes. Mister High and Mighty. We all bow down to your greatness," Kai said from beside him in a high-pitched voice.

Greeve socked him in the arm. "And so, these guys have been teasing me for ten years now, even though they're the ones who made me do it in the first place."

"I still think it's amazing that you won." Wren beamed at him.

I looked closely, but her words were purely friendly. I doubted she could see them as anything more than brothers after all the years they had spent together. They seemed like a family unit.

"So, did anyone actually find food earlier?" I asked.

"Yep." Kai jumped to his feet. "It's not much, but it should be okay for one meal. If we sleep tonight, we can hunt in the morning when we can actually see what we're doing. For tonight, it's just these three birds."

They started to pluck them for the fire, and I dug around in my pack. My knuckles grazed the hidden book, and my body jerked in response. No one noticed. I pulled wrapped loaves from my pack. "I've got a bit of bread left from my friend's mother."

"I would trade you Fen's whole bag for a single bite of actual bread," Kai said.

"I'm sure he'd love that." I smiled at Fen. When his fiery eyes met mine, I stopped and pretended to shift around in my pack again. Shit was getting awkward.

Before long, the birds sizzled and my mouth watered for fresh, hot meat. Kai leaned forward and rotated the bird, and I noticed a familiar phoenix symbol tattooed on the inside of his arm. At first, I thought I may have imagined it, but after several times, I knew for sure I had seen it. I studied the others, wondering if they too knew about the rebellion. I wouldn't mention it until we were alone, but I needed to ask him about it.

After eating the most fulfilling meal I'd had in a while, I yawned and could barely keep my eyes open. Especially now that I was comfortable and felt somewhat safe with the southerners close by. It was unexpected but welcomed.

"I'll take the first watch. Try to get some sleep." Fen stood, picking up his sword and sheath from the ground beside him.

"Yes, Father," Kai said.

"Kai takes the second watch," Fen ordered.

"I take it back."

"Too late," Wren added with a yawn.

I rolled my blanket out and put my pack under my head. Fen moved closer to the tree line, and the rest of us lay down to sleep. This was the first night I'd slept without Fen right by my side. I felt that absence like a fresh wound, or maybe just a scar. It didn't hurt, but it didn't go away either. Still, within minutes I was standing in the middle of that gods-damn field in my recurring nightmare. I tried to force myself to wake up, but I could not.

I ran, tearing up my legs, but I was shoved from the towering cliff and drowned until my shredded body was lost in scorching flames and turned to ash. I screamed and thrashed until I heard him call to me.

"Ara. Shh. Wake up," Fen said, shaking me. "It's just a dream."

I opened my eyes to the entire group surrounding me. "I'm so sorry," I whispered, throat raw.

"Are you okay? What happened?" Kai asked. Genuine worry flashed across his handsome face.

"I'm fine. It was just a nightmare. I'm sorry I woke you."

"I'm pretty sure you woke the whole forest," Greeve said, eyeing the tree line as he pulled his weapon.

"Kai, take over watch," Fen ordered.

Everyone else went back to lie down except for the prince.

"I'll sit with you," he offered.

"You need to sleep too, Fen."

"Want to tell me about it?" He poked the fire with a stick until the end caught flame, and he played with it, letting the flames dance like tiny fire pixies.

I stared until I felt him watching me. "There's nothing to tell. It's not real. It's just terrifying."

He sat down beside me. "I'll just sit here, and you can lean against me if you want."

I couldn't help it. He brought me comfort, and no matter how much I fought it, I fell asleep again. I woke the next morning still resting on him as he slept sitting up. I peeled open my eyes and saw Kai sitting near the fire.

"Morning, new mother," he grinned.

I rolled my eyes and sat up. No nightmare.

Fen shifted, realized I had moved, and jumped to his feet, eyes wide.

"Careful, broody fae. I'm right here."

His shoulders dropped, and he took a long breath in and out before he stretched. I wrapped his blanket around me as he crossed the clearing to the pond, pulled his shirt off, and dove right in.

"Mornings can be hard for us male fae," Kai smirked.

"It's too early for sexual innuendos, Kaitalen," I said just to mess with him.

"It's never too early for sexual innuendos."

"He's not afraid of the water wraiths?"

"Doesn't look like it." He lifted a shoulder and wiggled his eyebrows.

"Can I ask you a serious question?"

"Sure." He straightened.

"How long have you been a rebel?"

His eyes narrowed on me, and I didn't think he would answer. He looked around the group of sleeping fae. "We all support the rebellion, Ara. We don't like to advertise it in the north but most in the southern kingdom do, though not all." He lifted the sleeve of his shirt to show me the phoenix insignia I had seen the night before. "Wren's is on her shoulder, mine is on my arm, Greeve has his entire back done and Fen's is on his chest."

"And Lichen?" I asked.

"Lichen is here when we travel because King Tolero requests it. When we are home, it's usually just the four of us. Sometimes Wren's sister Sabra tags along, but we had these done in a traditional inking ceremony with the dracs when it was just the four of us."

"I see."

"The better question is how do *you* know about the rebellion?"

"I helped a bunch of lesser fae escape some slavers, and they revealed themselves to me. Have you heard of the Weaver?"

He breathed in deep. "You know the Weaver?"

"Yes. She is one of the fae I helped and who, in turn, helped me."

"She's a legend in the south," Kai said in awe. "She's the one who killed an entire horde of her own kind to try to help her lover escape."

"I knew she had a story. I just didn't ask what it was."

"You have to introduce me one day. I think I love her." He clutched his chest.

"You really are a child, Kaitalen."

"You wound me." He fell over, faking his own death.

I let him flail around for a while and then asked, "Do you think we'll get out of this forest today."

"Yep." He sat up. "We're near the edge. If you listen closely to the birds, you can hear the faint echo of their calls. That sound is bouncing off the side of the mountains way in the distance. I'd wager we will be out of the forest before mid-afternoon. It might take us a couple of days to get to the base of the mountains, but then we can follow them west until we find the Western Gap."

I heard a splash and watched Fen get out of the treacherous water. Fearless. I wished I could watch that sight over and over again. His trousers hung low on his hips, and I'd never envied beads of water until I watched them glide down his tanned body. I snapped my jaw shut and

229

managed to swallow as he ran his fingers through his jet-black hair. He must have felt my gaze because he turned to look, and I wished I was strong enough to look away, but I didn't have it in me. I could nearly feel his prideful satisfaction as he smiled knowingly at me.

They didn't come in a prettier package, but the minute he smiled, I melted into the ground. He knew exactly what he was doing to me and was not even kind enough to catch me as I fell for him.

Bastard.

Kai snorted. "Remember that time when we were just sitting here having a nice conversation about my future wife and leaving the forest behind and you literally forgot about me because Fen appeared? That was such a good day."

I rolled my eyes and stood. "It's time to get out of this damned forest. If I never see another tree for as long as I live, I'll die happy."

"Famous last words, Princess."

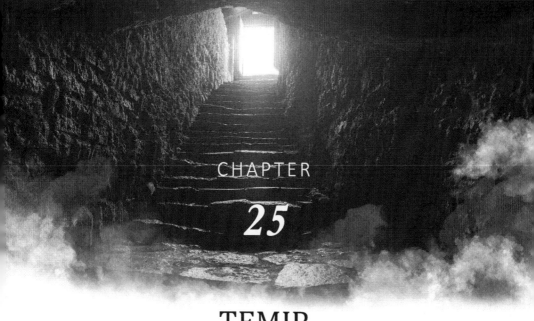

CHAPTER

25

TEMIR

*W*e had one extra guard, so the male with the ax and injured ankle took the back position while the rest of us moved as quickly as we could down the tunnel. Just moving instead of sitting still waiting brought peace. Come what may, now we wouldn't be caught unaware.

We inched ourselves down the hall and probably only made it a hundred agonizing paces before the calls from the soldiers began.

"Behind us. They're behind us," the winged female whispered.

"Keep moving and stay quiet," I commanded.

The fear helped speed everyone up as we moved. Soon, the tunnel ahead split off into multiple routes and we had to rely on the injured guide to direct us. We followed his directions and had just come around a corner when from somewhere ahead, militant shouting filled the silence.

"Back up, back up," I ordered.

The space was barely wide enough to rotate the gurney. We moved into a dusty tunnel and continued farther back into the shadows. We heard the soldiers ahead of us as they passed by and I think everyone held their breath, hoping they wouldn't turn. Once it was quiet again, we shuffled back to the path and hustled down.

"Wait," I called. "This way."

"No, the entrance is to the right. We still have a long way to go," the male on the gurney said.

"I know. But I think I know where we are. Holy shit. I do know where we are. New plan."

I could smell the fruit from the trees in the castle above us. I hadn't put it together at all. When Oleo and I had the tree nursery built, we wanted it on the ground level so the trees could grow as tall as possible. The nursery had windows all around the top of the room. But the bottom? The bottom had to be above us.

"Move into this side hall and stay here. Two guards come with me. We will be right back."

The female with the staff and the male with the ax stayed behind, and the other two came with me.

"What are we doing?" one of them asked.

"One of these tunnels has collapsed. It happened when we started our tree nursery, and we never knew why the ground caved in. Apparently, it was because of the passageways below. We find the collapsed tunnel and start digging. We only filled it with dirt and planted a bush over it. It shouldn't take us long to dig it out."

We searched for less than five minutes before we found the cave in. No light seeped in from the castle above, but right in the middle of the cobweb-filled tunnel was a pile of dirt that reached the ceiling. We were close. I could smell the sweet passion fruit and fresh pina.

"You dig here, I'll go get the others."

As a group, we climbed into the nursery from the old tunnels. It took all available hands to lift the weighty gurney. "How are we supposed to get out of the castle?" the winged female asked.

"No one will enter these rooms. I want everyone to fill this hole back in with dirt if you are able. Then, you're to move along this wall and stay silent until I return. Understood?"

"Please don't leave us," one of the injured said.

"I'll have you back with the rebellion a lot faster this way. I just need you all to trust me a little bit longer."

I didn't wait for their reply. I washed my hands, changed my soiled clothes from the supply I kept there, and walked out of the rooms as if I'd been there all night working. I tried to keep my heart calm and my footsteps languid as I walked through the castle halls.

"Temir," the king called from behind me.

My heart leaped into my throat.

"Yes, my king," I said, bowing.

"So devoted. Working after dinner again I see. You know what's wonderful?" he asked, slurring his words. He reeked of wine, and it turned my stomach. "Death. Do you know why death is wonderful, Temir?"

"No, my king."

"Because it is a mystery I will never know, and yet I'm happily delivering it to my enemies as we speak."

"Are you?" I asked, rubbing the back of my neck.

"I've told Eadas if he doesn't deliver the heart of the rebel leader to me by morning, I'd take his instead."

"Rebels, my king?"

"Ooh. Right. I haven't told you yet. Apparently, a group of lessers think if they come together, they can stop me. But I have much bigger plans, Temir." He rested his hand on his favorite golden knife at his hip. The only weapon he carried that I was actually terrified of. It was charmed to never miss.

"No one is strong enough to stop you, my king."

"Quite right. No one." He looked into the distance for a moment and then walked off as if we hadn't been talking.

I headed straight for Gaea's rooms.

"What is it, Temir?" she asked, tying a robe around her waist and yawning.

"I need your help, right now."

A calm washed over her, as if she'd found a new resolve. "Give me a minute to change." She joined me in the hall moments later.

"Before we leave, you need to know something." I leaned in to whisper in her ear. "I've got injured rebel refugees in the nursery, and I need to get them out of the castle as soon as possible. The king found—"

She grabbed my wrist. "Let's go."

We popped into the nursery, and the rebels went completely still as we appeared.

"You're playing with fire, Temir," she said as she dropped my hand. "Where am I taking them?"

"Do you know where Bryer's Keep is?" I asked.

She shook her head, crossing her arms. "Bryer's Keep is gone. There's nothing there."

"Can you get them there?"

"I've never been," she answered. "I've been close, but they will have to walk for a bit to get the rest of the way."

"I'm not sure if that will work. I'll have to heal them, and we need the rest of the rebels to get there first. Can you take them to the island? Just for tonight? Then we can take them to Bryer's Keep tomorrow."

"At least they will be warm."

"I can't stay, I've got to go back for Rhogan. He doesn't know about the soldiers in the tunnels. I have to warn him."

"You can't Temir." She grabbed my arm. "What if you're caught instead?"

"I won't be. I'll be careful."

"Promise you'll come back. Say it."

"I promise I'll come back, Gaea." I hugged her tight until someone from the corner cleared their throat. "This is Gaea. She will take you to a place that is safe for the night. She will come back for you as soon as possible and get you close to Bryer's Keep."

"Who's going first?" she asked, her fingers lingering on my own.

I turned and walked out. I moved carefully through the halls, searching faces for any servants I recognized from the rebellion. I needed Roe, but I couldn't find him. I went down to the kitchens and found Iva. I motioned to her from the doorway, and she stepped out.

"Can I get you something, milord?" She curtseyed before shoving me into a corner.

"Where's Roe?" I asked hurriedly.

"He and a few of the others went down to check on the compound. Why?"

"Shit. How long ago did they leave?"

"Only a few minutes. You should be able to catch em' near the stables."

"Don't let anyone else go to the compound, Iva. We've been discovered. Spread the word," I was off before she could respond.

If someone saw me running in the castle, I'd be found, and if Roe and the others made it to the tunnel entrance, or anywhere near it, they would be found. I had to take my chances. Unfortunately, the stables were on the opposite side of the entrance where I could catch Rhogan, and he would likely be back soon. I slowed my pace to a painstaking walk each time I was near someone. I made it to the stables, but it took me longer than I would have liked, and I didn't see Roe anywhere.

"Hey, Tem." River bounced over to me.

"What are you doing up right now? You should be in bed."

"Everyone's on the move. I've had to ready all the horses and brush down the ones that have come back."

"Right, well stay in the barn tonight, okay. Don't come up to the castle."

"Okay, Tem."

"I'm looking for some friends of mine. One's named Roe. He works in the castle. He's a lot shorter than I am. About to my waist. His red beard nearly touches the floor."

"Oh yeah, I know him. He just left. He's with some others. They keep some tools in the barn sometimes."

"Which way did they go?" I asked, already walking out.

"To the rebel compound, of course."

I stopped short. "What did you say?"

"You know, the rebels."

I walked back to him, dropped to my knees and took his hands. "Listen to me very carefully. Never, ever again say the word rebel out loud. Do you hear me? Don't even think it. You'll be killed for it. The rebel compound is gone now. You can never go there, do you hear me?"

"Okay, Temir. I'm sorry. I didn't mean to make you mad." His eyes filled with tears.

"No, River. I'm not mad. You just shouldn't know about the rebels or their compound."

"Then they shouldn't talk so much when they think no one is around," he said, his face falling.

"I'll be sure to pass along the message." I ruffled his hair and ran toward the tunnel entrance I knew Roe would use. I caught them before the soldiers, thankfully. "Roe, stop," I panted. "You can't go to the tunnels. They are being raided. You have to go back to the castle and make sure you're seen."

"What about the others?" one of his friends asked.

"We got everyone out. They are meeting at Bryer's Keep, but I need your help with something else."

"Anything." Roe stepped forward.

"It's going to be dangerous," I warned.

"Perfect." He moved his hand through his beard as he waited for me to continue.

I explained to them exactly what they needed to do, which included sneaking into my rooms for supplies. I didn't have time to stay back and help them though. I still had to get to the other tunnel and hope to the gods all these delays hadn't cost Rhogan his life.

I wasn't sure where the other entrance was other than somewhere on the opposite side of the castle. As I ran, I considered what River had said. Could it have been rebels just unaware of his eavesdropping, or did we truly have someone within the rebellion who was that careless with information? We would need to be far more careful going forward. The rebel compound would now be days from me, so I wouldn't be able to attend meetings there. I wondered with it being a less central location if they would call meetings to different places scattered throughout the north.

I moved to the edge of the forest on the other side of the castle and searched for footprints in the snow. The soldiers had come to this entrance, so there must have been proof somewhere. I searched until I realized I hadn't gone far enough. I could hear rather than see a group of males huddled together in the distance. They were hidden within the tree line, which meant if I went closer, I wouldn't be able to watch the skies for Rhogan.

I crouched low behind a tree with a wide trunk and waited. Watched. There was movement ahead as soldiers exited. I recognized very few of them until Eadas himself walked out grinning like he'd won a crown. He carried a log chain over his shoulder, and I didn't have to look to know what—who—he dragged behind him.

They had tied Rhogan's hands in front of him and dragged him on his giant black wings through the thick forest. He had broken arrows coming out of every limb, and when I heard him groan, my body lurched toward him. I couldn't save him though. There was nothing I could do. I'd never be able to fight all of the soldiers unarmed, and if I tried to free him, they'd know my involvement. Doing anything for him would be suicide, and the hardest part was knowing that it was my fault. I was the one who had sent him for more supplies. I had rushed him out the door before considering the king's moves. Whatever happened to Rhogan from this point forward was on my hands.

I knew who they thought he was. A massive male caught trying to enter the tunnels with supplies? Eadas thought he had caught the rebel leader. Which meant his heart would be delivered to the king on a gods-damned silver platter.

When it was safe to leave, I snuck back to the castle, crossed the bailey, and waited behind the stables where I had told Roe to meet me. It took him forever. I'd begun to pace and rub my knuckles, worried he had been caught, but when he rounded the corner, my heart stopped as I took in his condition.

"It was only a tumble, Tem. All is fine."

"The traps are set?"

"Just as you told us," he answered. "The others are just waiting for the signal."

"You're sure everyone is in place and your friends were able to sneak back out?"

"Gron had a bit of trouble, but I made sure everyone is ready."

"Are there still soldiers in the tunnels?"

"Yes, but there's no telling how many. They weren't guarding all the entrances anymore, but we could still hear them inside."

"Okay, time to start the show," I said. "Are their soldiers at this entrance?"

"There were three. They weren't paying attention. I was able to get past them easily."

We carefully moved toward the entrance he and I had always used, where three casual soldiers stood several paces away, drinking and laughing. We circled around them and snuck into the tunnel opening.

"This one has more than the others?"

He held up two fingers.

I struck the flint he handed me, and it sparked but missed the fuse. I held my breath and listened for the soldiers to rush inside, but they didn't. "This lights, you run." He nodded, and I struck again. The fuse sizzled, and the flame moved down the tunnel. "Hurry," I whispered, pushing him forward.

We ran out of the tunnel and slipped off to the side undetected. Eadas' soldiers were terrible guards. We ran back toward the barn and got about halfway before the explosion shook the frozen grounds. I'd given Roe and his friends access to dangerous chemicals, and when mixed with the flame, they would not only close off all the tunnels, ensuring no rebel was caught trying to reenter unaware, but it would also send a message to the king. The rest of the planned explosions followed shortly after, and the only tunnel left open was the one that led directly below the castle. The tunnel where Rhogan was taken prisoner.

"Better get back to the castle and join the others trying to figure out what just happened. The king is going to call me in to heal the soldiers they can pull from the tunnels. He's about to find out I'm out of magic."

"Meet me in your solar," Roe called, heading toward the castle. "Try to beat the king, I have a plan."

KING TOLERO

*T*he castle was silent as I moved. As they always did, the visitors reveled in the city the night before the Trials began. I left the gates to the castle and made my way into the boisterous crowd that danced and sang. Laughter filled the air like a song. I stepped back into a dark alley and closed my eyes, remembering my once youthful days. Life was so much simpler then.

I nearly crashed into two lovers deep in the throes of frantic love making, but I kept my eyes to the ground and swept past them as the female cried out. On this night, if you closed your eyes and listened, you would know what the land of fae was always meant to sound like. Alewyn was supposed to be a haven to faeries. A place to drink, celebrate and love as freely as the air we breathed. I wasn't sure what it had turned into, but it was far from that.

I placed my hands upon a familiar shop door, and it let out a tiny squeal as it inched open.

"Finally," Murtad called from across the space. "If I had to wait any longer, I was going to waste away. How are ya, King? Where's your minion?" He looked behind me.

"Murtad," I said in greeting.

"Oh, right. Right." He gave me a superfluous bow, waving his hand nonsensically as he dipped.

Always the character, this one. He reminded me of Kai with his antics. Thoughts of the boys struck a chord, and I felt a deep sense of loss, missing Fen. If he were here now, I wondered what he and his crew would lend to the situation. He had always told me to befriend the gifted. I wished I'd listened to him more.

"Why have you summoned me?"

His tone turned serious. "I've come to update you. King Autus has learned of the rebellion and is actively hunting them in the north. He sent some soldiers to destroy a small township, to send a message."

"What will you do?" I asked.

"I believe we may need to send some rebels north to help secure passage for rebellion refugees to move to the southern kingdom, if you will allow it?"

"I'm glad someone asks my permission these days."

"About that, I have additional news for you. Your kingdom is flooding with sea fae. Pun intended. My guys have been watching selkies everywhere. The fae act as if they cannot see them."

"Yes, I've seen them myself. They act as if they cannot see them, because Morwena has been enchanting my people. Removing their ability to see them as if they were invisible. I'm guessing the rebels have been immune because she hasn't gotten to you, yet. I'm working on it."

"You should go to Gillie's Tavern. My guys have spotted them in there a few times. So far, we've avoided them. I've told the rebels to remember their locations but steer clear. We can't let them know how far the rebellion has stretched. We hope they think it is just a few rogue fae in the north."

"And what is it, if not that?" I asked.

He pursed his lips and cocked an eyebrow at me. "A movement."

Indeed. "I will allow the fae to continue to enter the southern kingdom, if you agree to two things, Murtad. First of all, you do realize that I could enchant you right now and take the rebellion for myself, do you not?"

"That's assuming I speak and make the calls for the rebellion, King. I've never admitted to either."

"Fair point. Shall we find out?" I asked, taking in a big dramatic breath as if that's how it was done. I knew better. My own council had a rebel. She reported everything.

"No, no. Not necessary. What are your two requirements?"

"When it comes time—and surely it will before this is all said and done—the rebellion will not stand against the southern kingdom. I'm not asking you to join me, simply to refuse to kill my fae."

"And number two?" He looked to his hands as if I bored him.

"The rebellion will owe me a favor when I call upon them."

"Will you increase our food rations and the coins you donate?"

"I will increase the food rations when you provide me with solid numbers."

"Fair enough," he said. "The rebellion will not fight against the southern court unless the king begins to turn on them, and we will owe you a favor for harboring the refugees."

If he didn't trust me, he wouldn't leave that opened ended favor on the table, so I knew we were on the same page. He needed me far more than I needed him. For now, anyway.

"Will you attend the Trials?" I asked.

"We'll be around, King. Now I must be off. I've got a little lady to see before the world falls apart." He sauntered out of the shop and left me standing there with my own thoughts.

Feeling particularly reckless after the events of the long day, I decided I'd follow his advice and head to Gillie's

I loathed sitting in a crowded tavern surrounded by drunken fae having loud conversations with each other about things no one in the nearby vicinity cared about. I drummed my fingers on the table and watched the door as I waited for my drink to come. I would not indulge, but it would help me blend. Being in the city undercover the night before the Trials was easy because of the careless drinking and the cloaked fighters who sat heavily in their seats discussing their techniques for the next day. Some of them I actually looked forward to watching. If I could ever take a minute to enjoy myself knowing the storm was brewing around us.

The door opened and closed so many times as fae came and went, but it wasn't until the end of the night that I finally watched a selkie stalk in. Her long hair looked as if it flowed in unseen waters, and her shiny skin reflected the lights throughout the tavern. Not a single fae looked to her as she entered, smiling as she crossed the crowded room.

I watched her lift a finger and draw it across the back of a large male's neck, and though he shifted, he acted as if she were not there. She moved like a wraith to an empty seat at a full table and leaned in, listening to the fae talk as she batted her eyelashes and smiled, though none could see her.

The reality of what this meant was more alarming than her eerie presence. She had no possible way to enchant the minds of the southern fae. Only one sea witch could do that, and that meant one damn thing: Morwena had been spending an exuberant amount of time in my kingdom, enchanting my fae. Her enchant had always been powerful, derived from the sea. But this was still a feat.

She was the poison. Not only was she enchanting my fae to be oblivious to her spies, but she was also planting lies and making it seem as if I were at fault. The guards from the barn? That was because of her. I'd bet anything on it.

I stood from my seat, removed my hood, and waited as the fae in the room slowly realized their king sat among them. The moment the whispers grew louder, the selkie's head snapped to mine, and we locked eyes. She stood and darted for the door. I should have stopped her, but I let her go. I'd get to her eventually.

The room dripped with animosity toward me. Faces reddened, lips curled, someone growled from the back corner. There was not a kind eye in sight. The laughter and celebrations had twisted to rumbles about burning down that farm and killing fae. About hiding in my castle for years.

"Silence," I belted, letting my enchantment ricochet around the room. "Raise your hand if you have seen the sea queen." Every hand in the room shot to the ceiling. Angered eyes and vicious sneers greeted me. "Raise your hand if you have seen the sea queen on this day." All of the hands dropped.

"You will forget all of the toxic lies she has told you. Every word from her mouth will leave you, and you will have no memory of it. Whatever she has demanded of you, it is gone now."

The fae visibly relaxed. The ire melting from the stone-cold faces.

"You did not see me here tonight. You will not spread lies about your king any longer. You will go home, and tomorrow, when you wake, you will make sure every fae you know in my kingdom shows up to watch the Trials."

I stood, pushed back the exhaustion from enchanting so many, and exited the tavern. I stormed the darkened streets as thoughts poured from me.

She had stood beside me. Morwena. When I watched my mate's pyre drift off into the ocean. She had stood there and offered condolences. Coro was there. Autus stood beside him. But Morwena? She had reached for my hand, and yet Efi had died at hers. She had poisoned her like a coward, knowing it would be the most crippling thing she could have done to the Flame Court.

Southerners were a dangerous enemy. Snakes in the sand that bite when angry. Had she poisoned me, she would have had the wrath of my kingdom to deal with. Instead, she broke me and let them watch my degradation. Let them doubt me, until their minds were easy to turn against me. If her plan came to fruition, she would have a willing kingdom delivered on a silver platter.

Morwena. The thought of her name sickened me. The snake of the sea came into my home and destroyed one of the only good things in this world for her own rise to power. She had shed tears. Had seemed genuinely sorry. Caused our son to suffer the loss of his mother. And for what purpose? She was no closer to the throne now than she was fifty years ago. Did she really think Autus loved her? That their marriage was anything but a political move? No. Likely, she didn't, but that didn't matter.

For each step I took, that tiger pounded within me, guiding me, building me taller. I heard Efi's laughter in my mind and watched her sleeping peacefully in my memories as I remembered the way she reached for me, called to me when I made love to her. I saw her dance in the halls with the staff and stumble into bed when she'd had too much wine. I remembered the way she would curl into my body and stroke her finger across my chest deep into the night. No female had ever loved a male the way that one loved me. And she had been ripped from my hands by a coward. An evil, lying coward.

Lost in the maze of my own mind, I found myself standing at the crest of the tumultuous ocean. "Morwena," I yelled, sending my voice as far across the ocean as it would carry. Perhaps it wouldn't need to come down to a war between the kingdoms. Perhaps we would settle it tonight, right here between the two of us. "Morwena," I screamed again and again until my voice had nearly left me. Somewhere in the distance, I heard her. A cackling, cringe-worthy laugh riding the foaming waves that crashed to my feet. "Come out, you spineless sea hag."

"Ohhh." She leaped from the water and laughed as she spun, the scales of her leviathan body catching the moonlight before she dove back in. "We're calling each other names now?" She laughed again.

"Tell me why."

"You'll have to clarify." She waded in the water as it lapped around her waist.

"Why did you poison Efi? Why would you take her from me?"

"Finally." She moved her hands through the sea as she smiled. "It took you ages to figure it out. I nearly thought I was going to have to write you a full confession letter."

"Why, Morwena?"

"Oh Tolero, did you really think you could sit in your hole all the way down here and we would just forget about you? What have you been doing since Efi died? While we have been building armies and putting our plans into motion, where has the Flame Court been?"

Her ice-blue eyes glowed in the darkness, and for one small moment, regret slid through me. Would she just kill me now? Did I care? "What will you do, Morwena? When you've married Autus and conquered the world? What then? When your own mate finds you and you're married to that beast? I knew your parents before you ruled the seas. Even they would have detested him."

"Yes, well now they're dead and they don't matter. Just as you will be. Just as your son will be. My selkies have become quite fond of your little kingdom. Perhaps I'll set them loose and let them devour your people after I've killed you." She paused, moving her hands through her saturated hair. "You'd like that, wouldn't you? To join Efi? I see you spend so much time on that little isle. Perhaps I'll destroy that favored landmark of yours just before I end you."

There was a time when I would have begged her to kill me. When I had wanted nothing more than to be with Efi. Things had changed. Efi was still with me, and this kingdom—my kingdom—needed me.

"Come to shore, Morwena. Let us settle this between ourselves."

She huffed. "Oh no. I've got pieces all over the board. I might have taken you out before the game has begun, but I still have great plans for you, Tolero. I'll see you soon, my pet." She leaped out of the water, her body contorting into her true form as she laughed again and disappeared.

The tiger within me roared, and I stalked off. She was gone and would not be back. I didn't have a plan. I had no idea what I was doing, but I knew one truth: I'd have to catch that fish in a net. And that meant letting her think she had the upper hand until the very last second.

Walking back to the castle, I knew I wouldn't be able to sleep in my own bed tonight. If I slept at all, it wouldn't be in the place I had shared with my love. I'd failed her. So thoroughly. I couldn't protect her from my own enemies, and she had paid the ultimate price for it. But so had Fenlas. I stopped before I opened the door and looked to the starry night sky wondering where in the world he was. I could only hope his mission was proving more successful than mine—that his mate would never leave him and he would never know the pain of life alone.

Trotting up the stairs to the rooftop, I stood for a long time looking out over the beautiful city. Thousands of reasons to join this fight slumbered below me. I was ready.

I stepped carefully to Asha's shelter, walked inside, and laid on the floor beside her. Though I thought she slept, she pulled her wing over me and curled in, her deep warm breaths protecting me from the crisp night air.

CHAPTER 27

ARA

"So, hunting?" I asked as we all sat around the fire, preparing to leave the forest.

"Hunting," Fen answered.

"Oh, should we make it a competition?" Wren asked.

"Might as well." He shrugged.

"Girls against boys?" I asked, smirking.

"I'd hate to give the new girl unfair odds." Kai pursed his lips to conceal his contagious smile.

"Challenge accepted. Nothing so big we can't carry it through the mountains," I leaped to my feet.

"Deal," Fen said, grinning at me as he rose and slung his own weapon behind his back.

We separated from the guys, Wren and I going one way, them going the other.

"Shall we go invisible?" she asked.

"Might as well use our advantage."

We walked back-to-back, me checking the treetops and her scouring the ground.

"Bunny," she whispered, pulling an arrow.

"Got it?"

She nodded and shot it right through the eyes.

"Nice shot," I whispered.

We kept moving. I took down two birds before she had another, and again, her shot was perfect. I hadn't given her credit for weaponry skills. But she was a southerner, of course she would have them.

"Deer," she said.

"Too big," I answered.

We moved forward, and she yanked on me. "Troll."

I should have known from the sour smell in the air.

"I have an idea," I said with an evil grin, though she couldn't see it. "How far do you think the guys are?"

"Hard to say, but they have Lichen. I bet we can find them. He is hardly quiet."

I picked up every small stick and rock I could find before the troll got too far away. I threw a rock, and he stopped, turned toward us, and took a few steps.

"Start moving in their direction, I'll get him to follow. Fen will see us, so we still have to stay behind the trees."

"Trolls are that dumb?" she asked.

"Not all, but some are. I don't think we have a real winner here. His trousers are on backwards." I paused. "And definitely inside out."

"You seriously want Fen to hate you, don't you?"

"Something like that." I threw another rock.

We wound our way through the scattered trees. The troll stopped three times. Once to use the bathroom, once to smell a tree and the third time to try to catch a firetipfly, on which he burned his hand, whined, and kept coming. I had to replenish my rock supply four times until I finally heard a twig snap up ahead.

"There," Wren said, quieter than a breath.

They were spread in a circle moving slowly inward as one, using their hand signals to communicate. I tossed the final rock right into the middle, and Wren shook with silent laughter as the small forest frugho they were trying to catch, with its giant furry ears and medium-sized body, scampered off in fear of the troll.

"Fuck." Kai stomped his foot.

The troll turned toward him and waved, scaring off all the birds in the trees above.

"Yes, hi. I see you, ya big oaf," he grumbled.

Fen motioned for him to be quiet, but Kai just gave him a crude gesture and crossed his arms.

"Is that our fearless tracker throwing a tantrum?" Greeve asked from the canopy of trees above.

"We can't let two girls beat us," he said.

"They were probably too scared to go back into the forest alone. I'm sure the squirrel we caught is still more than what they got. How much time do we have left?" Fen asked.

I elbowed Wren and leaned in, "We're taking that fucking squirrel just for that comment."

We carefully began to move, avoiding Fen's peripheral.

"Five minutes left," Lichen said, holding out the squirrel. "Should we use this as bait?"

"No. Keep it," Fen answered.

We were nearly to Lichen, who was tying their only catch to a lead so he could hang it from his hip when Greeve snapped his fingers.

I looked up to see what he was pointing at.

"BIRDY!" the troll yelled, clapping.

It took every single ounce of self-control I had not to completely lose my shit. Wren was shaking so bad I knew we had seconds until she gave us away. I reached forward, snagged the squirrel off Lichen's rope with a knife, and yanked Wren away. We were not quiet, but we ran back to the clearing as fast as we could. The minute we were out of the forest, Wren burst into laughter until four sourpuss faces walked out.

"How'd it go?" I asked, trying to keep a straight face.

"Lichen lost our fucking squirrel," Kai whined shoving past poor Lichen.

"This looks awfully familiar," Fen said, lifting my hand so everyone could see the squirrel still half tied to Lichen's rope.

"Birdy!" Wren yelled, and everyone but Kai laughed.

"You cheated," he pouted.

"I don't know what you mean. We were too scared to go back into the forest alone." I looked Fen right in the face as I mocked him.

He shook his head, pushing away the smile that threatened to show.

Kai stepped forward. "Next time I'm on the girls' team."

"How did you get the troll to the circle?" Lichen asked, looking at Wren.

"Wouldn't you like to know," she answered.

"When you're ready, children," Greeve interrupted. "We have a long way to go."

We cleaned the meat and started off.

I had a better sense of who everyone was now, so leaving today with them felt a lot more like I fit. Somehow. We left the forest behind and walked for several days as the flatlands outside the forest gradually changed into steeper hills, mimicking the looming mountains in the distance.

Kai kept his exhaustingly jovial attitude and Wren was proving to be more and more of a badass, even out hunting me. Lichen was Lichen. Still full of a thousand questions. Greeve was driven and quiet. The prince was still the beautiful male struggling to let me have some space. I'd worked out each day, and though he'd given me freedom the first day, by the second he wanted to come along and by the third, we were practicing sword fighting pretty fluidly and he had yet to beat me. I still had nightmares, so I tried to keep myself a little farther from the group, but

Fen would always end up beside me. They never came when he was there, but I didn't want to tell him that.

"Did Mom kick your ass again, Dad?" Kai asked as we joined the group one day after a particularly sweaty workout.

"You try fighting her," Fen answered.

"Oh, come on, she's tiny."

"Pick your weapon." I wiped the sweat off my forehead.

"No, I couldn't. If I hurt you, Fen would kick my ass."

Fen snorted. "I'll give you a pass."

Kai shook his head, his messy blond hair falling into his blue eyes. Clearly, he thought the idea was completely irrational. I read the unspoken question on his face. How could a female beat a commander of the southern army? Still, as Greeve slipped three coins into Wren's hand and nodded to Kai, he couldn't back down.

"Fine. You wanna fight, I'll kick your ass. But don't come crying to me later when it hurts. I say hand to hand combat. No weapons. First to tap out loses."

"No other rules?"

"I promise I won't just sit on you. Does that work?"

"Thank the gods for that." I started taking off my weapons. I first dropped the sword from my back, then I took each of my throwing knives and dropped them in the pile. I pulled the dagger from my boot and let that one fall, then twisted my wrists and let those hidden knives pop out so I could drop them too. I pulled the flap at my back and removed the last small dagger I had hidden.

"What the hell? You just walk around with an armory attached to you? Wait, you actually sleep with all of that?"

I shrugged. "Your turn."

He dropped the sword he kept strapped to his back and patted himself down dramatically. "That's it for me, I guess."

I stood in front of him and held my fists up.

"Are you sure you want to do this. I don't want to hurt—"

I jumped and kicked him in the face, his crazy hair went flying.

"You ..." he croaked.

Fen burst into laughter behind me and Wren was already slipping the coins into her pocket.

I dropped my hands while he reset. I perked an eyebrow and waited for him to make a move. He pulled his fists close to his face, jumped back and forth on his feet and stepped in to swing, but I dodged and cracked my elbow across his face.

A little sniggering behind me made me smile as I waited for him to reset again.

"That should be a good enough head start, don't you think?" Greeve asked. "Time to get serious, Kai," he joked.

Kai spit to the side and brought his hands up again while I did the same and waited for him to strike. He didn't. We circled a few times, and I blew him a kiss right before I kicked the inside of his thigh, causing his leg to twist as he fell to one knee. Before he could react, I brought my own knee up to his nose, and though he tried to block, he wasn't fast enough.

"This is like the hottest thing I've ever seen," Wren said. "Aside from watching you chuck knives at the wall blindfolded and practically naked. Oh, and when you were drunk dancing around in Fen's shirt." She clapped her hands over her mouth. "Sorry."

I tried to catch Fen's face, but he was looking away and tremoring. I don't think he wanted his pseudo brother to know he was genuinely laughing at him. Or me—hard to tell.

"Give up?" I asked, moving my feet around.

"No," he cried behind bloodied hands as he stood. He let his nose run as he set his stance once more. I got too cocky and moved in to punch him again, but he caught me. He struck me right in the side, but I could tell he was holding back.

"I'm not afraid of you, Kai. You can hit me like you would Fen or Greeve."

I bounced around on the balls of my feet, waiting for him to make another move. He swung wide, and I ducked below, taking a groin shot. It was cheap, but ... no rules. He fell to the ground, and I plopped down right on top of him.

"You didn't say *I* couldn't sit on *you*, right? That wasn't a rule?" I looked to the group standing back watching, and Fen smiled that smile at me, and I couldn't help but beam. I felt his pride, and that was the best compliment he could have given me. "Tap out yet?" I asked.

"You're a fucking beast," Kai said. "I give. You win."

"Yay." Wren clapped her hands.

Greeve came over and offered me a hand up. I took it, and he shoved Kai over with his boot. "I can't wait to tell Tolero you got beat by a girl."

"Asshole," Kai groaned.

"She's hardly a girl," Fen said, studying me. I'd never felt so exposed. I immediately started strapping my weapons back on. Naturally.

"I let her win," Kai said, getting up.

"You're bleeding and took the fetal position on the ground." Fen stood beside me. "I'd say she beat you fair and square."

"Where'd you learn to fight like that?" Lichen asked, the suspicion clear on his face.

"I told you yesterday, I trained with my father. The one I knew. Did you ever meet him?"

"I did, but I never had the pleasure of watching him fight."

"I bet he was amazing," Wren said.

"He was," Fen answered. "Ask my father. He could tell you plenty of stories."

"He could?" I asked, wishing I truly could ask the elder king.

"My father knew your real father and the one who raised you. They were both amazing. Someday, you should ask him."

"If I ever go to the Flame Court, I will," I said.

"Of course you'll come home with us," Wren said. "Won't you?"

"I honestly don't know." The high from my win left as quickly as it had come. "I have a lot to figure out, I guess."

"Speaking of figuring out where we are going, where exactly are we headed from here?" Fen asked Kai.

"I have a map here," Lichen said, pulling a folded piece of oversized paper from his pack. "We've just come clear of the maze forest and crossed this clearing here. You can see the hills we're in right now. As a point of reference, I think if we traveled straight south, we would reach Hythe in the Marsh Court."

"Aren't we going north?" Wren asked.

"Yes, so if we travel through the rest of these hills, we will hit the Wind Court by nightfall and be standing right at the base of the mountain range. We then follow the mountains west until we find the gap. It's going to get colder than any of us can possibly imagine. I hope everyone is geared up for that."

"We'll have to make the best of it," Fen said. "Kai, take the lead. Ara and I will bring up the back end while we work on her magic."

"Going to work on her from the back end, eh?" Every tooth Kai could possibly show gleamed as he dodged Fen's flying fist.

"Go soak your head," Fen teased. "Be sure to find the deepest part of the ocean."

"Not an insult to our little sea enthusiast—he'd love that. Let's not forget his penchant for mermaids," Greeve chuckled, pulling him into a headlock.

"Don't even act like you guys aren't curious. I just want to know where to put it. Still waiting on you to get me that answer," he said, shoving out of Greeve's playful grip.

Fen laughed louder than I'd ever heard him. "Kai saved a sea fae when he was a boy. Just a little fish. She gave him something to remember him by, didn't she, pal."

"You guys can make fun of me all you want, but someday, I'm probably going to become a sea God and you'll all be sorry," he said, flashing the opaque sea glass ring he kept on his little finger.

"Right." Wren giggled. "And someday I'm going to learn to fly."

As the group pulled away, still glowing from teasing Kai, I waited for Fen to say something. He had distanced us for a reason.

"Everything okay?" he finally asked as his smile melted.

"Yes."

"I saw your face when Wren invited you back home."

Home? I didn't have a home anymore. I had burned the only one I'd ever known to the ground. I really didn't know where I would go after I found Nealla. I hadn't thought that far ahead, and the truth was, I was afraid to even consider it.

"You could have asked me that in front of them, you didn't have to send them off."

"I wanted to respect your privacy."

"If you wanted to do that, you wouldn't be here." I looked away. "I intended to make this journey alone."

"I'll always be here." He leveled his chin, and his eyes flicked back and forth between my own, searching for something I wasn't ready to give.

"I don't need to talk about it. I'm fine."

"Clearly you're not, but I'll give you some space to sort it out. If it's The Mists you're worried about, we'll figure it out together."

He started to walk away, and I stopped him. "It's not about the mountains, it's not about The Mists, it's not even about what lies beyond. I'm afraid of the truth if I'm being brutally honest with myself."

That wall I'd kept up became a bit thinner. As much as I hated to admit it, he made me feel safe. Like the point of a blade, a balled fist, a razor-sharp mind, I cherished that feeling. And I think he knew that. I didn't need to be saved from the world. Just myself. If nothing else, he was giving me that.

He turned and looked at me, then stepped closer. I held my breath as he lifted my hand. "Whatever fate befalls you, I'll be there. Your future is my future. It's written in the stars, in our blood, in the very core of this world. Nothing about my commitment to you is fleeting, Ara. I would promise you, but I'd rather prove it to you."

"They're staring," I responded blandly, looking at the group that had turned to watch us.

"Let them." He lifted my hand to his beautiful lips.

"So, about that magic ..." I pulled away.

"Yes, the magic." He grinned. "I have a plan."

"And what is it?" I asked.

"It will be purely scientific, I promise."

"Spit it out, Prince. What's the plan?"

"We will stop, the group will carry on and Greeve will come back to get us at nightfall."

"What's the point in making them leave us?"

"You'll see," he answered with a grin.

"Why are you making this so mysterious?" I laughed. "Just tell me what we're doing."

He waved to the group, and they began walking again. Apparently, that was the signal that I was a sucker. I crossed my arms and stared at him until he gave in.

"I'm going to try to overwhelm your senses and see if I can cause your magic to come forward. If you'll let me."

"Is this some kind of creepy torture plan you're scheming? Because if it is, I'll cut your balls off and eat them for dinner, Prince."

"Like I said. It's your choice."

He knew I'd agree. How could I not? If I had magic like his, I'd really be able to fuck some shit up. "Do your worst, Prince." I spread my feet and bent my knees, fists up.

"If at any point you want me to stop, just lift your hands or say stop."

"I'm not a baby, just do it already." He closed his eyes and the lengthy grass began to grow, weaving in and out of my legs, up my arms and across my body. I couldn't move. "Nothing's happening."

He pushed a gust of wind forward, and it blew so hard I couldn't catch my breath.

I tried to think about the bucket of magic and pull it forward to meet his own, but everything inside of me was quiet, still. "How am I supposed to raise my hands when you have them tied down?" I yelled over the vicious wind whipping my auburn hair around.

"Your mouth still works," he smirked. "What's the matter, Princess? Can't beat your way out of this one?"

"Taunting me won't work when I literally just kicked your ass."

"I wasn't trying," he lied.

"Maybe not with your magic, but I saw the sweat. You couldn't touch me with a sword."

"I can touch you with fire."

Suddenly a burst of heat ran up my legs, through my core, up the back of my neck and through the ends of my hair. He hadn't intended it to be arousing, but it was.

"Do that again, Prince."

"Did you feel it?" he asked, shooting the heat through me once more.

"I felt something." My husky voice betrayed me.

His ears perked up, and he took a step back. "Focus."

Water poured down on me as wind tore at me, but still my limbs were strapped down. He pushed that heat through me again.

I arched my back and tried to let his water wash away the growing need. "I don't think this is going to work. At least not in the way you want it to."

"If you want me to stop, break free."

I pushed and pulled at the vines, watching the careful lines of his face, studying him as he watched me struggle. I should be pissed, but I wasn't because a wicked idea had formed. I began to move my hands inch by

258

inch until I had enough space to twist my wrist, engaging the throwing knife secured within my clothing. I was slow at first, so he could not see. I cut a few vines at a time while we locked eyes and he let the rain soak me.

"Concentrating?" he asked me.

"Entirely." As soon as I could move my arm freely, in one swoop I cut the vines and launched myself at him.

"Gods-damnit, Ara," he said from below me as I tackled him to the ground. "That was not the plan. Magic. You're supposed to use magic."

"I have another idea. Purely scientific." I crawled backward and sat in front of him. I'd been holding back. So many emotions had buried themselves for so long within me. The longing I'd been suppressing rose to the surface, but this time I didn't shove it back down.

"What is it?" His anger melted into intrigue. The southern prince continued to surprise me.

"If my magic is pulled forward by a powerful emotion, and you can't make me mad at you when I know you're trying to, maybe you could try a different emotion."

"Which one?" He rubbed the stubble on his cheek, and something in that movement, in the way he responded to me, lit a fire.

"I think you know, Prince." I crawled toward him until I was inches from his face. "I am fae. If not rage, what else would call to me?"

"You test my self-control, Princess."

"Maybe you should test mine instead."

"Purely scientific?" he managed, although I could see him struggle.

"If you say so," I purred.

"Stand," he ordered. The vines crawled up my body again. "Try to remain still, little vixen."

"I promise nothing."

He cleared his throat and faced away. A smile threatened to appear, but I pushed it away. This was torture for him and me both. Invisible hands moved across my body like an instrument he intended to play, the fingers of his magic trailing below my ears, across my neck, and down my spine.

I squirmed.

"Eyes closed," he ordered. "Think about your magic and imagine it coming forward to meet my own. If at any point you truly want me to stop, say stop."

Gods help me, I tried. But concentrating on anything while he commanded my body was impossible. His magical heat circled me, and I felt it lick a distinct line up my thigh. The closer it moved to my core, the harder my traitorous heart raced. Water still dripped from my fingertips, heightening my senses. "Careful, Prince."

"And if I'm not?" His lips were inches from my ear.

I hadn't heard him move at all.

"Then these vines may not hold me."

"Come and get me then." His deep voice resonated through me as purely as his magic did.

I peeked an eye open. His were closed, and he was standing only inches away.

"Are you picturing me naked?"

"My imagination is not that tame." His voice shook.

The fire magic moved closer until every part between my legs was wet, trembling, and I could feel the pressure building inside of me. My breaths began to fall short as his winded fingers moved down my chest and over my sensitive nipples. I gasped, and his heat plunged deep within me. I tried to move, to buck, to bend, to do anything. But I could not. I was entirely at his mercy.

"You can only use your magic to push me away."

"This is definitely kin to torture," I panted.

"It is only pleasure, Princess. Use that feeling as a conduit for your magic. Answer my own."

He moved his fire magic up my body, and I couldn't help but moan out loud as the desire for a moody prince rolled through me. Magic? It was nowhere to be found, but as the heat stroked my body and those illusory gentle fingers moved down my front, I thought I might fall from the indulgence.

"Release me, Prince," I whispered.

"Focus," he strained to answer.

"Release me." I wouldn't use his safe word. I hoped he never stopped.

"Release you how?" he purred in my ear from behind.

I opened my eyes as he circled me like easy prey.

"Those sounds you make will be my undoing," His gaze was fierce as he took me in. Instead of stopping, he came at me with a vengeance. I felt his heat moving through me in waves.

I moaned louder as the pleasure mounted. I was inching toward orgasm, and he was relentlessly stroking me. I tried to think about the damn bucket of magic, but the only thing I could see when I closed my eyes was his large body wrapped around mine. I imagined him full and hard and deep within me as I leaned back into him. I felt his very real growth and rubbed against him.

"Ara," he warned. "I only have so much control."

"Then let it go."

"Is that you asking me to stop?" he asked, pausing entirely.

"No. But I would like my hands, please."

The restricting vines fell to the ground, and I spun and wrapped my arms around the prince of the southern kingdom. "Purely scientific?" I asked, inches away from his face.

"You're going to be the death of me."

"Probably." I closed the space between us. His lips were everything I imagined they would be, and as he brought his hands up to gently hold the side of my face, I felt the real contradiction of who he was. There was an invisible line between us, and somehow within our endless kiss, I saw him. Who he pretended to be to the outside world and who he truly was with his friends. His family.

I pulled back, catching my breath and searching his eyes. Had he felt that too? That invisible line.

"Okay?" he asked carefully.

I nodded and kissed him once more. That intense passion had always been there. It might have been masked as hatred, but there wasn't a single moment between us that wasn't deeply emotional. His lips massaged mine before he nipped at me as his hands roamed more of my sensitive body. Somewhere along that line, I'd lost the divide between his need and my own.

He planted his hands on my hips and pulled me closer to him, then ran his fingers through my hair and made a guttural sound as I moved against him.

"Shit," he whispered against my collarbone. "This isn't how I planned it at all."

"No, but isn't it so much better than torture?" I asked, lips still pressed to his.

"It is exactly torture." His heated gaze stole my breath.

"Wait." I pulled away. "You aren't going to tell the others, right?"

"Gods no." He smiled.

I heard a grunt behind us, and then someone cleared their throat. I pressed my forehead to Fen's shoulder and squeezed my eyes closed. "If we ignore them, will they go away?"

"What is it?" he bit out.

"I'm sorry to interrupt, Fen," Greeve said. "I can just wait over here until you're ready?"

"Absolutely not." I jumped off Fen, immediately putting five feet between us.

His face was taut, and I knew Greeve was in for a fight later.

"Someone better be dying," he said.

"There's something I need to discuss with you. Alone."

"Hey. I thought I was part of the team now," I protested.

"You heard her, Greeve. You better tell us both."

"Right. Sorry, Ara. For interfering with your magic lesson."

My cheeks reddened, but I absolutely refused to look away.

"Get on with it," Fen said.

"While we were walking, Kai thought it would be good for me to cleave ahead toward the Western Gap so we could travel in a straight line instead of walking all the way to the mountain range and then going west. I agreed."

"What happened?" I asked, putting my pack on my back.

"I didn't get all the way to the Western Gap, but when I got close, something felt off. Dangerous."

"I think we all assumed there would be danger," Fen answered.

"We should go around. Head down to the Eastern Gap, cross the range where everyone else does and then come back down. Avoid the Western Gap altogether."

"For so many reasons, that's a terrible idea," I said.

"I'd rather scale a mountain than get that close to the Gap again, Fen. I don't know what's there, but even the wind pushed me away."

"Leave us for five minutes. Let Ara and I decide together and then come back."

He bowed and vanished.

"What do you think?" he asked. The fact that he made it our decision and not his own was not lost on me.

"If we go all the way east, we will lose days, weeks if the weather is bad. We will have to travel all the way back across, trying to remain undetected in the northern kingdom. If we can make it through the Western Gap, we will still have to travel through the Wind Court but not for nearly as long. I don't see that we have a real choice here."

He nodded. "Whatever the danger is, going the other way is likely still worse. Let's stick to the plan and be extra diligent about watching our surroundings."

"Do we need to discuss this," I said, motioning between us, "before he comes back?"

"Purely scientific." He took my hand and winked.

I found comfort in his answer. I was confused and trying to figure myself out, and not having to think about the prince or what could be between us was certainly the easiest approach.

Greeve used his wind cleaving magic and carried me back to the group before going back for Fen.

"What the hell?" Kai asked. "I thought he was headed for the Western Gap not back for you guys?"

"I'll wait for them to get back, and then we can talk about it as a group."

"Hungry?" Wren offered me a piece of dried meat.

I took it eagerly, and it was half gone by the time the others arrived. Magic lessons wore me out.

"What happened?" Kai demanded as they came to meet us.

"There's something dangerous in or near the Gap. Ara and I talked and decided we should still take that route. I'll offer again for any of you to stay behind if you want to."

Everyone turned to look at Lichen.

"I'm with you," he said, less than confidently.

"I would hear your advice, Lichen," Fen said.

"Tell me what you felt, Greeve."

"Something large, living, and dangerous. I didn't get close. The minute the air became thin, I turned back."

Lichen pulled out his map and studied it for several minutes. Fen sidled up beside me and leaned down to whisper, "I hope you understand why I have to ask his advice as well."

I nodded as I watched Lichen search his map for any way around whatever the danger was.

"I think we will have to continue with our plans, just as you have decided. The closer we get to the Eastern Gap on the other side, the closer we get to Morwena, Coro, and Autus. I'd rather take our chances with whatever's scaring Greeve."

Wind whipped through us.

"You'll watch your tongue," Greeve said, leaning in with hardened fists. "I am a draconian. We do not fear, but it is my job to keep the prince safe."

He could be scary when he wanted to be.

"Did you at least figure out what the direct path to the Western Gap is?" Kai asked.

"Yes, this way," he said, pointing.

And so as one, we moved toward whatever danger Greeve had found, and this time when Fen held my hand, I did not pull away.

CHAPTER

28

TEMIR

I stood in my solar waiting for whatever plan Roe had come up with. Unable to stand still, I sifted through and reorganized the various elixirs on the packed shelf. Roe and the others had been here to retrieve the supplies they needed, and I didn't want the king to notice a single thing out of place. He'd been here enough times that I couldn't be too careful. There was a soft knock at the door, and I opened it to find Roe with a high fae soldier barely standing.

"Hurry," he said.

I grabbed the soldier and laid him on the table.

"He looks fine," I said to Roe.

"Exactly. He's just knocked out."

"You're a damn genius," I told him, pushing him out the door.

I frantically ripped at the soldier's clothing and even used a clean knife to draw blood. Just as I set it down, I heard the barreling voice of the king hollering from outside the door. Still drunk. I placed my hands on the fae and bowed my head as the door slammed open.

"Who the fuck is that?" he yelled.

"I'm not sure, my king. He came in looking like he'd been through the grinder. Someone dropped him off. Said you'd be in after to wipe his memory, but he's still unconscious. It took everything I had to heal him."

"But I've got a whole fucking cave full of soldiers that need to be healed." He narrowed his eyes on me.

"What happened?" I asked, feigning shock.

He shook his head in confusion. He probably still couldn't believe someone had actually made a move against him. One he hadn't seen coming. And now he didn't have a healer to help.

"It's not important right now. How long do you need to restore your magic?"

"I'll need until morning," I said, stretching. "I'm completely wiped out. I'm sorry, my king."

"Fuck." He slammed his fist into the wall. "Get out of my gods-damned sight."

I left the room and wandered back to mine. It had been the longest night of my life. Even if I wasn't completely drained of magic, I think I could have slept for days, but as I opened the door, Gaea launched herself at me. I held her so tight, I thought we'd never separate again.

But she backed away and then shoved me so hard I stumbled. "What the hell were you thinking, Temir?"

"I can't talk about this right now. Rhogan got caught, the king is pissed at me and if I don't lie down, I'm likely to pass out from exhaustion. I'm almost completely drained. The only reason I'm alive right now is because the king plans for me to keep him immortal."

"Bed, now," she ordered. "But I'm going to kill you as soon as you wake up."

I turned, dragged my feet to the bed, and fell face forward, the last of the adrenaline leaving my wracked body. Seconds passed before Gaea shook me awake.

"Temir, you have to wake up."

"Can't," I moaned. "Not yet."

She pulled the blanket off me, grabbed my hands, and made me sit up. I cracked my eyes open. Amber sunlight shined through the drafty window. I must have been asleep longer than I thought. I could tell I hadn't replenished my magic. Not fully.

"How long?" I asked.

"It's only been six hours, but the king has ordered us to the throne room." All color left her beautiful face, and I could see the worry within her stunning eyes.

"Did he say why?" I asked, getting out of the bed.

"No, but what if he knows? What if someone saw you? What if someone knew I was involved?"

I suddenly remembered Oleo's vision of me in chains in the castle.

"Shit."

"He won't kill you, Temir. But he will kill me. I'll die today. I told you not to get involved. Why couldn't you just listen?" She stood and walked to the window, placed her elbows on the sill, and stared out to the bailey. "You've caved in half the grounds. Did you know that? Maybe he knows you're the only one with supplies to cause that kind of reaction." She turned and tears had fallen down her cheeks.

"I'll tell him they were stolen."

"You won't be able to talk your way out of this. The last thing Autus is, is reasonable. We have to leave, Temir. It's time for us to run."

"I can't just leave, Gaea. I have a purpose now. I've committed to the rebels, and I'll keep that commitment."

"You would see me die for the love of the rebels?"

"No, I won't see you die. Let's go to the hall, see what he has to say, and if anyone makes a move toward you, you spirit away and never come back. Take this." I handed her a vial of our truth serum. "Use it if you need to find someone to trust."

"I'll come back for you," she said, taking the vial. "I'll find some place for us to go, and I'll come back, Tem."

268

"I have to see this through. I have to. To whatever end the rebels find, for the sake of all the lesser fae out there dying without just cause, I have to do what I can to save them."

"The same way you saved Rhogan?" she snapped.

"Too far," I answered, walking to the closet to dress.

I couldn't believe she meant to cut so deep. She didn't know I was responsible for him dying. I hadn't had a chance to tell her. I would never say anything to intentionally hurt her, but again, she didn't hold me to the same standard. I felt the distance between us take a heaping step backward, and my heart hurt more than it did before.

"Ready?" I asked, walking to the door.

"Temir," she said, reaching out to me. "I'm sorry. I didn't mean that. You're just being so reckless and I'm terrified."

"I think you did." I grabbed a small dagger and left the room.

I walked the halls alone, and the closer I got to the throne room, the faster my heart beat. I dropped the knife into my boot. I had to put my relationship with Gaea behind me now and stay alert. Observant. If I was about to be put in chains, I wasn't going down without a fight.

I entered the hall, surprised to hear my footsteps echo. The space was nearly empty, and Autus loved crowds for executions. Gaea walked in quietly behind me. She kept a stagnant distance between us. King Autus sat on his large throne at the top of his dais, and beside him, Eadas stood confident and grinning as Evin took the other side, void of emotion. The dark twins were absent.

"Ah. Temir. Gaea. Come forward," the king called across the great room. He looked like he hadn't suffered a single loss.

I walked deliberately ahead until I was at the foot of the stairs and looked up to Autus, expecting malice and loathing, but instead, a wicked smile spread that was so much worse.

"Bring it forward," he said. Two sentries came from behind us and sat a small wooden box on the steps between us. "Open it." He was absolutely thrilled with himself.

He watched our reactions carefully as the guard lifted the top of the box. I knew instantly what I was looking at. A fae heart. Rhogan's heart. My breath stalled, but I forced myself to remain calm and appear uninterested. "You've killed the rebel leader, then?"

Autus stood and walked down the steps. He pulled the bloody heart from the box and held it out to me. "This is a symbol. A message. Can you guess what that message is, Gaea?"

"No, my king."

"No?" he shouted, and she flinched. "I am untouchable. I am everlasting. What are the lives of a few lesser fae to me? Absolutely nothing." He was yelling so loud spit flew from his mouth, and his hands shook as he dug his bloodied fingers into the heart, ripped it in two, and threw the pieces across the room. The squelch of the splatter destroyed me. "I don't have time for rebels," he roared. "I have much bigger plans for this fucking world. Leave us."

"But Your Grace—" Eadas protested.

"Don't fucking start with me."

Eadas cowered, limped down from the dais, and scurried out of the room with Evin right behind him. I hoped his limp meant Rhogan fought until the end.

"I don't have time for bullshit or explanations. I need you two to complete a task for me, and I don't want you back in this fucking castle until it's done. Which means do it quickly."

"Tell us what must be done, and we will do it," Gaea said, unwavering as she stared straight ahead.

"Finally." He let out a long breath. "Someone that doesn't question a gods-damned thing."

Gaea and I exchanged a glance while the king's back was to us.

"I'm looking for something specific, and I believe only the two of you will have the ability to acquire it. I've heard a tale of an ancient flower. It's called the adda. Have you heard of it?" His voice was calmer as he turned to me.

The relief of a task and not death at his hands was so powerful I could hardly speak. I pinched the bridge of my nose, giving myself a second to recompose. "I know the legend of the flower and its description, but I did not know it still existed."

"I'm told by a prophetess the flower can be found in the Ruins of Durante." He turned to Gaea. "You're to take Temir to the ruins and help him locate the flower. Be hasty but thorough."

"Yes, my king," Gaea said, bowing.

Without another word, not even a dismissal, we walked out of that room, each step a reminder that we were the fortunate ones, even though death incarnate had his eyes upon us as we left.

"Something's up," Gaea whispered to me in the halls.

"Not here, not now. Gather whatever you need and meet me in my rooms as soon as you can."

"Twenty minutes?" She stepped closer and placed her hand on my arm.

I met her eyes for a brief second and pulled away, nodding. I rounded the corner toward my rooms, and my whole heart dropped into the pit of my stomach as the breath was yanked from my lungs. She was there. In the hallway. Her red hair was losing its shine. She looked to me, her face gaunt with deep violet circles below her eyes. Nadra was living in some kind of hell with the king. I moved close to her without control of my own body. Moving slowly, I pushed a sweet curl from her face, and as my finger touched her cool skin, she released a soft moan. Then, as if the moment hadn't happened at all, she looked away and hurried down the hall in the opposite direction while I stood, frozen.

The king had been trying, to no avail, to persuade her mother to join the wielders in his collection. Clearly it wasn't going well. Did she have no regard for how he took it out on her daughter? I'd have to find a way to save her when we returned.

Later, Gaea stood in my room while I gathered books from the study and put them in a pack I had put together. I dressed in several winter layers and a cloak made of fur. I tied an extra blanket to the bag and threw it over my shoulder. I had no idea what we were going to face, so I strapped a sword to my back and hoped Gaea had a better plan.

"Ready?" I asked.

"Damn, Tem. I thought we were picking flowers, not going to war."

"What was the last thing you heard about the ruins?"

"I haven't heard about them at all in recent years. I've never even been. We will have to travel for about half a day."

"Exactly."

She huffed. "If there is trouble, we'll just spirit away. You probably aren't going to need that thing." She pointed to the weapon.

"I hope not, but I won't get caught without it again," I said, remembering the sound of the lavrog's claws ripping the flesh from my bones. I held out my hand formally and saw the discomfort cross her face at my actions, but we were in a weird place now, and if nothing else, this was going to be a relationship-defining journey.

"Temir." She pushed my hand down and stepped close enough that her feline eyes stilled me. "It doesn't have to be like this. This is our chance. We could get River and go. They wouldn't even come looking for us for days, and by then we could be anywhere. Anywhere we dreamed."

I hadn't seen this coming, but I should have. I'd denied her this morning already. Had she asked me this months ago, I would have said yes in a heartbeat. I would have begged her for it. But now? Everything was different.

"I've said I would help the rebels, and I meant it. I have to see this through."

"But this is what you've wanted for so long. This is our chance."

I shook my head and watched her heart break in front of me while I felt mine crack in my own chest. "This is not the right time."

"This is exactly the right time." She shoved me. "The rebels will only get you killed. They are careless and dangerous, and they have giant targets on their backs."

"Exactly." I threw my hands in the air. "I have to help save them, and then I have to help them beat him. It's the only way, Gaea. If we don't take him down now, while he is weak, he will rule the world, and no one will be able to touch him."

"Fuck, Temir. Do you seriously think a bunch of untrained, rogue fae are going to be able to get to him? We need to go south. That's what we need to do. The south breeds warriors. They kill for sport. Northern fae fight to live while southern fae live to fight. That's where we need to be. You can start your own rebellion. Build a damn army and then kill him for all I care. But you can't do that here. You'll never win, Tem."

"Listen to what you're saying. If the south is full of warriors no one has seen in ages, do you honestly think some random fae, a lesser, is going to go down there and do anything?" I tilted my head down to show her my horns. "Don't forget what I am just because you've forgotten what you are."

She crossed her arms. "I am not lesser, Temir. I am different, but I'm not less than them. I never will be."

"Don't you think I know that? I hold you above everyone else in the whole damned world. You're the first thing I think about in the morning and the last thing I think about at night, Gaea. The king himself is less than you. But everything is broken now. There's a mountain between us, and don't tell me you don't feel it too."

She dropped her head. "I feel it. I'm the one who put it there."

I took a step forward, put my hand under her chin, and forced her to look in my eyes. "There will be other times to run. I know you're afraid. I know losing Oleo crippled you. But I also know there's a smart ass, lovable vixen hiding somewhere in there, and I hope someday she returns to me because that strong, relentless warrior would not back down from this fight."

She brought her hands up to my arms. "Maybe he's done it. Maybe he's already won. Maybe he knew taking Oleonis from us would shatter me so thoroughly I'd never be able to repair myself. And maybe he saw us together that night. At the ball. And realized if he broke me, he'd break you too."

"Perhaps he thought that's what would happen, but instead he lit a fire in my soul. I am not irreparably broken, but I am forever changed. I'll never be the male I was before, and maybe that's added to the space between us, but I won't go back. I'll never be his to command again. I have to do this, and I'm sorry if you can't understand it."

"I understand it. You were always the best of us all, Tem. You've always said your true nature was to heal, and I honestly believe that. But not just a single fae or even a group. I think you'll heal the world."

Without another word, she carried us away.

"A bit overdressed, aren't you, healer?" a voice from behind me asked.

I pivoted on the sandy beach and quickly counted heads.

"Do we have to leave?" one of the injured rebels asked, tilting her head back into the warmth of the sun.

"It is lovely, isn't it?" Gaea responded.

"I can't believe this place exists," the male whose leg I had healed said. "Clearly, we need to get out of the north."

"Trust me," she answered. "It's not all sunshine and soothing waves in the rest of the world. Are you all ready to go?"

"I'm ready," the male that had readily carried an ax said, stepping forward. "This is all beautiful, but it's unsettling to just sit around waiting. It's time to fight."

"Unfortunately, I didn't have enough time to fully restore my magic before I was called in by the king. I'll examine you all, do what's best, and Gaea here will take you one at a time to a spot near Bryer's Keep."

"Well, I'm fine, so I'll go first," said the female with the staff.

We worked our way down the line until I came to the female with the wing I had taped up. "I see you've taken off the bandage."

"Can you still heal them?" Her cracked lip quivered.

"Yes. Healing a wing does not take a great amount of magic." I smiled and placed a hand near the crease in her wing. She sucked in a breath between her teeth and I let my magic free, pushing through the tips until her shoulders dropped and she sighed in relief. "All done."

She flapped them back and forth, and a smile grew across her face. "Thank you, healer," she beamed.

Once Gaea had taken the whole crew, she placed her hand in my own. "Do you want to see them through, or do you want to head to the ruins?"

"Did you see that ax? I think they will be okay. Let's see if we can find this flower and then decide what to do."

"Can we talk about the flower?"

"Sure. It's called the adda. The flower itself looks like glass, like ice, but the leaves resemble flames. It's the stuff of legends though. I'm not even sure we can find it. I've heard of it and brought a few books, but even Oleo had never seen one. He told me about it ages ago, and that's the only reason I know of it."

"Don't you think it's odd that the king has us, two of his prized fae, hunting down something as ridiculous as a flower? I think he's planning something, Tem. Something bigger than anyone ever saw coming."

"I'm listening." I removed the heavy cloak before I started to sweat.

"Well, remember when I told you Autus made me take Thane on a hunt, but he wouldn't tell me what we were searching for? And then the business with Ragal and The Bog? And now we are hunting down a flower that's only heard in legends? Sounds like a recipe to me."

I remembered Oravan telling me about the sword he had demanded from him. I'd never thought to ask if he finished it before the rebellion took him and his family into hiding. I hadn't considered it might be for anything more than an ornament for a king during war.

"You're right. So, we find the flower but don't hand it over? Or we find a fake? I doubt the king knows what the flower physically looks like. It's a risk though. I can't be sure."

"Let's see if we can find the real flower, and while we journey, you see if you can remember or find anything in your books that might pass for it."

"Okay, let's go." I flung my heavy cloak back around me and lifted the deep hood until my face was completely hidden. Gaea did the same. The bite of the frozen air mixed with the sound of the whistling northern winds created an atmosphere that did not encourage small talk.

I considered what Gaea had said about healing the world and wondered if she knew the truth of my magic, if she would condemn me to annihilate it. Could I use my magic against the king, or was he too strong? Would the risk be worth finding out if I could stop a war? But then I also remembered the sea queen and knew I'd never be able to stop the war, even if I could defeat him. As long as the courts had the royals they did, this world was condemned whether by my hand or the king's hardened fist.

We trudged through the deep snows and quickly realized the blizzard whipping around us was going to not only slow us down but would be terrible through the night.

"Let's get as far as we can, head back to the beach to sleep for the night, and then spirit back in the morning. There's no point in trying to sleep out here in this," Gaea yelled over the rushing winds.

We kept going until we crested a hill. I tried to keep my face down as much as possible to keep the air from piercing my skin, but luckily, she was paying attention. She grabbed my arm and yanked me down, pointing to a small cottage in the valley below. A fire glowed from within, and we watched as two fae dressed in black circled the small house, looking into the old windows with weapons drawn.

Gaea drew her thumb across her neck and pointed again. I nodded slowly, and we crept down the hill. I wasn't certain who was in that little home, but they were about to be robbed at the very least. We got all the way to the cottage until the wind could no longer mask the screams from within.

"A child!" Gaea yelled.

She shot up and ran for the cabin, pulling her own hidden knife out as she slammed through the door and disappeared. I yanked my sword free and followed, hoping she hadn't just run right into a trap. As I entered the small home, I saw one male with his knife held to a child's neck and his arm around her mouth. Lesser fae. The child's mother, with buds of a stag's horns similar to my own, screamed and thrashed about as the other fae tried to hold her down.

"Get the fuck away from her," Gaea said to the male with the child.

"Only if you'll take her place, pretty kitty," the male said.

"Deal."

"Gaea," I warned.

"She's a child." Her voice was calm, low and dangerous.

The male holding the mother grunted as she made contact and jolted free of his grip long enough for me to rush forward and step between them. "Who are you?"

"Who the fuck are you, lesser?" he spat.

"I'm here on the king's order to take these females to the castle."

"Well, too bad he's not here to help ya." He pulled his own sword from a sheath strapped to his back.

I had hoped my lie would cause him to pause, but as he stepped forward, I realized he was a sea fae and threats of the king would do nothing to cause him fear. The sea fae believed themselves invincible in the northern kingdom because their queen had Autus by the balls. Or so they thought.

He slammed his sword into mine. I planted my feet ready to counter. The space was small. He swung his sword and I moved back, causing him to gouge the cracked wall with the tip of his blade.

"Just give me the child," Gaea said from behind me. "I promise you can have me instead." I heard her knife hit the floor and turned just in time for my opponent to swing and nearly take my arm off.

"Give me your word," the sea fae told Gaea.

"I promise," she said, sticking her hand out.

"Gaea, don't," I said as I continued to fight. I knew what she was doing, but if they thought I was worried about her, they might mistake her for easy prey. I hoped they did.

The mother continued to scream as the four of us filled her tiny home with lethal violence.

I jammed my foot into the thigh of the fae across from me at the same time as the other fae shoved the girl across the room and captured Gaea's hand. One moment he was smiling, the next, they were gone.

"Where the fuck did they go?" the one left shrieked.

"She took him to hell. Be sure to give him my regards." I jammed the tip of my sword through his stomach and lifted until he was nearly cut in half. He fell unceremoniously to the blood-soaked floor. For a moment, time stood still. I'd killed him. And though I searched for my essence to lash out at me for defying my true nature, there was nothing but silence. I slowly turned to the frightened female.

"Tian. Run," she screamed again, yanking her child toward the door. "I won't go with you, demon. I won't let my child near that monster."

Gaea popped back into the room, and though she panted, she was unscathed.

"I'm not here to take you to the king. Please," I lowered the sword. "I only said that hoping they would be scared off. I am like you. Do you see my horns?"

"The king has a stag fae working in his castle," she spat.

"Yes, that is me. But I'm also part of the rebellion. Have you heard of them? Do you know of Rook?"

She narrowed her eyes and evaluated me. She was a fierce female to be sure. "I've heard of the rebels. They've been around looking for males

278

to join them. They said I could join too, but we're safer here. Away from that."

"This is safe?" Gaea looked at the dead body bleeding all over the floor.

The child stepped forward. "We cannot travel safely. We tried, but it is just me and my mother."

"Tian, mind your tongue."

"I know you don't trust me, but I could take you to the rebels if you truly want to go there. You could pack only what you need and quickly," Gaea said.

She wouldn't join the rebellion, but she still believed in them. She would never take a child there if she didn't think they could keep her safe.

"Do you mean it?" the girl asked with doe eyes locked on Gaea.

"I do." Gaea smiled, her face tender and kind. Her love of children was greater than anything I'd ever witnessed. Perhaps she had acquired that from Oleonis.

"We won't go," the mother answered, pulling her child back. "You take your weapons and get out of my house."

"But Mama," the girl cried. "This is our chance to leave. Next time, what if no one is here to save us?"

"You let me worry about this, child. You don't know if these fae can be trusted. Never trust anyone. How many times have I told you?"

"Trust is fluid in Alewyn."

Everyone turned to see a strange old female standing at the door. She had long white hair and carried a staff with braided leather hanging from the top. Her face was wrinkled and her eyes were unnaturally large.

"Aibell!" The child crossed the room to her.

"*The* Aibell?" Gaea whispered, looking to me with her mouth gaping wide.

"Speak up, child of the wind," the old female snapped, slamming the bottom of her staff into the floorboards.

"A-are you really Aibell?"

"She really is." Tian looked to the older female as if she were a god.

"We have not called you, you may take no payment from me today," the mother said, voice shaking.

"You must leave, or you never will." She stared down the female, then moved closer to me. She walked carefully around me, judgement as heavy as her steps.

"Ah. There you are. In there," she said, tapping her staff to my chest. Gaea and I exchanged a glance, but no one moved. "You will lose all hope, but I remember, and so will you. Your magic is what you make it, Temir."

"I didn't realize I had lost myself," I snipped.

"Time is relative," she answered.

"What does that even mean? Who are you?"

"I am Aibell," she answered before disappearing.

Gaea looked as if she had seen a ghost. Her slackened jaw snapped shut, and she turned to the girl. "Do you know who that was?"

"Yes. That was Aibell," she said, giggling. "She has ponies, and I got to ride them with my friend Ara one time."

"Quiet, child. You may take us to your rebellion headquarters," her mother said.

"Is there anything you wish to take?" Gaea asked.

"There is nothing here for me anymore," she said. "I will dress, and we can go."

A short time later, I sat on a hard wooden chair, waiting for Gaea to return and considering the old female. She couldn't have been the Aibell from the nursery tales. She would have had to be ancient. But the child was so sure.

The cottage was nothing to be attached to, if not for the obvious memories it had provided the mother and her child. A layer of dust sat along the crooked shelves, furniture was sparse, and the only things holding most of it together were crooked nails and answered prayers. There were no photographs, no plants, not even a blanket on one of the two small beds in the single room. They had lived in this home, but only just.

I looked at the dead sea fae lying on the ground. He didn't deserve a funeral pyre, but I wasn't sure I could leave him here either. I considered trying to bury him, but the Wind Court ground was and always would be frozen solid. I dragged him outside instead to let the animals do what they would with him. Perhaps travelers could use the house for shelter.

"Always the chivalrous one, Temir," Gaea said, leaning against the door frame.

"Does it still count as chivalrous if I imagined his body being shredded to pieces while I moved him?"

"Yes." She smiled "Shall we go?"

"How much farther do you think we have?" I asked, looking out of the tiny broken window as I watched the layer of dust swirl in the draft seeping through.

"We could probably still get an hour in tonight, and then we should be there by mid-morning if the storm doesn't slow us down too much longer," she said, looking at me pointedly.

"Why are you looking at me like that?"

"You're slow."

"Your magic comes from the wind. It will never work against you. I, on the other hand, feel like I'm pushing against a mountain just to take a step. Believe me, I'm the normal one here."

"So you say." She walked out the door.

"Did we just have a normal conversation?"

"I think so." She placed her hand in mine, and the moment she touched me, the storm calmed. I could still see the snowfall and visibility was still limited, but I moved easier and the wind didn't bite into my skin.

"I knew you were cheating."

"Just come on, you big baby." She tugged my hand as she sped up.

CHAPTER
29

KING TOLERO

"Mother above, Your Grace. We've been searching for you everywhere," Inok called, yanking me from a dreamless sleep.

I moved and groaned.

"Yes, I suppose sleeping on the cold hard ground next to an animal would make for a sore morning. You're not a young boy anymore." He put his arm under mine and helped me to my feet.

"Thank you for the gentle reminder." I grunted as I stood.

"Long night?" he asked.

"You have no idea."

"Loti is a mess in the kitchens. She was worried sick when I showed up without you and no one found you in your bed."

"Best get down there and get that sorted out. It's sure to be a long day as it is."

"We've got a few hours until the start. Better get a bath as well." He pulled away from me.

282

"You first."

Though I knew it was hard, and likely he had been just as worried as Loti, he still smiled at me as we descended the steps and crossed the castle to the crowded kitchens.

"Well, by the gods," Loti said, jamming her hands onto her hips and pursing her lips. "Where in the heavens have you been? And don't give me that 'I'm a king' speech. I've been out of my mind. I had to prepare a feast for all the extra people, and all the while my heart was in my throat." She grabbed a cloth and dabbed her forehead for good measure.

"I'm sorry, Loti," I smirked.

"You wipe that smile off your face." She swatted me with her towel. "Sit down and eat before I have to wallop you."

Inok and I shared a look and promptly sat at the counter.

"Asha's back, Loti. Could you make sure she is fed?"

"You heard your king, get upstairs and feed that animal," she barked to her full staff.

"But what do we feed her, miss?" a young maid asked.

Loti jutted her chin forward in disbelief. "Asha is a cetani. Take her a goat."

"A full one?" another asked incredulously.

"Unless you'd like to chop it in half for her first?" she snapped.

"No, miss," the fae replied, curtseying, and rushing out of the kitchens.

"If you aren't going to be nicer to them, we'll have to find new help by the end of the Trials."

"Oh, aye," she agreed. "It's hard to find good help around here though, so good luck."

She was in a mood. I shoveled the eggs into my mouth and hoped I could get away before she tried to put me to work. Inok must have been thinking the same thing because he finished before I did. We set the dishes in the sink and just as we were about to leave, she caught me.

"I'll expect you for dinner, or would that be too much for an old female to ask?"

"I'm more than twice your age, old female. I'll be in the hall for dinner, I promise."

"See that you are." She shooed us out the door.

"The next time I cross paths with Morwena, remind me to bring Loti," I joked with Inok as we walked down the halls.

He stopped immediately and turned to me.

"What do you mean, the next time?" he asked.

"Oh right, I should probably get you caught up." I looked to the full hallways of fae bowing and otherwise avoiding me. I shook my head. "Not here, Inok. Best come to my rooms."

After telling Inok everything that had happened with Murtad, the tavern, and finally Morwena, it was safe to assume he'd never leave my side again, whether I ordered him to or not, but we carefully laid out a plan just in time to stop and see Brax before the Trials began.

"How do you feel?" I asked him as he swung a sword back and forth.

"I feel lucky, Your Grace. It's quite an honor to be chosen as your champion, especially since I don't work in the pits." He sheathed his sword.

"I've watched you grow from a boy, just as I watched my own son. You're a good lad, Brax. Just keep an eye on that right side of yours and leave your emotions out of it."

"Okay," he answered, hopping from foot to foot.

"Remember what I told you," Inok added. "You've been trained like a soldier, they've been trained like street fighters. They won't fight with honor, so don't expect that from them. You watched Greeve last time. Attoc's males are especially ruthless. Keep your eyes open. Even when you think they are down, they probably aren't."

"Got it."

"The first fighter will have naught but his upbringing for training. He will know how to fight, but not well enough to best you. He personally slighted your king, and you're there to teach him a lesson. Think you can handle that?"

He stopped his warmup and looked at me. "With pleasure."

"How have your mornings with Muth been?" I asked.

He just shook his head and laughed. "Fun."

"I'm glad to hear it. Good luck, Brax. You've got my whole vote today! You'll do well, son." I patted him on the shoulder. "I'm sure Fenlas hates that he can't be here."

"Probably not as much as Greeve." He smiled. "He'd be down here barking orders at me the whole time."

"And Kai would be taking bets," Inok laughed.

"They'll be home soon enough. It's time we let you go. Eyes open."

"You got it." He dipped his head before we walked away.

The amphitheater was a circular stadium with seats stacked several stories high lining the outside. I sat in front of the fighting pit atop a stage that stood at ground level along with several council members, including Inok. We all wore the traditional attire: lighter clothing for the females, exposing their midsections, and robes of all colors and prints for the males. Most were draped in jewelry, and even the crowd glistened from the sunlight. There was something about the tradition of it all that felt like home. It reminded me that after all of these many, many years, the land of faeries still honored something sacred.

"Did you find Umari?" I asked Inok, leaning to the side so my voice didn't carry.

"She knows the plan, Your Grace. She and the draconians will stay tonight in the castle and remain for the closing ceremony."

"We have to get through this day first," I whispered.

"Fortunately, Brax fights first. That should keep us on our toes."

"Indeed." I sat back in my chair until it was time to start.

"We are ready, Your Grace," a soldier called from the side of the arena.

I stood and walked to the edge of the stage. "Welcome," I called. The acoustics of the arena carried my voice like a song.

As one, the fae rose and took a knee, even the council behind me, and though I couldn't see the entirety of the crowd, hateful faces still greeted me.

Morwena had played her hand perfectly. My people outright hated me. They believed I killed for no reason, they believed I hated them, and they all believed I was the worst king to sit atop the flame throne. They knelt from fear alone. This couldn't go on much longer, or I would have rioting and assassination attempts.

"It is with honor and pride that I open the Trials of the Flame Court. Today we bring together the many fae of the south and celebrate as one. Today we honor what our fathers' fathers have left behind—a legacy. The Trials are a passageway into history for this kingdom. Some of the greatest fighters to emerge have been immortalized in our stories and our memories."

I took a step closer to the edge of the platform.

"Today I would ask a favor of my people. We have many new faces joining us from the north. Welcome them. In the south, we honor battling with skill and showing mercy. Fae life is precious. You will not witness death today."

I could see the uncomfortable movements in the crowd and only hoped I was right. All eyes were on me as I continued.

"The Trials are about more than bloodshed, more than carnage and killing. They symbolize our dedication as a kingdom to learning the skill and art form of different styles of combat. Let us begin."

"Hooh. Hooh. Hooh," the draconians called from the sky as they soared on the backs of the cetani and landed in the battlegrounds. The crowd stood and cheered as the beasts marched in circles around the draconians.

As one, they put on the most spectacular show, swinging their bos and flying through the air with dangerous acrobatics. Even I sat on the edge of my seat as one cetani took her rider and dropped him from the sky, just to soar below him and save him from death.

Umari landed in the ring and the crowd went still and silent. Her kohl-lined eyes searched the crowd as she performed. I knew they looked at her and saw Efi, their former queen. Just as I had done. It did not make her performance less powerful. If anything, there was excitement and passion building in the anxious crowd as she moved.

For the grand finale, she jumped onto the back of her cetani and soared straight up into the sky, letting loose a scream. Asha bolted in from the side and twirled higher and higher and then nosedived to the ground, landing on her feet, as cats do, just before impact. Asha pivoted to face me in the center of the pit and bowed low, and all the cetani followed. Then the draconians moved in front of the beasts and bowed as well.

"Today we honor you, Flame King," Umari announced.

Silence filled the air. No one clapped. No one moved. I doubted anyone took a breath. The tension was so strong it began to hum. Finally, Inok stood and clapped, and I joined him. Only a handful of the fae in the crowd did as well. From the looks of it, it was mostly the new northern fae—the refugees. Things were worse than I had anticipated.

Umari didn't skip a beat. She turned to the crowd and dipped again, and the spell was broken as they all cheered and screamed once more.

"How right you are to honor our king with silence," she yelled as she mounted her cetani and shot into the sky.

That wasn't what they had done at all, but she had planted the thought in their minds, and that was enough for me. Those that were not enchanted by Morwena would not question the silence, hopefully.

Up next were the fire dancers, who leaped through flames of colors, and for their finale, a faerie with fire magic created the illusion that the entire arena burst into indigo flames and a great phoenix soared from the ashes.

Slowly, I noticed the draconian fae slipping into the seats above. One by one, they moved in like anchors in the crowd. My hidden warriors.

Brax was announced, and he got mixed reactions from the gathered fae as he entered with his guard uniform on. Muth's announcer, however, was well received. I looked to Inok, but he didn't take his eyes off the pit. I didn't doubt Brax for a moment, especially against this poor excuse for a male.

The two circled each other before Brax leaped forward. The announcer yelped and jumped backward. The crowd laughed, and even Inok chuckled. Brax did not choose a weapon for this fight, but the announcer had, and for some reason that choice was a long sword that looked too heavy for him to lift. The lack of knowledge with a weapon could be just as fatal as a full education. Brax would still need to be careful.

The announcer groaned as he lifted the tip from the ground and thunked it back down as the hood of his plated armor slammed shut on him and left him blind. Again, the crowd laughed as he made an absolute fool of himself.

Brax shrugged, and while the announcer tried to lift the hood, he snagged away his sword, strolled across the arena, and handed it to me from below.

"Shall I go on?" he whispered as I took it from him.

"Just a bit longer," I snickered.

He walked back to his opponent and planted his heavy boot on his bottom until he fell over, headfirst into the ground. The crowd roared with laughter, and I could see even Brax biting back a laugh as he waited for the announcer to figure out how to stand in full armor. He flopped around like a fish and yelled until Brax grabbed his hands and pulled him to his feet.

He removed his obnoxious helmet and threw it across the opening, then lifted his fists and shuffled his feet. Brax smirked but mirrored the announcer, waiting for him to make a move. He jabbed a few times until Brax looked to me again for guidance. I gave a subtle nod, and he slammed his fist into the announcer's nose one time. One single time.

288

He cried out in pain and screamed for mercy. Brax took his bow, and the crowd he had won over cheered for him. He walked a bit taller as he exited the arena.

I had always liked that kid.

The rest of the day was full of tiers of pit fighters. Brax was right, they didn't seem to be as committed as they had been in years past. I'm sure it was hard to fight when you had been enchanted to hate the king you were to perform for. I doubted they cared much at all.

By the time we rose to join the feast, I was not only famished but stiff as a board. Sleeping on the hard floor next to Asha had not been my brightest idea.

The long banquet table waiting in the hall had been decorated with tall billowing flowers and hundreds of wine glasses. The fae in the room lined the table and talked amongst themselves in soft whispers. I pulled my chair in and they followed, taking their seats and digging into the feast Loti and her staff had prepared. I held a drumstick of meat in my hands and a spoonful of potatoes was halfway to my mouth when Umari caught my attention from along the wall. She tilted her head toward the door, and I knew she meant for me to follow.

I nudged Inok under the table, giving him the signal.

"My king," he called out. A little louder than necessary, but I never pegged him for an actor. "Are you well?"

"I'm afraid I must take my leave. My head is aching from the heat of the day. Please, enjoy yourselves."

I stood, as did the faerie court. They may hate me, but they still followed the rules of propriety. I leaned over to Inok and whispered in his ear, "I better have three full plates of food in my rooms by the time I get there or I'm firing the cook."

He nodded, trying to bite back his smirk. My love of food had never left me, but he knew I'd never fire Loti.

CHAPTER
30

ARA

"Holy. Shit," Wren said from beside me.

She was invisible, and I had my dark cloak pulled up, hoping the shadows hid me well enough.

"Well, good news and bad news," Kai whispered. "The good news is I don't think The Mists are the reason fae never return. Bad news is I'm, like, ninety-nine percent sure it's the dragons."

I could hear Lichen's small whimper from behind us as Fen laid a firm hand on the small of my back. We had crossed a boundary during that magic lesson. I just didn't have time right now to process what that meant.

"Let's get back to camp and make a plan," he said.

I couldn't move as I watched the substantial number of scaled creatures fill the entire expanse of the Western Gap. The jagged, snowcapped mountains to each side looked like peaked hills to the creatures. Large billowy clouds filled the sky and yet were infinitesimal in comparison. The air was filled with the mephitic fumes of sulfur, and as the beasts crawled around, shifting their powerful wings, I stared into the bloodshot eyes of the one closest to us. It was too dark to determine color or quantity, but I had no idea if dragons were nocturnal. If they weren't, it was possible they already knew we were there.

I crept slowly backward, keeping my body pressed firmly into Fen's as we moved. Once we were back to our camp, a small cave inside the mountain range we had been following, I walked away from the group, moving farther into the cave than everyone else. Where the moonlight wouldn't reveal the fear blossoming over me.

"Ara," Fen whispered behind me.

He grabbed me and forced me to turn to him, yanking me into his arms and holding me firmly. I wanted to push away. I wanted to reestablish that boundary. But I was terrified. Not to die. Not to fight dragons, but to be responsible for one more person's death. I buried my face in his chest, and he didn't say a word, only held me and waited until I was ready. Something my father would have done. I could still feel my mother's concerned eyes watching me as I held him, though.

"I can't let any of you go any farther," I whispered. "I can't be the reason any of you die."

"You don't get to decide that. I won't let you cross that gap alone. You know that. We can figure this out together."

"We made a deal, Fen. If I said you couldn't come any farther, you couldn't."

He moved until I was pressed up against the wall, then lifted my chin and kissed me so gently it was like a whisper.

"What if they die? What if you die?"

"Draconians don't fear," he answered, leaning down to look into my terrified eyes.

"Fae do."

"Do you want to turn around? We could walk back down the mountain range, cross the other gap, and come back on the other side."

"You would do that?" I asked.

He brought his forehead to mine so I could just see the outline of his face in the dark. "I would move this mountain one rock at a time for you, Ara. I would slay a thousand dragons. I would travel to The Mists a hundred times. Whatever you wish of me, I will do it, as long as you don't ask me to let you go alone."

"Okay, Prince." I held him tightly. "Let's go make a plan."

"Five more minutes," he protested, kissing the tops of my sensitive ears.

"So, I guess science is out the window?"

"Was it ever really there?" He ran his hands down my arms, and I stood, stunned. "Have I ever told you about what happened the first time I saw you?" He leaned in and kissed my neck. My very sensitive neck.

"You might have mentioned something vague about a sea queen and a rage-filled prince."

"You enthralled me the moment I laid eyes on you. I spent my whole life wondering what you would be like, what you would look like, but never in a million lifetimes did I think you would be as beautiful as you were the day you turned around and walked out of that ballroom, straight toward me."

"Did you know?" I asked. "Did you know it would be like this between us?"

"I had hoped for it. But then I thought I'd screwed all of it up trying to protect you. When you were in Aibell's cottage and wouldn't wake up, I didn't sleep at all. Kai and Greeve had to get me roaring drunk just so I didn't lose myself in that rage. You were so beautiful and I assumed delicate. I thought for sure I'd lost you before I even had you."

"And when you saw me in the tavern?"

"I thought I felt you there the night before, but I couldn't be sure. But the next night, when you were barely dressed and sitting at that table, I could have killed every male there who wouldn't take their eyes from you."

He shifted, brushing his fingers down my cheek.

292

"When we watched you punch that male and drag your friend out, that was it for me. That was the night you won Kai and Greeve over. They had watched that asshole bring female after female into the tavern, get them drunk and haul them home. The moment you took the proper stance and clocked him, I had to convince Kai he wasn't actually in love with you."

"Your five minutes are up, Prince. Are you trying to distract me right now?"

"Is it working?" he asked, moving his hands gently down my body.

"Nearly," I whispered. "Come on. We have a horde of dragons to slay, Prince Overwhelming."

"How many nicknames do you have for me?" he chuckled.

"Get me past those dragons and I'll tell you the first one."

"Let me guess. Prince Asshole?" Kai asked as we joined the others.

I smiled as we sat down. "No, but close."

"What's the plan?" Greeve asked, getting right down to business.

"We thought we should work on the plan as a team," Fen said, saving me from showing how worried I was.

"Well, obviously we can't go through the Western Gap," Lichen said.

"What do you know about dragons?" Fen asked him.

"Surprisingly, not much. Dragons haven't been around since before the Iron Wars. We didn't have to deal with them much in the south. I know they will capture you long before they eat you. They prefer to play with their food first which is why you can't make a bargain with them. Ever."

"That's not helpful." Wren shook her head and let out a long-measured breath.

"We aren't actually considering going through," Lichen asked.

"It's best if we do," Fen answered. "If we find dragons here, who knows what we'll find on the other side of the mountain. They do fly, after all, which means we may run into them either way."

"Okay, so what if I take each person through using my magic?" Wren offered.

"I think we would be going too slow," Fen said. "We're better off using Greeve's magic and he can take us to the other side one at a time. If we go fast enough, they won't see us at all."

"Can you manage that?" I asked.

"I can." He stood strong. No fear.

"So, the order?" Lichen asked.

"Ara first, to make sure she makes it through. Then me, so I can stand guard. Then Wren, Kai and Lichen last."

"Why should I be last?"

"Because if there are any kinks, we will work it out in the first few passes. That way you can come straight through with no problems."

"I think Wren should go first, then me, and so on," I said.

"Ara, no. I'll be fine. I can keep Lichen and I invisible while we wait for our turn."

I didn't like leaving her behind, but there was no point in arguing if we were all going to the same place anyway. "Okay. Do we go tonight or in the morning?"

"I think it's best if we stay here for the night and wake early to get through the Western Gap and to The Mists by nightfall tomorrow," Fen answered.

"I'll take the first watch," I offered.

"Let me take it," Greeve said. "You've had watch duty for the last two nights."

"But what if I have that nightmare again?"

"Maybe if you told us about the nightmare, it would help," Lichen said, getting his notepad out.

"Do you think?" I looked at Fen

He shrugged. "Couldn't hurt."

I took a deep breath. "It started the day I opened Nealla's book. I had to read it though. I needed to figure out how to find her."

"What happens in the dream?"

"I'm standing in a field, but the grass turns to snakes and they are biting my legs, then they change to blades and begin to shred my skin. I run through the field until I get to a cliff. A wind shoves into me, knocking me into the sea, where I drown until the water becomes flame and I'm burned to nothing but ash."

"Well, that sounds terrible," Kai said. "My nightmares are about running out of food."

Fen slugged him in the shoulder. "Any ideas?" he asked Lichen.

"Yes, actually. I'd wager it's your magic calling to you."

"So, you do think I have some?"

"It would make sense," he answered.

"But we've tried everything, and I can't get to it."

"Perhaps it just isn't time yet," he said, closing his notebook.

"Maybe now that you know what it is, it won't happen."

I didn't mention that the nightmares didn't happen when Fen was touching me. I wondered if he had figured it out though. Because he always took watch when I did and always slept right beside me.

"Let's get to sleep," Fen said. "Tomorrow looks to be a very long day."

I laid out my blanket and covered myself with my cloak, closing off the cold in the air. Fen laid his out beside me, but within minutes, he was under my cloak and throwing his blanket over the top of us. He had done his best to filter his magic, slowly keeping us all warm as we traveled, but each day he grew more tired, his eyes more wary. I snuggled in close to him and felt his warm breath caress my neck, the sensation trickling down my spine as he yawned. Keeping us warm was draining him. He slept so soundly when he could and never seemed fully rested in the morning. I was sure when this was all over with, he'd need to sleep for days. Apparently, that's how magic worked.

"Are you okay?" I whispered to him.

"Just tired." He yawned.

He wrapped himself around me, and within minutes his breathing had slowed. I could hear my mother's voice warning me. I shouldn't trust anyone. We had come leaps and bounds from that first day in the forest, but the rush of feelings? I wasn't ready. I never wanted to be mated, but I hadn't thought I wanted to fall in love either. Still, Fen was starting to feel like home. And it wasn't just him. It was all of them. They had grown on me.

I woke to Kai shaking us.

"Time to go," he said, ever the chipper fae.

I rotated in Fen's arms and trailed a finger down his ear until he smiled and opened his eyes. Our noses were nearly touching, and he pulled me in closer.

"Good morning, beautiful Ara," he said.

"Good morning, Princey Poo. Time to go slay those dragons for me."

"Lead the way, Princess."

We walked through the plan one more time and stood together as a group watching the dragons for longer than I think any of us had planned. Saying we were going to just easily travel through them was a lot more difficult than actually doing it.

Eventually, Greeve came up behind me. "Ready?"

Fen squeezed my hand. "Wait. Maybe I should go first. Just in case it doesn't work out the way we think it will."

"Honestly, Fen. Ara could kick your ass. If anyone is going to slay a dragon today, it's going to be her," Kai said.

"And besides," Wren added. "You have to take over an entire kingdom one day. It's not like your life isn't important also."

He nodded but yanked me into his arms for one last hug. I could feel his desperate heartbeat before Greeve grabbed my hand and cleaved me away. I closed my eyes and wished for it all to be over as soon as possible. The wind was disorientating, and I didn't particularly care for this means of travel, other than it was fast and hopefully undetectable to the winged beasts.

296

We landed on the opposite side of the horde in a small crevice in the mountainside. Nestled within the walls, I couldn't see a thing happening outside.

Greeve didn't take a moment to catch his breath. He ordered me to pull out a weapon and, in an instant, was gone.

I couldn't see the horde from where I was, but a few circled above, filling the sky. I tried to stay hidden, pressed up against the rocks, while I held my breath and waited for Fenlas. When he arrived, he pulled his sword, nodded to Greeve, and didn't say a word as he turned and blocked the outside view. Again, Greeve disappeared and we waited. I thought he'd turn to me. Reach for me. Something. But instead, he watched the opening as if his life depended on it. His friends were like family, so not being able to help protect them must have been so hard on him.

An eternity passed. And then another. And when I felt Fen's panic, I knew something was wrong.

"Where is he?" I whispered.

"Something's happened. He would be back by now."

I reached for his hand. "Let's give him a bit more time. Maybe he had to wait to get through."

He nodded, but I could feel his hesitation. We waited even longer, but after an hour had passed, it was obvious something had gone wrong.

"I'm going to have to go get him." Fen clutched the back of his neck, muscles strained.

"What's our plan?" I asked.

After several moments of careful silence, he looked at me, took my sword and set it with his against the wall, then took both of my hands into his, leaned his forehead against mine and closed his eyes. "I won't pretend the thought of you in danger doesn't terrify me too. Just promise me you'll be careful."

"I will be."

"We'll have to get out of this crack and around the corner before we can make a real plan. I'll use magic to keep our scent hidden. Whatever you do, Ara, do not make a bargain with them. No matter what they promise, it will never be worth it."

"Fen, I'll be fine."

We grabbed our weapons, and he carried his in front of him as I strapped mine to my back.

"You might want to keep that out."

"What's a sword going to do against one of those things? I bet it wouldn't even penetrate their scales. We're going to have to be a lot more creative than that."

He let out a deep breath but kept his weapon in front of him as we inched ourselves around the wall.

"Watch out for those guys." I pointed to the airborne ones.

He nodded, and we continued at a snail's pace while taking everything in. It looked similar to the other side of the gap, only this side had one massive green-and-blue-marbled beast sleeping with his long, spiked tail wrapped around him. With each snore, he exhaled a plume of smoke that filled the air above him. Beyond him were several more reptilian bodies. The head of the sleeping dragon would have taken me several minutes just to walk around quietly.

I could feel the steady air moving around us as Fen used his wind magic to create a seal of our scents and any accidental sounds. We crept forward, trying to hide behind the southern wall as we moved. We came around the curve, and I saw them instantly: Kai was pinned to the ground with a dragon's sharp talon holding him and Greeve was trapped by another. I surged forward. I didn't have a plan, but they had minutes until they were lunch.

"Ara!" Fen snapped from behind me.

I was filled with a foreign rage. I looked back to the prince only long enough to see the murderous glare on his handsome face.

"Ara, no," Greeve called. "They have magic."

Still, I thought if I could distract the beast holding Kai down, he could pull himself free long enough to make it to Greeve, who could then cleave them through the Gap while Fen and I ran behind them. But I was wrong. So wrong.

I hadn't noticed that Greeve was cuffed until I was closer to them. The moment I could reach Kai, the dragon holding him down took in a deep breath, turned to me, and exhaled just as Fen threw himself and his magic in front of me to shield us both. He was furious, wouldn't even look at me, but still, he saved my ass. I got up, and we ran toward Greeve.

"I'm cuffed. I can't touch my magic."

Four treats, a voice hissed.

I slowly turned to see a giant yellow snout inches from my face.

Fen reached for my hand, but before he could pull me away, cuffs identical to Greeve's locked around his wrists. He gasped, and I knew the void from his magic had hollowed him.

A cage appeared around the three of us, and we watched in horror as Kai remained pinned to the ground. The dragon dug his claw into his shoulder, and he screamed in agony as we all held onto the metal bars and watched his ruthless torture. Without Fen's magic, the temperature dropped, and if we stayed here long, we'd freeze to death. Fire-breathing dragons or not.

"Now would be the time to access your magic," Fen breathed into my ear.

"Why didn't they cuff me?" I whispered back.

"Because you haven't given them a reason to."

I nodded, closed my eyes, and tried like hell to push my magic forward. I envisioned it coming from my core and out of my fingertips. I imagined the heat from the dragon's breath as my own as I pushed and pushed.

"That's it," he said, stepping in front of me.

I could feel something in my palms, and I knew I was on the cusp of drawing it forward. It was right there. But the moment Kai screamed again, I lost my focus and it slipped away. We were officially trapped with no means of escape.

"Damn it," he bit out and paced like a tiger watching its prey. The gate flew open, and before we could even get to the door, Kai was violently dragged across the ground by invisible hands and thrown in with us.

What are you? the dragon said into my mind. *You do not smell like the others. You are different. Worldly. Will you come to me on your own? Be my pet if I let your friends go? I think I'd like to keep you, strange one.*

I looked at Kai writhing on the ground, Fen pacing like a wild beast, and Greeve rigid and still. I could save them.

CHAPTER

31

NADRA

ould our minds be broken? I thought they could. He looked at me today. The one with the horns. He always did that. But I didn't want him. I wanted my king. I needed my king. He wouldn't love me though. Not yet. My mother was to join him, but she would not, and I wasn't allowed to ask her. He said he would continue to punish me if I did. He let me touch his arm yesterday. I was supposed to like it, but it was nothing. Just like me. I'd bathed in despair and found solace in my own familiar nightmares. He told me of his plans. He knew I'd take his secrets to my grave. The shallow grave I'd already dug in my broken mind.

CHAPTER

32

TEMIR

*A*fter traveling as far as we could through the tundra of Alewyn, Gaea and I headed back to the comfort of the tropical island. I had my books spread around me in a circle as Gaea wandered deeper into the island looking for food. Somehow, I'd found peace with where we were. We had both laid everything bare, and now we could only grow. She no longer distracted me from living, and I hoped, if nothing else, we could form a friendship.

I caught her watching me a few times, but that pull to her was no longer there. I knew she felt it too, and I think we both found comfort in the possibility of friendship. The pressure was gone.

"Find anything?" She picked up a book and set it to the side so she could sit beside me.

"Nothing yet, but you know, I've been thinking."

"Nothing new there." She handed me a bright green fruit. "I don't see what's so special about a flower anyway."

"This isn't just any flower. It's the adda. It's like the king has asked us to capture a star from the heavens. Things that are so rare are always powerful, Gaea. I think the king needs that flower for something terrible, and that means it's not going to be something we will easily find. It also means we need to start trying to figure out what he's doing."

"We know what he is doing. He's trying to conquer the world by whatever means he can."

I took a bite of the bitter fruit. "Aren't you curious to find out what it is?"

"Not really. You've always been the bookworm and I've always taken a hands-on approach. Let's just focus on trying to find something to fool him with, destroying the adda so he can't use it and figuring out what our plan is from there. You have the rebellion, but I don't know where that leaves me."

"You could have the rebellion too," I offered.

She shook her head. "Have you told them? About the truth serum?"

"Not yet. I don't have enough made for it to be very useful to them. I'm committed to helping them, but I need more time."

"So, you don't trust them?"

"I trust them. I just want to be sure the serum doesn't fall into the wrong hands."

"So, you don't trust them." A smile lit her eyes.

"I don't trust them the same way I trust you. Let's leave it at that for now."

The hollowness from my magic and the exhaustion from the long day creeped up on me as I tried to read in the silver moonlight, and the words moved around on the page until they were utter nonsense. I laid my book down, covered myself with my cloak, and rested my head on my pack beside Gaea, who was already asleep.

I was almost to sleep when I got an overwhelming feeling that someone was watching me. I opened an eye and scanned the shoreline. Empty. I rolled over and nearly jumped out of my skin when I saw the old female, Aibell, standing in the distance staring me down. She held out a hand and crooked a finger for me to come to her. I put my cloak over Gaea and walked across the white sand beach to where she stood.

"What do you see, boy?" she asked, gesturing to the ocean.

"Why are you here? Who are you really?"

"You know who I am, and I'm here to help you. What do you see?" She was abrupt, jamming her bony hand on her hip as she leaned into me, waiting for the obvious answer.

"Water."

"And who commands the water? What lives within?"

"Morwena and her sea creatures," I answered.

"She watches you even now with eyes that aren't her own. This isle is not safe for secrets."

"How do you know?" I asked, dropping my chin.

"Always the scholar." She clicked her tongue. "Clouded vials clear with time and it's my business to know. Now listen, winter child, there is a glassmaker in the Marsh Court. His name is Alavon. You must find the Weaver. She will show you the way. The glassmaker is who you must seek to replicate the flower. You'll find nothing in those books to help you now, Temir."

I swayed backward, raising my voice. "How do you know about the adda?"

"For being a male of reasonable intelligence, you are not very bright. Do as I've told you. And one more thing? You must let her go." She looked to Gaea and back to me. "She belongs to another."

I felt a pain at those words and turned to the female sleeping where I'd left her. I looked back to the old one, but she was already gone.

"Gaea." I rested my hand on her shoulder and shook. "Gaea, wake up. We cannot stay here."

She jerked herself into an upright position and searched all around me for immediate danger. She paused and shook her head. "There's nothing, Tem."

Without warning, an overwhelming wave of deep sadness consumed me, and I could not explain it. I rocked back on my feet and had to push away the baffling feeling so we could get to safety. "The old female came back. She said this island is being watched by the queen and is not safe. We need to get to the rebel headquarters."

She pursed her lips for several seconds, her mind racing. "Why would we go there?"

"I need some information on someone, and I think the leader there might know who it is. You won't have to come in. They won't even have to know you are there."

"Should we get the flower first? Then go to the rebellion?"

I thought about it for a few moments and nodded. "You're right. Let's see this done and then try to finish quickly with the rebellion before the king grows suspicious. Perhaps we should go back to the cottage, stay for the night, and then continue from there."

"Better get your warm clothes back on." She yawned.

I looked down and realized I'd slipped out of my boots and taken two layers off. "Right."

We spent the rest of the night in the drafty cottage with the wind whistling and blowing through. I did my best to sleep, knowing I needed to regenerate magic, but Gaea, on the other hand, stayed up and kept watch by the door. I'd offered to do it, but she knew I needed rest.

We were on our way the next morning, and just as she thought, we made it to the ruins in a few hours. The moment we crossed the broken stone archway, the wind died and everything was silent. Gaea and I exchanged a glance, and she pushed me forward.

They were ruins for a reason. The scattered stone pillars and buildings were hardly more than broken stones holding each other up by fate alone. No snow fell within the barrier, and though it was freezing cold, the ground was covered in hundreds of species of spring flowers that spread across the ground and crawled up the broken statues. The stone was nearly dust, as if it might disintegrate when touched, but the air smelled like spring in the Marsh Court.

"I wish he was here," Gaea said beside me. "Do you think he knew this existed?"

"I'm sure Oleonis knew of the ruins, but I'm not sure anyone would have guessed the flowers would be here. No one travels this far northwest because of the weather."

"Are any of these the adda?" she asked.

"I don't think so."

There was a single leaning building we could walk into, but it was dark, and if ever there was a place that gave off a danger signal, it was there. The entire thing was made of perfectly carved stones, and if one fell, the whole thing would. Still, we walked carefully inside. The air was stagnant, but somehow, an eerie glow allowed us to see through the darkness.

"Where is the light coming from?" I asked.

"Temir, look at the walls." She ran her delicate fingers through the deep grooves and dangerous cracks, pulling the thick dust away.

"Be careful what you touch. This whole place could come down."

"Do you think they mean anything?"

"I'm sure they do, but I wouldn't know how to read them."

"They are pictures. Look, this is a tree and that is a fire."

"Perhaps it tells a story." I leaned in for a closer look. "Maybe it will tell us what the king is doing. Maybe the adda's power is etched in the walls, Gaea. Stay here and see if you can make anything of it while I go below." I pointed to the door on the floor.

"Are you sure?"

"I'll be fine." I pulled out my sword. "I'll try to hurry."

I edged down the stone steps leading into the expanse below the shoddy building, knowing I needed to hurry before the entire thing collapsed on top of me. The ground was made of compacted dirt and smelled of rot. A glow illuminated everything in the ramshackle building with no obvious source.

I followed the narrow walkway until I entered a small room with similar etchings on the damp wall. The intricate marks were worn farther down than the ones Gaea had found above. Barely legible. But the ground was again covered like a mossy garden, and I had to kneel to sift through the aromatic plants. I worked my way through the room until I got to the corner at the far back wall and pushed aside a thorny bush of sapphire lilies. There, below the long blades of grass that had grown with no sunlight, was the loveliest flower I had ever seen. I reached my hand forward to touch the delicate petals, but a masculine voice stopped me.

"You may have it," a deep voice said from behind me.

I nearly hit the ceiling in surprise as I whipped around to see an ethereal being standing in the doorway, glowing with the soft light from the rest of the room. His haggard face held centuries of treasured wisdom, and though his colorless eyes were kind, they were also stern.

I sucked in a breath. "Who are you?"

"I am the keeper." He swept a translucent hand around the room. "This is my garden. You've taken such care not to trample, I thank you. The last soul who dared enter was not so fortunate."

"The northern king has asked for me to deliver this to him. What say you to that?"

"I would ask you not to." He drifted forward. "That flower has powerful, powerful magic. I have raised it, and now you must protect it, as I cannot."

"What kind of power?" Standing, I moved away from him.

"It is a piece of a puzzle. A formula. Once the puzzle is complete, even the world cannot save you. You must guard it."

"I will do my best." I put the sword in my hand away.

"You must do better than that," he answered before vanishing.

I reached down, and as my fingers connected with the glass-like leaves, I felt a surge of ancient magic course through me. I had not slept well enough to regenerate all of my power, but as soon as I pulled my hand away, I was full of healing magic and my heart raced. I pulled the sturdy flower from its roots and felt a dip in the vibration of magic and pushed a bit of healing into the stems to try to keep them strong.

"Run, Temir," I heard the voice of the ghost echo in my mind as the unsteady ground shook.

I bolted down the hallway, and the stones crumbled as Gaea screamed. I took the stairs two at a time and frantically searched the room above. The walls were caving in. She was pinned below half of the collapsed ceiling. I put the flower in my bag and ran to her, pushing and pulling the stone until it gave way enough for her to slide herself out.

I threw her over my shoulder and ran for the exit as the rest of the building caved in.

"Keep going," she screamed.

I ran until we were outside of the eerie magical ruins, which were now being sucked into the ground. The building was demolished, and even the flowers, vibrant and thriving moments ago, began to wilt as the cold air sucked the life from them. Whatever magic that kept the place protected was gone. I sat Gaea down as carefully as I could and immediately called my magic forward as I placed my hand on her forehead and forced her to sleep, knowing this was going to hurt like hell. She had several broken bones, had sliced into an artery, and from what I could see there was also extensive nerve damage.

I closed my eyes and worked as fast as I could, guiding my magic through her body. The old female may have said she belonged to another, but she would always also be mine. Maybe not in the way we had both hoped, but my devotion to her would never falter.

Once I was done, I sat, knees to my chest, waiting for her to wake. I didn't risk bringing the treasured flower out of my pack, so instead, I opened it to look inside. It was exactly as I had heard it would be. Like fire coated in ice. But there was no coolness or heat when I touched it— only that commanding vibration of power that once again replenished what I had used to heal Gaea. With this, I could heal the world and never deplete my stores. The king couldn't pay me enough to hand this over. I could only imagine what he would do with such a thing. And it wouldn't be good.

"Did you find it?" Gaea asked, sitting up. Her tattered clothing was soaked in her own blood. The color had returned to her cheeks though.

"I did. Are you okay?" I moved to help her stand.

"I'm much better now. Thank you, Tem." She wiped her hands on her torn shirt.

"Did you decipher anything from the hieroglyphics?"

"Not a thing." She rubbed her head. "Just some random symbols. That's it."

"Let's get out of here. Something about this place rattles me."

"Could it be the literal quake that just wiped out the ruins?"

"Could be." I smiled. "Let's get to the Keep so I can figure out what our next move is."

We landed in typical scenery for the Wind Court: snow-covered grounds with scattered trees and the promise of something far in the distance to break the wind. She pointed to a phoenix symbol carved into a nearby tree. Finding another, we followed them until we reached a broken cart sitting back in a tree line some distance away from the actual keep.

"Something I can help you with?" a male with the nose of a hound asked crawling out of the cart.

"I'm here to see Rook," I answered.

He looked to Gaea and back to me. "Never heard of him."

"You move headquarters knowing hundreds of rebels don't have a clue where to go, and you refuse to let them in, even though I've given you the leader's name? Not really welcoming for the fae we are out there trying to recruit."

"Don't know what you mean." He took a sharp bite out of an apple and leaned a shoulder against the side of the broken cart. "Care to help me with this broken wheel?"

I slowly nodded, hoping he'd give me more information.

"She okay?" he whispered, pointing to Gaea's ripped and bloody pants.

"She's fine."

"No, I mean she's not forcing you here by the king's orders, right healer?"

"Oh, no. She isn't. She will not be going in either." I turned to her. "Could you meet me back here in say twenty minutes?"

"Happily," she said sharply and spirited away. I hoped she didn't go to the island, but if I knew her the way I thought I did, she was going to check on River.

"This way," the male said, moving into the tree line. He shifted a large branch and revealed a hidden door in the ground.

"Why does everything have to be underground?" I mumbled.

"Hard to find?" He shrugged.

The door creaked as I pulled it open and walked down the narrow galley of stairs.

At the bottom, a sentry stood watch with several weapons. "Name?" His detached voice was a replica of his impassive face.

"Temir."

He finally lifted his eyes to take me in as he stumbled backward. "Come with me. Rook's been waiting on you." He led me through the rebel's new headquarters, and though it was quite a bit smaller, it was a far cry from a cave in the ground. The walls were plain flat stone, there was proper lighting with individual meeting rooms, and I believed we passed a few bedrooms as we walked. Even though we were underground, the air was crisp and clean, and I would have never guessed this was beyond a door covered with a dead branch.

"Temir." Rook stood from behind an empty desk and held his hand out for me. The room was bare aside from the single piece of furniture, but it was clean. I grasped his forearm in greeting and took the seat opposite of him.

"Rhogan?" he asked.

I shook my head.

"Damn it." He bowed his head, a brief pause the only mourning I would see from him. "I have a mission for you, Temir, if you can manage it."

"I've got my own mission, right now. Maybe we can help each other out. Tell me what you need."

"There's word that soldiers are storming Volos in two days. I need to send someone I can trust with them, willing to try to protect the city."

"That's on the other side of the kingdom. They would have had to leave days ago to get there in time."

"They are already gone, but they do not have a leader. With the loss of Rhogan, I need someone there calling the shots. Can you make it work?"

I ran my hands through my hair and felt the rough texture of my growing horns. I closed my eyes and tried to figure out how I could do it all. "I will do everything in my power to meet them, but I can't travel with them. I have to find someone called the Weaver in the Marsh Court."

"She's one of ours. What do you need her for?"

"It's complicated," I answered. "The only reason I was able to leave the castle is because the king sent me on a mission."

"She won't do a thing for the northern king, Temir."

"It's not for him. It's to help me trick him."

"She lives in Hythe. She is called the Weaver because she owns a basket shop there. Tell her I sent you and she will help."

"Thanks, Rook. I'll do what I can to meet the rebels outside of Volos."

I left the new headquarters in the same manner I had come, and Gaea appeared not long after. "Can you get us to Hythe?" I asked as soon as we were far enough away from the fae in the cart.

"Yes. I've been there. Autus made me travel all the way down the King's Road. That's what they call it in the Marsh Court. Take my hand."

We spirited away, and I envied Gaea's magic. "Thank you, Gaea." I kept her hand in mine after we arrived. "I'd be lost right now without you."

She bumped her shoulder into mine. "Glad you finally noticed."

"Are you hungry? We could eat before we hunt down the Weaver. We've got to go through the shops here anyway."

"I'm famished," she said, pulling me into town. We had lunch in a rugged tavern and then walked the main road until Gaea spotted the shop. "Is that it?" she asked, pointing to a shop with glass windows and baskets and ropes hanging from the ceiling.

"The Weaver's Inn," I read on the carved sign. "Let's go."

The soft sound of a bell filled the store as it clanged against the heavy opening door. Gaea searched through the scattered wares—baskets perfectly aligned on shelves and different woven ropes hung from the low ceiling—as we waited for someone to assist us. Within minutes, a naga slithered out from the back of the store. Her dark kohl-ringed eyes matched her curly hair as they watched us. She moved behind the counter.

I pulled a small piece of paper from my pocket, unfolded it, and laid it on the counter. The Weaver looked at the phoenix symbol for less than a second and then stared blankly at me.

"I seek Alavon," I whispered. She stared at me, the depth of her hard eyes showing that she would reveal nothing. I leaned across the counter and whispered, "Rook sent me."

She kept silent, tilting her head toward the back of her store. She moved and we followed, stepping between the piles of baskets and ducking so my horns did not get stuck in the low-hanging net. The Weaver slid a long hanging tapestry to the side and stepped behind it.

In a small room in the back of her craft shop, covered with sharpened hooks, half-finished ropes, melted candles and spools of twine, we waited while she searched behind books and under tools. "Here." She handed me a small map and pointed to a building just outside of town. "Follow this road, turn at the dead end. You'll find a farmhouse with a large barn. If you knock, he will not answer. See yourself in, climb the ladder to the loft and speak to his mate. She will assist you from there. He will not know of Rook. You'll need to speak my name to get any assistance from them."

"Thank you."

She thumped her fist to her chest and dipped her chin. "I wish you luck." She held the tapestry aside so we could leave.

"At least your rebels are taking their secrecy more seriously," Gaea laughed as she walked to the barn the Weaver had sent us to. "That one was creepy though."

I couldn't help but smile because that sound, her laugh, was so beautiful. "Shall we?" I asked, stepping toward the barn.

She took my hand. "Together."

We walked into the barn and stopped dead in our tracks.

"What *is* this?" Gaea asked.

"Be extremely careful not to break anything."

The inside of the massive barn was covered in delicate glass statues and towering fixtures, but perhaps the most beautiful thing of all was the carved grand staircase leading up to the loft. It was unlike anything I'd ever seen. It was a wonder the glassmaker was able to keep his skill a secret. Planted lights were strategically placed around the expansive room to reflect off the beautiful statues and walls that were covered in colored glass shapes, twinkling like stars. I tried to imagine what the barn would look like if it were not paneled in wood on the outside. The sun would caress the gentle curves of Alavon's handiwork, and fae would travel just to glimpse the beauty he crafted. Maybe in another lifetime that could have been his fate.

"It's like a dream," Gaea said, touching the meticulously carved banister made from glass.

We crept up the steps. I looked to the floor below my feet and gripped the banister tighter. The glass was so clean we could have been walking on air.

"Hello, dears," a sweet voice said from the top of the stairs. "Welcome." A slender female with a pressed apron and perfectly pinned hair beamed. The fur covering her long ears twitched as she waited for us to say more.

"The Weaver sent us," I said as we made it to the top. "We seek Alavon."

"Of course," she said, smiling. "How else would you have found us?"

"Right."

"He's right this way."

The loft was full of glass items, and the glassmaker's mate touched nearly every piece she could as she guided us to him.

"They're here," she said in a high-pitched voice.

We stared at the back of a lanky male with long blonde hair and pale skin.

"Thank you, my dove." He turned to look at us, his eyebrows as bushy as his wife's ears. "Tea would be wonderful," he said as if answering an unasked question.

"My name is Temir, and this is Gaea. We've come to ask a favor."

"A favor from strangers is quite a bold statement." He pulled out a seat.

We sat across from him in glass chairs.

"My mate has had a visitor who told her you would come. A persistent old female, I must say."

"So, she's been here as well." I pictured the old crone stamping her staff around the glass like she didn't have a care in the world.

"She has. I will help you if you will do something for me in return," he said.

"Name it."

"First, show me what you'd like me to replicate." His eyes were too eager, but I had no choice.

"I'd actually like to ask for two things, if it's possible." I carefully pulled the adda from my bag, and that familiar power coursed through me. Setting it on top of the table between us, I watched his eyes double in size as he sucked in a breath. "It is quite remarkable, is it not?"

He reached for the flower.

I pulled it away before he could touch it. I did not want to share the secret of its power. "The flower is dying. I can heal it, but its life will only fade again. I would ask that you not only replicate the flower as perfectly as you are able, but I need a glass case for it that can hold my magic to heal the flower as needed. It is the only way."

"Yes," he breathed. His fingers twitched at his side as the pull of the flower drew him in.

"And your task?" I lifted the flower and placed it back in my bag.

"Forgive me." He shook his head. "It is quite powerful. I ask in return that you examine my mate. We have been trying for over three hundred years to conceive a child and have yet to be successful. Twice she has lost a babe in her womb." Raw, painful emotion swarmed him like the sea as he swept his hair back and tried to hide those feelings.

"This is a fate that all fae have, Alavon. I am afraid I may not be able to help. However, I would be more than happy to take a look."

"The old female has told us that you will find a way. She said that it would be unconventional, but we wish for a child so badly, we will do whatever it takes."

I nodded, fully understanding what my role would be. "Tell us about your life here, Alavon. If you would. It might be helpful."

"It's just the two of us. We spend most of our time here in the barn or working for the rebellion. We have plenty to offer a child, and as you saw, my Eliana is the kindest, sweetest soul." He smiled as he thought of her, and I longed for that level of companionship.

"Can you give us a moment, Alavon?"

"Take the time you need." He stood, paused for a moment and then stepped away.

"What is it?" Gaea asked, her eyes flicking about the loft covered in more statues.

"You were awfully quiet," I answered.

"I think I'm in awe. They adore each other so purely."

"That's what we need to discuss. I won't be able to heal his wife. She is not wounded. I have a solution but I don't think you're going to like it."

"No," she said firmly. "That is not a solution. He is not a pawn in a game."

"River would be safe, loved and cared for here. Most of all, he would be away from Autus. This male has remained in hiding his entire life. Over three hundred years. And you've been here now. You can visit him whenever you want. He would have a warm bed and meals and a family who would love and cherish him."

"I love him." Her voice broke.

I clasped her hand and willed her to see reason. Of course, I also cared for the boy. "I know you do. That's why you know, in your heart, that this is the best thing we can do for him." She nodded but looked away. "I won't do it if you tell me not to. I'll try to think of something else."

"You know there isn't a better solution. I won't be selfish." She bit her lip as the tears fell down her flushed cheeks.

"You're the best person I know, Gaea," I said, wiping them away.

She turned her back to me. I would take the very last thing she loved in the world and give it away, and this would be the action that broke the last bond between us. Even though she knew it was for the best, it wouldn't matter.

"Tea?" the glassmaker's wife called, walking up the stairs and setting her tray on the table.

"You can tell your mate to join us. We've made a decision."

316

The four of us sat at the table. I reached for Gaea's hand but she pulled it away. "May I examine you?" I asked the beaming female.

She nodded, and I laid my hand, palm up, on the table. She placed hers within mine, and I closed my eyes. I called my magic forward and searched for anything to save Gaea from this sacrifice, but it was as I thought. There was nothing wrong with her apart from the fertility problems that all fae faced. It was a matter of avoiding overpopulation in our world with beings that lived such long lives. Only the Mother could change that fate, and the gods rarely interfered in our world.

"Your mate is quite healthy. There is nothing that can be done, but as the old female explained, I have an unconventional solution." I squeezed my hands into fists below the transparent table. "There is a boy in the Wind Court who needs a home. He has been under our protection for some time now, but as the unrest within the world grows, I believe it is time to find him a safer home. Somewhere that he will be loved and cared for."

"He has the kindest soul and will be such a good boy," Gaea's voice cracked as she wiped another tear.

"I would not take a child from someone who loves him so deeply," the female said, reaching for Gaea. "It would not be right."

"No," she answered, swallowing her emotions. "I cannot protect him and teach him and care for him the way you can. He needs you as badly as you need him. I only ask that you allow me to visit when I am able and make sure he knows how much we love him too." She stood and walked out, and the female followed her.

I could feel the gaping void growing in my aching heart as she left. For him. For her. For the world that would never make sense and would continue to cleave the hearts and souls of good fae.

"Thank you," the glassmaker said. "I will need a few days to complete the two objects you've asked for. You may stay here if you wish."

"I have another task from the rebellion, but would you allow my friend to stay with River, the boy, for that time."

"She can stay for as long as she needs." He stood, and we walked out of the barn to find the glassmaker's wife embracing Gaea.

"How will we get him here?" he asked, placing his hands into his pockets.

"Temir and I will go now to get him. We will be back soon."

Gaea held her hand out to me and I took it, knowing it would be one of the last times she allowed me to do so. We spirited to a dark corner of the stable just in time to see Marte strike the boy.

Gaea dropped my hand and moved to step forward, but I grabbed her. "Let me," I growled.

"I don't fucking care what that asshole says, when I tell you not to leave, you don't. I am still your master."

"River, go to Gaea." I stepped between them and watched him crawl across the floor in the direction I had come from. "I told you what would happen if you ever touched him again."

"I'm not scared of you. I could have crushed you when you were a child."

"Well, I'm not a child anymore." I pulled my sword and shoved it into his gut. "You should have listened." I yanked it free and stepped away as he fell to his knees. I watched him slowly fade away and felt no remorse. None. He was a stark contrast to the family who would take River in, and it solidified my difficult decision.

"We have to go. Before we are seen, Temir."

Within minutes, we were back outside the glassmaker's barn.

"You have to listen to me," she said, kneeling before River and wiping the blood from his swollen lip. "You can't stay in the Wind Court anymore. There are nice people here that will take care of you and keep you safe."

"What do you mean?" He pulled away from her to look into her eyes.

"Temir and I can't always be there to save you. Bad things are happening, and we want to make sure you are going to be with someone who will love you the way we do. Do you understand? We have to leave you here." Her voice trembled. She gulped.

River threw himself into her open arms. "I don't want to stay here. I want to go home. Let me stay with you," he cried.

"I wish I could," she said into his ear.

I knelt beside them and pulled him from her. "I've always taken care of you, haven't I?" Giant tears streamed down his face, enhancing the ice faerie marks upon his pale cheeks as he sniffled and nodded. "I'm still doing that today, and I will still do that tomorrow. I will think of you in everything I do, River. You are the reason we are trying so hard to fix the world. You will be so loved here, and these people," I gestured to the fae behind me. "They have waited for you for a very, very long time."

"Don't make me stay, Temir. I'm sorry. I'm sorry I was a bad boy and left the barn. I'm sorry you had to protect me. I'll be good, I promise. Please take me back."

He launched himself at me, and I held him in my arms as he cried.

"Can I show you something magical?" Gaea asked from beside us.

He nodded but still clung to me. She tried to pull him away, but he shook his head and buried his face in my chest. I stood and carried him into the barn.

"Open your eyes, River." Gaea brushed her hands down his back.

His head lifted from my shoulder as he took in the room. "What *is* this?" He wiped his nose on his sleeve, those marks catching the light as they so often did.

I sat him down and turned to the glassmaker and his wife. They stood hand in hand, staring at River in greater awe than Alavon had when examining the adda.

"These are my friends, and Alavon has a magical power that helps him form glass. I bet he could make you anything you ever wanted."

"Lemon tarts?"

Alavon's wife giggled and stepped forward. She knelt before River and said softly, "I can make you lemon tarts."

"And chocolate?"

"All the chocolate you want, my dear. After dinner, of course."

I looked at Gaea and noticed she wasn't breathing as she watched them. I grabbed her hand and squeezed. I thought she would pull away again, but she didn't move as tears pooled her beautiful feline eyes. She would never let him go. Not really. She would always come back to him.

"You can stay," I whispered to her. Still, she didn't move. "You don't have to go back. You could stay with him."

She shook her head. "I couldn't lead him here. He would hunt me, and if he found me, he would kill them all."

I nodded. "For a few days, then? The king doesn't know we have the flower, we could convince him the journey took longer?"

"You wouldn't mind?"

"Not in a million years." I squeezed her hand. "In fact, I have something I need to do for Rook, and the replica is going to take a couple of days anyway. If you would take me to Volos, I could finish that task and you could stay with him. Make sure he gets settled in?"

"Why would you want to get that close to The Mists?"

"Rook."

"Temir, it's dangerous. Have you no care for your own life?"

"Look at him, Gaea. Look at him and tell me you wouldn't do the same."

"I'll take care of things here. You go." She grabbed my arm.

"Wait." I pulled away. "Let me say goodbye." I strode to River, who was holding the hand of the glassmaker's wife as she showed him the complex statues. "Come here, boy." He stood tall and walked slowly toward me. "I have to leave now. Promise me that you'll take care of Gaea for a few days and don't let her cry. I'm counting on you to be a good soldier. Can you do that?"

He nodded. "Will you come back?"

"I'll come back in a few days, and then I'm not sure when I'll be able to return, but I will see you again someday. I promise."

"Then why are you saying goodbye?" he asked as his rigid stature began to break.

"Because tomorrow is not always promised, Rock." I ruffled his hair.

"Hey," he cried out, trying to smooth it back down. "That's not my name."

"I'll see you around, kid," I told him, holding my hands out.

"Can this be a promise?"

"Yes."

He hugged me, and though I didn't really want to let go, I knew I had to. I tried to ignore the tears in Gaea's eyes as she spirited us away.

"Be careful?" She nudged me with her shoulder and forced a slight smile.

"Always," I answered. "I'll meet you right here in three days."

And then she was gone.

It took me no time to find the rebels scattered through the modest village. I made them gather and meet me outside of the small town so we could plan. They received confirmation the soldiers were, in fact, coming, and as I looked around at the group of six males, I hoped I could keep my promise to River.

CHAPTER

33

KING TOLERO

nok was a male of his word, so when I got to my rooms hours after Umari had pulled me from my evening meal, food lined the dresser. Even the bed had two trays. I couldn't eat this much if I was starved for a week, and he knew it. I gave it my best effort though, plowing through the sausage and savory gravy, the sweet cakes and soft breads. Eventually, I was so full I moved the food and crawled into bed with my clothes still on and fell hard and fast to sleep.

"How are you not five hundred pounds?" Loti's sharp tone woke me in the morning.

"What are you doing here?" I yanked the blanket up.

"Half my trays are in this room, you old coot. I've got breakfast to serve. Best get up and get ready for the day."

"Don't you have staff for this job?" I rubbed my temple.

"Oh, posh. Inok had to do something at the stables and asked me to wake you. I needed the trays, so I said I would. Now up and out."

"When did you get so bossy?" I asked, stretching.

"Yesterday. I got bossy yesterday. Up, up." She yanked the covers off me and shoved me out of bed. "It's a blessing to us both that you don't sleep in the nude." She laughed. "Breakfast in an hour. Will you take it privately or in the hall with the city folk?"

"I suppose I better take it in the hall. Maybe you should spike the cider."

"I would never." She gasped.

"It is a joke, Loti. I'll be down soon."

"Hm. I didn't know you still knew how to do that."

She left me as disheveled as she had found me. I worked my way out of the rumpled clothing I had fallen asleep in, bathed quickly, redressed and joined the crowd of fae in the dining hall. I was surprised anyone had come. Though I chose not to let the people stay in the castle, they still appreciated a free meal and the chance to look around, especially if they were spying for the queen, I supposed.

"Good morning, Your Grace," Inok greeted me.

"Are you ready for this day?"

"More so than tomorrow, I think." We crossed the room and took our seats at the head of the long table. Nearly half the fae who had come to last night's dinner were gone.

"Tonight, we will have a feast at the castle, with dancing and music to follow, in honor of the winners of the Trials."

Forks clanged to half full plates as several of my fae stopped eating and acknowledged me. They turned toward each other, their poisonous whispers spreading like wildfire as they discussed my news. The high pitch of hissed secrets reached the end of the table as several guests stood and left the room.

"Have the draconians follow them," I said to Inok behind my drink.

He motioned to a watchful guard at the open door. Even though the guard was dressed appropriately, he was not one. He was a draconian. He darted out of the room, and I settled back into my seat. Although I'm sure Morwena didn't mean to, her ghastly game with the cetani had backfired

323

on her. Umari and her dracs were now her biggest threat and my biggest ally.

"I want a small council meeting before we open today's Trials. Bring them all to the study."

"Yes, Your Grace," Inok answered.

Some time later, I sat at my desk waiting for them to arrive, debating involving them. But what was a council for if not to be involved? They filed in one by one and stood before me, Inok closing the door behind him. I sank down into my power and called it forward. These were strong minds. It would take quite a bit of magic.

"Those who have had direct or indirect contact with the sea queen over the past few years, please step forward."

Unsurprisingly, Madu, the boarder lord, stepped forward, but also Sabra, the refugee liaison and Igrer, the scribe did.

Gasps and accusatory glances came from the rest of the council. I'm sure my magic assisted in that reaction.

"Madu, tell me when."

"She came to me before my rotation was to begin on the council."

"And what precisely did she say to you," I asked as I rose from my seat.

"She told me to make sure the lesser fae were not welcome here."

"Is that all?"

"She told me I was to report any information about war or anything spoken in the council that would be of relevance to her. She told me to make sure everyone knew you were not worthy of your crown. I was also never to speak of our encounter."

"What have you done on her behalf?" I asked.

"I've only spoken against the lessers, I swear. And I told her Sabra was protecting them. You've barely held council meetings. I've had nothing to report otherwise. I've also spread lies about you through the city." He clapped his hands to his mouth to try to muffle his words.

"Put your hands to your side and leave them there." I took a deep breath. "Tell me any other moves against my people you have made on your own behalf."

"I've ..." He tried to stop himself from talking but was unable. "I've posted signs and killed three lessers who entered my property."

"Do you admit this has to do with your own decisions and beliefs and nothing to do with mind-altering magic?"

"I do."

"Why did you agree to join the council, knowing I could procure this information from your own lips?"

His face remained impassive, but his words were hateful. "Because everyone knows you don't use your magic. I'm not afraid of the docile king."

I jerked my head up as a vein pulsed. I willed that anger down. If only to finish the meeting. "You are to forget the queen's enchantment upon you. I release you from my own."

He sank to the floor, the braided rug dampening the sound as he did. He remained there, sobbing in fear, as I moved down the line.

"Sabra, you will tell me when the queen contacted you."

"Only days ago, my king."

"And what did she say?"

"She told me that I was to tell her where the northern refugees are staying and that I was to stop assisting them in any way. I was not allowed to give them food, coin or clothing, and I was to tell them this was your order. She told me to convince them all to go home and forget that I had seen her."

"Inok, you need to get word to Umari and have her send half of her draconians to guard the refugees. Go now."

I realized I had just enchanted him, unintentionally, but when it came to him, he would always do as I asked, magic or not. Still, I hated that power over him.

He ran from the room.

"Sabra, tell me anything you have done to sabotage me or my people on your own behalf."

"I haven't, my king." She shook her head.

"You are to forget the queen's enchantment, and you are released from mine."

She sank at the shoulders, and then tears streaked down her face.

I stepped in front of her and placed my hand on her arm. "Do not feel bad, Sabra. You could not control those actions. You are a loyal member of this council, and I'm happy to have you here."

"But what if the refugees are harmed?" she cried.

"Did you see them this morning?"

She nodded, sniffling.

"Then they will be well. I've sent guards we can trust to watch over them."

"But how do you know she hasn't enchanted the draconian guards?" Jacon asked from the back of the room.

"Because they still bow to me and cheer my name. They still look to me as if I am worthy. She has been focused on the city." I stepped in front of Igrer.

He shook in fear. He knew what was to come, but before I could say a word, he lurched forward, and I saw the knife seconds too late. He planted it all the way to the hilt in my stomach.

I inhaled a sharp breath as the searing pain was followed by warm blood soaking my robes.

"King Tolero," Sabra screamed.

Igrer rushed for the door.

"Stop, Igrer," I sang, gasping for a breath.

He froze in his tracks.

I swayed forward and landed hard on one knee. The room began to fade. "Jacon, get the healer," I ordered, falling to the ground.

I woke to Inok leaning over me with concern and anger written in big letters across his forehead. "You enchanted me. You made me leave your

326

side. I would have sent a guard and been right back to protect you. What were you thinking?"

"It's nice to see you too, brother." I moaned, my side aching.

He held a hand out and I used it to pull myself up on the table. A slow burn coursed through my stomach, and my limbs shook as I willed my eyes to focus on the dark room lit only by flickering candles and one small lamp upon a cluttered desktop. The familiar room took me back to so many moments in my life. Some were more painful than others. This was where we discovered Efi had been poisoned. She might not have died in this room, but as the walls closed in on me, it sure felt like it.

"King Tolero you must lie down," the healer said from behind me.

"Have the Trials started?" I asked, trying to hide my memories.

"Yes, my king. We've told the people you had urgent business to attend to."

"I suppose that's true enough. Inok, help me to my feet."

"But, Y-y-your Grace ..." the healer stammered.

"Now's not the time, healer. You've patched me up. I must be out there."

"Are you sure?" Inok asked.

I nodded, wincing. "I'll manage."

"Fine, fine, but at least let me give you something for the pain." He handed me a salve and grabbed my other arm as I stood from the table.

"Get a different robe for me, Inok."

"Sabra brought something from your room. She is outside the door. She will not leave."

"And Igrer?"

"Dungeons," was all he could say behind gritted teeth.

"And Madu?"

"Same."

"We will deal with him later," I said. "Let's go."

Inok pushed the door open, and Sabra soared up from the chair she sat upon. "Oh gods, are you okay?" She reached for me, fussing as females did.

I took the robes from her hands. "I'm fine, Sabra. Headed out to the fights. Would you care to join us?"

"You would still have me join you?"

"Sabra, you've done nothing in your own control. You and your sister are powerful members of this court. You must let your actions go. Do not drown in the past."

"Do you need help to walk?" Her voice remained unsteady.

"I can't let them see me injured. I must walk out there and act as if nothing has happened, and you're to do the same."

She dipped her head and followed us out.

By the time we made it to my platform, spots flecked my vision. I happily sat down as my council gathered around me. The crowd was silent as they watched. No king had ever missed a part of the Trials before. Perhaps it would just give them another reason to think me incapable of ruling. I didn't care. I looked into the concerned eyes of my reverent council members.

"I've been distant. I should have been more diligent in leaning on my council for advice during this time, but as you all know, I've not been myself since Efi ... left us. I can only ask that you trust that I'm working on that now more than ever. I've been reminded today that I don't not want to die just yet.

"As you have seen, Morwena has been enchanting my people. She has been planting seeds of hatred and sitting back to watch them grow. War is creeping up on us, and we need to be prepared. I have a plan, but you're all going to need to trust me more than ever as I draw out the sea queen. You must not let the people know I've been injured. You must sit here and act as if all is right in the world. Do you understand?"

They nodded.

"Let us get on with this day, then."

"What will you do with Igrer and Madu?" Jacon asked.

"I am still deciding. Please, sit."

I took my padded seat and gestured for the event to continue. "How long until Brax fights again?"

"We are down to Muth's top guy, Attoc still has two in, and Brax. Attoc's fighters will battle each other next, then Muth's male will fight Brax, and the winner of that match will take on Attoc's top fighter."

"So, three fights and then the traditional Rites begin?"

"Yes, and then you can go back to the castle and rest."

I shook my head. "I've announced a ball, in case you've forgotten."

"So, you intend to move forward with the plan? Injured?"

"I do." I faced forward as Attoc's fighters walked out.

"Where did that beast come from?" I asked Inok while gesturing to the massive male swinging two broadswords like they were rapiers—akin to my own weapons of choice.

"That's Attoc's top fighter, I think. The one Brax told you to pick. I believe he has come from the Wind Court. Giant for sure."

"Hm. Let's see what he can do with those swords."

The opposing fighters faced each other and bowed. They were from the same pit, so I imagined they had fought before. They took a step away, and the larger male swung his sword in great arches again. The sound of the swords whooshing through the air was beautiful.

The smaller contender held a shorter sword, and though it wasn't something I would have chosen against the giant, I had to believe he knew what he was doing. They circled each other for a few minutes until the crowd buzzed, urging them to move. But rather than do anything, the smaller opponent took a knee and placed his sword in the sand. A forfeit.

The fae in the stands booed and hissed as the two fighters exited the arena. A forfeit was allowed in the Trials, but it was rare and usually came once defeat was imminent. I could tell that was Attoc's order. Although it was cowardice, he wanted to keep his top fighter uninjured and energized for the final match.

"You know the people are going to eat him alive for that later," Inok said.

"Yes, quite so, but it was smart."

There was a small break between the next two fights, and I used that time to meet with the draconians once again. I didn't move fast and had to apply my salve before I could go back, but I had faith in the plan and had to see it through.

"All set?" Inok asked me.

I shrugged. "As much as we can be, I suppose."

He nodded and faced forward as Brax and his opponent stepped out.

CHAPTER
34

ARA

I *know you consider my offer, strange one*, the dragon continued to hiss in my mind. *Tell me, what would it take to keep you?*

I held my face neutral so that Fen was unaware, and somewhere deep within my mental shield, I tried to think of a way to turn this in my favor. Could I outsmart a dragon? I moved between the layers of that shield, attempting to find a way out of this. I turned to see the pale face of Kai as his wound continued to bleed. It wasn't fatal, not for fae, but it would hurt like hell, and if we did nothing, eventually the wound would be.

"There," Greeve said so that only the three of us standing at the front of the cage would hear him. His eyes shifted to the left, and Fen and I watched as the ground subtly changed, small footprints left behind.

"Don't move," I said loudly to Kai, who was already not moving. "I bet that big fucker sleeping back there has the keys. We'll never convince him to give them to us with you squirming like food." Wren, hidden behind her magic, stopped and inched away, Lichen in tow. They were slow, but I watched their footprints press into the ground as they went.

He would never give them up, the dragon said just outside of my mental shield.

I made eye contact with the lemon-colored beast and watched a smile creep across its giant serpentine face as it felt my submission. Fen was already pissed at me. If he knew, he'd lose his shit.

I will make a deal with you, beast.

I felt him sliver around my mind, and I said a silent prayer that this would go to plan.

Do tell, he said.

I will agree to stay here and be your pet or whatever you want without ever trying to escape or leave you if you can answer three questions correctly.

And if I lose, strange one?

I pulled back several layers of my mental shields as I prepared for my first question, setting the trap as carefully as I could. *If you lose, my entire group will be allowed to pass through this gap whenever we wish, and you will owe me one favor.*

Deal, he said eagerly. A deep shimmer of ancient magic crossed my body. I had just made a magically binding deal with a dragon on a hunch. It was our only chance though.

Ask your question.

I lifted my chin. *Who is my king?*

You would try to trick me, strange one, but you didn't know I could see into your mind. Though you look to be southern with tan skin, you smell southern, and you travel with the prince of the Flame Court, your king is King Coro of the Marsh Court.

Fen cleared his throat beside me. I ignored him as he took an exaggerated breath.

How could I have thought I could trick you? We might as well just give up.

You cannot. Futile as it might be, you must complete the bargain.

I looked down to my hands, casually examining my nails as my heart raced. *Well then, I guess it doesn't matter what I ask you. What is your name?*

Heat filled the air as my question settled over him. *That is not a truth of yours, but a truth of mine. I will not answer.*

So, you will agree to set us free?

I will not.

Then you have to answer the question, beast. I lifted an eyebrow and pursed my lips.

Fen had asked Lichen what he knew of dragons, but he never thought to ask me. I knew a few things. A dragon's name was his freedom. He likely thought there was no one left on Alewyn who remembered this truth. Even though I hadn't believed they existed, I was still taught the legend. I pushed more memories toward the doorstep of my mind, just in case I did get to my third question.

There was an eerie clicking as the dragon's massive scales brushed together. He roared and launched himself into the putrid air.

"Are they back yet?" I asked quickly, knowing the dragon would have to return soon.

"Not yet. What are you doing, Ara? Has he asked you to make a bargain?"

"Can you shield your minds?" I asked.

"Of course," Fen answered. "Though it is more difficult with a dragon."

"Do it now and do nothing else but reinforce your shields until we are out of this fucking gap. He cannot find the answers in your minds."

"What the fuck did you do?" Greeve growled.

"Don't make me kill you in a cage, Greeve. You will not speak to me like that. I'm trying to save our asses. Have some faith in me like you asked me to have in you."

Fen stepped between us, but the rage within him was palpable. He was as mad as the dragon. His silence was a lethal weapon, as sharp as a blade.

Greeve said, "If you just bargained off my life—"

"Don't," Fen warned, staring him down. "If she did, it was because she had to."

You've angered the prince, the dragon said, shaking the ground below him as he landed.

I don't care. He's nothing to me. Will you free us now?

I will not. I will offer my name to you, strange one. It is of no use to anyone anyway. His lie was so believable I would have doubted my own memory had it not evoked an initial reaction from him. *My name is Pathog.*

Your full name is required, dragon.

Pathog the Unyielding, he snapped. *It has been ages since I've thought of my own name, I've nearly forgotten.*

Liar. One more question and I had him right where I wanted him.

"Wren," Fen breathed in my ear. A subtle nod and I continued knowing the only reason he hadn't already scented her and Lichen is because the dragon was so distracted by our game.

Okay, you've gotten two questions right. One more and we can be done with this silly game and I'm yours forever. The male who raised me was tall, strong, brave, and bright. He was everything to me as a child. What was my father's name?

Your father was Thassen. I win, he said, rising to claim his prize.

Relief flooded my ears. "Oh shoot," I said out loud. "You're wrong. Thassen was not my real father."

"What?" he roared. "Liar. I've seen your memories, strange one. That male is Thassen."

"Yes." Fen stepped between us. "But she tells the truth. Thassen was not her real father. Search my mind for proof if you wish."

The beast leaned down and breathed Fen in so deeply I thought he might suck him through the cage. "This cannot be!" he roared.

"A deal is a deal. You must let me and my friends go. You can show yourself now, Wren." She and Lichen appeared, and I looked at her empty hands. She subtly pointed to her bag. She had the keys.

"I only agreed to give the ones in the cage passage, and I never said I'd release them from their cuffs."

"No, the bargain was: if you lose, my entire group will be allowed to pass through this gap whenever we wish and you will owe me one favor, but I think we both know you will do as I wish now, don't we?" *Pathog the Unyielding.*

He took two steps backward. "But how could you know of that?" He bent his long neck forward so he could press his enormous eye to the top of the magical cage.

"That's my job, dragon. I know things. Remove the cage and the cuffs."

He huffed and the cage disappeared but the cuffs remained. "Those cannot be removed unless one wields the keys. As it happens, I am out of keys."

"No matter, let's go," Wren said.

Greeve and Fen lifted Kai, and he moaned in pain.

"Just let us get out of here and we'll stop and help you," I said to him.

"So, we just walk out?" Lichen asked, his eyes locked on the fuming dragon.

"Yes," I answered, stepping away. "See you on our way back, dragon."

We made it to the other side of the gap in careful silence. The other dragons watched us but did not move as we crossed. The minute we were out of their sight, Fen held his hands out to Wren. "Get these things off of me."

We were all frozen, but Kai's lips were blue. Our breaths filled the air, and even Greeve rubbed his fingers together for warmth. The cold caused Wren's hands to tremble as she pulled the stolen keys from her bag and removed the golden cuffs from his wrists. She dropped them to the ground, moved to Greeve, and did the same.

"Extraordinary, aren't they?" Lichen said, holding the contraption up to examine it. "I didn't know such things existed."

Fen rounded on me. "What were you thinking?" He roared louder than the dragon. "You carelessly ran in without a plan, and you did the one thing I specifically asked you not to do without even consulting me."

"Back the fuck up, Prince. I am not one of your subjects. I couldn't consult you. There wasn't time. I admit I might have been a tad hasty in my rescue attempt, but—"

"A tad? You didn't have a single weapon in your hand like you were going to fistfight a dragon."

"I thought if I distracted it, Greeve would use his magic to help Kai escape. I didn't know the cuffs were there. And did you see them? What the fuck was a sword or a knife going to do? Scratch them?"

"And the bargain?" he asked.

"If I had said anything out loud, he wouldn't have taken the deal. I had to do the best I could with what little resources we had. My mind was the only thing I had."

"What if you had lost?" Greeve asked, clearly still mad at me, as his constant wind circled through his hair.

"I only told him he could keep me. I didn't mention you guys unless I beat him."

"Stop fighting and look around you. We've made it to the Wind Court. That was the goal. We're here. Let's see if we can get Kai fixed up and keep going," Wren said.

"Take care of it, Wren," Fen ordered, grabbing my hand and pulling me away from them.

I planted my feet after we were far enough away and yanked my hand out of his. "I'm not a child, Fenlas. You can wish for me to follow your orders until I'm dead, and I never will. I'm not going to be caged by your dreams of what you hoped we would be. I told you I don't want a mate. I don't want an overbearing lover either. My life, my rules. I get to control something." I bit the inside of my cheek to keep from going on as I glared at him.

"Ara, I didn't order you at all. I asked you. You act like your life means nothing, but it does. Even beyond my own feelings, you're important to this entire world. And you may not like that truth, but that doesn't change it. Why bring us on this journey if you aren't even going to take the only part of the prophecy we do know seriously?"

"I didn't bring you. You chose to come. I tried to stop you."

"Guys?" Kai called.

"I do take the prophecy seriously. I know it's important, but nothing makes my life more important than anyone else's."

"Guys," Kai said more firmly.

"What?" we both yelled.

"We have company." He pointed behind us.

We turned as one to see two males watching us with weapons out. "Who are you?" one of them shouted.

"Who the fuck are you?" I answered, jamming my hands across my chest.

"None of your business, you high fae bitch."

Greeve was instantly behind him with a knife to his throat. The other one turned and tried to swing on him, but ferocious Fen was already there, blocking the blow. He heaved in breaths as he forced himself to hold back. He wanted to kill that fae, and there was something so sexy in that protective nature. Annoying, but sexy.

"Not a great time for this," Wren said, holding pressure to Kai's shoulder.

I stepped closer and watched as Fen pounded the other male on the ground. He wouldn't use magic when he needed a punching bag. He was angry with me, but the stranger was taking the brunt of it. That ragey ass male was out of control again. "Stop," I yelled. "Everyone, stop."

The lesser fae at Greeve's knife tip hissed but didn't struggle. Fen held the other pinned to the ground with his fist in the air ready to strike again.

"Look at their coats. Stop. Release them."

"Rebels?" Fen asked, looking at the phoenix symbol sewn into the gray coat of the one he had pinned.

"What do you know of the rebellion?" the one Greeve still held asked.

He threw him to the ground and showed him his tattoo.

"You're a rebel?"

"I'm the prince of the Flame Court, you stupid, mouthy asshole." Fire erupted in a circle around us.

"Ain't no Prince a rebel," the one on the ground said.

Fen lifted his shirt and showed him the tattoo on his chest. "I've probably been supporting the rebellion longer than you have. What are you doing here?"

"Temir," the one on the ground shouted.

The flames dissipated, and several more rebels crested a hill behind my pissy prince.

"Everything okay?" the one with horns called from a distance, presumably Temir.

"You better get over here," he shouted back.

Greeve shoved the mouthy one away and came to stand beside me. I gave him a look, and he smirked. "Just because I'm mad at you doesn't mean you're not family now." I smiled and he wrapped his heavy arm around my shoulder. "Just don't go running in to fight dragons without a weapon again, okay?"

"Okay," I answered.

Fen walked over, still reeling while we waited for the rest of the rebels to meet us.

"They say they're rebels," the one Fen attacked said.

Stag horn guy must have been the leader.

"Do you have proof?" he asked.

338

Everyone but Lichen and I showed their tattoos. He nodded. "What are you doing near The Mists?"

"I could ask you the same question," I answered. "Wait a minute. I've seen you before." I pulled out my sword, and instantly my group, aside from Kai who struggled to stand, did the same. "You're one of Autus' collected wielders."

Fen tilted his head to the side. "You've let your horns grow."

"I belong to no one. The king thinks he owns me. He does not."

"How did you escape him?" Lichen asked. I was surprised he didn't get his notebook out.

"I remain on his council as a spy for the rebellion."

I dropped my sword again. "Why should we believe you?"

"It's true," Aibell said, appearing seconds before she spoke. "And you will not waste time with this now. The king's soldiers are nearly to Volos, and if you're to save even a single person, you will make friends and play nice."

"Do you enjoy this game you play, old female?" the male asked.

"This is not a game," Aibell warned. "Fates and flames are coming soon."

"Use care when you speak to her," he told me. "She is odd, this one."

"Trust me, I know," I answered, pursing my lips.

"Temir, heal this one," Aibell said, pointing at Kai. "Then get on with it."

He took a step forward, but I blocked his path. "You hurt him, and I'll have you mounted on the wall of my future home."

He pushed past me and laid a hand on Kai, who moaned. I tried to walk forward, but Fen grabbed my arm. "You must listen to Aibell. She wouldn't be here if it wasn't important. We have to help them."

"Oh, so you're talking to me and not yelling anymore?"

"Later," he answered as we watched the stag heal our friend.

"Time to go," Temir said, turning back to us. "We've got only the seven of us."

"Do you have a plan?" Fen asked.

"The entire village is made up of only fourteen homes. We've evacuated everyone to a cave just there." Temir pointed toward the mountains.

"We need someone to stand guard to make sure they are safe. Aside from that, we'll arm ourselves and enter the homes of the fae, pretending like we are the villagers. When the soldiers come in, and we don't know how many there are, we will surprise them. We will still have a fight on our hands. I imagine the six of you plus the eight of us would give us a better chance."

"Unless the females would prefer to wait in the cave," a rebel said from behind Temir.

"You don't know our females," Fen said. "You'd be better off caging a grendel."

"We must leave now, then," Temir said.

"Finally," Aibell grumbled and disappeared.

"You get used to her," Fen told Temir as we moved.

He sent two of his rebels, and we sent Lichen, to guard the cave. The rest of us crossed the frozen terrain and descended into the tiny village. We left several homes unoccupied, deciding to work in teams. Fen and I took a home, Wren and Kai took one and Greeve insisted on being alone.

We marched into our chosen cottage and it was like stepping into someone's memories. Carefully knitted blankets covered the aged furniture, paintings hung crooked on the vibrantly painted walls, and for a moment, it was cozy. Until Fen shut the door behind him and rounded on me again.

I pushed my chest out and raised my chin. We'd been here before. This was all too familiar territory. "Now is not the time for your asshole male issues."

"You're right. Right before a fight I should absolutely not say a word about your desire to constantly self-sacrifice."

"My life is my business. My choices."

"Again with the choices." He pinched the bridge of his nose, shaking his head at the floor.

"Yes. I should get choices just like everyone else does."

He stopped, opened his mouth to say something and then stopped again.

I didn't want to fight with him. He needed to understand though. I stepped forward. "As soon as we reach her and I find out what I really have to do here, all my choices are gone. Fate doesn't negotiate. I'm stuck with it no matter what. It's that or I die. I need to have choices. I need to have the freedom to make my own decisions for as long as I can. I hope you can at least try to understand that."

"I am a prince and the Guardian. Few people understand that more than I do, Ara. It doesn't mean you have to stop considering yourself and your safety."

"I'll work on it."

He nodded, but there was still that wall between us.

I heard the horses outside before he did. "It's time."

We moved to the window, and he carefully pulled the floral curtain to the side. "Twenty. At least."

"Perfect." I pulled my sword. "Let's worry about this later. Bet I can take out more than you."

"You're on." He moved to the door just as it slammed open. He reached around, grabbed the soldier by the collar, yanked him forward onto his blade, and pushed the door shut. "One for me."

The door crashed open again, and I flicked my wrist, pulled a throwing knife and took out the next one. "Tie game." I stepped over the body of the first fallen soldier. "Let's go."

We left the comfortable house and entered full-blown chaos outside.

The rebels fought hard, but my team was absolutely brutal. Wren probably took out more soldiers than anyone. They never saw her coming until her knife was across their throats. Kai moved with fluid grace, but a pure, solid weapon. He was definitely holding back when we fought last time.

I couldn't keep track of Greeve at all. He was all over the place. He might have beaten Wren's body count. I watched Fen fight two at once while I took on a third. He didn't break a sweat as he moved like a dancer with an irresistible smirk on his face as he counted his kills. He made it look so easy, and in that moment, I realized the fierceness that was my team.

After it was over, the rebels had lost two of their own and the village was laden with fallen soldiers. The king of the Wind Court had sent over forty males. The rebel leader healed a cut Greeve had gotten in the fray, and we traveled together to the cave to retrieve Lichen, our bags, and the occupants of the village. I'd beaten Fen's kill count, but he never asked. He didn't use his magic, so it wasn't really a fair contest anyway. But if we were counting, I won.

"The king will realize his soldiers did not return and will send twice as many next time," Temir said. "The best thing you can all do is either travel south or join the rebellion and help yourselves."

"My name is Fenlas. I am the prince of the Flame Court. My father will allow you to seek refuge in the southern kingdom if you can travel. I urge you not to use the Western Gap."

Wren stepped forward and, in the kindest voice I'd ever heard, pleaded with them all. "Please consider this. We have a committee ready to welcome you when you cross the border. My sister, Sabra will see you to safety and comfort. It's no longer safe here."

With that, we parted ways with the rebels of the north and started toward The Mists. We'd survived a giant, dragons, and the king's soldiers. It couldn't be worse than that.

CHAPTER

35

TEMIR

"You're sure it was the prince?" Gaea asked as we stood together outside of the glassmaker's barn.

"Yes. And several others working for the rebellion."

"This is huge, Tem. It means the rebels stretch across the world. It means that you might actually have a chance."

"You could still join us."

"Someday." She looked away. "For now, we have to get back to Autus before he has us hunted for sport."

"Have you told him goodbye?"

"Not yet," she said.

"It's time."

"I know he is safe here and so well looked after. They already love and adore him, but I selfishly want to take him home. I suppose the castle isn't really home anyway, and I could never offer him what he would have here."

I waited while she worked up the courage to leave River.

When we walked into the barn, he yelled my name and sprinted to me. I flinched as he weaved through the pieces of glass and leaped into my arms.

"You're here," he said.

"Only for a few more minutes, River. I've got to get back to the king."

"I did just what you said and made sure Gaea was happy the whole time you were gone. And Mr. Alavon made me a practice sword with glass and said if I was careful and didn't shatter it, he would teach me how to use it. And they have the best lemon tarts ever here, but don't tell Cook I said that. And did you know if you want you can slide down the banister on your butt and you won't even fall because it has magic?"

"I did not know any of that," I said, smiling at him.

"Glad to see you made it back in one piece," Alavon said as he approached us. He placed his hands on River's shoulders and squeezed until his neck disappeared and he giggled. "That's the best sound in the world."

"I'm glad he'll be safe and cared for. Did you get the items finished?" I asked.

"I sure did. I just need to attach the final glass piece after we place the actual flower inside."

I turned to Gaea.

"I still have it," she said, grinning at my slight panic.

I had given it to her before she left me in Volos, knowing I wouldn't be able to guarantee its safety. She reached inside her own packed bag and pulled it out carefully, then placed it in my hands.

I turned to the glassmaker. "Ready?"

"Let's go up to the shop and see this finished."

He set the box on the table inside and waited while I gently set the adda inside. "Now place your hands on each side and push your magic in while I form the final piece." I did as he said, and as the last piece of glass closed on the tiny box, I felt a silence fill the air. I hadn't realized the power of the adda resonated so strongly until it was muted. "The box can only be opened by you, Temir. The magic sees your soul and will not release it unless you wish it."

"And the replica?" I asked, putting the glass box in my bag.

"It's here." He pulled it from his pocket.

Gaea gasped. "It's identical."

"Did you doubt me?"

"They always do, my dove," his mate said, coming up the stairs with a full tray. "Tea?"

"No, thank you. I'm sorry, but we have to go." I lifted the replica from the glassmaker's hands and nearly dropped it in surprise. "The vibration. How?" It was so similar to the actual flower. It didn't touch or fill my power, but the motion was there.

"Magic, of course. It does nothing, but the king will assume the vibration is power. Eventually, he will learn the truth, but I hope this buys you the window that you need."

"So do I." I reached my hand out to him. He clasped my forearm and then placed a fist to his chest. I did the same and wished them all well.

"It's time," I told Gaea.

"I know," she said sadly. She looked down to River, who squeezed her hand. "I must leave you now, my precious boy. You do all the things I told you and mind your manners. Life here will not be like living in the stables. You'll have to listen well and be helpful."

"I will. Promise," he told her.

She lifted him into a hug and held him for several minutes, then sat him back down and placed his hand into the glassmaker's wife's. "Take care of my boy," she said softly.

"With all my heart," the female answered.

She reached out, touched my arm, and in the next moment, we stood back in my rooms at the castle. It felt like an eternity had passed since I had been here last. She turned to step away and I reached for her once more. "Will you ever forgive me, Gaea?"

She paused, her eyes locked on the floor. "There's nothing to forgive." She lifted her gaze and I wiped the tears that fell down her cheeks. "You made the right choice, Temir. It wasn't the easy one, but it was right." Her voice was thick with sorrow as her shoulders began to shudder. I pulled her into my arms and willed her sadness to become my own. "I've done everything wrong. I should have loved you even when it hurt. I should have let you in when I could see you wanted me to. But I didn't. And I'm sorry. You're all I have in this world. If I let myself love you, and you die too, then what do I have? I let the wedge build itself into a wall because I didn't know how to get back to this. How to just let myself find peace in your arms. I've spent all this time thinking that if I had happiness it would be a betrayal to him. Because he never got to have that."

I put my finger below her chin and forced her to look at me through her tears. "Loving someone would never be a betrayal to the man that taught us how. I can't imagine he'd want anything more than that."

She sniffled. "I know. I let that tiny seed of doubt become something so much bigger and I've ruined everything between us because of it."

"We are not ruined. Grief doesn't come with directions. I'm still here. I'm standing right here waiting for you to see me."

"I see you now." Her voice was like a promise. Those four words held so much more meaning than she could ever know. I knew she was hurting and maybe I was the selfish one as I condemned her for her sorrow, but somewhere within our own mistakes, was a buried love.

"I see you too," I whispered as I leaned into her. I wouldn't push her. I'd waited for this moment for so long, I let her close the distance. She pressed her lips to mine and I waited for my heart to roar to life, to remind me why I'd loved her so ardently. But it remained silent.

She stepped away and smiled and for a moment I saw the fae she was before, but something was wrong. Because I wasn't the same either. And though she'd finally opened up about her true feelings, as mine came crashing into me, I realized nothing was better, in fact, it was so much worse.

"Ready?" she asked, wiping the remnants of tears away.

I set my packed bag with the glass box in my study below my desk, and we strolled through the bustling halls of the chilly castle as if nothing had happened. This was the final piece of our careful plan and we had to set everything to the side, for now. If the king even detected the flower was not authentic, he would have us killed or imprisoned.

As we approached the doors to the throne room, the twins stepped into our path. "The king is busy and asks not to be disturbed," one said.

"Tell him we have returned," Gaea answered, putting on the annoyed face she wore so well.

"Wait here." He slipped into the room.

We stood for several moments outside of the guarded doors. We had never been ordered to remain outside before. I kept my face calm and tried not to look at Gaea as I wondered if our plan was foiled before we had even a chance to trick the king.

After several moments, the doors flew open and the seamstress stormed out with her chin in the air, and shortly after that, her tearful daughter followed with her face buried in her hands. Instead of walking around me, her small framed slammed right into my chest and I sucked a sharp breath between my teeth as I grabbed her shoulders, righting her before she fell to the floor.

"Forgive me." Her voice was tender and she was even thinner than last time, with knotted hair and torn rags for clothing. Whatever had happened, she was far more distraught than her stubborn mother. Everyone around her felt it. My hands lingered on her arms as we had a silent conversation. Something within me needed to know that she was alright. That I was not standing idly by as the king took another victim. Her honey-colored eyes held mine for an eternity until she dipped her chin and pulled away. I watched her until she rounded the corner and Gaea cleared her throat. My head snapped back to her, but she would not meet my eyes. She looked straight ahead, waiting for the king to summon us.

We stepped into the empty throne room, and I chanced a glance at the king. His face was red. Whatever had happened with Nadra and her mother had set the stage for our potential demise.

347

"It's been days!" he screamed, standing from his throne. "Where have you been?"

"Forgive me, my king." Gaea bowed low. "I had not been able to travel as close to the ruins as I had hoped. We were caught in a dangerous blizzard."

"Once we were able to finally get to the ruins," I said, telling him what we had practiced. "We had to search and search for the flower. We did find it, but the ruins caved in, and we were trapped below for a long time."

He waved his hand, not caring about the process. "Just give it to me."

I stepped forward and pulled the replica from my pocket. I treated it as gently as I had the real adda, walking up the dais stairs and placing it carefully into the king's out-turned hand.

His frown was instantly a disturbing smile. His hard eyes widened as he held the flower up to the light. "So, it is like glass," he whispered, mesmerized by the depth of flames within the petals of the flower. "Do you see, Eadas? This is what delivery looks like. This is what happens when you give an order and those who are loyal to you actually follow through."

"Yes, Your Grace," Eadas said from behind him.

"If only I could get that fucking seamstress to do the same."

"If you would just enchant her," Eadas said back.

The king whipped around so fast I thought he might drop the flower in his hands. "Do not tell me how to rule my kingdom. She will be loyal to me because she chooses it. I will not spend my days puppeteering my court. Do I not provide for you? Do I not give you any fucking thing you need? She should be grateful I'm even entertaining her gods-damned wretched daughter. She wanted a husband for her. Well she got a king."

Eadas flinched, and a fire roared within me at his words. My heart slammed in my chest. I needed out of this room as fast as possible, or I would give everything away. He thought everyone worshipped him. He thought he was due a lover just because he ordered it. He thought every single fae in this whole world should bow down to him, but I would not. I could not sit back and watch much longer. He was the epitome of everything sick and twisted in the land of fae. I was done. Fucking done.

Gaea moved slightly and took my hand. "Calm," she whispered. "Are we dismissed?" she asked in her usual tone, though I could tell she was nervous.

"For now," the king said without turning back to us.

He had Eadas in his sights, and I'd gladly leave them to it. Gaea spirited us to my rooms, and I heaved. I doubled over trying to push the anger and sadness from my body. I'd never felt such rage.

"Temir?" Gaea placed a hand on my back.

"Leave me," I snapped, unable to control the fury.

Without another word, she was gone. I stomped into my study, slammed my hands on my desk, and shoved every damn thing to the floor. I pulled my packed bag up, unloaded all of the clothes and shoved anything I thought would be helpful into it. Books, journals, as many elixirs and leo flowers as I could. And then I sat, waiting until the sharp anger left me, and deep sadness finally faded to utter exhaustion. I watched the sunrise from the window and laid my head on the desk.

I dreamed I could be as free as the southerners. I wished I could be as free as the lesser fae in the northern kingdom, even. I wished to be anyone but myself. I felt a soft breeze and woke, expecting to see Gaea standing before me. Instead, a folded piece of paper sat on my desk.

Temir,

I wished on every star for you and my heart is shattered to admit I am afraid for you. I'm afraid for me too. I've lived in that fear my whole life at this castle. That fear has controlled me for so very long. There were times when I didn't recognize it for what it was, but now I see so much more clearly. You know what the future holds for you, yet you press on.

If only the rest of the world had your heart and compassion to see beyond their own fear. I love you but I'm not strong enough to sit by and watch your decisions ruin you. I'm also not strong enough to watch you fade away from me. I felt it in our final kiss. I know our love will never be what we both dreamed and I will never blame you for that.

It seems that destiny has something else in store. I thought I'd love you and you would love me and I hoped that would be enough. But it wasn't.

Something on the wind calls to me. Just as something in your soul calls to you. I hope one day you find peace. Save her.

~G

All sound faded. The blood drained from my face. My breath halted. "No. Shit. No. Gaea." I crumpled the paper, hoping she was in spirit form, watching. But she wasn't. She had left. My final words to her had been to leave me, and she did. She finally found the courage to leave the king, and I knew, with every fiber of my being, that I had pushed her over that dangerous edge.

I wasn't sure what to do. Save her, she had told me. I imagined she was talking about Nadra. The high fae female I had no business even touching, though the thought of her had begun to consume me. I couldn't save her. I couldn't even save myself.

I bathed, washing the days of travel, battle, and stress from me. I had no idea where Gaea had gone, but I'd have to let that go for now. I dressed, and just as I was about to hunt down Roe, my door slammed open and three guards filed in.

"The king requests your presence. Now."

"Of course he does." I followed the guards out of my rooms and back to the throne room. He had probably discovered the truth of the flower. At least Gaea would be safe.

The throne room was filled with fidgeting people. Like a great cathedral for the ancient gods, the rows of fae stared ahead to the dais, as if Autus was one. A beam of warm light poured through a window above, landing perfectly on the angry king as he slumped in his throne, thrumming his fingers upon the arm. The entire castle's population must have been called in.

There were no introductions; he didn't use flowery words or build anything up. He simply waited for me to stand before him, rose from his throne and descended the stairs until he was inches from me. "Where is she?"

"Who?"

He slammed his hand across my face. "Do not play games with me, Temir. Where is she?" I stared at him. "Where is Gaea?" his melodic voice demanded.

"I do not know, my king."

"I've got a missing stable boy, a dead stable master, a missing blacksmith, a fucking rebellion on my back, the captain of my guard was mysteriously killed, and now I'm missing another magic wielder. What the fuck is happening in my court? Morwena is doing great, powerful things, and I can't even keep a fucking stable boy!" I looked at him blankly as he ranted. "You will not move," his magic called.

He smashed his fist into my gut. It took everything in me not to swing back. Not to move. I could not betray the magic in the ring I wore. I had to stand there and take it. He swung again, striking my face, but I remained still. I could feel the blood seep from my nose.

"You will not use your power," he sang.

Again, he swung. I couldn't feel it anymore. I was numb. The absolute hatred had built a shield around me. A thousand eyes watched, unwavering as he struck. I held my chin higher and waited. Blow after blow. I could no longer see out of my swollen eyes, could not breathe through my broken nose. Still, I stood. If I ever found Gaea, I'd never tell her of this moment. Of the beating I'd taken for her.

"You will find her. And you will bring her back to me. You will not step foot in this castle again until you do, but you'll wish every night to sleep in your bed and have my forgiveness," he sang.

I did not move. Did not breathe.

"The seamstress conspires with the rebels and is now in my dungeons. They will come for her and I will trap them all," he announced across the room. "I am tired of insubordinate fae. From this moment on, if I even think you may be working against me, you will die. All of you." Sweat glistened on his head that was not there before. His hands shook as he turned back to me. There was a weakness in his power.

"Get out of my castle. You may not return to your rooms."

I turned and strode away. He had enchanted me not to heal myself and never took it back. If I hadn't had my protection, I would have never been able to save myself again. He was getting reckless, and that was an extremely dangerous thing.

I ran the halls searching for Roe, healing myself little by little. I could not find him, but I did find Nadra wandering like she was lost, searching for something. Or someone. I finished healing myself, knowing I was still covered in my own blood. I pulled a flask from my pocket. "Drink," I demanded, giving no other options.

She took it from my hands but did not drink.

I grabbed her hand and pulled her into a small cove. She weighed nothing and likely didn't have the strength to fight back even if she wanted to. "Drink it." I slipped the bracelet Oravan had given me for helping him join the rebels over her wrist.

"You watch me," she said, tilting her head back and forth. "You watch me, but I am broken."

Putting my hand on hers, I took a long deep breath. I needed to slow down. I needed the world to slow down for just a moment so I could make a new plan. She was here. Standing before me. And I had to do something. I felt her. Her spirit. Her soul. It was broken. Completely shattered into a million pieces, and that wasn't something I could heal. I pushed my magic through her anyway. She had bruising below her rags, and I knew the king had been beating her. I healed everything the eye could not see, and she stood straighter, broken ribs mended.

"Drink," I said again, softly. She lifted the serum to her lips and tipped her head back. When every last drop was gone, I pulled it from her hands. "Tell me everything the king has enchanted you to do."

I didn't want to hear it. I didn't want to know, but as I watched her, felt the bond between us, I knew I had to do this. She had to be released from him even if she would not feel the same pull to me.

She opened her mouth to speak but closed it. Squeezing her eyes shut, in the smallest voice she could muster, answered. "He has told me that I love him fiercely and want only him. I am not to ask my mother to join him but I will take her punishments if she doesn't." Her eyes filled with tears. "Why would he do this to me? He is an animal. My mother wants me to marry so badly. Why would she not give in to the king?"

I kept my tone soft, letting out a heavy sigh. "She was likely enchanted by King Coro not to work for another and doesn't even know it." I reached for her before shoving my hands in my pockets to resist.

"What is your name?" she asked.

"My name is Temir." A clattering in the hallway reminded me that I couldn't stay here with her. I may put her in danger by association if I was caught. "We don't have a lot of time. I need you to trust me. I need you to listen."

She nodded, and her honey-brown eyes watched me carefully.

"This bracelet will protect you from the king's enchant. You can't let him find it. I've given you a truth serum so you could retrieve the memories of what he has done to you. You must try to leave the castle. If you can steal a horse, try to find a servant named Iva. You need to get to Bryer's Keep, and she can tell you how to get there. Once you are there, I will meet you and protect you from him. You cannot stay here. Do you understand? The king is using you to trap your mother. You must eat, Nadra. You must."

"Okay."

"I will meet you there. Do you hear me?"

"Yes," she said as she squeezed her eyes shut.

"Take this." I gave her the antiserum so she would no longer have to speak the truth.

"I know his plan," she whispered and stepped away from me.

I ran toward my rooms, but guards were standing outside. The adda was in that room and I could not get to it. I only had one vial of serum left in my pocket. This was a disaster. I should have been more prepared. I ran to the stables to find Roe waiting for me with a fae horse already saddled.

"What's the plan?" he asked.

"I've got to get to Bryer's Keep. I'm going to have to come back for some things and you're going to have to get me in. Please ask Iva to help keep an eye on the king's ward. The red-haired female. As soon as you can get away, meet me at the Keep."

"Take him. He is the fastest." He handed over the reins. "Be safe."

"You too, Roe."

I rode as fast as that thunderous horse would carry me. I entered the rebellion headquarters in a flurry and pulled Rook from his bed that night.

"What is it, Temir?"

"I need to show you something. It cannot wait."

I reached into my pocket and pulled out the final vial of truth serum.

CHAPTER
36

KING TOLERO

*B*rax wore black-plated armor this time, and as he held his
sword before him, I knew he took the Trials as seriously as
they were always meant to be taken. He was a proud young
fae, and I saw so much of my own son in him. As he faced the naga before
him, he did not show concern.

"What's Muth's top fighter named?" I asked.

"That's Seel. He is from the south and as vicious as the naga are
known to be." Inok kept his eyes forward, indulging my curiosity, but
still incredibly invested in the show.

"Do you think Brax can beat him?"

"Yes, but if he does, he will have to fight that giant, and that's where
my concern comes in. This won't be an easy fight, but following it with
that, I don't see how he can manage."

The drums beat loud, signaling the beginning of the final two fights.
A horn blasted through the air, and my heart raced. The crowds shifted
forward as electricity crackled through the air in anticipation.

The naga coiled low as Brax brought his sword up. They wouldn't
fight to the death, but nearly. Until one of them stopped moving or

forfeited. I knew Brax's honor would never allow him to, but I prayed he didn't end up with severe injuries. Inok was right. I hoped Brax didn't win this fight. Until it began, and then I could never root against him. I had placed him there. I would see it through with him.

I clenched my fists and forced short breaths as they attacked each other. The naga held a slender sword, similar to a rapier, while Brax fought with the standard sword issued by the royal guard. Brax was quick, but his opponent was faster. Being able to coil and rotate quickly gave him the upper hand. They had countered each other's swings for so long they both had slowed and tired.

Brax rolled behind Seel. He swung from his knees. The naga countered with a blow to his head with the side of his sword.

"Come on," Inok growled from beside me. "His left."

Of course he'd noticed. The naga had left his left side wide open, only blocking his weaker. Again, Brax lunged, missing completely. The naga slithered sideways and knocked him down. Before he could react, Seel had his blade pressed into Brax. He whispered something to him.

I thought that was going to be it. The final battle would come down to the naga and the giant after all, but Brax slammed the side of his sword into the male, and it knocked him off balance. It was enough for Brax to get to his feet. The anxious crowd cheered and yelled for their favorite contestant as Brax stalked forward. He blocked every blow and continued to inch closer until he reached out and grabbed the naga by his neck and squeezed.

Seel tried shoving Brax away, tried to slither backward, even tried bashing him on the head, but nothing worked. It was like he had been possessed by a male scorned and seeking revenge. Whatever the naga had said to him was his own undoing.

Eventually, Seel tossed his sword into the sand and forfeited the match. The entire stadium erupted, filling the air with chants of Brax's name. Like they didn't remember that he would now have to face the giant.

"Can we buy him time to recover?" I asked Inok, grabbing my side as I remembered the injury.

"You're the king, I think you can do whatever you want, but I'm not sure how the people will feel about it. It would show favoritism, and he is already your fighter."

I waved, gesturing Brax to approach. He jogged across the arena. "Can you fight the giant?" I asked. He nodded. "You're sure? Do you need a break?" He shook his head. "Do I even want to know what the naga said to you?"

Fire lit his eyes. "No."

"Don't fight him with the sword," Inok leaned in, pinning him with a look.

"What should I use?" he asked.

"You need to stay out of his reach, which is expansive. Get him to his knees and then don't let him get up."

"I've got a plan." His eyes lit up with whatever had struck him.

"Off you go, then."

He walked out of the stadium as, once again, the drums pounded through the space. One by one, each fighter filled the area below, lining the walls of the pit. Standing on shaking legs, I stepped to the edge of the stage and turned to Umari. She rose from her seat. "Are we sure everyone is here?"

"Every last fae in the kingdom, Your Grace. We've flown in those who stayed behind, though there weren't many."

"And the hunters?"

"We believe we've found them all."

"Perfect."

I faced the crowd and took in the great size of my growing kingdom, tens of thousands. Every single fae was here. As one, the drums stopped and the crowd halted their cheers. I tugged on my magic and let it move through me as I started with my normal voice, letting it build. I held my hand over the charm around my neck I'd put on this morning. I needed everyone to hear my voice. This would be the greatest amount of power I had ever used, and even then, I wasn't sure if it would be enough.

"Tonight, one winner will be announced as the champion of the Trials. Following the battle, we invite anyone who would like to join the guard to come forward for presentation. After that, I welcome you all to the castle bailey, where you will be served a feast and can celebrate with our new victor."

I let the magic come forward.

"You will no longer remember your encounter with Morwena, the sea queen, or her selkies. Any feelings toward me that were not authentically yours prior to meeting with her are gone. Morwena killed your queen. She has poisoned your minds. I restore those to you now and order you to attend tonight's gathering."

I took a step backward and let the truth of what happened settle among the crowd. Pure exhaustion radiated through the void of my unjust power. Some cried out, others were silent for many moments until they all—the crowds, the pit fighters, and even the council behind me, including Inok—took a knee and bowed their heads. Finally, I had restored my kingdom. There was only one piece of the plan left. Waiting until all fae were gathered was difficult, but it was the only way.

"Let us begin anew," I said to my people.

This time they stood and cheered. For me. For this small battle we had won. I went back to my seat and waited for the sands below to clear of fae until it was only Brax and the giant. He more than doubled Brax's height, and I hoped I had bought him enough time to catch his breath before he began again. Unlike he had in the other fights, the giant took a knee and dipped his head to his opponent. Brax did the same.

"Finally, a fight with honor," Inok said from beside me.

"Remind me to give you a vacation after this is all over," I whispered.

He looked at me and glared. "Would that be before or after your stab wound is healed?"

"Still mad, then?" I asked.

358

"I'll still be mad at you on your four thousandth birthday."

"Why would anyone want to live that long?" I winked at him.

"I would. Just to be pissed at you."

I laughed, forgetting my wound, and winced in pain.

"Make that five thousandth," he snapped.

I shifted in my chair and smiled. "If only we didn't have a queen to capture first," I said under my breath.

"If only," he answered.

The crowd roared in applause and drew my attention back to Brax. He had chosen the throwing knives this time instead of the sword. Wise, though dangerous. It was evident there would be bloodshed.

The giant swung his swords as he had done before and crouched into his ready position while Brax clapped a powder on to his hands and did the same. The giant sprung, running at Brax with his sword swinging wildly. Brax easily dodged to the side, and the giant barely stopped in time to keep himself from barreling into the side of the arena's barrier wall.

Using that to his advantage, Brax whipped a throwing knife into the back of the giant's knee. He wailed and spun to remove the knife, but Brax threw another, slamming it into his hand, causing him to drop one sword. He scurried forward and grabbed the giant's discarded weapon. It was far too big for him, and he knew he couldn't keep it, so he ran and tossed it to the far edge of the arena, knowing the giant could still retrieve it, but it would cost him.

He did just that though, running for the sword. Brax threw another knife and was short by half the distance. The problem with throwing knives was arming your opponent and disarming yourself. You had to be precise, as every throw counted.

The giant halted and ran back for the throwing knife before jogging off to get his sword. I finally realized what Brax was doing. Inok laughed beside me as he put it together as well.

Brax hadn't missed with that knife. He was wearing the giant out. Forcing him to run back and forth. That still didn't solve the problem with the number of weapons the giant now had in comparison to Brax. He'd thrown three knives, which meant he had only three or four left.

"Think he can do it?" Inok asked, never looking away from the fight.

"I don't know. The giant has slowed for sure, but that's all he has achieved so far, and he wasn't that fast to begin with."

The fighters circled each other once more, and I noted the three knives left in Brax's hands. The giant, unable to keep the throwing knives and two swords, dropped the extra knives at his feet and stomped on them until they disappeared into the sand. He then looked at Brax, and his belly laugh echoed off the walls. He definitely thought he had outsmarted my soldier. I still couldn't help but smile at the giant's infectious laughter. He was enjoying the fight, and that was what the Trials were supposed to be.

Brax smiled with him but then turned and ran to the other end of the arena. I didn't think he'd be able to throw far enough to hit the giant before he moved out of the way, but he did, planting a throwing knife in the giant's shoulder.

The giant's smile faded as he roared in pain, dropping a sword again to remove the knife. He then charged after Brax, who kept his feet planted and waited until the very last second to jump to the side as the giant crashed into the wall.

Brax ran to the general area, where his other knives had been buried, and frantically dug, thinking he would have time to find them before the giant recuperated.

"Behind you," a female screamed just as the giant grabbed him by the neck and lifted him off the ground.

Brax swung a knife out, but because his back was to the giant, he couldn't reach him. He couldn't slam his knife into his hand because if he went too far, they would go through the other side and into his own neck.

360

The crowd gasped as the giant threw Brax across the arena. He landed with a thud and groaned, rolling to his side.

The giant dropped his sword and ran over to him, kneeling. He pushed his arm under Brax and helped him to his feet. He then bounded back across the arena, picked his sword back up, and crouched once more, smiling. The world needed more giants.

Brax regained his bearings and limped toward the giant in the middle of the pit, took a knee, and held his sword up to him. It was the most honorable forfeit I had ever seen.

The crowd jumped to their feet and applauded as the two fighters shook hands. They came to stand before the stage, and Inok and I walked to the steps to greet them.

"What's your name?" I asked the giant.

"Greywolf, sir king," he answered

"Where do you come from, Greywolf?"

"The Winterlands, sir king." He pressed his lips together.

"I've not heard of them. How do you like it here?"

"It's hot. But nice, sir king."

"You fought with great honor today."

"Thank you, sir king." He bowed low.

I turned to the roaring crowds. "It is my pleasure to name the winner of the tiered fights, Greywolf of the Winterlands. The very first fae from the north to ever win the Trials. Please join me in congratulating him." Again the crowds cheered, and I looked to Brax. He grinned from ear to ear and patted Greywolf on the back as the giant also clapped for himself. "And now is the most special time of all," I called. "Should any of you wish to join the guard, please come stand in the middle of the arena."

The crowds shifted as males and females made their way to the center.

"Brax, please join us in evaluations," I said.

"Are you sure?" He looked between Inok and me.

"I'm sure." I stepped down to the sandy bottom.

The folk formed a line across the arena, and I was happy to see Greywolf join them, right in the middle of the prospects. We stood before him first.

"Are you sure you want to join the guard, even though it would mean leaving the fighting pits?"

"Fighting is good. Sir king is better," he replied.

"Welcome to the Flame Court, guard Greywolf. You'll report to the castle tomorrow morning."

"Yes, thank you, sir king." He smiled and nodded his head in earnest.

"I'm happy to have you," I reached up to pat his massive arm before I moved on.

We finished going through the rest of fae, some showcasing weapons skills, some with hand-to-hand combat skills. We then turned to the magic wielders. I thought of Fenlas and where he would rank among the gifted. I hoped he'd found his charge and would be home soon. I considered what it might mean if Morwena caught him before he could make it back to me. His prophecy had loomed over him since the day Alewyn's Promise was born.

Through these volunteers, the world has giving us the gifts we would need to take on the northern kingdoms, should it come down to that. I didn't collect or imprison magic wielders, but my adversaries did. I recognized how dangerous that could be as I watched a fae move the world below him.

"Are you ready?" Inok asked when we were finished, knowing what was to come next.

"More than ever."

"Do you think it will work?"

I shrugged. "I guess we'll see if we truly can catch a fish in a net." I turned to the crowd and spoke for the final time. "The Trials are over. Please join us in the bailey of the castle for a feast."

ARA

*T*he northern kingdom was beautiful. Though I knew I'd only seen a fraction of it, in the stillness of the frigid air and the white-capped mountains, a single voice, a single song, could echo through the entire kingdom. And so it did as Greeve stood on the crest of a hill and sang into the endless winter. The melody of his song was soul-wrenching and his pitch and vibrato were perfect. The rest of us stood back, shoulder to shoulder, waited, watched, and listened.

We stood on the cusp of the abyss. A straight line of fae staring into the distance as we listened to his melodious song carry us away. Away from The Mists lurking behind us. Away from the journey ahead. A male as beautiful as Greeve with a voice like a god should never have existed. If Fen wasn't holding my hand, anchoring me to him, I think I would have fallen in love in that one single moment. His dark hair blew gently in the breeze, and though he sang with his eyes closed, he opened his spirit to sing that ballad. Of all the moments and memories in my life, however long it may be, I hoped this one would always stay with me. The moment a southern fae lost his soul on the wind of the northern kingdom.

"They used to be from here, you know," Fen whispered in my ear, bringing me back from wherever Greeve had carried me off to.

"Who?" I asked, still watching him.

"The dracs. They lived in the north until the Iron Wars forced them to the Flame Court.

"Do you think something calls to him here?"

"His magic is of the wind, as is this court. This is where his people, my people, came from. I would say something within him probably feels at peace here in these mountains."

"Do you? Feel at peace here?"

He stood before me, putting his strong hands on my arms. I looked up into his fierce eyes and let his words settle over me. "I know you can't see this right now, but you are my peace. Whatever it is Greeve feels standing in the Wind Court, I feel that ten times more strongly standing beside you. When you take my hand," he said, kissing my fingertips, "when you smile at something stupid Kai says, when you don't back down no matter the odds, when the thought of you brings me more pride than anything I've ever done, that's my peace. It's not a place, it's you."

His words lifted my soul like a prayer. But a tiny seed of doubt remained. He'd been so intense for so long, flawed and angry and possessive. But so was I. Maybe I didn't want a mate, but I did want someone in my corner. Someone who would have my back no matter what. Someone who would look at me the way he did.

"Attention whore," Kai coughed into his hand as Greeve rejoined us.

"Don't listen to him," Wren said. "That was so beautiful, Greeve."

"Where did Lichen go?" I spun, searching for him.

Wren pointed. "He's down by the fire with his nose in a book, I'm sure. I think that's all he packed."

"Glad I don't have to carry that bag," I said as we made our way to the bottom of the hill. We moved to sit around the warm fire, giving Fen a magic break. He claimed it only took a trickle to maintain our warmth, but a trickle would eventually run him dry.

"Lichen, what the hell?" I jumped to my feet. "That's my book. What were you doing in my bag? You shouldn't have opened that!" It was too late though. I felt a foreign surge of anger and then a scream. Eerie laughter covered the remnants of Greeve's song in the air. I whipped my head around and scanned the horizon. Nothing. "Give me the book," I growled. "Show me what you were reading."

"It's quite interesting actually," he said.

"No the fuck it isn't. You don't know what this book is. It's not a toy or a resource for your curiosity. You've just unleashed something that should have stayed trapped. How? What did you do?"

"What are you talking about?" Fen surged forward.

"What is that?" Wren inched her way toward Greeve.

"The book." I threw my hands in the air. The haunting scream echoed again. "Listen," I said, pulling two knives, "I got that book from Coro's library. It had information about Nealla which I needed. But apparently Aibell also needed me to retrieve the book, and I was supposed to hold onto it. She told me there were creatures locked away inside. I have a feeling Curious Cathy over there just let one free."

"You've been carrying that around this whole time and didn't think to even mention it?" Fen asked.

"Don't start with me, Prince."

"Awesome." Kai reached for a weapon. "So, before we have to enter the land of doom and gloom, and right after we fight dragons and soldiers, we have to hunt and kill a creature our ancestors could only lock into a book?"

"Aibell," Fen roared.

"Don't blame her," I told him. "She didn't open the book."

Everyone looked to Lichen.

"Sorry." He looked to the ground.

"We'll be having a chat about going through my shit later." I shot daggers through my glare.

"Tell us what you were reading about," Wren said, trying, as she always did, to ease the tension.

"I believe that is the scream of a banshee," he answered.

"Are you fucking kidding me?" Greeve asked, pulling the long, curved sword from his back.

"Does anyone have any ideas on killing a banshee?" Fen asked, looking directly at me.

"Not a gods-damned clue," I answered. "The only thing I've ever heard is that if you hear a banshee cry, you have under twenty-four hours to live."

"Super awesome." Kai stared down Lichen.

The banshee's scream was closer this time and again followed by a haunting cackle that made my hair stand on edge.

"I only read the words in the book. How was I supposed to know?"

"You couldn't feel it? The magic?"

"No." He shrugged, his shoulders still heavy.

I would think about why an evil book with magical creatures inside called only to me later. For now, I had to think quickly. "Can anyone see it?"

"I can't see it, but I can feel it on the wind," Greeve replied, watching the skies.

"Can you intercept it?" Fen asked.

"Possibly."

"So, we just send him up there on his own?" I turned to Greeve, who grinned and disappeared.

"Attention whore," Kai coughed into his hands again.

"Maybe, but I'll still save your ass," Greeve answered from somewhere above.

Fen pulled his sword and took a step away from me so he had clearance to swing if he had to. We waited in uneasy silence, all ready in case the banshee showed itself. The scream rattled the sky. I felt a gush of wind as Greeve flew past me, and then another shriek as he made contact.

Lichen yelled and grabbed the sides of his head as deep red blood poured from his nose.

"Shit." Kai moved his weapon haphazardly through the air, though he could not see the attacker.

"Kai, stop, you could hit Greeve," Wren scolded.

No one moved as Lichen fell to the ground with his ears covered, still screeching in pain. Then Wren followed him. Instinctively, her magic came forward and she was gone, but we could still hear her cries from the ground.

"Gods-damnit. Come on, Greeve," Fen barked.

"It's fast," he called from above.

I felt him move back and forth across the sky with bated breath. Another scream. A terrible, gut-wrenching, vomit-inducing scream. Blood poured from Kai's ears, and he also yelled, trying to cover them. Fen grabbed his temple and groaned, trying to resist whatever was happening, but he still fell hard to one knee. I felt a rush of Fen's own power as he tried and failed to pin the banshee.

"Stop, Fen," Greeve begged. "You're pushing me around."

"Tell me how to help. I can't just stand here."

"Try your magic," Fen said through gritted teeth.

I closed my eyes and tried so damn hard to find some kind of foreign source of anything within me that I could push forward. A trickle of something small and so far away I could barely reach it flashed through my mind. I held on and tried to drag it forward. Nothing. The screaming continued, and Greeve grunted as he passed.

"It's not working," I told anyone who could hear me at that point.

The banshee shrieked a never-ending cry of pain and panic, and then Greeve landed on the frozen ground, heaving, the snow-covered ground stained with fresh blood.

"Gone," he panted.

He was completely tattered. Whatever the banshee was in corporeal form, it had shredded the wind cleaver. He bled from a thousand slices all over his body. The other's screaming faded, and Fen crawled across the ground to Greeve. He made it as far as he could, reaching out his hand to clasp Greeve's.

"Wren?" I asked tentatively.

"Here," she moaned, revealing herself in the fetal position on the frozen ground.

I walked over to Kai and knelt beside him. "Are you okay?"

"Never better. So glad we had Greeve to save our asses." He grunted and sat up.

Fen stood, pulled Greeve to his feet, and dug through his bag until he pulled out a tin of salve. It was exactly like the one my father had kept in our barn. The only one who needed it was Greeve, but he barely used any. He changed his clothes and joined us around the fire. I'd never questioned Greeve's intensity. He carried a dark mystery with him, wrapped in the breeze that flowed, but now? Now I knew he was a creature of legends.

"Anyone else carrying anything they want to talk about?" Fen asked.

The whole group turned to me.

"Oh no you don't. Lichen should have never gone through my things."

"I'll admit, I am at fault. The book slipped out when I had everyone's things in the cave with me. Curiosity got the best of me. Speaking of curiosity, isn't it strange that the banshee did not target you?"

"Is it? I don't know the rules of a fucking banshee. Maybe my birthright protects me. Maybe you shouldn't deflect the blame."

"You felt your magic though, didn't you?" Fen asked.

"How did you know?"

He shrugged and looked away.

Wren cleared her throat, and my eyes snapped to her. "What was it like?" she asked Greeve, but I noted the subject change. They shared a secret and weren't telling me. Nothing would hold my wall up better than lies and deceit.

"No. Don't change the subject. How did you know?"

"I didn't," he said. "I just assumed you tried, that's all."

I read him carefully, but he didn't flinch.

"Let's just get some sleep. We've got a long day of dying ahead of us," Greeve said.

"Hey, that was my line." Kai threw his blanket at Greeve.

"Yeah, but I'm the hero, so I can say what I want."

I walked over to my bag, pulled out my blanket and laid down separate from the group. I felt a wave of heat move over me, but Fen kept his distance. There was definitely something he wasn't telling me.

As I drifted off to sleep, I fell into my nightmare. Only this time inky hands covered my mouth and I couldn't make a sound as I was forced to go through the motions.

Nealla's seductive voice echoed in the background. "You are nearly there, child. But do you need your friends? Should you drag them through the unknown? You don't need them. You only need me, right now. Come, child. Come through The Mists."

I woke, drenched in sticky sweat and heart racing. The sun had not yet risen, and Lichen had fallen asleep during guard duty. I stood carefully, pushed my blanket into my bag, and took Nealla's advice. I'd only continue to endanger them if I brought them with me.

Two snow-covered hills later, I stood face to face with the ominous wall of dense fog. Even in the pitch-black night, with only scattered stars and a distant moon to light the world, The Mists still moved in a gray shadow of a wraithlike haze. There was nothing gradual about the divide between the Wind Court and The Mists. I lifted my hand to reach beyond the barrier, preparing myself for searing pain or total encapsulation as I made contact.

"Stop!" Fen shouted from behind me. "What in the world are you doing?"

I dropped my hand and my head. "I'm going on by myself, Prince."

"We talked about this. We're a team now."

"Are we? Really? Why would Lichen go through my bag, Fen? Did you ask him to spy on me? That book didn't just fall out. I had it hiding in the very bottom."

"I'll talk to him." His voice shook with desperation.

"No, it's not just that. You're hiding something too. I saw the way Wren looked at you earlier. I know you aren't telling the truth."

"Ara, no. I'm not hiding anything from you. I don't know what you thought you saw, but you didn't. We can leave the others, that's fine. But let me come with you."

"Greeve would kill me if I took you into The Mists without him."

"You think he wouldn't kill me if I let you go alone? You matter too."

"Stop saying that. Stop trying to convince me that I'm important to them. They are only here because you have some score to settle with fate and they are stuck with you. The only role I play is the line leader as we all march to our own fucking deaths."

He reached for me, but I stepped away.

"You think that banshee tonight was bad, Fen? Every one of you were on the ground from that one damn creature. Nealla wants me, begs for me to come to her. I don't know why. I don't know what she's going to do to me, but I know that even if the second half of my prophecy doesn't matter, I still have to try to save this gods-damned world. I can't even save myself. What right do I have to drag anyone along?"

"You aren't dragging. We choose it." Wren appeared out of nowhere.

"You don't know what you're saying. You could die."

"Yes, and I could have died a thousand other ways in my life. If I die fighting to make the world better, then at least it meant something. At least I didn't sit back and watch it burn."

"You go, I go," Greeve said as he and Kai landed beside me. "I don't choose Fen, I don't choose the southern kingdom. I'm not here to be anything but your friend. I choose you, Ara. You walk into those Mists, then I'm following right behind you."

"I know it doesn't seem like I take it seriously, but I do. Just like everyone else. It's not just your journey anymore. It's all of ours." Kai stepped closer. "We've come way too far to let you leave us behind now. I fist fought a dragon. I mean, I totally lost, but I did that shit. I just got ear fucked by a banshee for gods' sake."

"You guys are all fucking crazy," I said. "When we die, don't say I didn't warn you."

"I hope there's dessert in hell." Kai winked. Greeve smacked him in the back of the head. "What? You can't tell me you don't miss Loti's kitchen right now."

Fen faced me and held his hand out. He didn't step toward me, and I knew he was asking me to meet him halfway. To let that gesture be a truce between us as we faced a legendary unknown. I looked carefully at each of their faces. I knew I'd regret it, but I slipped my hand into his. "Together, then."

"Are you going to stop trying to leave us behind now?" Wren pursed her lips.

"Probably not."

"Are we just going to leave Lichen sleeping on guard duty while we go?" Kai asked as we stared down The Mists.

"It would serve him right." Greeve crossed his muscled arms.

"You guys are being too hard on him," Wren answered. "He said he was sorry, and we've all done way worse things than read."

"I'll go talk to him," Fen said. "I don't think anyone is getting any more sleep tonight anyway. We might as well get this over with."

"I'll take you," Greeve said, grabbing his arm and disappearing.

"Bet you a bottle of wine he doesn't want to come," Kai said, elbowing Wren.

"You're on," she answered.

Minutes later, Fen and Greeve joined us without Lichen in tow. Apparently, the banshee had scared him from coming any farther, and I didn't mind at all. I didn't want to have to watch out for an old fae who would likely get us into deep shit the minute his childlike curiosity peaked.

"Should I stay with him?" Wren asked, ever the mother hen.

"He's not a child," Greeve answered. "You can do what you want, but I'm sure he can manage just fine. He will be there when we get back."

"Shall we?" Fen asked me.

In that moment, I realized Fen was about to walk into The Mists. His mated father had lost his wife, and this was where widowed fae came to die. He had probably spent the last fifty years hoping his father would never stand in this exact spot, and here he was, ready to walk in for me. I forced away the lump in my throat.

"No time like the present." I stepped toward the wall of doom.

Fen grabbed my hand, and I reached for Kai's. He took Wren's, and she held Greeve's. As one, we took a single step into the Mist.

Nothing happened. I looked back and forth through the glow of the unknown, but aside from the weight of moisture in the air, we were fine. Still gloomy within, there was nothing to see beyond thick fog.

"That was anticlimactic," Kai said, dropping our hands. "I thought for sure we were going to die."

"We've taken one step." Greeve pulled his sword out. "This could go on forever."

"Just stay together and keep walking." Fen drew his own blade.

We separated enough for everyone to be properly armed and moved as one through the legendary Mists. It grew denser as we moved, and after an hour, I realized the sun should have risen. Nothing had changed except the fact that I could barely see them beside me as we walked farther into the abyss.

"Fen?" Wren's worried voice pierced through the silence.

372

"Still here, baby bird," he said.

I pushed away an annoying ping of jealousy at their long history. I didn't even know she had a nickname, and I blamed myself for not being more observant and not trying to get to know them better.

"We should talk," Greeve said. "To make sure we're staying together. I can't see shit."

"How far do you think this goes?" Kai was farther from me than he should have been.

"You'd be the one to ask, tracker." Fen answered.

I heard the sharp sound of his sword sliding into the sheath and felt his hand brush mine. I grasped it tightly but felt the pull of him slipping through my fingers.

"Kai," Greeve shouted in the distance.

"Here," Kai answered from farther away.

"Ara?" Fen's hazy voice was frantic.

He was right beside me a moment ago, and now I could barely hear him. In fact, the last sound I heard was the distant scream from Wren before the entire world was a massive cavern of empty moisture. Chasing my destiny had inevitably led to chaos, as I knew it would.

"Fen!" I screamed into the emptiness.

No answer. I turned and ran backward, closing my eyes to focus on sound alone. My heartbeat filled the emptiness like thunder. He was gone. They all were. I turned and ran back the way we were going, or at least the way I thought we were going, hoping that we might have been near the end and would soon come out the other side.

I wandered for hours with my hands held before me. I couldn't see my fingertips. I screamed and screamed into The Mists until my throat was raw. No one answered. I wished for a drink of water so badly, if I wasn't so deathly afraid of whatever The Mists were made of, I might have started sucking on my damp pack.

I walked and walked and ran and ran to no avail. I felt like I was moving along a wheel on a spindle. I had never been so grateful for

Nadra's mother as I was in that moment. Her magic was keeping the moisture away from my skin, and the warmth never left me. I was sure the others weren't so lucky.

Eventually, I became so tired I realized I must have walked alone the rest of the entire day. I wouldn't stop to sleep, but my feet dragged along the ground, and it became difficult to keep going. Still I walked. I yelled as often as my tattered voice could.

I was desperate. I had done this to them. If they would have just listened and let me go alone, they would all still be safe and not lost within the fog. But maybe they found each other and I was the last one left. My emotions were erratic as I walked. Anger bled into fear, carrying me step by step as I wondered if it would ever end.

There became a point where I could no longer walk. I was so tired, so sure it had been more than a day, possibly even two days of walking, searching, and begging for the end of that horrid place.

I thought of Fen. The others too, but mostly him. Not having him here with me was unsettling. I wasn't sure when that switch had happened, but I realized I just couldn't fight the way I felt about him anymore. The idea of never seeing him again was the worst thing I could imagine. I had no one else. I hadn't thought I'd be scared to be alone until I really was again. I was going to tell him how I really felt. Just lay it all out there and let him make the decision. He'd been a dick, but he'd more than made up for that, and it was time to really let it all go.

I couldn't sleep. I wouldn't let that nightmare of Nealla call to me again. Instead, I lay on the ground and did the only thing I could think to do. I tried to call on my magic. I had no distractions, no other choices and an endless amount of time.

I closed my eyes and let the muddied world fall away until I was completely weightless in my mind, searching deep within me. I jumped to my feet as I realized I hadn't felt my magic, but Fen. It felt like he was right beside me, comforting me, though I knew he wasn't.

"Fen," I screamed, but only silence answered.

I sat back down, closed my eyes and concentrated. Again, I could feel him. Sense him, though he wasn't there. I tried to reach out to him. Nothing. I even tried taking down my mental shields. I only felt naked, exposed. Still no sign of the others. I shoved my shields back in place and focused solely on the magic I knew was within me.

I reached for that drop I had recognized before. Only this time it was more than a drop. A shallow bowl. I called it forward and felt it rush through me and into the world like a thunderclap. My hair stood on end as I looked around and realized I'd cleared The Mists around me in a large circle radius. The barren ground was only compacted dirt, but I could finally take a full deep breath without the feeling of soggy suffocation. I vaulted to my feet. My palms sweating, heart pumping and eyes blinking rapidly. I'd done it.

I ran to the edge of the circle, closed my eyes and tried again to pull that magic through me. It was more strenuous this time, but when I did, and The Mists cleared, I saw a figure in the distance. From here, I could see the ink on his tan skin and his long black hair draped over his broad shoulders.

"Greeve," I screamed.

He turned, saw me and was by my side in an instant. "Are you okay?" He searched me for wounds, spinning me around and then crushing me into his chest.

"I'm fine. Only tired and hungry."

"Here." He reached into his pack and handed me a hunk of grilled rabbit. I hadn't realized just how hungry I was until I inhaled the meat, barely even tasting it. "If I'd known we were going to be separated, I would have sorted out the meat for everyone."

"How long has it been?"

"Days, I'd wager. How did you ..." He waved to the clearing.

"I'm not sure. I think I used magic, but I don't know what kind. It wasn't fire though. I just pulled on it and this happened."

"Can you do it again?"

I bit my lip. "I could try."

We walked together to the edge of the circle I'd cleared, and I repeated the process. When I opened my eyes, the clearing had nearly doubled in size, but it was bare.

"Again, Ara. But stay away from that final drop, do you hear me? Never use that last bit of magic."

I nodded. My fatigue had grown exponentially by the fourth try, but as it happened, Wren appeared. She wailed and leapt into Greeve's arms. "I thought I'd never see you all again. I was certain we had made the biggest mistake coming here."

"I'm not so sure you were wrong," I answered.

Greeve handed her some meat, and she ate it about as gracefully as I had.

"How?" she said with a mouthful of food.

"Ara's using her magic," Greeve answered, pride lighting his eyes.

"So, it's true? You really do have it. What kind?"

"I don't know. Mist clearing seems to be working so far. Does that count?"

"This time when you try, see if you can get the same results using less." Greeve looked around us, recognizing that eventually that small bit of magic would be gone. If I didn't learn quickly enough, we would never get to the others.

"I don't know how. I'm not in control of it."

"Just imagine one drop will clear all of The Mists. You put the power into the process and see what happens," Greeve said.

"No promises," I answered.

I did as he said and tried to imagine what the area would look like completely void. I felt the unfamiliar magic rush from me and opened my eyes as Wren gasped.

"Holy shit. That's remarkable." She spun in a slow circle.

I hadn't cleared the area like I had hoped, but again, I'd opened a massive piece of it, revealing Kai napping on the ground. Wren went to get him while Greeve stayed planted by my side. "Only Fen left, Ara. Can you find him?"

"The little bowl of magic is almost gone. I can probably do it one more time, but that's all of it." I could feel my palms sweat as panic rose. If I couldn't find him, I'd never be able to tell him how I felt. But what if my magic just wasn't strong enough?

"Wait," Wren said, jogging back to us. "Ara, try reaching out to him."

"I've tried, I've tried reaching out to everyone over these past few days. It doesn't do any good."

"No, I mean see if you can feel him like you do your magic. As soon as you feel him, try sending your magic in that direction instead of just letting it pour from you."

"I'm not in control."

"Just try it." She stamped her foot.

I bit the inside of my cheek to keep from sniping at her for ordering me about. She meant well, so I tried taking her advice. I let my heart call out to his. I pictured those beautiful green eyes and his tanned skin, the way he pulled himself out of the water, and the way he smiled when he looked at me. I heard his voice as he made promise after promise to me. *You're my peace.* I played those words repeatedly in my mind. The moment I thought I felt him, I pushed the magic, just as Wren had said.

"He's there," Greeve pointed.

In an instant, we ran to him. He was farther than the others had been. The moment he realized The Mists were clearing and he saw me, he dropped everything and bolted. We crashed into each other. Physically and on some other level as well. Something within me wrapped so tightly around him, in that moment, I knew I'd never truly be able to let him go again. I pulled away from him only to look into his eyes. To silently convey the feelings I didn't know how to put to words. I felt the tears fall as he nodded in understanding.

"I thought the worst had happened." He held me so tight I couldn't take in a full breath.

"Thanks, Fen," Kai yelled. "I'm fine by the way. In case you were wondering."

I gave him a crude gesture. No matter what issues lay between me and Fen, no matter how much I didn't want to fall for anyone, I hadn't realized how much I'd missed having him here beside me until he wasn't anymore. My mother's warning to trust no one was a lifetime ago. I was foolish for thinking I couldn't have faith in the one male who was sent to protect me. If he said he was hiding nothing, then I needed to swallow my pride, my fears and believe him.

CHAPTER
38

NADRA

itting on the edge of my fine silk sheets in a room that was not my own, I realized the lesser fae with horns had released me from the hell and prison that was my own tangled mind, or at least he had tried. The king had used his magic to destroy me. My thoughts hadn't been my own in so long. But I was still a prisoner. To my memories. To the hands that beat me. I would have begged for him without the enchantment and tried to win his heart. But everything was different now. I'd seen a true piece of the cruelty that festered in the world. It had changed me beyond recognition. Once a bubbly socialite, now hardly a female at all.

I ran my fingers along the soft fabric and refused to look at my harrowing reflection. Had my mother seen how I looked and been tortured by her inability to save me? The only one who could save me gave me power over the king. I knew his dangerous plans. The darkness in my mind beckoned me. Coaxed me to live in hatred and betrayal. Convinced me that I was nothing and no one and the world would destroy me. The king would. But if I told him of the lesser fae's revelations. If I gave him the bracelet and told him of that serum. If I told him about Bryer's Keep and that there was a worker here named Iva that was also a rebel? Would he let me go?

CHAPTER

39

TEMIR

"I don't understand," Rook said. "What is it?"

"Just drink it and let me show you." I folded my hands on the desk between us.

He drank the entire tube of truth serum in one swallow and handed it back to me.

"Try to lie. What is your name?"

"S ... Rook." His eyes went wide.

"Are you loyal to the rebellion?"

"Yes."

"Are you trying to lie."

"Y-yes," he answered, rapidly blinking as his mouth fell open.

"It is a truth serum I've created. If we give this to any of our rebels, they won't be able to lie. We can keep traitors out of our ranks."

"Do you have more?"

"I do, but unfortunately I don't have the antiserum with me. So don't talk to anyone you planned to lie about anything to until it wears off."

I walked back and forth through the tidy room and tried to make a plan, rubbing my hands together as I stared at the ceiling. "My stores are in the castle with something far more valuable. I need to get back in without being detected, and if I can have some males come with me, I'd appreciate it. I've got a lot of seeds and flowers we will need to make the serum, but if we cannot get to those, I'll never be able to make it again."

"Can your friend use her magic to get you in and out?"

I'd refused to think of Gaea the entire journey to the Keep. I couldn't process the way I felt. I wasn't sure if I was angry with her for leaving the way she did, or if it was all my fault and I deserved every emotion I'd felt the moment I realized she was gone. But none of that mattered anymore. Not one second of it.

"She is gone. I will have to ride back. Roe is supposed to monitor the status of my rooms at the castle and meet me back here with a plan to get us back in."

"Okay, follow me." We walked together down the dimly lit stone hallway all the way at the very end. "It's not much, but it's a bed. Get some rest, Tem. You look like shit."

I closed the door behind him. The room was more of a closet with a folding cot, but it was clean, and I didn't need anything more than that. I'd fled the castle. I would go back, get my things and for once in my life, those grounds would no longer be my home. If I could be sure the king wouldn't find the rebellion, then I could be sure he would never find me.

I slept long and hard, and I only woke because Rook banged on my door. I sat up, stretched my arms and remembered where I was. I threw the door open.

"Roe's here," he said.

"How long was I asleep?" I asked.

"Nearly a full day. I figured if you slept that long you probably needed it. He just arrived."

We walked into the empty meeting room, and Roe jumped to his feet. He'd been sitting at a large round table surrounded in empty chairs. "We need to leave right now. There's a small window of time I can get you into your rooms, but if we don't race, we aren't going to make it."

"Let's go."

"There's one thing though." His shoulders dropped as if someone had just crushed him. I looked at him expectantly, but he kept his head down as he held out a large metal file to me. "If you enter the castle with your horns, I'll never be able to conceal you."

He was right, of course. My horns had grown so mighty, I'd be recognized immediately. "Thank you," I said, taking the file.

Roe and I left immediately. I held that hoof rasp in my hand for quite some time. Before, I'd have to put myself in a place mentally before I could degrade my stag horns. The difference today would be that I no longer hated myself. I did not blame myself for the cruel actions of the unforgiving world—of the wicked king. I was proud of my own convictions. But as I tilted my head down and began to file, it still took every ounce of self-control not to scream through the blustering night.

I filed and filed right through the pain. I thought of Gaea leaving me and filed. I thought of the king beating me in front of the entire court and filed. I thought of all the fae in Volos who had to leave their homes forever just to live. And filed. I thought of that single female in that slain village who used her fire magic to disintegrate the bodies of everyone she knew and loved, and I filed.

Roe remained silent on his horse beside me as we rode, and I appreciated him more for that than anything else he had ever done for me. Roe had become my friend. He was now the only one I could count on, no matter what, and though he was a lesser fae like me, he was a male of great character, and I was beyond proud to be his friend.

We rode through most of the night and watched as the golden sun crested behind the castle. We went through the gates easily, disguised as servants. Crossing the bailey was not difficult either. The real trouble came when we entered and I had to navigate the halls full of fae who would recognize me.

"Up here, you take a left and go directly into that empty bedroom. As soon as the guards leave and before the next shift comes, I'll give you the signal and you go to your rooms. Grab what you need and get out, Tem. You'll only have a few minutes. Then, meet me back in the empty room."

"Thanks Roe."

"I don't know exactly how long until the switch. You'll have to just hide until then."

"I've got it, Roe. Don't worry."

He dipped his head once, his beard sweeping across the floor as he hustled away. I slipped into the vacant room, pressed my palm to the door and rested my forehead against it, breathing in and out slowly while listening to the other side for Roe to give the signal.

I could feel her. I could nearly see that bright red hair and those golden eyes somewhere in the castle. I knew what it meant. I think I had known what it meant for a long time. Gaea did too. Maybe that's why she had left. How cruel it would have been to make her sit and watch as I discovered, saved, and sacrificed everything for my mate.

I reached for the bond that had formed in my mind. She was on the other end of it when a wave of absolute terror washed over me. She was in trouble. Without thinking, I grasped the door handle, then pulled away. I would have one single shot at acquiring the adda. If I left this room, I'd lose it. But if she needed me, I had no choice. I would have to find another way into my rooms.

I yanked the door open just as the guards walked away.

"Roe," I whispered. Nothing. "Roe," I called again.

The tension released from my shoulders as he finally answered. "Here, Temir."

"I need you to get the things from my room, Roe. I have to find Nadra, the king's consort. I can't explain it right now, but I think she needs help."

"Let me find her. I can walk the castle. I promise, I'll bring her to you. I don't know what to get from your rooms. Trust me with your mate, Temir."

"You knew?"

"You rode all night to get back to your rooms for something. I imagine only a mate would be worth sacrificing it for. Hurry now."

He ran off down the hallway, and I bolted into my rooms. My mind was not here but with her and the terror and heated anger she sent me through me. Something had happened.

I threw my entire stash of leo flower seeds into a bag, then placed all of the dried leaves I'd been working with in as well. I took as much care as I had time for, wrapping full vials of serum I'd made. I pulled the formula book from the hidden tear in my sinking mattress and added that and the adda's glass box. I took all of my dried herbs and as many helpful journals as I thought I might need, then threw as many books and journals into the fire as I could. I didn't pack a single personal item.

I wondered if that's why Gaea had kept her rooms bare for so long. It hadn't occurred to me until now that I would never see any of these things again. I packed two bags full and threw them over my shoulder. I cracked opened the door and peeked around the corner. Still no guards. I snuck out and went back to the empty room I'd been waiting in before.

I paced. I sat. I paced again. They did not come. Hours passed. Absolute dread seeped over me like a cloak, and the most horrid revelation occurred. I lost the feeling in my face, the strength in my legs. I'd told her everything. Literally every single thing she could have used against myself and the rebellion. I knew she was my mate, but what if she didn't? If she refused the bond? I could have sealed my fate in a moment of panic. I froze as the entire world around me came crashing down. I'd put my trust in a stranger, and as the minutes turned into hours in that damn room, I realized I may have made the biggest mistake of my life.

CHAPTER

40

KING TOLERO

The bailey around the castle was so full of fae I wasn't sure it could hold more. The staff exited the castle carrying heavy trays of savory food and sweet wine as thousands upon thousands of fae stood upon the red sands, oblivious to what was to come. The threat approaching the castle, if everything had gone to plan. Inok did not leave my side as we took turns glancing to the wide-open unguarded gates, waiting impatiently. She would come. She was too desperate, too hateful to do anything else.

As if my thoughts were cast into the night, selkies filed through the open gate. Inok grabbed my arm in warning as Morwena followed close behind. She searched the crowd until her eyes landed on me, flickering to Inok's protective grasp.

"What a foolish king you are indeed," she jeered from above the throng of fae. "To stand amongst your people in the open night. Have you been so busy crying into your pillow that you could not even see that your entire kingdom has turned on you?"

"I'm not sure what you mean, Morwena," I answered, stepping behind Inok as if in fear of her.

She cackled and gestured to the crowd. "These are my people now, Tolero. My warriors. They were all so eager to join me."

"Were they?" I tilted my head to the side, the corner of my mouth lifting.

"Now!" Umari yelled a few feet away.

The selkies stepped away from the sea queen in unison and turned to face her with their harpoons out.

"What is this?" she demanded. She opened her mouth to enthrall the crowd, but before she could make a sound, the cetani filled the sky above with roars so loud her voice was lost in the roaring.

Asha swooped low and dropped the tightly woven net over her. She did not see it coming at all. I could tell she was screaming, but as the cetani continued their feline chorus, no one could hear her. Or anything else.

Umari stalked closer, staring down the female who had killed her beloved daughter. My heart pounded as the tiger within me roared, wishing it could be me but knowing this was Umari's moment. My wound would not allow me to strike her without also hurting myself. It would be worth it though.

Morwena scrambled backward, further tangling herself in the net, and tripped, falling to the ground. Umari held her bo loosely at her side, spun in a circle, and slammed it across the sea queen's face. Morwena hadn't stood a chance. She crumpled to the ground. The cetani stopped roaring, but Umari did not as she struck the queen again and again.

Eventually, I stood beside her and placed my hand gently on her taught shoulder. "We must prevent her from speaking when she wakes. Please, let Inok bind her."

She stepped back, shaking, but let him wrap a cloth around the sea queen's mouth and a rope around her limp hands.

The selkies stood frozen, watching.

"She must be taken to the dungeons, and no one is to go near them. Everyone stays away, or she will enchant your minds to do despicable things. Is that understood?" I looked to the soldiers behind me.

They clapped their hands to their chest, and Morwena was lifted from the ground and taken below the castle.

"I can't believe it worked." Inok shook his head.

"Glad to see you still have faith in me." I smiled. I had just captured the sea queen by playing her own game. Unable to relish in the victory, I faced the selkies. "You will march yourselves to the dungeons behind your queen and keep your mouths shut until further notice. You will allow my soldiers to muffle your hearing, and you will not make a move against me or my kingdom ever again. You will make no attempt to aid Morwena of the Sea Court in escape." I used the last bit of magic I had, avoiding that final drop.

They turned and followed the soldiers to the dungeon.

Umari moved to my side. "What will you do with her?"

"I'd slit her throat right now if I could. But, if I did that, the Wind Court would rain down upon us, and I don't believe we are ready."

"They would never know," she countered.

"When a king or queen dies, all of their people feel the loss at once. The sea fae will know when their queen is dead. You likely didn't feel the loss of your former king because you had already made the conviction to leave before he died. The loss of a king or queen—no matter how horrible they are—is still a great loss to the fae."

She studied the ground and the faces of the stilled crowd.

"Will you join me?" I asked. "I'm going to tell Efi we've finally avenged her."

"Not this time." She took my hand. "I'm taking the draconians and the cetani back with me. It's time to prepare our fae for battle."

"Thank you, Umari. I couldn't have trusted anyone else with the task I gave to you and the draconians these past days. You've saved us all."

"It's what she would have wanted. What she deserved." She walked away.

I knew then that Umari and I had a new respect and understanding for one another, and we would forever be bonded not just because of Efi, but also because we were both leaders who had opened up in our most desperate time of need and helped each other.

"Inok, call the small council into the study for a quick meeting."

I turned to the crowd and raised my voice. "Please help yourself to food and drink. Dance and celebrate this night, my kingdom. Today we have won. I think together we have learned that individually we may not always win, but when we come together with conviction, we can change the trajectory of a losing battle. Let this night be a reminder that in the south, we do not bow down. We will never stop fighting for our lands, our people, and the kindness this world needs now more than ever."

A bit later I sat at my desk as the council, short two members, entered. "I'll start from the beginning." I walked them through the discovery of the cetani and the realization that the fae in the kingdom were being enchanted.

"But I still don't understand how you were able to pull off her capture," Adom said.

"Well, we knew Morwena had been sending selkies through the crowds, and each person she enchanted had been told they could not see them. I can see through her enchantment though, so I knew they were growing into a problem as we realized they were spying and reporting back to the queen.

"I ran into one in the tavern, and that's when I knew. So, during the Trials, the draconians hunted through the crowds and captured them. I snuck away, as I was able to without raising suspicion. I took a page from Morwena's book and enchanted the selkie in two batches. The first batch were to convince the queen not to come to the Trials. That she would risk being caught by the draconian fae if she did. The second round of fae were to convince her that her tactics had been so successful that the guards had agreed to leave the front gate unattended at the castle tonight, so the entire kingdom could ambush me. They were told to wait until the moment they heard Umari's signal, and then they were to step away from their queen and remain still until I released them."

"But how did you know she wouldn't enchant her own selkies."

"I didn't. It was a risk we had to take. If nothing else, they wouldn't have shown up, or we would have had to fight the selkies first. We considered the risks and decided to take the opportunity. And as I'm sure you guessed, the cetani were there to mute her until we could capture her. It wasn't graceful or pretty, but now we have the sea queen captured in the dungeons."

"And Madu and Igrer?" Sabra asked.

"Ah yes. I will question Igrer, and if he was only enchanted and holds no ill will of his own, he will be forgiven. And Madu?" I pinched the bridge of my nose and thought for several moments, considering the right course of action with him. "Madu will divide his lands along the border and donate them to the northern fae who enter this kingdom with nothing. He will learn the hard way what it means to have nothing, as they do. Sabra, I will put him in your charge and ask that you report to me with any problems."

She bowed her head. "And your wound?"

"I will recover. I think we can all agree that Igrer isn't the greatest warrior. I'll be right as rain before you know it. Unless anyone has any questions, that's all for now."

They filed out of the room, and I wandered down to the kitchens. Loti was darting all over the place, barking orders to her staff as she tried to keep food hot on the trays before sending them out to the hungry crowds. "You could have warned me you invited the entire kingdom," she snapped as she lifted a whole chicken and dropped it on a plate. "The cooking isn't pretty, but at least it's food."

"Should I apologize now or later then? When you have more time."

"Best make it both," she answered, pausing long enough to smile at me. "I won't feed her. She can sit in that hole and rot for all I care."

"So, you heard about the queen?"

"Well, I'm only in the kitchens, Your Grace. Word spreads like butter in a hot pan around here."

"I'll be back in a while, Loti. I'm going to visit a pretty girl, but I wouldn't be too upset if there was cake when I got back." I smiled.

"A girl?" she asked.

"Yes." I walked out of the kitchens.

I climbed the stairs until I reached Asha, the most beautiful girl I could find. "You stayed?" I whispered, slowly approaching her. She had a clean shelter once more, and I was glad she hadn't left me yet. "I know you can't be here forever, but I'll take one more night."

I buried my hands in her fur as she purred in my ear. The sound was like a song. One filled with sorrow, forgiveness and a kindred spirit. There was just something about her that made me feel whole. Like half of me hadn't died. I stood for a long time nuzzling her, letting her long, soft mane glide between my feathers.

"Can we fly, girl?" I asked. "I'm hurt, so you'll have to take it easy on me, but would you take me to the skies?"

She stood and stretched her neck high, then walked to the open rooftop and extended a feathered wing to me. I crawled to her back and held on at her neck just as I had before. She roared and leaped off the rooftop, diving toward the fae still filling the bailey below. She extended her wings, and we lifted into the sky.

The Flame Court at night was pitch black. I thanked the stars Asha could see where we were going as we coursed the darkness. Several times she roared as a warrior, and each time, the tiger responded. They spoke to each other on a spiritual level, and I wondered if Efi had always planned that. Had always known that the beast within me would respond to hers so fluently.

It hurt a little less now. Being here with Asha made it feel like she was here as well. Like she watched from the Ether, sending us love in her own way.

I closed my eyes and breathed in. "Are you here?" I whispered to Efi. "Are you with us now, my love?"

I am always with you, my tiger, I heard her say into my mind.

The hair on my arms stood straight as I felt her wrap around me.

"Would you forgive me, Efi? If I didn't want to join you just yet? If I wanted to stay here with our son and see this through? Would you wait for me?"

An eternity, her otherworldly voice answered.

"We've done it, Efi. Your mother and I have captured the sea queen. She waits now in the dungeons."

Be careful, my love, she warned. *A fish out of water would do nearly anything to return.*

"I'll worry about that tomorrow. Tonight, let us soar through the sky and fly as one."

And so we did.

ARA

"*I*f you need rest, just say it," Fen said. He had been trying to get me to stop for over an hour, but the magic hadn't depleted, and everyone was ready to get out of The Mists. I'd used the magic as a stream and let it loose little by little as we walked, but we weren't getting anywhere fast.

"You're sure this is the right way?" I asked Kai for the thousandth time.

"I'm sure it's northwest, does that count? I'm not magical, just a genius."

"I suppose it has to," Wren answered for me.

Nearly there, girl.

I jerked as I heard Nealla in my mind. It was enough motion to warn the others, who instantly pulled blades and looked around to see what I had seen. I felt the pull then, like greedy hands upon my free will. Nealla beckoned me.

"What is it?" Fen stepped closer, his jaw tightening.

"I know where to go. She's calling to me."

"Have I mentioned lately how much I hate her?" Kai asked.

"Only a hundred times over the last hour or so," Fen answered. "Lead the way, Ara."

Letting the magic trickle through me as we walked, The Mists dissipated and as one, we stepped out to the other side. I wasn't sure what I was expecting, but it certainly wasn't the view in front of me.

The ground was covered in a sea of sun-bleached, broken and whole bones, like chipped shells along a sandy shore. In the distance was an unearthly, still body of water that looked like glass as it reflected the beaming sun above. My body vibrated. Something physically pulled me as I stepped forward, but Greeve grabbed my shoulder. He looked at me, and then down to the bones, then back to me.

"I get it. But we can't just stop here. I have to keep going."

"You'll be cursed. You can't just walk over the grave of fallen fae."

"He's right," Wren said.

"The bones lead all the way to the water, how am I supposed to get over there?"

"If there was a clearing, I could take you."

"No," Fen said. "These are our brethren. Fae folk who have chosen to end their lives for whatever reason. None of their souls have been released."

"Can you burn them?" I asked.

"No. Nope. Absolutely not." Kai stepped backward. "Terrible, awful, bad idea."

"Care to elaborate?" I lifted a brow to him.

"Lichen opened a book and a fucking banshee came out to play. You start lighting these bones on fire, I'm guessing something way worse is coming for us."

"I'm open to suggestions, then." I turned back to the water. "We're going to have to cross that too."

Fen dropped his pack to the ground. "We've had a really long few days. Let's rest right here and see if we can figure it out in the morning."

"Okay, but I'm not sleeping a wink." Kai knelt to observe a cracked skull. "This is by far the freakiest thing I've ever seen."

"I bet you a blind date you're the first to fall asleep," Greeve said with an ornery smile.

"Fuck that. Last time I lost a blind date bet, you set me up with a Crowl cousin. I'd rather have dinner with that guy." He pointed to a full skeleton in the eerie pile.

"Counter?" Greeve asked.

"Fine, I'll take the blind date bet, but if I win, I set your blind date, and you can't back out this time."

"When you're done, children." Fen tapped his foot on the ground.

"Yes, Dad?" they asked in unison.

Wren and I burst into giggles.

Fen scowled and looked at Greeve. "Are we out of food?"

"No. Almost. We have half a rabbit left and a bird."

"Can you hold The Mists back so we have a bit of a clearing?"

I shrugged. "I'm not sure how long, but sure."

We spent the evening resting just inside the small clearing. Everyone took turns sleeping except for Kai, who watched the bone graveyard as if it would come to life, twisting the ring on his finger. I didn't understand him fully. Kai was dangerous. Tall, broad shouldered, an absolute weapon on the battlefield. But that wasn't who he really was. He was the guy who filled the uneasy silence with a laugh because it was how he dealt with awkward situations. As I laid on my back and watched the sky, I caught myself wondering about his life. What made him tick? Why was he terrified of bones, but not of killing someone?

I considered what I knew of Greeve. Strong, traditional, fiercely loyal to his friends. He had way more tattoos than the others, but I'd guess that each and every one had a story. A meaning. Greeve had a mysterious depth to him, but I found myself so grateful for his unwavering friendship. I wasn't sure I'd done a single thing to deserve it, but he'd followed me blindly and would be the first to step between me and danger aside from Fen.

But then there was Fen, who had me more confused than anyone else. I knew the passion, the chemistry between us was raw and real and palpable. When it came to Fen, with his beautifully exotic completion and his deep, dark features, I was insatiable. There were times when I looked at him and thought I'd forget to breathe if I wasn't careful. But why did I feel like I was forcing myself to trust him? Why did it feel like he and Wren were hiding something from me?

"Can't sleep or won't?" Kai came to sit beside me.

"Both."

"Nervous about tomorrow?" He poked the fire with a stick.

"I haven't even thought about it. I was trying to figure you guys out, actually."

"What about us?" he asked, ditching his stick while he readjusted to face me.

"I mean, isn't it strange? You don't know me at all one day and the next day you'll follow me straight to hell?"

"Wrong," he said, shaking his head. "You don't know us at all, but we've known you your whole life."

"You *all* have?" I asked, surprised at his admission.

"Age means nothing, you know that. But if we're keeping track, you were a baby when you were sent away, but we watched them take you. Greeve handed you to your new mother the day your family left the southern kingdom. He lit your real parents' funeral pyre."

No wonder I'd felt so drawn to Greeve. As if he were an old friend I'd somehow forgotten. "I had no idea."

"I think the big piece of the puzzle you're missing here is Fen. If Fen woke up right now and told me to go swimming in that creepy lake, I'd do it. I'd walk right over these haunted bones and leap into the water. He's my brother. I'd do anything for him. But he'd do anything for you, Ara. That's his destiny. We're just the lucky baggage."

"But that's the problem, isn't it? You're here because of him, not because of me, and he's here because of destiny, not actual choice. If I do something reckless, it's not just my own life at stake. It's the four of you also."

"No one's got a choice here." He stood and stretched. "You've got to let that guilt go. The dracs believe that nothing is a coincidence. I'm here and you're here because we were meant to be. Wren was right. This isn't just your journey, so stop thinking like that. It's our journey."

"For being the funny guy, you're full of wisdom tonight."

"I'm funny because it's needed. You can't take life so seriously."

"I'll keep that in mind the next time you're ear fucked by a banshee."

"You have a sick sense of humor," he said, chuckling. "And I like it."

I'm not sure how, but eventually I ended up falling asleep. I felt myself teetering on the cusp of Nealla's nightmare when pain hit my stomach. My eyes flew open, and I was face to face with the wrinkled face of Aibell staring me right in the eyes, her staff in my gut.

"Wake child. The clock has stopped."

I sat up and looked around. The Mists were pushed back even farther than they had been last night, and a clear path had been made through the sea of bones.

"What happened?" I asked.

"Nothing yet. Nothing happens when time is obstructed."

"What am I to do from here?"

"First, you must release the book into the water, child. Go alone and do not touch the water. It is made of souls and you'll never find yours if it's lost in the chasm. You must make a blood sacrifice to the water, the Soul Repository."

"If you could come here, why didn't you just bring me? Why make me go through all of this?"

"The journey is important." She looked to Fen. "I am one. This war will take more than that. Greater things must happen."

"Anything else I should know before I keep going?"

"Plenty," she said before disappearing.

"Old hag," I yelled, just as the hold she had on time released and I woke everyone but Kai, who sat with his knees to his chest watching the bones. As if it was a game we played, they all jumped to their feet, weapons ready.

"Sorry. Sorry. Just Aibell here to crash the party."

"Where is she?" Greeve searched the horizon.

"Oh, she's gone now. She came to be a pain in my ass and then off she went."

"I see she left us a path." Fen stepped forward.

"No, wait. She said I had to do the next part alone."

"We talked about this," Kai said.

"I know. I promise. I'm not trying to be the hero. She said I have to release the book, and I have to do it alone. Just wait here. I'm sure it will take me like five minutes."

"If I get to six, I'm coming after you, Princess," Fen warned.

"Calm your rage. I'll be right back."

I reached into the bottom of my bag and pulled out the alluring book I'd carried. Something about this place must have spoken to it because I could hear the voices screaming at me not to go farther toward the water.

As I did, I realized Aibell was right and it was not just water. It truly was a deep basin full of haunted souls. Or at least that was what I had to assume they were, based on the troubled faces floating by. I knelt, and just before I stuck the book into the water, a high-pitched scream came from within its pages. Then a deep, dark voice laughed. I dropped the book without a splash and watched as the souls swarmed it, devouring it.

Still kneeling, I looked back over my shoulder. The team stood watching me carefully, but no one came forward. They had respected the boundary, even though they hadn't liked it. I could see the anguish on Fen's face. I carefully slipped a blade across my palm, dripping my blood into the water.

398

The souls within scurried away as if I'd used a weapon to threaten them. I realized I'd heard of this water before. I hadn't thought it was real. The Water Beyond The Mists was a poison from my bedtime stories. So deadly a fae would die nearly on contact. No wonder Aibell had told me not to touch it. I shuddered as I remembered the rumors that said this was the water that took Fen's mother from him. I took a small step backward and watched as a familiar face crested the water.

"I know you."

"Shy little Ara has come a long way, I see."

"Why are you all the way up here, Mikal?" I asked, staring at the water nixie from the Neverwood lake in the forest behind my parent's cottage.

"Why are you?" He leaped out of the water, a trail of droplets following him. "You've brought friends this time. Didn't your mother tell you to trust no one?"

"He's my Guardian, they are my friends," I said through gritted teeth. "Tell me why you are here."

"I have been called by Nealla to guide the way for you, little Ara."

Again, he dashed into the sky, changing from a mermaid to something with tentacles before landing without a splash. "Only you and your Guardian may pass, so please call him forward."

I turned and motioned to Fen. He prowled forward ready to attack Mikal. The moment he stepped away, The Mists returned, engulfing the others.

"Don't touch the water," I warned Fen. I turned a lethal gaze onto Mikal. "What happened to them?"

"They will be fine. Waiting there just as you left them when you return. Hello, Fenlas." Mikal looked at him oddly. He twisted his head back and forth and tsk'd. He waved his hand, and a small boat appeared before him. "You must take this boat across the Soul Repository. Nealla waits for you on the other side. However, if any secrets lie between you, now is the time to set them free, or the boat I have crafted will disintegrate. You must truly be one to cross."

He jumped into the air once more and slipped into the water, not splashing a single drop of the deadly poison.

"Ready?" I asked, lifting my foot over the edge of the small boat.

"Wait," Fen said, stopping me. "We can't go yet."

I turned and saw the panic on his face. Something twisted in my gut. Something I'd pushed aside, distracted by his smile and those damned eyes. Nausea rose as I took in his face, pale with fear. I forced the painful words out. "So, you are hiding something?"

"I didn't want to scare you away." He reached for me.

"Tell me," I said, feeling the panic set in. "What are you hiding?"

"Honestly, it's not anything you shouldn't have guessed already."

"Tell me right now, Prince."

He dropped his broad shoulders and looked to the ground. His mistake was written across his face. "When our fates were read, when you were a baby, the prophetess said something else that I haven't told you. I didn't want it to matter. I wanted it to happen naturally, like you did."

"Spit it out," I snapped, moving away from him.

"It's just..." He scratched the back of his head and looked away. "We're mates, Ara. That's why I could feel your magic before, that's why you could find me in The Mists. It's the reason I scented you in the tavern in Hrundel."

My entire world crashed in around me. The breath left my lungs as everything around me faded away. A loud humming filled my ears. "No," I whispered.

"Ara, It's okay. It's only something that—"

"No, Fenlas. It's not okay. You lied. And not only that, it's just another thing in the long list of things that I get no choice in. My life is not my own. Not now and I guess not ever. But you knew. Wren knew."

He shook his head and moved to me, but I backed away again.

"Everyone probably knew, except me. Because I'm the idiot. I wanted to trust you. I even brought up not wanting a mate. You could have told me right then. You could have told me a thousand times. You're a liar, Fenlas. I don't want this. I don't want to be your mate. I reject the mating bond." I stepped over the edge of the boat, sealing off his own despair with my ire.

Fen fell to his knees, and I felt a deep pit rip into my soul. "No!" he screamed as I grabbed the only oar and pushed away from the bank.

"Keep your secrets, Prince. Apparently, you didn't care about me enough to share them." I turned away and rode the boat across the deadly waters alone.

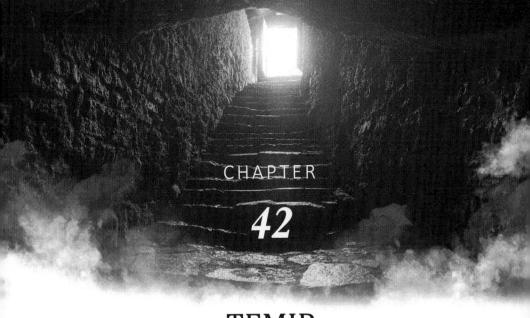

CHAPTER

42

TEMIR

*P*acing and pulling on the mating bond were the only two options I had as I remained hidden in that room in the castle. I'd listened outside the door for a while, only to realize the guard rotation had been completed, and now, even if I could leave this room, they would see me. My horns may have been gone, but I was still a tall, recognizable male lurking in an empty room in the castle.

I had no idea where Roe had gone. But I couldn't believe he would have abandoned me if he had a choice. Which made me worried for him. I'd given Nadra Iva's name, so I worried for her too.

I wished I knew her, or if I could trust her. I tried to tug on the bond. I tried heaving on it. I tried sending magic down it. I tried everything I could think of, but the only thing I got in return after the rage had settled was absolute silence.

"Yes, I'm sure the king won't mind at all dear," I heard a muffled female voice call from the hall. "Right this way."

I realized the doorknob was turning and leaped behind the heavy curtains just in time as someone entered the space. My heart raced as whoever came in shut the door behind them. For moments, the room was still. Silent. Just when I thought I'd imagined it all, I heard her.

"Hello?" Nadra whispered.

I ripped the curtains back and crossed the room in three strides. "Have you betrayed me?" I barked.

She flinched, shook her head, and stepped away from me, trembling.

I felt the fear move down our bond as if it were my own. "I'm sorry. Please don't be afraid." I was an animal. I hadn't meant to scare her.

"I nearly did tell him, but he locked up my mother and deserves nothing." She took another step back. "I'm sorry." I looked at her shrunken form and doubted she had eaten anything even though I had begged her to. "Can you help me?" she asked. "I know what the king is planning. I will tell you."

I stepped toward her and lifted her chin. I looked into the depth and despair of her hallowed eyes and realized it must have taken a great internal strength not to give in to the king when he had tortured her so badly.

"Will you come with me? To safety? I can protect you."

She shook her head again and crumpled to the floor, burying her head in her hands and sobbed. That overwhelming sorrow bled into me, and I felt her all-consuming sadness as my own. She didn't want to be here. She barely wanted life at all. I felt the need to rip something to shreds, to try to breathe life into her in anyway I could, to light a fire within her and beg her not to leave me. I tried to calm myself as I sat before her on the floor.

"I cannot leave her. You don't understand. She is all I have."

"If you will let me take you from this place, I promise I will come back for your mother."

"Can't you see that I am broken? A promise means nothing to me anymore."

"I see you, Nadra. I've been broken before. I know what it feels like to know if you died tomorrow not a single soul would know or care. That you wouldn't care. Being broken is like a storm. It's all consuming while it lasts, but it's never permanent. Even the clouds run out of rain. Please let me help you." I reached out to take her hand.

She pulled away. "Please don't touch me."

Fiery rage blossomed like a struck match. I would kill him. If it took my own death to see it through, I would do it. "Nadra, we cannot stay here. It isn't safe. Do you know of servants named Iva or Roe? We need them to help us get out of here."

"Iva waits outside the door. She has been with me since you left me in the hallway."

I stood and opened the door enough to see a familiar short female standing there, worrying her hands as she watched the guards.

"Iva," I said, loud enough that only she would hear.

"Oh, for goodness sake," she called out. "I'm sure it's under the bed. Let me help you." She stepped into the room and shut the door, pulling me down into a hug. "I've been so worried," she said. "I've taken care of your mate, Tem. But she is not well. She will not eat."

"Thank you, Iva. I need to get us both out of here. Roe was supposed to come back and he didn't."

"He was called to serve in the dinner hall. He sent a message, and I did my best to get down here as quickly as I could."

"Can we walk out the front doors? Will we be noticed?"

"I'd imagine if you keep your hoods up, you'll have no problem. Most are at dinner right now."

"Can you have Roe meet me at the Keep as soon as he can get away?"

"It might be a few days. He's been gone a lot, and I'm worried someone's noticed."

"As soon as he can. That's all I ask. Don't take a risk. You should probably think about packing up yourself, Iva. It's not safe here."

"It's never been safe here, Tem. But ask yourself, where would you be if we weren't here?"

"I'm grateful. I am, but I don't want to get news of your death. Please be careful."

"I'm always careful."

I looked down at Nadra, and Iva patted my arm. "Just give her some time," she said, helping Nadra to her feet. "Come, dear. It's time to go. You'll be taken care of. Just stick with Temir. You couldn't have gotten a better male."

She said nothing, withdrawn into her shell, but she let me take her hand.

"I'll distract the guards, see yourselves out as quickly as you can without drawing attention. Be safe."

She left the room, and I watched out of the cracked door until the guards turned away. There were only seconds until they turned back. We made it down the hall easier than I'd anticipated. We left the castle and moved within a small crowd until a guard called to me.

"You there. Take off your hood."

I felt the fear through the bond mix with my own as I reached up and inched my hood down. I locked eyes with the guard as a rebel snuck up behind him, whispered in his ear and winked at me. The guard waved us on. I pulled Nadra through the gate and to the horses that Roe and I had left tied in the tree line.

"You'll have to ride with me. Roe will need his horse. Is that okay?"

She didn't say a thing, but when I mounted and held a hand down to her, she took it and let me help her up. She sat still and silent in front of me as we rode toward the Keep.

"You are my mate." She was quiet and a million miles away from me in her own frayed mind.

"I am," I answered truthfully.

"Sorry."

My heart dropped. "For what?"

Again, she didn't answer. There was peace and turmoil battling a war within me. Knowing I had a mate and she was safe in my arms settled me, but the moment I thought about the outside world, exposing her to a single fae, an indescribable madness threatened to consume me. I wrapped my arm around her tightly and kicked the horse into a run. It would be a long ride, and I hoped to get to Bryer's Keep as quickly as I could. I needed to get her to safety. Especially if I had to find a way back to the castle—again.

"I see you've made it back in one piece," Rook said as he eyed the female I brought with me.

"I did. And I've brought what I could to create more of the truth serum."

"Good. I suppose you're going to need a bigger room?" he asked, still watching Nadra.

I stepped in front of her and narrowed my eyes. *Mine*, my mind screamed.

"A mate, then," he answered with a smile. "Congratulations."

I dipped my chin and turned to Nadra, but she looked less than thrilled. Less than any emotion. Her face was blank, apart from the red circles below her eyes from crying. I would have to make this as temporary and comfortable for her as possible. "Do we have another room to spare, Rook? I'm not sure she would be comfortable in mine."

Nadra squeezed my hand, and I turned to her. "Don't leave me alone," she said.

Something in that simple phrase, mixed with my protective nature of her, roared to life, and the bond between us vibrated in response. I wanted her. I couldn't control that beast.

"I've got one room with a double bed and that's about as much as I can offer. We are working on expanding, but it's still much better than what we had."

"That will be fine." He led us down the stark white hallway and into a simple room. Just as he was about to shut the door, I paused. "One more thing, I'm going to need some rebels. Nadra's mom is in the dungeons and I intend to save her."

406

"I'm not sure I've got them to spare," he said.

"The king imprisoned her for being a rebel, Rook. Even if she isn't, I've got to try. She's a seamstress with magic. She could be helpful."

"A seamstress? What's her name?" He looked back at Nadra.

"Megere." His face lost all color. "Do you know her?"

"We've met," he said curtly and walked out the door, agreeing to nothing.

I watched Nadra carefully as she sat on the edge of the bed. The small room was plain. A bed, small chest of drawers and a covered lamp. I set my loaded bags down gently and began pulling out the items I'd retrieved and covered the top of the chest with pungent herbs and essential elixirs. I lined the wall with the small number of books and journals I'd managed to save and I filled the drawers of the chest with all the materials I could bring to make as much truth serum as possible.

"You did not pack clothes?" Nadra asked as she watched me.

"Books were more important."

"My mother would disagree." She turned her head, staring off into nothing.

"I believe she would." I smiled. Crossing the room, I sat beside her on the bed. "Would you allow me to heal you, Nadra?"

I held out my hand and waited.

She looked down to it for several moments before she rested her own within.

I called my magic forward and gently moved it toward her. The moment the magic coursed through her, she gasped, and I continued until she looked less pale, less gaunt. I knew it would not heal her heart or her mind, but the lack of proper nutrition would be gone.

Her beautiful red hair began to shine, and the circles below her honeyed eyes faded away. As I pressed my magic deeper into her, I sent feelings of happiness and encouragement. Nadra's eyes drooped. She needed sleep. I pulled my hand away and helped her lay down. I slipped off her shoes and covered her with the blanket.

Mine. She was mine, and my baser instinct told me to take her. To make her mine in all ways. I had to pull back. I had to remind myself that her pull to me was not as strong as mine was to her. That she was still fragile and would need time. If I forced it and she refused the bond, my soul would be ripped in two, and I wasn't sure how anyone could survive that. I lifted the second pillow from the bed, turned off the lamp, and found a spot on the floor. I listened to her soft, slow breathing until I fell asleep. I woke to Nadra nudging me. "What's wrong?" I asked, bolting upright.

"I'm hungry."

My heart leaped for joy at those beautiful words. Eating meant she had found a will to live, and I'd doubted that would happen several times the day before. "Let's go see what we can find around here."

"Thank you, Temir. For everything."

We scoured the underground building until we found a small kitchen. There wasn't a lot, but there was enough to make eggs and toast. Watching her eat was pure satisfaction. To know I had fulfilled a simple need for her caused the mating bond to vibrate. We went back to our shared bedroom, and as soon as we entered, I double checked to make sure my bags were still there and then set down the pitcher of water I'd brought from the kitchens. I sat on the floor and began the tedious process of making an abundance of serum.

Not a single person knew the rebel compound held one of the king's most sought-after possessions. I had to believe that if he would send two of his prized wielders after something that even the creator had asked me not to hand over, then it really was as powerful as I felt it was.

I felt the void of Gaea's absence more acutely now. I trusted her with my life. I knew her. Nadra had admitted she would have given the king my secrets, and for that reason alone, I could not trust her. I could protect her, but right now, I had to keep my secrets close.

She had been quiet all through breakfast. Withdrawn. I became more and more consumed with the thought of her and the mystery of who she

408

really was as I worked. I'd mixed the ingredients I needed and closed my eyes, infusing my magic into the plucked leaves before starting the oil extraction.

She tugged on the bond, and my world stopped. I looked up to meet her curious eyes.

"You can feel me?" she asked.

"Just as you can feel me." I set my work to the side and moved to sit beside her on the bed. "Close your eyes."

She did, and I tried to stay focused while studying the lovely outline of her freckled face. The mating bond thrummed within me as I studied her. She was captivating. She always had been. I closed my eyes and accidentally sent a wave of desire down the bond. Her eyes flew open, and she scooted away from me on the bed.

"I'm sorry." I soared to my feet. "I didn't mean to do that."

She looked at me and used the bond to send a wave of anger.

"Is this how you want to tell me how you're feeling?" I asked.

She was silent.

"I am a male who has just discovered his mate. Every ounce of me wants to claim you as mine. I'm doing everything I can to hold myself back," I said firmly. "I am trying to resist it."

She looked away.

I stood and left the room. She wouldn't understand. She was a high fae female in all ways. I stopped, realizing something that should have occurred to me so much earlier than this moment. She had apologized. I'd spent my entire life living directly on the divide between lesser and high fae. The fact that neither of them would ever accept me had monopolized my thoughts for so long. I wasn't sure how I hadn't even considered that her being a high fae and me being lesser might have felt like she was trapped with someone below her. Maybe that was why she had apologized. Maybe she had already decided she would not be able to accept the bond between us. Maybe I was not worthy of her.

I faced the bedroom door from the hall. Perhaps if I begged her, pleaded with her to give me a chance, to let me love her, she would try. But no. No one should ever have to beg for fated love. She hadn't been my choice, and I hadn't been hers. Fate never cared for choice, but I'd never heard of a lesser fae bonded to a high fae.

I walked down to the meeting room and let myself in. It was empty. I sat alone at the desk and ran my hands through my hair. Could nothing be easy?

"Temir?" I heard her call from the door.

I hadn't shielded my emotions from her. Everything I'd felt had been sent right down that bond between us. Still, I did not want to see her. I did not want to hear the rejection. I had enough to worry about. I still planned to save her mother, even if I had to do it alone.

I heard her sigh and walk back down the hallway. I'd have to protect myself from her. I would fall hard and fast, and I had no reason to believe she would do anything but watch me crash.

I waited alone in that room until Rook let himself in. "There you are," he said.

"I need to get back to the castle."

"No. I can't allow that right now."

"I'm not asking for permission. I've done every single thing you've asked of me for the rebellion, no matter what it cost me. I've shown you what I am able to bring to the table. I took the lead when you cowered at the king's attack. Now is the time you repay me, Rook. Now is the time you give me something I need."

He growled but submitted. "How many rebels, Temir?"

"Ten."

"Five."

"Six and horses to get us there and back sooner."

"Stay here," he said, rising from the table. "But if anyone asks, this was my decision and not your own demand. Do you understand?"

I nodded.

410

He returned with five males in tow. "What's the plan?"

I jerked my head back. "You will join us?"

"Yes, but you will lead, Temir."

"I have an idea. I thought we should wait for Roe to get back to Bryer's Keep, but I think it works in his favor if he is not missing when all hell breaks loose. He and Iva have no plans to leave the castle, so if we storm in and surprise everyone, they won't be associated with us."

"We aren't outfitted to storm the castle," Rook said.

"We won't be. The tunnel entrance that runs under the castle is still open."

"The dungeons are not connected to the tunnels."

"No, but at least we can sneak into the castle. I say we split into two teams. Team one will free the fae horses in the barn, causing a distraction. Then they light the barn on fire and try to lead the horses out of the gate in the chaos. If we are able to steal any of them, great. If we aren't, then at least they will have provided a distraction while team two, with me, sneaks into the castle through the tunnels. There's a way in from there. Once we are inside, we'll need to find the hall that leads to the dungeons, get down there, free the seamstress, check for any other rebels and get out as fast as possible."

"I know where the dungeons are from inside the castle," a male sitting across from me said.

"Great. Rook, do you want to form the teams?"

"I'll come with you and Ven," he said, indicating the male who had spoken up. "Everyone else can work on the barn. We won't want too many in the castle trying to sneak through it."

"When can we leave?" I asked.

"Right now." Rook stood and turned to the team. "This will be our first move against the king without provocation. Reports say he's already discovered we killed his soldiers in Volos. You'll need to use extreme caution. If you're caught, you might consider taking your own life. It may be an easier death than what he will offer."

411

I searched the determined eyes of the rebels in the meeting room. I realized what I asked of them and why Rook hesitated to do this. If we made it out, we'd won a small battle, but if we didn't, we had sacrificed the lives of so many for a single female.

We rode at a steady pace. I hadn't taken the time to check on Nadra. I had penned a message and left it to be delivered after we left. Hard as I tried to push her from my mind, I could feel the moment she held that letter in her hand. The connection she felt to it, even though she didn't want to. She didn't want me, and when I returned, I would have to deal with that. For now, I focused on the mission I had created on her behalf.

Heavily armed, we split paths and left our horses in the trees beyond the tunnels. When we left, we'd need to be able to mount them and get back to the compound swiftly. Rook, Ven and I moved easily through the tunnels without speaking. We found the collapsed passageway that I had used before and dug our way up into the tree nursery. No one had been here. The trees were not yet dying, but they would soon. The fruit had already begun to rot. Years and years of hard work and memories beside Oleonis had turned to mush.

"What a waste," Rook said from beside me as he reached up to touch a rotten rhogula pear.

"Do you know where we are in the castle?" I asked Ven, turning away from the deserted trees.

I had a vague idea of where the dungeons were, but nothing precise enough to get us there efficiently. The king kept them tight lipped and under lock and key. We stood at the door and waited for chaos to begin outside. Within minutes, the screaming began, and we let the commotion build.

"I do. Time to go," Ven said, taking the lead.

We followed him through the castle, keeping space between the three of us so we would not draw attention to ourselves. Twice he rounded a corner and I thought I'd lost him, but eventually we made it to a part of the castle I had never been in. Perhaps I'd subconsciously avoided it, knowing the violence that took place here.

"How did you know this was here?" I asked as we watched the dark twins standing at the door at the end of the hall.

"I make it my business to know." He winked at me before turning the corner and running straight at the guards.

I expected a struggle. Something. But before they had time to call out, Ven had knocked them both out and waved to us. We followed as he lifted the keys from one of the winged fae's belts. He tried several until one finally clicked and the door opened to a dark and narrow set of stairs. We moved silently, pulling the fallen guards onto the landing and shutting the door behind us. Lit sconces showed us the path as we went down and down until the air was heavy and humid. The stone walls seeped with stale water, and the floor was slick with new blood, barely concealing the old. Two more guards stood rigid at the bottom of the stairs.

Ven took one as I took the other. I searched for more keys on their fallen bodies, but there were none.

"Over here," Rook called, his voice strained as he stood in front of a cell.

We ran to him and found a female, curled up and lying naked on the dirty floor.

"Megere?" I asked. She barely lifted her head. Rook immediately took his coat off and threw it to her between the bars. "How do they open the doors?" I asked, looking at the untouched tray of bread and water in the corner.

I heard a moan from the next cell down. Ven moved to check the rest of the room.

"I don't know," Megere answered. "They've taken my clothes to prevent me from freeing myself." She sat upright and wrapped Rook's jacket around her, holding the fabric close and taking a deep breath.

"Rook?" she asked, moving to her feet. "Is that you?"

"It is." His voice cracked.

"Guys, you might want to see this," Ven called through the dark prison.

I stepped away and walked down the hall. I looked into the only other cell occupied and nearly dropped my sword. "Rhogan?" The male didn't move. His wings had been shredded, his skin scarred. Chunks of his blond hair pulled from his scalp. "But I watched the king ... your heart."

I realized then that the king had been testing me. He had wanted me to react, and I had not. Instead of the death he'd promised, he locked Rhogan in his gods-forsaken dungeon, and Eadas or one of his sentries, had been torturing him for information. From the looks of him, they hadn't gotten what they had wanted.

"How do we get them out?" I asked.

"I'm open to suggestions," Ven answered.

"Rhogan? Can you come to the front of the cage? I can heal you if you can make it."

He crawled. Inch by inch he dragged his broken, battered body across the dank cell until he was close enough to the door that I could reach for him. I healed him slowly and with great effort. His entire body had been broken in such a way that he was only on the cusp of life, left dangling.

He stretched, and as his pain subsided and his wings were restored, he stood slowly. He transformed before us from a shell of a fae into a massive, angry male with a giant score to settle.

"Release me," he ordered.

"Do you know how? Where are the keys?" I asked.

He grabbed the bars and tried to pull them apart, they did not budge.

"How did you resist the king's enchantment?" Ven asked.

He pointed to his tattooed arm. "The ink has metal shavings from the blacksmith."

"Temir," Rook called. I walked back to him, and he pointed. "She can free them," he said. "She will use my jacket."

414

I watched as she ripped a piece of the material and tied it around a bar. She kept herself as covered as she could and touched the fabric. Her magic rippled through it, and the bar cracked. She tied several more pieces. and I tore the bottom of my own shirt to assist her. Ven began tying pieces of his shirt to Rhogan's cell. Once Megere had freed herself, she ran to Roghan's cell and touched the fabric on the bars, cracking them as well. His large frame required a lot more space, which meant time. And as it was, time was precious.

The moment Rhogan was free of his cell, he stepped out and pulled the half-naked fae into his arms. "I told you we would get out of this together." She shook with tears in his arms. "What's the plan?"

"Well, it's not great. We have to get back through the castle and down the tunnels without getting caught."

"That's not a plan, that's a gods-damned death wish," he said.

"It's all we've got. If we get separated, take her to Bryer's Keep."

"Let's go," he said, keeping a tight grip on Megere's shaking hand.

She held the jacket closed and looked back to Rook as they walked past him. He didn't say a word as we fell into line, went back up the stairs, and into the hall with no issues. We used the same tactic as we had done before, keeping a distance between us, but hiding a giant winged fae and a half-naked female proved to be more difficult. Several fae watched us as we walked, and my heart raced. A cascade of worry drifted down the bond, and I knew Nadra was responding to my own emotions. I'd tried to shield them, but when they came so strong, it was hard to worry about that. Rook and Ven led the group at the front with a good gap, then Rhogan and Nadra's mother with me trailing behind.

"Traitors," someone called.

"Rebels in the castle," another said.

And then fae were screaming and running, and while we tried to hide in the chaos, it didn't work as we had planned. Ven and Rook disappeared down the hall, and as the soldiers came running, Rhogan roared, grabbed

Megere and jumped out of an oversized window. I watched as they disappeared into the sky, leaving me alone as the soldiers surrounded me.

"Well, well, well. What do we have here?" Eadas jeered, joining his males.

"A rebel," the king answered from behind me. "Cuff him."

And suddenly Oleo's vision had come to pass.

CHAPTER 43

ARA

I had to be careful not to splash a single drop on me as I rowed across the poisoned water to the other side. Though I tried, I couldn't stop thinking about Fen and that shattered look on his beautiful face when I'd denied the mating bond. But he only felt the way he did about me because the universe had forced us together. It wasn't me he was infatuated with. It was his own idea of me. And I'd never live up to those perfect expectations. I couldn't handle the pressure. It was just too much.

I could nearly feel him standing on the outside of my mental shield, even now, begging me to come back for him. I wouldn't. Couldn't. This was about me, not him, not us. Just me. I moved the oars carefully through the water and watched the shore grow closer until I heard the bottom of the small boat slide over the small pebbles and gritty sand.

Stepping out of the boat, I pulled two knives and studied every detail. The moss-covered ground was a direct contrast to the endless winter I had left behind. The largest trees I'd ever seen in my life loomed high above me, and a small path of broken stone stairs invited me deeper into

Nealla's Island. As I walked, I kept my mind as clear as I could, listening to the deafening silence. There were no birds. No animals. There was not even wind.

Come.

The sound of Nealla's voice filling every crevice of my mind was pure agony. Nothing else existed but her hypnotizing pull on me.

Come.

"Yeah, yeah, I'm coming," I managed, though my head pounded.

I continued to climb the ivy-covered stairs until the fresh air thinned, and as I reached the top of the hill and settled within the treetops, a small, dilapidated cottage covered in tangled vines appeared. I didn't pause. Didn't stop to give myself time to turn around. I charged forward and slammed the door open.

"You're late." A cloaked figure, hidden in shadows, folded her hands and placed them on the round table before her.

The cabin held a faint stench, reminding me of my parents and a time I would rather forget. Perhaps it was the Soul Repository, but it reminded me of the death and decay of the forest. The room was completely bare apart from the simple table with three chairs. Mine, hers and presumably one for Fen. The female's silky smooth skin was the antithesis of ancient, but her face was covered with a beautifully woven scarf and a hood that covered her hair. Her eyes glowed from within, and I wasn't fooled for a second. She could murder me with a single thought.

"I didn't realize I had a schedule to keep." I pulled out a chair and plopped down like I owned the place.

"There's always a schedule, child."

"I won't bore you with the details. You wanted me, so here I am, Nealla. Tell me what I need to know."

"Where is your mate?" she asked, cocking her head sideways.

"I don't have a mate."

"So you say."

418

I ignored her response. Maybe she didn't know everything then. "I've come for answers. I got rid of the book just like Aibell told me to. I traveled through The Mists. Tell me what I need to know. Tell me everything."

"Ah, the book. Simply a conduit," she said as her eyes flickered.

I pulled away from her. "What do you mean?"

"You've gotten rid of a means for those beasts to enter this world, but not the beasts themselves. Should another door be opened, they would still come."

"Fantastic." I swung my feet up onto the small table and leaned back in my wooden chair. "Also not my problem."

"Yet. But perhaps we should start from the beginning." She looked pointedly at my feet and then the two legs of my chair still on the ground.

Without so much of a flinch, my chair went flying, and I crashed to the floor, landing hard on my backside.

"Respect will be given in this home, child. I've done much for you."

"What specifically?" I stood and dusted myself off, threw my hair over my shoulder and raised an eyebrow, waiting for her telling response.

"Sit," she said as the third chair moved away from the table.

I sat and leaned forward, resting my elbow upon it. "Happy?"

"It's a wonder your mate and his friends made it this far with you. You have always been a selfish brat. I am timeless. The laws of magic don't even apply to me, yet you still test my patience."

I sighed. "You're the one who told me to leave them behind in the first place. Can we get on with it?"

"As you wish," she said, standing. "Come."

She walked out of the cottage, and I followed her. The island changed into a flat, sandy desert with nothing in any direction for as far as the eye could see. I turned back to look at her, and she was no longer the hooded female from the cottage. She was not a female at all. That was when I realized the stories had gotten it wrong. Nealla did not ride a beast through the night, she was the beast. Massive black paws with razors for claws moved toward me. I looked up to see the face of a creature plucked from my nightmares. Distorted face and corded veins, she had clawed herself from the depths of hell and stood in her beast form, ready to devour me.

She roared, and I took several steps backward. She stood on four feet but towered over me. Her thighs were the size of my entire body. Horn-tipped wings ripped from her back, and the only remnant of the fae she had presented herself as was the glowing yellow eyes staring down at me. She leaned over as saliva dripped from her razor-sharp fangs.

"Is this because I put my feet on your table?"

Show me that you are worthy of your title.

"I'm not in the mood for games."

She roared once more and batted a long claw at me. It shredded the skin on my chest and I was thrown backwards. Warm blood poured over my abdomen.

"Fine. Have it your way." I pulled out my faithful throwing knives and ran my fingers down the intricate design embedded in them. I'd trained my entire life for this. I shut my mind down from the distractions of the outside world, from the pressure of the future, and focused solely on Nealla, planting my feet and holding my knives loosely.

I threw a knife, and she moved with pure grace, dodging it, then tilted her head backward as the makings of a mangled laugh escaped her. She spun and struck me with the barbed end of her tail, sending me flying again. I barely managed to get to my feet before she hit me again. Blood pooled in my mouth, and as I spat on the ground, it sizzled in the heat of the sun. I watched it turn to steam and vanish then realized what I was meant to do. It wasn't about the weapons I had brought. It was me. I was the weapon.

I bowed my head and called forth the small bit of magic I had. She hit me again. This time, with the wind knocked from my desperate lungs, I went down and stayed down. I lay there and pulled on that magic.

Get up.

420

I wouldn't. I shoved the magic from me and hoped and prayed it did what I needed. The moment the monster was struck, I jumped to my feet just in time to see the beast form melt away and the female saunter forward.

"Oh yes, I forgot," she said as she approached me, moving over the top of the sand like a serpent.

I pulled my throwing knife, and she looked at me, daring me to throw it. I didn't take that dare. I let her walk right up to me and place her palm on my forehead as she whispered into my mind, *gan cheangal.*

Everything went dark. The pain of a thousand deaths tore through my body as I felt myself fall through the world and land over and over again. There were no words, no sounds, no emotions. Only pain. So much pain I knew for certain that I had crossed the world only to die. I felt the blood leave my body until I was drained of all life. I felt my soul, recently damaged. I felt everything and nothing as the shadow of the reaper dragged me to hell.

The only thing that kept it away was the small flicker of light within me. I knew it wasn't mine. Nealla had taken everything that was a part of me, and whatever was left was something else. Someone else's. But it was just enough to keep the God of Death at bay. I lost myself in that small flame. That foreign fire that tied me to the land. That tiny promise that I was not like the others. That I was meant to do something greater than die at the hands of a wicked being that had once promised to protect me.

Do you see? I heard her say. *He is still there. He is the only thing that holds you now, girl. Your will to die costs him. You have no sense of self preservation, but still, he protects you.*

A numbness settled over my body as my soul reached for that little flame and wrapped itself around it. In the endless pit of despair I was currently suspended above, the only thing that mattered, the only thing that held me, was him. Fen. I didn't know how or why after I had left him, but he refused to let me go, and somewhere within that conviction was my entire heart, no matter how much I fought it. I wanted everything that broody fae would give me. Flawed as he was, he was mine. A peace settled over me the moment those words filled my mind.

All at once, I was shoved back into my broken body, and the anguish from being rebuilt encapsulated me so thoroughly my back arched and a foreign scream left me. I cracked my eyes open to see that once again I laid on the floor of Nealla's empty cottage.

She stood above me, staring. "You are unbound."

I groaned and rolled to the side. I felt the same yet wholly different. Something within me had changed.

"Sit," she demanded. I crawled over to the chair, pulled myself up and laid my head in my hands on the table. "Shall I begin?"

I wanted to slap the laughter from her, but I could barely move.

"When the seven gods came together and created this world, the first faerie also became the first king of Alewyn. He was elven and lived and breathed for the immortal fae of this world. However, after conquering the land from the creatures, the fae became bored, so they began to bicker and fight until the entire world was divided. The first king began an arduous journey of hunting many sacred artifacts to create a blood oath to the land. He bound his oath by sacrificing the precious immortality of the fae. In return, he asked for a promise. When the lives no longer mattered and hatred ruled the lands, a fae would be born in secret to save the world."

She shifted in her chair and reached for my hand. I lifted my head, gasping. She filled me with an emotion of complete love and adoration. Within that touch I heard the first cry of a newborn, the first laugh of a babe, a long embrace from a father's arms, a mother's smile, a first kiss, the devotion of lovers.

"This is the message that king left for you. No words other than this feeling. To remind you that hatred is not the only way forward. He promised a Guardian to protect you as you completed your destiny, child. And so, you will see that you cannot sever the bond between you and the

Prince. You are mates, but you are more than that. Though the king pledged you to the world, he vowed your Guardian to you."

The truth hit me like a blow to the chest.

"You may have spoken out of rash anger, but your heart never denied him. You accepted that bond when you found him in The Mists. However, the bond between you is special. It is a bond that can never be broken, no matter how foolish or reckless you are."

There was comfort in her words somehow. Because even though he'd lied, I knew him. He had done it because he thought it was the only way to protect my tumultuous heart. He might have known I'd chosen him in The Mists, but I'd chosen him before that. A hundred times. And that's all I'd ever wanted. A choice. He'd given that to me the only way he knew how, and now that I'd left him behind, I wondered if he would ever forgive me. I'd never let her know that, though.

"Is that all, then?"

"When you were born, the prophetess told the sea queen the Promise was born. You then revealed yourself to her, as your raw power is far vaster than hers. Look within yourself to see the truth."

I stifled the groan as I closed my eyes and searched for my magic. No longer a small basin, but seemingly an endless pit swirled within. It lit my veins and pumped my heart. The magic was so vast, it pressed at the seams, overwhelming me the moment I became aware of it.

"Control it." Nealla stood and latched onto my arm. She knew I couldn't.

"I'm trying," I ground out.

"That magic is as pure as the magic of the first faerie king. It is your will alone that rules it. Remember that. Just as I bound the tongues of the fae from speaking of you, I bound the magic from you, but the closer you got to me, the closer you got to your true power."

I could barely concentrate on the words she said as the pressure continued to rise.

"Control it, girl," she said again as her eyes glowed brighter within her cloak.

"I. Can't," I answered seconds before the bomb exploded within me. In a flash, we were back in that desolate desert as my magic poured.

I watched her change from terrifying beast to mysterious fae and back again as she was struck with my magic.

"You must close off your magic in the same way you seal your mind. Bind it yourself. Hold it to your will." The moment I considered binding it, the pressure subsided. I truly was in control. Kind of. "Don't destroy the world, girl. The living wielders in Alewyn have but a fraction of the power you do. You must never lose control."

I concentrated on breathing until the control began to slip and the pressure began anew. I thought of Fen. Of what would happen to him if I ever lost control when he was near me. I pictured Kai's laughter and Wren's smile. I pictured Lichen's books and Greeve with his fiercely dark nature. I could control it. If for not myself, then for them. Because even though they all likely hated me right now, they were still all I had in the world.

"Yes," Nealla said from beside me. "You are now ready."

"For what?"

"To hear the second half of your prophecy. You will either fulfill it or die first. Those are your options." Though I couldn't see her face, I could still feel the wicked smile.

I nodded. I would not be afraid.

Again, we stood in the cottage as Nealla circled me like a predator. I was absolutely still as she traced a pointed finger up my arm, across my back and down the other as she moved. Her voice became distant, a phantom of her own as the demon within her surfaced.

"Four thrones, four crowns,
North, South, Sea and West.
One Fae, One Will,
Must kill them all and free the rest."

424

The final word was spoken, and again, the world around me drifted away into darkness. I opened my eyes to find I was laying on the beach with an emerald-eyed fae prince staring down at me in utter torment. I reached for him. He crashed to his knees, face full of worry as our souls melted back together with the heat of that tiny flame that had never wavered. I'd never wanted a mate. But on some level, I'd always wanted *him*. I was stubborn in all the worst ways. Prideful in all the best. But I wasn't stupid. I saw him. He'd loved me my whole life, and I needed him. Forever.

It was finally time to tell him how I felt. "I'll never find the words to give you the apology you deserve. I am sorry. You saved me. You've always saved me. You've always thought of me, of my safety, of my heart, and I've not been as fair. I choose you Fenlas. Until the last star falls from the sky, until the final grain of sand is blown from the very last beach, until my heart stops forever, I choose you."

His shoulders drooped with relief. His lips brushed mine, but before I could demand more, he shoved his arms under me and lifted. As I lay my head on his broad chest and listened to his heart beat in tune to my own, I let him carry me away, realizing only then that I was going to have to find a way to tell my mate, my Guardian, that I had to kill his father.

End of Book Two

Fate and Flame

Would you sacrifice yourself for the world?

Ara's found her soul mate and accepted the bond, but now she must journey south with her team, keeping her secret while fighting against the power that's threatening to destroy her and the world at every turn. Though fate is non-negotiable, can she find a way to escape it? Or will she have to do the unthinkable before she becomes the victim? The hunted?

It's over for Temir. He's lost everything, including his freedom. His mate, who has refused him, has all the answers but can he escape the king and find a way to get that information from her? How can he save the world when he can't even save himself?

It's time for war in Alewyn and fate has decided that no one is safe.

One Savior. One Prisoner. One Epic Battle.

Fate and Flame

FAE RISING

3

WOULD YOU SACRIFICE
YOURSELF FOR THE WORLD?

MIRANDA LYN

Acknowledgements

I think I'll always stop and thank the reader first. It was always you that pushed me to keep going. To write when I hadn't slept, to plot while I paced my kitchen, to create these characters that would mean the most. Chaos and Destiny was the book that Ara stole away from me. I'd had other plans for her, but she always knew where she wanted to go, where we were supposed to land and how to set up the final book in this trilogy. So, thank you for getting this far with me, and I hope you'll still be around for the finale.

To my husband, this book is for you. For every morning you woke up at some ungodly hour to go to work. For every laugh, every hug, and every time I wanted to chuck that headset out the window. We'll chase our dreams together! Promise.

To my girls, my little dreamers, thank you. For inspiring me far more than I'll probably ever inspire you. For knowing random things that no human should probably just know. For snuggling with me, even though you are far beyond your toddler years. One day, you're going to be my age and think, "Someday, I want to do this." And whatever that is, my girl, do it. Start right now. Never wait for your dreams to happen to you, chase them. So hard.

To Tristopher, this was the book I wrote in tandem with you. Each day, we pushed each other to keep going, to work through the tough parts. But it was always more than that for me. You have always been the friend I never knew I needed and I'm forever grateful for the change you've brought to my life. Richard is in our sights!

To Jess, round two, girl! Thank you for reading every word so many times and for still loving it alongside me. You're my favorite cheerleader. There's not a part of this journey I ever want to be on without you. We dreamed about this, remember? When I was writing and still not sure about publishing, what it would be like to talk about these characters with other people. And now we get to do that every day. Thanks for dreaming with me. For pushing me to keep going. Thanks for being the best alpha anyone could ask for.

To Michael, you still haven't given up. You're still helping me behind the scenes. I assumed once the website was built, I'd be on my own, but you've stayed for the ride and I'm glad you're here. But you've always been here, even when we were kids. You've always taken on that role and I'm grateful for you.

To Darby, I don't know how to thank you. You helped me pull this book into a stronger story, but you've done so much more than that. You've loved these characters and the Fae Rising series from the first pages all the way through the end. That love has inspired me and pushed me to make it better. <insert that one emoji>

To Claire, who whipped through this book so fast and then had to turn around and help whip it into shape. I am so grateful for you and our friendship. You always make me laugh and I can't tell you how much I respect you as a working mother. You do it all so gracefully and I'm so proud to know you. And Evanna.

To the BRA ladies, the Book Readers Anonymous that discuss so much more than books. I can't believe I've found this group of incredible, empowering women crushing their life's goals. You inspire me every single day and I'm so, so thankful for you all.

And finally, to my street team, Amber, Anber, Claire, Ivy, Kristyne, Niki, Sara, and Whitney, my voices, those that carried these books in their hearts before everyone else got to read them. I love you all so much. I thought you would just read and post, I never imagined you'd become the marketing powerhouse you have. Or more so, my friends. #justiceforoleo I'm not sorry.

And one extra thank-you because I can. To bookstagram. To every single one of you that takes time out of your day to post pictures of books, reviews of books, and creates this wonderful environment of booklovers around the world, thank you. I may not effectively use my hashtags, have the most creative questions of the day, or always have a cohesive theme, but I'm still in awe of you every day! Thank you for loving on these books with me.

About the Author

Chaos and Destiny is Miranda Lyn's second novel. She grew up smack dab in the middle of the United States with nothing to do but dream up stories of fantastical creatures and powerful heroines. Now married with three children of her own, an idea sparked a buried passion within her to follow a dream and teach her children that anything is possible if you're willing to work hard for it. Be sure to check out her social media!

Instagram: https://www.instagram.com/authormirandalyn/

Facebook: https://www.facebook.com/authormirandalyn/

Twitter: https://twitter.com/AuthorMirandaL

Check out our website for extras, character art, and exclusive content. www.faerising.com

Also, click here to sign up for the mailing list and get access to more exclusive content and giveaways!

https://www.faerising.com/subscribe

Made in the USA
Columbia, SC
05 March 2021